The shuffling, blank-eyed things had been people once, before the xenos had gotten hold of them. Damn frickin' xenos! They'd come and hauled off people and messed with them. He used to think that the people they caught were just killed. Tortured, probably, maybe even eaten. But he knew better now.

They were up there. A hundred of them, maybe more, and he'd been caught away from his doss with only a couple dozen of his best slugs. Stupid to fight when the odds weren't in your favor. Stupider to fight when you didn't know the odds.

He had found a good hole where he'd hidden from the bastards before. Jones and a few others crawled in with him. If they all stayed quiet, the frickin' xombies would go right by.

Problem was, he could hear something else up there. Something that didn't move like a xombie.

Jones heard it too. "Sounds like there's a machine up there."

That would be bad.

Above them, at the top of the stairs, the door rattled as something tested it. The bar they'd placed in the crudely welded brackets held. No damn xombie, even as strong as they were, was going to bust it open. Nothing human was going to bust it open.

Nothing human did.

Also by Richard Fawkes

FACE OF THE ENEMY

NATURE OF
THE BEAST

RICHARD FAWKES

An Imprint of HarperCollinsPublishers

EOS
An Imprint of HarperCollins*Publishers*
10 East 53rd Street
New York, New York 10022-5299

To JS,
who,
like a good Eridani,
does the difficult daily.

NATURE OF
THE BEAST

PROLOGUE

2316
RIM WORLDS ECONOMIC UNION (DEFUNCT)
PACIFICA, KILAWA ISLE, PALISANDRA

Sue scanned the low-hanging clouds, but nothing revealed itself to her probing eyes. The wind was light and from the west, just the conditions they liked. Where were they?

"You see anything, Ren?" she asked.

The boy gave a slight shake of his head. His young eyes were better than Sue's at a distance, and he was uncannily good at spotting the least motion. If he couldn't see something, it wasn't there to be seen.

Sue fretted. The timing was right. The weather was right. Could she have picked the wrong place to await them? It would be bad if she had. She'd pulled people away from the harvest for this, and with winter coming on, they couldn't afford to lose any resources.

At the thought of loss, her eyes shifted north, toward Bartie's territory. There had been hardly any trouble from those bullies this year. She couldn't help but think that it was overdue, that soon there would be an unwelcome bill to pay for the peace they'd had all through the growing season.

A flash of light snared her eyes. The signaler was on the northern edge of their territory, posted there to watch for the very raid Sue feared. But this warning wasn't about raiders. This was something else.

Machines were coming from that direction, striding through the park that had once belonged to the Serenten embassy. They were the usual sort, with broad, wedge-shaped hulls that Jesse said were "fighting compartments" even though everybody else called them torsos or bodies. Those armored hulls were replete with concealed sensors, tools, and horrific weapons. Spindly legs carried the five-meter-tall machines with a gait that evoked a primeval predatory bird on the prowl. They moved a lot like Sue had used to imagine the ancient carnivorous dinosaurs of Old Earth had hunted. That, and the fact that no one had ever seen their operators, probably explained why she tended to think of these things more as fantastic creatures than as fighting machines.

Sometimes she thought of them as demonic monsters. And why not? Hadn't the aliens brought hell to Pacifica?

She remembered the confused reports of the first contact, when the aliens had, without provocation, attacked and destroyed the first ship to encounter them. There had been a lot of speculation about misunderstandings at first, but the aliens hadn't cared what humans thought. They closed in on Pacifica, destroying as they came. The night sky had burned with fire when the invaders obliterated Pacifica's orbital station and every ship that dared oppose them. Then they brought their terror to the planet's surface, their striding machines in the vanguard of the conquering wave that had swept across Pacifica.

With human society overthrown, the aliens had stopped the mass killing. No one knew why. Instead, they burned a swath around Palisandra and built their Wall. The city, perhaps the last refuge of humankind on the planet, had become an unjust prison, its inmates a cross section of society chosen by the random fortunes of the aliens' war. Even now, after all these years, the alien overlords patrolled the boundaries, exterminating any who tried to escape the madness.

And madness was what life surely had become. Isolated, the people in Palisandra had been left to fend for themselves. Squabbling over resources and territory had begun almost immediately. Groups had coalesced, some successful, some not. Some trying to hold to civilized ideals, others not. Everyone did what they could to survive. Each year it grew harder as supplies dwindled and irreplaceable items—and people—were lost to the oftentimes savage struggle. Sometimes, when despair gnawed at her, Sue wished the aliens would just make an end of it. They surely had the power. Any one of the three monstrous machines stalking among the towering Radeyo pines had the power to put an end to her and all her people.

But this trio wasn't hunting, as their kind had during the first few weeks of the invasion. They moved steadily and unwaveringly, marching straight toward where they were going. Unstoppable. Fearlessly contemptuous of the humans who still scrabbled for their lives in the ruins of Palisandra. And why shouldn't they be? All those who had tried to halt them were long since dead.

The world had changed.

How odd to look upon those things and think the sight welcome. Which it was. Sue didn't doubt that these were the harbingers of what she awaited, for the otherwise almost never seen Walkers always attended a landing. But where, exactly, were these headed?

It was a matter of great import. Though Sue hated living on the charity of conquerors, she wasn't ready to give up living. And living meant food and medical supplies There was some food to be had in Palisandra along with ever-dwindling medical supplies, and some food could be grown, but not enough. And the only pharmaceuticals to be had were what the conquerors deigned to give. Handouts. Bones thrown to squabbling dogs. Charity—though she doubted the conquerors understood the concept.

There were only so many suitable landing sites in what was left of Palisandra, and since the path the Walkers had taken led them out of Bartie's territory, it wasn't going to be in his backyard. And it wasn't going to be where she had expected. So where, exactly, would it be?

Her vantage point let her see a good part of southern Palisandra, and watching the Walkers for a couple of minutes gave her the trend of their line of march. Projecting that path, she spotted a likely landing field: the Diamond Point Mall. The lot was big and flat enough. And luckily, it was within range of Ren's high-powered rifle and he'd have a clean shot at most of the field. He could give covering fire if necessary without having to relocate. But his support wouldn't be necessary if she couldn't get her people there on the ground to stake a claim.

She left Ren making the necessary adjustments to his scope and scrambled down what was left of the stairs. Jesse had seen her coming and was running to meet her. She cut off his questions and panted out her new plan. Together they got everybody moving double quick. They needed the carts to haul whatever they got, but they wouldn't get much if they didn't get there fast. Reluctantly, she split her people, pushing on ahead with her best fifty fighters and leaving the rest to follow with the carts. They reached the edge of the Mall lot just in time to see the last Walker stride into the cleared space. It picked its way across the crumbling asphalt to take up a station equidistant from its mates. All three machines turned to face toward the center of the lot. Sue didn't bother to watch them. She had her eyes on the sky.

Yes! There it was! A dark shape in the clouds.

She checked the periphery of the open space. Nothing. So far, hers was the only group to have made it to the landing spot. Good.

The familiar deep thrum, almost more felt than heard, drifted down from the clouds and grew louder as the shape came closer. Like the humans, the Walkers tilted their torsos up as if to stare at the great aerial manifestation emerging from the clouds. It was a sight! As ever, Sue was awed and revolted by what she saw. People called them "Carriers" for what they did. What they were, no one knew.

The first impression was of a grotesque and titanic grub, lit from within, that floated in the sky like some monstrous balloon. It was no balloon, nor did it simply drift. The noise it made came from a dozen iridescent wings, each big enough to provide lift for a small aircraft, beating in a frenzied blur and drawing it onward. Those wings were set in pairs that studded a spined, lumpy carapace on the front end of the thing. And forward of them sat the tiny questing head which made it clear that this thing was alive, some sort of insectiform monster. Overall, the thing looked a bit like a picture that Sue had seen once of a queen ant, an insect whose abdomen had swollen to hideous enormity until it dwarfed the rest of the creature, leaving the queen's body and head looking like little more than tiny, insignificant, useless appendages. Like that ant, this thing's bloated abdomen was so overwhelmingly mammoth that it seemed to be the all of the creature. But that immense bulbous mass was not a queen's egg factory but a gas bag—or so Professor Murch said—an organic zeppelin that supported the bulk of the insectiform and lifted the mass that its wings could not possibly support. It was tantalizingly close to transparent, and looking at it was a little like peering through skim milk—you could almost see through it, but like milk, this thing was too opaque, too real. There was a sense of darker things within the bulging mass, but nothing could be discerned clearly.

Shadow dropped across the landing field as the thing came closer. Its propulsive wings stilled and folded against its bulk. The fifty or more pairs of smaller wings that lined the side of the balloon-abdomen beat on in various rhythms, shifting the enormous bulk, turning it until its long axis lay parallel with the long axis of the clear space.

Tentacles uncoiled from the darkness beneath its forward body, extending, reaching toward the ground. Two wrapped themselves around old illuminator supports, but the rest found no such convenient mooring points. They slithered across the broken pave, snaking out away from the carrier's shadow. Somehow—whether by suckers or adhesive slime or tiny subsidiary tentacles, Sue didn't know—they gripped the dirt and grass and shattered asphalt and drew the great bulk down.

When it had hauled itself to within sixty meters of the ground, one of the Walkers stepped forth. The machine stood almost beneath the Carrier's tiny head—tiny by comparison only, for it was easily as large as the carapace of the five-meter-tall Walker. Panels opened on the Walker's torso, allowing strange devices to deploy. One long, multi-jointed arm reached toward the descending Carrier. As soon as the Walker touched it, the insectiform began to chirp, a bass resonance that Sue felt in her chest.

Under the Walker's guidance, the Carrier settled in. Peristaltic shudders rippled along its mass as the Carrier began to excrete slimy blobs of gelatin as if it were laying some sort of colossal eggs. The Walker led the Carrier forward, making room for the next deposit. Each was the size of a cargo hauler's container and when seven of them lay glistening and still on the field, the Walker released its grip on the Carrier and the chirping stopped. As the Walker returned to its post, the Carrier released it grip and retracted its tentacles. Free again, the Carrier bobbed up a good ten meters. It continued to rise, but much more slowly, until the great propulsive wings unfurled and buzzed up to speed, carrying the creature higher and faster than its own buoyancy could until it disappeared into the concealing cloud cover.

The Walkers, however, did not depart, which always made Sue nervous. Only once had she seen those silent sentinels interfere: the first and last time her people had tried to use combustion-powered vehicles to help with the hauling. On that day the Walkers had used their weapons, blasting the trucks and the dozens of people aboard them. Mercifully, most of the victims had died immediately, but some had lingered, suffering horribly from their wounds. Jack had lasted three weeks.

But the Walkers didn't seem to care about carts, even when they were made from old, unpowered vehicles. She'd heard that Jan Spicer's people had horses that they used to haul their carts, and that the Walkers ignored those too. The rigs that Sue's people used were rickety things, but they were a lot better than packing stuff out on one's back.

And those carts were finally arriving, to a total lack of acknowledgment from the Walkers. Sue could see that her people were winded from their rush, tired from pushing against the crossbars set across the traces, from doing what Spicer had horses to do. So far, their exertions looked to be paying off—no one else had shown up yet to collect the eggs.

What the Carrier had laid wasn't really eggs, but those slimy gelatinous masses would hatch what Sue's people needed. And as they drew closer to them, Sue could see the dark shapes of cartons, crates, foil packs, barrels, and cans within the viscous stuff. Within those containers would be foodstuffs, medical supplies, and occasionally other things— some useful, some not. None were things they could make for themselves anymore, at least not easily. All were the gifts of the conquerors.

Jesse handed her one of the flensing poles, and Sue drew on her feelings about the conquerors to apply the pole's sharp blade to the gummy barrier between her and the commodities. All around nearly three hundred of her people were doing the same, even the cart pushers. Cutting away the gelatin to get at the good stuff within was hot, sweaty work, but no one let that stop them. Compared to how they got much of their food these days, this was easy. Precious supplies were freed from their gelid packaging. The piles in the carts grew.

The jackals announced their arrival with a shower of arrows and a fusillade of gunshots. Three arrows burrowed into the Carrier's egg jelly beside her, but nothing touched her. Her people were not so fortunate. Dozens were down, dead or wounded. Their screams filled the air.

Seeing the ragtag raiders spilling onto the landing field, Sue screamed too, but not from pain. She screamed for blood, wanting to gut each and every one of the bastards who were hurting her people.

She ran at the nearest group of attackers. Something tugged at her jacket. A hot bar pressed against her arm. Heedless, she charged on. Men and women scattered before her wildly swinging flensing pole. One wasn't fast enough. The sharp blade cut through muscle as easily as egg jelly. Bone was little more resistant.

For a few moments no one came near Sue. Wildly, she

scanned the field. Everywhere men and women struggled. It was hard to make out what was happening in the swirling chaos, but a few facts were clear. A lot of the attackers wore black leather jackets and vests, suggesting that these jackals were part of Giatti's pack. They were scavengers and scroungers usually, and wouldn't take on a more numerous group.

But something must have gotten their courage up. Or maybe not. There were a lot of them. Maybe Sue's people didn't have a numerical advantage, for the feral attackers were everywhere. Had Giatti found allies? He must have.

A bare-chested kid in warpaint, not looking at all like one of Giatti's crowd, leaped at her. The boy had a wickedly curved knife in hand. Sue sidestepped the rush. It was too easy to sweep the shaft of her pole into the back of his knees and bring him down. A thrust with the butt stunned him. He looked so young lying on the ground. So vulnerable. So human. And so treacherous as he groggily cut at her. So much for the mercy she offered. Her blade flashed down and put an end to him.

All about her, individual struggles like the one she'd just finished went on. Men and women screamed, fought, were wounded, and died in the terrible hand-to-hand strife. Isolated archers and riflemen from both sides lurked around the periphery of the battle, looking for and finding targets, but most of those so armed had become embroiled in the more personal clash of blade and rock and clutching hands.

The pitiless Walkers simply observed the slaughter.

Unlike them, Sue was not divorced from the brawl. She found herself facing a huge man with a bandolier of scalps slung over his black leather jacket. She recognized him as one of Giatti's lieutenants, but she didn't know his name. He offered no introduction as he charged, notched machete high. Sue fended off his first rush, but he was persistent. She kept the flensing pole moving, using its deadly blade to keep him away. He was skillful and strong, blocking her fast, slashing attacks despite his weapon's unwieldiness. Their deadly dance went on until his machete caught her blade as she tried a disemboweling stroke. With her attack's momentum broken, he used the chance to close. Dirty fingers snatched a grip on her weapon's shaft. They struggled for control of the flensing pole. She couldn't match his strength. He began to force her down. All her defiance was inadequate, but she didn't stop fighting. Confident of his coming victory, he gave her a gap-toothed feral grin. She spat in his face.

Their contest came to a sudden end as half his head blew away in a spray of blood and bone. He might have been struck by some thunderbolt of justice tossed from on high. Miraculously, no one struck her down as she stood staring at the toppled corpse, stunned.

Slowly understanding dawned. Ren. The distant crack of his sharpshooter's rifle had been lost in the wild shouting of the melee, but it hadn't made his bullet any less effective. Ren had covered her just as they had planned. Just as she had planned.

She stared around her at the madness. Plans? Gone. Drowned in blood. She had forgotten too much. So had her people. One-on-one they were no match for the feral ferocity of Giatti's raiders. They knew that. They all knew that. But, like her, they had forgotten in the heat of the moment.

But now she had come to her senses. She was determined that they would too.

She spotted a clump of her people cowering behind one of the carts. She ran to them, shouting at them to get up and join her. "Up, up! Spears and flensing poles to the front!" They were slow to move. It took minutes—precious minutes in which more people died—but she got them into the formation they had practiced. Some stragglers joined them as they formed up. "Archers, shoot anyone who looks like he's even thinking of shooting at us. Bill, save that rifle for their gunmen. They'll be watching for you, so you just get them first."

She led them at a small knot of raiders half their size. She lost two spearmen, but none of the enemy escaped. The last went down with three arrows in her back.

"If they run, let them run," she snapped, but she was secretly pleased. These people needed confidence and their little local victory had won them a small serving of it.

The little band moved across the field, killing and driving off raiders. They gathered in more of her people. She found Jesse just as the small group he had gathered around him was about to be swarmed by forty or so of Giatti's brigands. Sue's formation charged and scattered the jackals.

"Thought I'd seen the last of you," Jesse said as Doc Shelly bandaged his arm. "Thought I'd seen the last of me too."

"The world isn't so lucky, you old war dog. Come on, there's still work to do."

Their combined force became the rock on which the battle turned. Several more times Ren made a crucial shot, taking down a seemingly unstoppable enemy or dropping a leader whose minions lost cohesion without him to goad them on. The swirling, formless melee starting taking on the shape of a real battle. The enemy clumped, their archers and riflemen whittled down. Sue's people formed a line of battle, as they had been supposed to do from the beginning. Ren still sniped.

Then, without warning the ripping blast of a pulse rifle burst from the trees, scorching across the sky and seeking out Ren's hiding place.

Sue's mouth went dry as ash. Where had they gotten that?

Her people had no answer to it. Clustered in their defensive formations, they would be easy targets. Her people were going to get toasted.

It didn't happen.

As one, the three Walkers reacted. Torsos swiveled in the direction of the shooter. Eye-searing beams sizzled the air. Trees exploded in shattering clouds of steam. Fires started.

There wasn't any more pulser fire after that.

Sue could see that Giatti's raiders were shaken by the obliteration of their pulse rifleman. Their morale hung on a razor's edge.

"At them!" she shouted. "Charge! Charge!"

She ran forward, waving her flensing pole. And her people followed. Raggedly, but they followed.

It was too much for the brigands. They broke. They ran, disappearing into the woods, into the streets, into the broken bones of Palisandra. Sue and her people held the field. The prize was theirs.

The wounded were theirs too. The dead belonged to both parties.

The Walkers stood unmoving, masters of it all.

PACIFICA SYSTEM
IDLS *CERVAL*

Jehan Walston sat quietly in the command couch of IDLS *Cerval,* as he had for every hour of the graveyard watch for the last ten days. He attended to routine business when needed, as was his duty when holding the con, but his true attention was reserved for the reports from Scan and watching the plot as each new bogey was added. Two had been confirmed as bandits, and most likely they all were, but passive scanning only yielded so much information. The important thing was that so far none of the contacts, bandit or bogey, had shown any indication that they were aware of *Cerval*'s presence in the system.

So far.

But despite his unease, each day that came and went without the enemy noticing them went a little further in making him feel a little safer. Not that his fears were going to go away completely. That wouldn't happen as long as there was a single bandit or potential bandit sharing the system with them. He knew too well how dangerous the enemy was.

Of course, *Cerval* was dangerous too. She was a warship, but a specialist one: a lurker, which meant that less of her mass was devoted to weaponry, armor, and screens than to surveillance equipment, stealth systems, and the shroud generator that was unique to her class. She'd have a hard time outfighting an ordinary enemy warship of similar mass.

Doctrine said that lurkers weren't supposed to get involved in stand-up fights. Unfortunately, out on the frontiers, doctrine didn't always have the last word. Things always were dicey in enemy-controlled space, which was where *Cerval* currently was. And so Walston worried, listening to Scan reports and watching the plot, waiting for the enemy to discover them.

Other lurkers, dispatched on missions similar to *Cerval*'s, had failed to return, presumably discovered by the enemy and destroyed. If there was anything Walston could do to prevent *Cerval,* and himself, from suffering such a fate, he'd do it. And so he listened and watched, looking for that first sign of danger and holding himself ready to act.

His shift was drawing to a close, the enemy still unaware, when ShipComp whispered in his ear, "Commander on the bridge."

At all stations, crew straightened to attention at the commander's early arrival. Walston unsnapped his harness and evacuated the command station. Locking his boots to the deck, he snapped a salute. Commander Rider drifted across the bridge to touch down precisely opposite the command couch from Walston. As always, Walston was awed by the elegance with which his Eridani commander moved. Like most of his breed, Rider was taller and more solidly built than ordinary humans, a phenotype that shouldn't be able to move with the feline fluidity that graced every motion he made. Rider's hand touched his forehead in a flawless salute, and his mahogany eyes requested a report.

"Ship status nominal, sir. On course. All quiet."

"Very well, Lieutenant." Commander Rider took his place in the chair. "I have the con."

Walston remained in place while the commander reviewed the ship's status and situation boards, waiting for Rider's inevitable questions.

"How is the evaluation of probe data proceeding, Lieutenant?"

Cerval had launched a series of probes just after entering the system; most had gone in-system ahead of the ship. The probes were fitted with a wide array of sensors, less capable than *Cerval*'s own, but quite proficient. They were stealthed and operating clandestinely, just like *Cerval,* but being un-manned, they didn't have the burden of maintaining an envi-ronment, and were less detectable than *Cerval,* thus they got the high-risk task of moving closer to Pacifica's eponymous colony world. Data from them had been coming in since their launch, correlated with *Cerval*'s own data. A picture of the Pacifica system was forming, coming into better resolu-tion every hour as the ship's technicians pieced it together.

"Scan and Eval are closing the probabilities on eight of the remaining eleven bogeys. They are almost certainly Re-mor. It looks like four more *Rukh*-class, three *Garpikes,* and a *Gorgon.*"

They had already confirmed one *Rukh* and one *Gorgon* in-system. Though all Remor ships were armed and had to be considered dangerous, only the *Gorgon* of all the classes identified in the Pacifica system could be considered a war-ship. Of course, a single cruiser-mass *Gorgon* carried more than enough armament to scatter *Cerval* into atoms if it caught her, and there were *two* of them here.

"We've also confirmed that several of the cold targets are wreckage. Mostly ships, but the largest of them looks to be what's left of Phillips Station." Phillips Station had been the gateway orbital waystation and transfer point for starships visiting Pacifica. The dead ships would be what was left of the doomed fleet that had tried to defend the station and the planet from the enemy. That battle had been fought ten years ago, one of the first clashes with the Remor and fought be-fore anyone really understood that humankind had begun a genocidal war with an alien species. Until now, nothing was known of the Pacificans beyond the fact that they had failed to stop the Remor.

"Enemy wreckage?"

"Nothing conclusive. A number of the cold targets have a high albedo. They might be Remor slag."

Bland lumps of uninformative slag that could as easily be cosmic debris were all that the destroyed Remor ships generally left behind, as enemy ships had an unnerving tendency to dissolve themselves after they had been rendered *hors de combat.*

"Slag doesn't do us any good," Rider observed. "Whether Intel is right about the Rim Worlds' fleet scoring against the enemy before they fell, it has been years. More than enough time for the Remor to have cleaned up."

Walston agreed. The hope that, in a secured system, the enemy might not have been tidy with their wreckage had been slim to start with, but the chance to recover unspoiled wreckage had been worth taking.

"I suppose it was a vain hope," Commander Rider mused. "It seems that the enemy's efforts in denying us any technical intelligence continue to be thorough. Well, I suppose it tells us something about our enigmatic foe that they are so careful even in a safe system. Maybe Intel can figure out what it means, for I surely do not know."

"We haven't classified all of the cold targets, sir. We may yet find something we can use."

"Optimism, Mr. Walston? I'm surprised."

Walston felt a flush starting. "I wasn't saying that we *would* find something useful."

"Ah. That's the Lieutenant Walston I know." The commander didn't give Walston's embarrassment time to grow. "What are we getting from the colony world?"

Striving for cool, professional detachment, Walston launched into a summary. "The first pics from orbit are in processing now. Should be up any minute. But even without them we've got definite signs of Remor presence: strip mining, forest destruction, craters where power plants used to be, that sort of thing. ScanTech McNally is certain she's spotted several of those harvester organisms that the enemy employed on Grenwold, but the resolution's still too low to be sure. The orbital pics will settle that one. The curious thing is that, so far, we've got no indication that the enemy have developed a spaceport, or established any large concentrations, for that matter. Power emanations from the planet are virtually nil."

"Which suggests that they haven't established a military presence."

"Judging by previous encounters, I am inclined to agree with you, sir, but—"

"But we can't count on the Remor to do anything the same way twice. I know, I know. Still. There's no reason for them to be hiding whatever it is they are doing on Pacifica, is there?"

"I wouldn't think so, sir, but they are Remor, after all."

That produced a rueful chuckle from Rider. "And we are the eyes of humankind. We'll continue looking."

Another week of careful data-gathering didn't change the basic picture. To all appearances, the Remor occupation force was minimal. There were no depots for battle machines, no combat support centers, no bustling enemy spaceports, not even any definite bases. To be sure, the enemy was present. McNally's harvester beasts had proven to be real. Remor domes and utility machines had been spotted on the mainland and on each and every one of the principal island chains. Remor shipping passed among the planets as calmly as sailboats upon Eusta's Great Bay. There could be no doubt that the enemy was making himself at home, both on Pacifica and in the local system.

But there was an anomaly. It seemed that, contrary to all expectations, humans still survived on Pacifica.

In the second week, the growing body of evidence stifled the last doubts. Detection had identified several concentrations of population, a significant achievement given that there was no electromagnetic traffic to intercept. Evaluation could offer only guesses as to why there was no EM, but they didn't even hazard guesses as to why the Remor were suffering people to live on what was now one of their worlds. The command staff, Walston included, didn't have any idea either. Commander Rider took in all the data silently, until at last the accumulating reports drew out a wolfish grin.

"What we have here, gentlefolk, is an opportunity."

Part I

Abstruse Lacunae

2319

"Good morning, Captain," the sergeant offered gruffly. "You're to come with me."

Anders Seaborg turned off the comp and swung out of his rack. As his bare feet slapped the floor, he was pleased to note that he felt no weakness in his right knee. The joint, slow in responding to reconstructive therapies, was finally coming around. His current situation offered him constant reminders of the trouble his conscience had gotten him into on Chugen. He didn't need more from his own body.

The sergeant's unheralded arrival most likely meant another "surprise" session, so Anders donned his dress uniform rather than simple shipboard coveralls. His choice was a part of his continuing small statement about the proceedings. The sergeant waited stolidly, making no comment. In the silence, Anders contemplated the fact that his improving physical condition was the best news he was likely to get today.

Anders sealed his tunic collar, tucked his cover under his arm, and said, "All set, Sergeant."

The sergeant nodded and led the way down the corridor.

Although the heavily built Holsteader sergeant, with the long service braid on the left sleeve of his tunic, was the sort of soldier with whom Anders normally got along well, he was even less communicative than other servicefolk with whom Anders had had contact in the last weeks. From them he'd gotten pleasantries, polite inquiries after health and condition, and reviews of food or some entertainment presentation when their duties brought them into contact with him. All inconsequential stuff—civil and courteous, but uninformative and distant. Just the way one would expect them to be, considering Anders's pariah status as a soldier under investigation for, among other things, disobeying orders in the face of the enemy and colluding in the escape of prisoners.

As was usually the case during Anders's forays from his stateroom cell, the corridors of Tarsus Station were nearly empty. A personnel scarcity planned by someone, somewhere, he assumed, for Tarsus was a sector headquarters and a very busy place. He also noted that those personnel he passed were rarely groundpounders, and even more rarely Eridani. The last time he'd been aboard the station, he'd noted that it was staffed by a higher than normal population of Eridani.

He'd found it comforting, then, to see so many soldiers from the home systems in one place. The small star nation of Eridan was one of the founding states of the Interstellar Defense League, more than willing to stand against the genocidal Remor. At the time, the Eridani Stellar Legion was one of the most experienced forces available, able to outperform the militaries of notably larger star nations. In truth, the League's few early successes were the result of Eridani leadership, troops, or the combination of both. Not surprisingly, the sons and daughters of Eridan quickly came to dominate the League's MilForce. MilForce was the better for it, but, as in battles against the Remor, there was a cost. Eridani were now spread thinly throughout MilForce, and the old comforts of camaraderie were growing harder and harder to come by. It was a difficult trial for a clannish people used to a harmonious community.

On the other hand, that cherished unity was surely why Anders was even more of a pariah to other Eridani than he was to the general run of MilForce personnel. The crimes of which he stood accused were crimes against honor, even more than against military law. Among Eridani, honor often outranked law. Even if he was acquitted, there would be some who would never forgive him. People who believed themselves dishonored by one of their own were rarely forgiving, and Eridani, despite being heirs of a superior genotype, were still people.

It was not an easy path Anders now walked. Nor, he realized as he looked around, was his physical route a familiar one.

Anders hadn't been knowledgeable concerning the layout of Tarsus Station before his confinement aboard it, but he'd had hours of time with computer access to nothing but unrestricted files. Eridani training had left him with an imperative to become familiar with his surroundings, and he had learned what there was to learn from those incomplete and sometimes deliberately misleading files. He could have hacked more—and more truthful—information from the system; he had the skill. But had he done so, and had his intrusion been discovered, it would have been highly damaging to his situation. The potential danger hadn't stopped him. What had stopped him was his own honor. One didn't break the rules without compelling reason.

"This isn't the way to Major Dillon's office," he observed.

Major Dillon was the officer in charge of the investigation into Anders's misadventures. The major's office and the exercise room were the only places Anders was allowed to visit when let out of his stateroom cell. And he'd already exercised this morning.

"You ain't going there today, sir."

When the sergeant offered nothing more, curiosity compelled Anders to ask, "Where *am* I going, Sergeant?"

"Ring 3, sir."

Ring 3 was command country. As the official descriptions of the station had it, it was the rotational section where the senior staff had offices and off-duty facilities. In truth, it held more than bunks and conference desks. For one thing, the main operations deck was in Ring 3. In point of fact, a number of crucial station control centers were in Ring 3. Anders suspected that the judicial hall was in Ring 3 as well.

And so, Anders learned, was the private office of Sector Commander Christoph Stone.

Stone had fought the Remor—bloodily, fiercely, and, as was all too rare for the defenders of humanity, effectively. He was a war hero with a reputation for being thorough and ruthless, a man with no sympathy for weakness. He was also the man who would pass judgment on Anders.

As he stood before the door whose name plaque read *Sector Commander,* Anders realized that this sudden summons could only mean a new phase of his tribulations had begun. It might even be the final phase.

A sector commander was powerful, essentially a military governor for the region of space under his command. Technically, he had only military authority, but in League space military authority extended to all things related to the war against the Remor. For practical purposes, that meant *all things.* When the hatch to the office slid aside, Anders got his first look at how such wide authority and broad power collided with the restricted space reality of a space station.

The sergeant conducted him across an antechamber the size of the four-man stateroom that served as Anders's solitary cell. Two officers sat talking softly in a corner. One was Colonel Hollister, sector executive officer, and the other was a general, an Eridani wearing StratCom flash. The passage of a disgraced 'pounder was insufficient to attract their attention.

As he passed through the arch to the next compartment, Anders noted that it was lined with receptor cells and other less identifiable ports and lenses. Beyond it they entered an expansive space. It was the largest full-environment compartment he'd seen on board save for the main operations center, but still small enough to be lost in a planetside facility of similar status. For one thing, the ceiling was set at the same 2.5-meters height as the rest of the station's habitable sections. The sergeant led him past a conference table of sufficient size to seat three or four full diplomatic delegations at once. Anders's surreptitious touch of the dark, polished edging that ran around the matte-black surface of the table's central holographic stage convinced him that it was made of real wood, and probably not just a veneer. The decorative moldings, hatch frames, and even the frames of the wall-mounted display screens were almost certainly just as organic, a touch of a real world imported to this artificial one at no small expense.

The chamber beyond the conference hall was their destination. Although larger than most compartments aboard the station, it was only a cozy alcove off the hall, dominated by a desk that might have been the offspring of the massive conference table. Two pairs of chairs flanked the desk, angled to face the single leather-upholstered seat behind it. A seat that was empty.

The Holsteader escorted him to one of the chairs and left him. With the sergeant's departure, the room was still, save for the faint huff of air in the ventilators. Anders was still too, physically anyway. Before long the lights dimmed, as they did when a public room's motion sensors convinced the controlling comp that no one was present. Were the station's machines starting to ignore him as thoroughly as the personnel?

Experimentally he raised a hand and wiggled his fingers. The lights returned to normal illumination in response. He didn't bother to trigger them again. There was not much worth seeing when the lights were on. The suite was sleek, all very tastefully designed to impress. It was also totally bare of any personalized touches. No family photos. No citations. No trophies. Spartan even for an Eridani. Wondering if Stone used this place often, Anders returned to his calming meditation.

Unexpectedly the room lights came up and almost immediately a previously unnoticed door in the paneling slid aside, revealing Commander Stone. Anders was at attention instantly. He snapped a salute.

Stone seemed not to notice as he strode into the suite, his broad shoulders nearly brushing the frame of the doorway. An elusive hint of gray in his close-cropped hair was all that suggested he might be older than Anders by more than a few years; Eridani genes kept a strong grip on youthful appearance. The commander's features were weathered and set in the constrained, slightly grim expression that had earned him the nickname Old Stone Face. Troops under his command swore that he'd no more crack a smile at an invitation from Miss Galaxy than he would show concern as his battle bridge shredded around him, and that supreme poker face offered no clues as he took his place in his chair. Only after he'd settled did he sketch a return salute and wave Anders back into his seat.

"You look fit, Seaborg."

"Thank you, sir. Trying to stay that way, sir."

"Any problems with the leg?"

Anders had not seen Stone since he had departed IDLS *Constantine* on the clandestine mission to Chugen that had ended so badly and brought him to his current predicament. He could not recall any visits by the commander to the infirmary, although there were parts of his stay in the hospital that were hazy and vague. Until this moment he'd had no idea that the commander had even been aware of the injuries Anders had sustained.

"Nothing to report, sir," he responded, denying the stiffness that had come back in his walk through the corridors.

Stone touched a control on his desk and turned his head to read the report it brought up. Anders got the impression that Stone was confirming something rather than learning it. The commander's gaze returned to Anders. "The station surgeon has lifted your medical restrictions."

"That's good news, sir." Or would have been had Anders's situation been different.

"Major Dillon said the same thing."

Medical disability barred an ordinary trooper from returning to active duty. It had also kept Anders from other things.

"Am I to face a tribunal, sir?"

"A sector commander has wide powers regarding discipline. As long as I am Sector Commander, I do not need to call a tribunal to deal with you." Stone leaned back in his chair and drew in a deep breath. When he continued, his voice was a couple of millimeters less stern. "One of the reasons I brought you on to my staff during the Chugen crisis was your experience on Cassuels Home and on Grenwold. Now that StratCom, in its infinite wisdom, has declared that the Chugeni indigs and their ilk are no longer to be considered the enemy, that 'expertise' is no longer pertinent. I also liked the initiative you showed on Grenwold. At the time, I thought you a credit to our homeworld."

Anders understood that Stone's opinion had changed.

"Seaborg, you had a good career opening in front of you. That was before Chugen. What you did there changed a lot of things, and not just for the Chugeni and their Pansie godparents. You disobeyed orders, colluded with outside agencies, aided and abetted the escape of suspected hostile agents, tampered with secure systems . . . in short, you showed yourself to be what Major Dillon calls you: a loose cannon. You have had plenty of time to think it over. Would you care to make a suggestion as to what I should do with you?"

"Whatever you deem appropriate, sir," Anders said without hesitation.

"Ready for the headsman's ax, are you? No excuses?"

Anders had no excuses—only a reason. "I did what I thought was right, sir."

"You overstepped yourself, mister," Stone snapped. "In a major way."

"Someone had to take action."

"So you acted. Why you, Seaborg? What made you the arbiter of right?"

"I was on the spot, sir. I believed that the mission orders were based on an erroneous premise and that execution of those orders would have unfortunate repercussions. Something had to be done."

"So you did it and damn the consequences."

"I thought the alternative consequences even more damning, sir."

Stone swiveled his chair a quarter turn. Though relieved of the commander's penetrating gaze, Anders still felt uncomfortable. He'd once enjoyed this man's patronage. Clearly he had disappointed. Anders was surprised to find out how much that hurt. Silence descended on the room, unbroken until Anders asked the question he'd been wanting an answer to since he had awakened in the infirmary aboard *Constantine* just before she boosted from the Chugen system.

"Am I to be cashiered, sir?"

"We are fighting a war to save our species," Stone said wearily. "We cannot afford to waste soldiers."

"Demoted, then?"

"And sent back to the infantry? You'd like that."

Actually Anders would. 'Pounders led a simple life.

"It's never that easy, Seaborg."

"I don't understand, sir."

Stone swiveled his chair back, settling his cool gray eyes on Anders. "You like to think of yourself as a simple soldier, don't you?"

"Yes, sir."

"Well, take a bit of advice from an older simple soldier. Forget understanding. MilForce never issues understanding."

Anders opened his mouth in confusion, but Stone cut him off with a raised finger.

"You're not the only one to rattle the tree with that business on Chugen, son. There are a lot of people unhappy with what went on there, and the waves are still spreading. Meantime, there's a restructuring going on within the League. The most obvious feature is that sector cartography is being retired."

The Interstellar Defense League divided known space into sectors radiating out from humankind's homeworld, although even within the human sphere, very little was under IDL jurisdiction. For while it was true that the star nations, associations, and independent planets that had banded together into the League to stand against the Remor threat were not small in number, they were only a fraction of humankind. Too much of humankind still ignored the threat to the species that the enemy represented.

"PoliStat is crowing about a new age of cooperation between star nations. As if changing maps will change attitudes. Point is, with no sectors, there can be no sector commanders."

But Stone still wore sector commander rank tabs.

"The orders haven't quite come through yet," Stone said. "Instead of sectors, we'll be operating in theaters, smaller jurisdictions within League-claimed space. Most of the commanders are retaining their bases. I am not one of them."

"No," Anders protested. "They can't blame you for what I did."

"Easy, son. I don't think they do. We all earn our own places in hell."

MilForce might not issue understanding, but Stone wasn't much better. "They can't be thinking of cashiering *you*."

Amazingly, Stone almost laughed. "StratCom is more subtle in its tortures. I've been given a theater command, such as it is. It is not a prime posting, so I am approving requests for transfers."

It was normal for disgraced commanders to try to give their loyal staff a second chance and, technically, Anders was still on Stone's staff. Was he offering Anders a second chance? It couldn't be so easy. Anders couldn't be getting off so lightly. It wasn't right.

"But I will not approve such a request from you," said Stone in confirmation. "We're both in the doghouse, Seaborg, and though I am not entirely happy with how you acted on Chugen, I'm going to give you the same chance StratCom's giving me. My new theater is in League-claimed space, but the Remor control it. If I can win it back, I win back StratCom's approval. It's not exactly a suicide mission, but it's close. What it is, son, is a chance at redemption. Either way, we get to pay for our sins."

Which was what Anders had expected to do from the day he'd crossed the line on Chugen. What he had not expected was a chance to go down fighting.

"Well, Seaborg? I could leave you to the keytappers."

"Sounds like all we have to do is beat the unbeatable."

"That's about it. You up for it?"

Anders was on his feet, saluting. "Sir! Yes, sir!"

Not unexpectedly, the door to Christoph Stone's office didn't close on Seaborg's departing back. The familiar silhouette of Chip Hollister, Stone's executive officer, filled the opening. With cool detachment, he announced, "General Wahlberg has arrived from StratCom."

General Winston Wahlberg's ship had docked with Tarsus Station three days before. Now his official persona as Strat-Com representative had arrived. Stone's grace period was over.

"Very well, Chip. Have him come in."

"Will do."

Chip stepped aside and gestured the visitor forward. Stone stood and saluted as Wahlberg's broad-shouldered form came into sight. The general looked older than when last Stone had seen him. He had solid gray at his temples, and the rest of his close-cropped hair was frosted with it as well, something that most Eridani didn't show till quite late in the game. Stress, Stone supposed. Wahlberg looked tired too, but he still carried himself with a poise born of the Eridani heritage that the two of them shared.

Though Stone's uniform collar carried the three stars of a marshal, one more star than Wahlberg's, the inferior to superior salute was in order, for Wahlberg's direct commission from StratCom held a higher authority than a marshal's, higher even than a sector commander's. And this visit was about authority, not rank.

Wahlberg looked a little embarrassed as he returned the salute and took a chair. Stone sat as well, waiting for the general to speak. Wahlberg didn't leave him waiting long.

"Seaborg the last of your loose ends?"

"The last."

"Then I guess it's time to make it official." Wahlberg placed a packet on Stone's desk. "I ought to tell you that StratCom wanted this to just go in the regular courier bag."

"Were the higher powers worried about my reaction? Why, I haven't cut the head off a bad-news bearer in at least a year."

"I expect some of them think you're overdue."

Stone picked up the packet, but he didn't open it. He already knew what was inside: his removal as Sector Commander. "Should I make them happy and send them your head in a box?"

Wahlberg smiled wryly. "That would make certain folks happy. Of course, most of those folks would be happier if I brought them your head."

"Gleason and Stroud?"

"Among others."

Strategic Commander Gleason of the Intelligence Staff and Strategic Commander Stroud of the Special Actions Staff had approved Major Ersch's Operation Chameleon for Chugen in all of its bloody glory, choosing it from among the alternatives Stone had presented to StratCom and ordering it forward. Like a good soldier, he had executed his orders, persisting even after the first screw-up. Only when it had turned out that the real-universe data didn't fit the assumptions on which the plan had been conceived did he deviate, doing—as Seaborg had—his duty as he saw it. The narrow vision of Gleason and Stroud hadn't seen things the way Seaborg and Stone had seen them. They had been among the loudest critics of how Stone had handled the situation.

Honor demanded that they admit their mistakes, but neither was Eridani, so he supposed they really didn't understand honor. They certainly hadn't admitted publicly to their roles. According to them, Operation Chameleon had been born, spent its ugly little life, and died strictly under Stone's command. It was all his responsibility, his mistakes, his failure. The innocent lives lost in the adventure were all on his head; the Casual Slaughterer had lived up to his name. And the media, especially that of star nations outside the Interstellar Defense League, had lapped it up. Accusing voices both inside MilForce and out didn't consider Stone's defeat

of the Remor fleet at Chugen to be sufficient atonement. And
to be honest, neither did he, though he suspected his reasons
were different than theirs.

Little matter now. Decisions had been made, orders cut.
Stone was no longer a Sector Commander. Soon there would
no longer be sectors. The timing was not coincidental.

Wahlberg cleared his throat. "You've got the Stone Face
on."

"Just contemplating my sins."

"If I have to wait till you're done, I'll get to see the heat
death of the universe."

"Sorry."

A frown of concern crossed Wahlberg's face. "It's not as
bad as it could be, Chris. You still have friends at StratCom.
Otherwise I wouldn't be here playing messenger boy."

Few people called Stone by his first name, fewer still
shortened it. Wahlberg was one of them. It was a privilege
earned when they had served together in the Eridani Stellar
Legion during the War of Autonomy. A lot of stars had sped
past the navscreen since then.

"And I am grateful for it, Win," he said honestly. The use
of Stone's Christian name had been a cue that he was speaking now to his old friend and not StratCom's representative.
"It's good to know the goffs aren't in total control."

"Not that they don't want to be."

It was a depressing old song. The bright promise of the
IDL was being continually eroded by a potent brew of self-
important martinets, embittered and short-sighted veterans
from Remor-shattered star nations, mules who still thought
warfare ought to be conducted with swords, vaccuum-heads
who thought the next shiny new thing out of R&D would
win the war all by itself, and grubby politicians. Goffs all.

"By St. Michael, Win, it looks more and more like they're
getting their way."

Wahlberg winked. "Looks can be deceiving."

"Would you care to elaborate?"

"No."

Something was brewing. Something that his old friend

felt Stone didn't need to know—at least not yet. But it was also something that Wahlberg thought Stone ought to be aware of, something of which Wahlberg felt he could not speak openly. Interesting.

"We should talk of other things," Wahlberg continued. "Wilson Horner sends his regards."

Horner was a name of their shared past. Ben Horner. Ben had also been on a first-name basis before he'd gotten himself inducted posthumously into the Order of Valor in the Davison campaign. He'd been a good man, a true Eridani.

"I don't know a Wilson Horner. One of Ben's boys, is he?"

"Youngest and last surviving son. Quite the rising star. He got transferred to the Strategic Staff last quarter and is settling in just fine. The boy's got a bright future."

"If the goffs don't beat him down."

"Not this boy, Chris. He's his father reborn with more political sense than you, I, and Ben put together. He'll survive."

If that evalution was correct, he'd likely do more than survive.

"Anyway, Wilson wanted to send his regards to one of his father's old comrades."

And Wahlberg undoubtedly wanted to give Stone a name of a partisan at StratCom.

They talked some more about old friends and life back home, all without any air of portentousness, before moving on to shop talk. Stone, happy to have a reliable confidant, used the opportunity to try out some of his ideas regarding his new theater command. Chip saw to it that they didn't starve as their discussion went on deep into the night.

2

PAN-STELLAR COMBINE
CYGNUS

Benton Mainwaring looked up from the screen to scrutinize
the personification of the data he'd been studying. This
Larsen Williams looked to be a right fine fellow. His tanned
skin showed him to be no idle indoors layabout, and the
sleeveless shirt he'd chosen to wear displayed firm and well-
defined muscles. There were calluses on his hands and scars
in the right places that fit the physical data. Whether he truly
had the rather impressive skills listed on his application
would be another matter, but the datapad was showing that
his references had checked out, so it seemed likely that he
was what he appeared to be: an excellent potential addition
to the team.

"So, Mister Williams, what can you tell me about yourself
that's not in this dossier?"

"Depends," he drawled. "What's in the dossier?"

Williams's accent struck Benton. "Your accent is a little
odd for a Combine citizen."

Williams gave an indifferent shrug. "When I was a kid my
parents were trading on Laurenten, that's in the Concordat.
Don't remember much about the planet, since we left before
I hit double digits, but it seems the accent stuck. Girls seem
to like it."

"Well, that's certainly something that's not in the data."

"Thought I put that Laurenten stay down in my application." Williams looked worried. "You're not gonna deny me
'cause I talk funny, are you?"

Benton chuckled. "The Laurenten sojourn is there in the record, Mister Williams. I was referring to your accent's effect on women. And don't worry, if we denied a berth to everyone who spoke oddly, we'd have an extremely small crew, wouldn't we, Master Lugard?"

"Whatever you be saying, Colonel Mainwaring."

Benton watched as Williams gave the grizzled old spacer a dubious look. Not surprising, since Lugard hadn't bothered to put on his uniform for the interviews. The man looked like some derelict tramp freighter pilot. It was fortunate for him that his skills in space far exceeded his sartorial ones. Benton felt a curious need to justify his choice of the man.

"This is Master Piet Lugard, he's my mandatory guild spacer. He may look a fright, but he is vastly experienced on the frontier. He will be responsible for keeping me from pressing the wrong buttons and evacuating our ships to space."

"That be about it," Lugard agreed.

"Master Lugard is also my fleet captain and second in command, so despite his laconic response, he does have a few other responsibilities even if he doesn't *yet* dress the part."

Benton hoped that Lugard would understand the hint of the *yet*. If he didn't, Benton would dock his pay and see if that made more of an impression. But that was a matter for another time; for the moment there were men to hire.

"Now, Mister Williams, I see that your employment record shows you to be something of a jack of all trades."

"I've knocked around some. I do the jobs I get."

"And well, it seems. Your application lists a preference for engineering. We're looking for good engin—"

A flash of robes near the back of the line of applicants arrested his thoughts. Though the robed figure's cowl was pulled up to hide her face, Benton recognized the Alsion initiate as Jasmine Coppelstowe. She was, he hoped, bringing the word he wanted. Forgetting Williams, he turned to face her as she came around to his side of the table.

"It is arranged," she said softly.

It *was* the word he'd been waiting for. "When?"

"Now."

Now? Surely Alsion had thought of that. Of course he had. Such a small thing could not escape the master of alinear sociodynamics. Still, it paid to be sure.

"But it will take time to get to the Institute. The meeting will be when we arrive, yes?"

"Of course. When else could it be?"

Benton grinned at the very Alsionite answer. He dropped the datapad on the table as he stood, waving vaguely toward the line of men waiting to see him. "Hire him if he seems good to you, Master Lugard. And any of the rest that suit."

The guild spacer grunted something in reply, but Benton didn't catch it. Nor did he care. The man was perfectly capable of doing the job alone and Benton had something better to do. He raced out to his car. Jones had the engines idling at ready by the time Coppelstowe, following more sedately, joined him in the passenger compartment.

"Let's go, Jones," he commanded.

The aircar lifted on roaring turbofans and, grinning still, he let gravity settle him back into the seat.

He was on his way to actually meet with Ambrose Alsion himself.

The Alsion Institute compound was virtually a city, and something of a fortified one at that. Although ground access to the public areas was barely restricted, flying into the Institute compound was unusual. Coppelstowe had provided the necessary clearances and codes to Jones and they zipped in. On the way Benton picked out the dormitory that Uncle Vincent had endowed and the library wing that Aunt Sharon had set up, right where they were supposed to be according to the family plans of the compound. He'd never felt prouder than he did today that the Mainwarings had had a hand in the good works of the Institute, working as partners with the renowned Alsion.

He caught his breath as Jones banked the car into the lane leading through the ring of the Fellowship, the nine towers that encircled the center of the compound, for there, in the heart of it all and nestled safely inside the Fellowship's protective ring, stood the famous *fidnaljef,* the gift unlooked for, from the Mimaks: Alsion's Tower. It looked much like a gothic cathedral from Old Earth, but then it should, since it had been designed by architects steeped in the architecture of Old Earth's religious structures and built by Old Earth craftsmen. No matter that Mimak credits had paid for it, Alsion's Tower radiated a sense of the cradle of humankind and glorified humankind's aspirations.

It was said that the design of the building had inspired Alsion's followers to adopt the positively medieval robes they wore, supposedly to meld with the building's dynamics. Benton wasn't sure about that, but he was certain that the robed initiate who met them on the landing pad and ushered them into the outer precincts fit perfectly in those surroundings.

Alsion's Tower was, of course, more than just a steeple, otherwise it would not have evoked the comparison to cathedrals. Like the true old cathedrals, it was a complex assortment of related structures, all interconnected and all serving very particular purposes. Their guide led them through halls and courtyards that were wonderfully alive with busy initiates and bustling scholars. Many of the scholars wore lapel pins showing their Institute association, though there was also a scattering displaying more esoteric signs of Alsionic status such as idiosyncratic caps or armbands. A substantial number wore robes similar to those of the initiates, though people in the know, like Benton, could distinguish the subtle differences in cut and detail that differentiated scholar from initiate. Other details displayed the level of sponsorship for the former and rank of the latter, but Benton was not as well versed in those nuances. Here and there in the crowds he saw several familiar faces. He nodded in acknowledgment when they looked his way and spoke greetings to those whose names he remembered.

A step through a triple-arched doorway and the crowds were gone, the bustle rapidly fading to a murmur as they strode on. They were in the private precincts now, coming ever closer to Alsion's sanctum. At last they arrived at a massive pair of double doors covered in red leather and studded and hinged with gilded metal. Their guide stopped and stepped aside. Coppelstowe took up a position opposite her on the other side of the doors. Slowly the doors opened. The guide indicated that Benton should proceed into the darkness beyond.

With his first step over the threshold, Benton's eyes began to adjust. It was not truly stygian in the chamber. A pale line stretched away from the door, a path. He took it.

Striding down the alabaster walkway, he took in the wonder of the place. The hall's darkness was a stage for two famous treasures. Ahead of him, the Glory Window shone with radiant light. In its center was what heralds called a sun in splendor, its smiling face smug with the secret knowledge of the universe that alinear sociodynamics offered. To either side the champions of light, rendered in astonishingly subtle stained glass, fought and vanquished the reptilian representatives of evil. A medieval splendor, but splendorous nonetheless. And above it was a greater wonder, the heart of *fidnaljef*: the Mimak Rose, an ever-changing rose window that focused light in endless variations as the very embodiment of the dynamic in the universe. It was said to be the pinnacle of Mimak biotechnological achievement and to incorporate secrets of their mystic philosophies. Benton's eyes were teary from taking in its beauty.

Benton could hardly believe he was actually basking in these wonders, seeing them as they were meant to be seen. But he was not given much time to stand in awe. A shaft of light speared down from the lofty gloom to illuminate an alabaster desk set in the center of the chamber. Behind it sat Ambrose Alsion himself, his bearded face calm and serene.

A second shaft winked on, spotlighting an ancient, leather-upholstered chair set before the desk. Benton accepted the invitation and sat. He had barely done so when Alsion spoke.

"Tell me now—in your own words and not those of the

underlings who drafted your request for a meeting—what is most important in your need to speak with me."

Alsion's tone was not unkindly but it reminded Benton of a teacher calling a wayward student to task. It had been a long time since anyone had spoken to him that way and it caught him off guard. He summoned his thoughts, groping for the best way to phrase his intentions. It had been a long time too since he had done that by himself in important circumstances. Much as he wanted to, he dared not use the carefully constructed phrases his public relations people had prepared to sell his idea.

"Since its inception, the Pan-Stellar Combine has been a model star nation. We have grown and prospered, demonstrating without a doubt that our competitive strategy of eschewing force as the principal extension of diplomacy in favor of exploiting the cold, hard realities of commerce is feasible, profitable, and wise. But dark times are on the horizon, although some, especially those on the Board of Directors, continue to blind themselves to the peril.

"For over a decade, the Directors have ignored the threat posed by the Remor. Until recently their policies seemed justified. The alien enemy's initial attacks were far from our space. We sat idle and let the most threatened star nations form the Interstellar Defense League and fight the enemy. Once, I agreed with that policy. The Remor's stab deep into the heart of human space at Chugen changed that.

"We are no longer safe hiding behind the League. If the Remor could strike at Chugen, so far away from their previous depredations, what is to prevent them from striking directly to the heart of the Combine and attacking Cygnus itself? Alas, none of the Directors to whom I've spoken want to hear it. Some, I think, will not believe in the Remor threat until the aliens vaporize their summer homes around their ears.

"I believe that the time has come for a demonstration. The Directors—no, the entire Combine—must be shown that idleness is wrong, and that we cannot ignore the threat of the

Remor any longer. The forces of the universe press upon us. The time for action has come! Someone must act!"

Benton's long, impromptu speech left him slightly breathless. He certainly had poured his passion into it. He didn't think he was telling Alsion anything that the creator and master of alinear sociodynamics didn't already know for himself, but he had expected some response other than silence. Alsion didn't even twitch. Clearly Benton had not said enough.

"And so I have organized—"

"Colonel Mainwaring's Expeditionary Force," Alsion finished for him. "A stirring name."

The compliment pleased Benton. "It does seem to have inspired some. Not always the right sort, I'll admit, but all in all the organization chart is filling nicely. Why, already—"

"You have taken the rank of colonel-in-command. Not field marshal? Not even general?"

"Well, field marshal just wasn't right and, well, general didn't seem appropriate either. I've read that oftentimes in human history when regiments were raised, the leader was a colonel, so I thought that would be suitable. And according to Interstellar Defense League rank structure, a colonel commands a wing or a brigade, which is almost exactly what my initial table of organization works out to be. Using League-style formations, of course. That did seem to be the best way to . . ." Benton trailed off. Alsion was staring silently at him. Had he made a mistake? "Do you disapprove? Is there something more apropos?"

"You are a being of free will. You, not I, choose your path. The universe, not I, will decide if it is smooth or rocky. Do you have good boots?"

Benton's eyes flicked down to the bespoke Robinsons that he wore before he realized the irrelevance and rhetorical nature of the question. Alsion was teasing him about his self-appointed rank.

Well, Benton was a big enough man to take a little teasing. What he called himself as leader of the expedition didn't really matter. What was important was the mission itself.

"I intend to join the war against the Remor. This is no time for true men to stand idle. Humankind itself is threatened! The enemy must be stopped!"

"With your small force?"

Was that mockery he heard in Alsion's voice? "We will fight alongside the valiant men and women of the Interstellar Defense League. Yes, we are a small force, but we are only a beginning. A beginning of the end for the Remor."

"All ends have beginnings, but not all beginnings have ends." Alsion shrugged. "At least not the ends envisioned at the beginning."

This was not going at all as Benton had hoped. "What is it that you want me to say, sir? What do you require of me?"

"You, sir? I require nothing of you, sir. People come here because they require something of me. You, sir, have come here, therefore you require something of me. But for the sake of old relationships, I will warn you that what I give is not always what is sought, even though it might seem otherwise. So, Benton Mainwaring, what do you seek? Answer honestly, and I will do likewise, as far as I can."

What Benton wanted was to be told that he was doing the right thing. "I was hoping for your blessing, sir."

"For your adventure?"

"Well, I would hardly call it an adventure," Benton sputtered. "You make it sound like an ill-conceived lark, some sort of—"

"And it is not a lark?"

Benton was on his feet. "I grow tired of your mocking, sir. What I do, I do for the sake and safety of humankind!"

"That a safe humankind means safety of your investments and patrimony is, to be sure, coincidental."

"Again you moc—"

"The truth stings, does it not? Sit, Benton Mainwaring, and calm yourself. Baser motives have led to greater goods. I find no fault in your reasons. Self-interest informs the dynamic and the dynamic informs the universe."

Chastised, Benton sat.

"Despite this," said Alsion, plucking at the robe he wore,

"I am no priest to give a blessing to anyone or anything. Nor yet am I a master of warriors to lead a host by your side."

"But you are said to be the wisest of advisors," Benton said, wincing at the whine he heard in his voice. It was embarrassing to have this calm old man twist him so easily out of his equilibrium. He wanted, needed, to get something from Alsion. "Have you no advice for me?"

For several moments Alsion was still, seeming a statue. His voice was small when he spoke.

"Shall I tell you to count your cash? No, you want something more specific. They always want something more specific, as if specificity were something to be plucked from the dynamic like an apple from a tree."

Alsion sighed.

"Right, then," he said more energetically. "Shall I then tell you that it will be darker before the light comes? Shall I tell you to be brave in the face of adversity? Shall I tell you to be prepared, to be vigilant, and to be wary of those who are not what they seem?"

Disappointment dragged at Benton. "I had hoped for something better than platitudes."

A shrug dismissed his disappointment. "We all have hopes, my good Colonel-in-Command Mainwaring. Some are foolish and some well considered. Many hopes are held in opposition to those of other dreamers. All hopes are fulfilled or dashed or simply left hanging in the continuum. Would it help if I told you that I see a butterfly in you?"

A butterfly? A butterfly! Gloom cracked and fell away from Benton. In alinear sociodynamics, the term *butterfly* was applied to pivotal figures upon whom the course of history would turn. He didn't understand a lot of alinear sociodynamics. Honestly, he didn't understand much of it at all, but he knew it worked. Using its predictive principles Alsion made himself the richest man in human space before retiring from business and setting up the philanthropic Institute.

"Hah!" Benton shouted. Alsion has just named him a butterfly. A mover. A shaker. He *would* be the one making a difference. "I knew I was doing the right thing."

"You do what you do," Alsion said quietly. "You are a ripple in the pond of the sea."

"What a lovely image! Ripples spreading out, each influencing others. I shall be your ripple, spreading and touching others. People will listen to me! They will see and follow my example! There is hope for humankind!"

Oddly, Alsion looked sad.

"Waves rise, and the shore will be changed," he said. "Go now."

The light above Alsion winked out, leaving Benton apparently alone in the dark chamber. The Glory Window still shone and rippling light shifted across the Mimak Rose. The stone of the walkway behind him dimly glowed, offering a path to the slowly opening doors.

He was being shown the way out.

3

SERENTEN CONCORDAT
SERENTEN

Sipping the morning's third cup of coffee, Danielle Wyss gave her attention to the Data and News Network's early morning news summary. As Premier Minister of the Concordat she had access to far more, and far better informed, sources of news than the DNN, but sometimes it was important to see for herself what angle her constituents were getting on the events of the day. DNN, despite its foreign home base in the Federated Star Nations, was the most widely scanned of the news media in the Concordat, and, also despite its home base in the self-involved FSN, usually gave good and balanced coverage to news of interstellar import. Idly she wondered if this morning's local lead story would get as much play on the core worlds of the FSN as it would on affiliates in the more far-flung parts of human-controlled space such as the Concordat.

As always, the briefing team seated in Danielle's office indulged her. They doubtless expected, from experience, that the interruption of the meeting would be brief.

"You've tuned to DNN," announced the traditional mellifluous voice as the screen filled with the earnest face of Serenten anchor Joss Mutabayo. The newsman covered the usual opening pleasantries before getting into "today's good news" with only the shortest of puff about DNN's diligent reporters.

"Last night a newly arrived diplomatic commission from

the Interstellar Defense League met with representatives of the Concordat government to formally announce an end to the IDL's controversial cartographic policy of sector designations, believed by many to be an implicit claim of hegemony over human-occupied space. The timing of this announcement has been coordinated to occur simultaneously at the capitals of major star nations and selected independent planets as part of a, quote, symbolic reminder that all humankind is inextricably bound by ties of origin and brotherhood, end quote.

"Further, in a prepared statement, IDL envoy General Whitcomb said, 'This new organizational structure is purely internal, subdividing the IDL space into jurisdictional zones called theaters, none of which include worlds of nonsignatory star nations or independent planets. We do this in an attempt to allay unwarranted concerns about the nature of the Interstellar Defense League. We exist merely to defend humankind from the threat of the Remor enemy.' Early critics, noting that Remor activity has been virtually nonexistent since the Battle of Chugen, have been quick to point out that several of these so-called theaters include worlds that never joined the Interstellar Defense League before they fell under Remor subjugation. This has caused some civic leaders to suggest that, despite soothing words to the contrary, the IDL remains expansionist."

He had more to say, but it was increasingly speculative. Danielle didn't need to bother with that, having hordes of speculators already reporting to her. She killed the feed and scanned the faces of her advisors.

"So how many of our good citizens care about this?"

Minister of State Henri Bouake wrinkled his grandfatherly face into a disdainful smile. "Outside of the government and a few communities of intellectuals, not many. Creeping fascists never seem as threatening as marching fascists. This victory probably won't even rate a footnote when some modern-day Shirer writes his *Rise and Fall of the Interstellar Defense League,* but at least we can sleep a little easier at night."

"Can we?" That suspicious question came from Security Minister Pamela Schmidt.

"Professional paranoia, Pam, or aware-anoia?" Danielle asked. Schmidt preferred asking questions to making statements, a fine characteristic for a person in the security business, but one that occasionally was a problem; she needed to remember that she also wore another hat as advisor to the Premier Minister.

"Nothing concrete to report at this time," Schmidt replied.

"But you have suspicions."

"She always has suspicions," Bouake stated. "It's in her job description and if it weren't, she'd have it written in."

Schmidt ignored the gibe. "For the most part, the change seems to be nothing more than a public relations ploy. The details supporting this conclusion are in my full report. In short, the shift to theater designations appears to be simply notional. We have observed no change in the martial law authorities granted to commanders, no change in strategic military postures, no change in strategic force allocations, and thus no change to the possible threat to the Concordat if the IDL is as expansionist as Minister Bouake believes."

"It is," he assured her.

None of the Concordat's intelligence services agreed wholeheartedly with Bouake, but enough of them saw danger signs that Danielle had her own misgivings regarding the IDL's benevolence. She recalled old advice from her father. *Know your enemies, so you will know where to hurt them. Know your friends better, for when the time comes that they become your enemies.* It had been political advice, but it applied between nations as well as between politicians. With the Concordat and the IDL sharing a border, an expansionist IDL could one day become an enemy. Danielle had no intention of letting the Concordat be caught unawares. Suitable protective vigilance was at the heart of today's meeting.

"There are, however, some new points of data to consider," Schmidt continued. "The roster of theater commanders is nearly identical to that of the sector commanders. One and only one is no longer in command of the theater that has replaced his sector."

"Who?" Danielle asked, though she suspected that she already knew the answer.

"Marshal Christoph Stone."

"So he has finally been cashiered for that Chamomile affair at Chugen," Bouake said.

"That would be Operation Chameleon," Schmidt corrected. "Unfortunately I cannot confirm that Stone has been removed from MilForce for that or any other reason. In fact, he appears to retain an active command staff, suggesting that he has been appointed some new task. I asked General Lockhart to prepare a briefing on what we know. General?"

Danielle was familiar with the general's far from brief briefings. "A précis will do for now, General Lockhart."

Lockhart frowned at not being allowed free rein and took a moment to organize his thoughts.

"As you saw in the last status report on IDL activity, IDL Defense Sector 32—ahem, excuse me, Tarsus Theater—has been downgraded from Red to Orange, indicating a reduction in Remor activity. As per IDL standard protocols, MilForce elements are being reassigned to more threatened areas. Simultaneously other fleet elements are heading for Tarsus Station. Since some of these are coming from low-threat sectors, it appears that they are not part of a force rotation to rest frontline troops."

"Then what are they, General?" asked Bouake, voicing the question to which Danielle herself wanted an answer.

"We don't know."

Bouake liked the answer no better than Danielle did. "Tarsus Station is too far away to threaten us. But it does border the Pan-Stellar Combine. Could the IDL be planning an attack on the Combine?"

"Possible, but unlikely," concluded Schmidt. "Sympathy

for the IDL is at an all-time high in the Combine, which is not to say that it is strong. The PSC Board of Directors is currently debating a resolution to join the IDL. This would be an injudicious time for the IDL to apply force."

"I concur," Danielle said. Of course, the quarrelsome and fractious PSC Board could go on debating until the stars went out. It might be that the IDL was getting impatient. The League's ruling junta wasn't composed of the most politically astute bullies on the block. "Perhaps the League perceives the situation in the Combine differently than we do. General, is MilForce actually increasing their forces in Tarsus Theater?"

"There is movement both in and out of the system, but it doesn't look like a significant change in combat power, Premier Minister."

"Which is anomalous for an operational sector just downgraded to an Orange danger rating," Schmidt added.

"Are they assembling a fleet?" Neither Schmidt nor Lockhart answered her at once. "Well?"

"We can't be sure, Premier Minister," Lockhart finally admitted.

"But you think so."

"Yes, Premier Minister, I do."

Danielle didn't need to ask Schmidt if she agreed with the general's assessment. She wouldn't have let him voice it unchallenged otherwise. A fleet. With no immediate Remor threat to oppose it.

"Where do they intend to use this fleet? Could there be a new problem on the fringe?" Danielle felt she was grasping at straws. "Tarsus is a frontier region. Pirates?"

"We can find no hint of any such threats," Schmidt said.

Not a comforting answer. Fleets were best assembled in safe, quiet harbors away from their intended targets. Tarsus Station was a long way from Concordat space, and might be just such a safe harbor. How unfortunate that Tarsus was also a long way from the Concordat's prying intelligence apparatus.

"We need to know what's going on."

Schmidt nodded in agreement, then smiled. "We believe we have an agent positioned to begin providing that information."

Danielle listened avidly to the details.

4

RIM WORLDS ECONOMIC UNION (DEFUNCT)
PACIFICA, KILAWA ISLE, PALISANDRA

Somewhere in the stinking darkness of the cellar, someone was crying.

"Shut down the noise," Bartie hissed, loud as he dared. "Or I'll shut you down."

His threat worked. The whiner stifled it. Bartie was glad. Sure, he'd have made good on the threat, but that would have made noise too. Noise was the last thing they needed.

There were xombies in the building.

Not ooga-booga magic-type xombies, but near enough. The shuffling, blank-eyed things they called xombies had been people once, before the xenos had gotten hold of them.

Damn frickin' xenos!

They'd come and hauled off people and messed with them. Bartie used to think that the people they caught were just killed or something. Tortured, probably,'cause that's the sort of thing frickin' xenos did. Maybe even eaten. Damned xenos would do that too. That's what he'd thought had happened to the bastards the frickin' xenos had hauled off, but he knew better now. He'd seen Gene and Howie and a couple of women that he'd caught once or twice shuffling along with a xombie hunting party. He knew then that the damn frickin' xenos had messed with them. Changed them. Made them into xombies.

He'd felt bad when he'd seen Gene and Howie. They'd been good boys. Good scroungers. Hadn't stopped him from putting his machete into the back of Howie's head twenty minutes ago when the frickin' Howie-zombie had chased a runner from Sheldon's gang right into the middle of Bartie's camp.

Howie had died easy enough. Not like xombies in stories—now, *those* would have been a problem. All these xombies died without having to be hacked to bits or blown to pieces. They were still tough, though. Small calibers didn't bother them too much. And they were strong. They were trouble, all right. 'Specially when there were a lot of them. Or when they had those damn xeno machines backing them up.

Damn frickin' xenos!

Everything was their fault.

"I can hear them, Bartie," Jones whispered. "They're up there."

Of course they were up there. There had been more than Howie cruising for meat. A hundred of them, maybe more, and he'd been caught away from his doss with only a couple dozen of his best slugs. The frickin' xombies had scared what seemed to be all of Sheldon's little gang. The whole damn, squalling crowd had come running through the camp. Caught off guard like that, there hadn't been much point in fighting. Stupid to fight when the odds weren't in your favor. Stupider to fight when you didn't know the odds.

So he'd called a retreat. Sheldon's people had run with them. The frickin' xombies had chased the whole mob. People had scattered into small groups and ducked in the nearest buildings. It was easier to find places to hide in the derelicts. The frickin' xombies had come right after them.

"Just shut up," he snarled at Jones. "They still got ears."

Bartie used his. He could hear the scuff of feet on rubble as the damn xombies searched the building for them. The things weren't bright. And they didn't stick with it. Easily distracted bastards, they were. Getting out of sight and staying there for a while worked.

Bartie had found a good hole where he'd hidden from the bastards before. Jones and a few others of Bartie's gang had crawled in with him. A few of Sheldon's weenies had gotten in before they could get the door closed. If they all stayed quiet, the frickin' xombies would go right by.

Problem was, Bartie could hear something else up there. Something that didn't move like a xombie.

Jones heard it too. "Sounds like there's a machine up there too."

That would be bad.

Damn frickin' xenos!

The damn xombies always worked harder when their frickin' xeno masters had them on a tight leash. The bastards were working hard now.

Above them, at the top of the stairs, the door rattled as something tested it. The bar they'd placed in the crudely welded brackets held. No damn xombie, even strong as they was, was gonna bust it open. Nothing human was gonna bust it.

Nothing human did.

The door screamed like a woman as metal bent and hinges tore. The locking bar gave. It tumbled down the stairs, bent and twisted. Bartie got out of its way. Somebody behind him wasn't bright enough. He yelped when the shaft clipped him.

Darkness shattered.

The harsh light stabbing down into the dark cellar made it hard to see. Bartie caught a silhouette. It was a damn frickin' xeno machine. Lotsa legs. It had found them. Like a hound. Hadda be. Then it had torn open their cover like a kid ripping into a candy box looking for a prize.

Its job done, the damn machine scuttled away from the opening. It was too big to fit through the doorframe anyway. The glare got worse with the frickin' xeno no longer blocking the light. A voice called out from above.

"Come out. Come out and you won't be harmed."

Like hell they wouldn't. Bartie took a tighter grip on his machete. It was a better tool than a gun for fighting the damn xombies in the darkened cellar. No muzzle flash to blind. No report to deafen. He'd chop the bastards when they came. They'd come. He was sure they'd come.

"That's Jim Breen," somebody said. She sounded shocked and surprised.

Breen was one of Sheldon's lieutenants. Or had been. There was a slur to the man's speech that Bartie didn't remember. Breen had to have been xombified. But if he was, he was a different breed of xombie. Most of them barely managed a mumble.

"We ain't comin' out," Bartie shouted in defiance. "You come down here and you ain't coming out either."

Breen didn't respond.

"What's the matter? You scared, you stinking xombie trash? You oughta be. I'm Bartie Lars and I sent every bloody one of you that ever tried to catch me to hell. You hear that? To hell! I'll do the same for each and every one of you if you come down here. You hear me?"

The answer was an avalanche of xombies.

He chopped the first one. And the second. Jones was there as well. And a few of his other slugs. The rest scattered into the cellar's recesses. Bartie cursed them, hoping their wet pants gave them terminal crotch rot.

His machete sheared through an arm and lodged in a rib cage. Before he could wrench it free, one of the bastards grabbed his arm. They struggled for possession of the weapon. Another slugged him hard. He saw stars.

Jones went down.

The bastards were crawling all over him. He lost his grip on the machete. He kicked. He punched. He gouged. He bit.

It didn't do enough.

There were too many of them and they wrestled him into snarling, cursing helplessness. Arms pinned to his side, he was hustled up the stairs. The light made his eyes tear, but he had no trouble recognizing the machine squatting in the midst of its xombie slaves like some lord of creation.

He spat at it.

It didn't care.

Damn frickin' xenos!

5

INTERSTELLAR DEFENSE LEAGUE, TARSUS THEATER
TARSUS V

Clad in an Mk. 17 Personal Battle Harness, Anders Seaborg couldn't feel the wind blowing across the alkali flats. He could see it lifting and spreading the dust kicked up by the blowers maneuvering toward the distant violet mountains whose humped shapes defined the western horizon. Without magnification he couldn't see the blowers either. As with the wind, he knew they were there from external evidence, free of personal experiential data. His hardsuit could tell him more than he cared to know about the wind's parameters, and it could give him pertinent data on the blowers; he had but to ask. The 'suit was a marvel of modern military technology. It enhanced his senses, offered a wide array of weapon and utility features, and was even stocked with an extensive library and an analysis engine able to unravel tactical problems.

Unfortunately it had nothing to offer Anders by way of dealing with the questions that plagued him.

He stood in the gun basket of a General Lift Turbines Mk. 8 armored scout car. It was a command version, outfitted with a selection of appropriate black boxes and commo equipment designed for command and control of an Eridani-style armored infantry company. The tactical identification burned into its IFF transponder marked it as the command vehicle for the 102nd Armored Infantry Company, Independent. The independent designation meant that the company was not part of any battalion, but an asset to be assigned as needed by the high command. A properly authorized request to a MilForce databank would reveal the relevant high command as a task group code named Balboa Rising.

A similar request would reveal that the commander of 102 ArmInfCo was one Captain Anders Seaborg.

Him. His blower. His company. His command. It wasn't at all what he'd been expecting when he'd left Stone's office. Not that he'd known what to expect.

Stone had said that Anders wasn't lucky enough to be a simple 'pounder and Old Stone Face had been right. There was nothing simple about command. But Stone had been wrong too. Anders was in a 'suit, in a blower, on the ground. He was being what he'd dreamed of being and trained to be, a soldier. There was not a desk in sight.

And that raised the question of why. Stone spoke of a tough, near-suicidal mission. So why had the forty souls of 102 ArmInfCo been tied to his fate?

Stone had also spoken of a chance at redemption. As commander, he was responsible for the men and women of the company. Was Anders now responsible for their redemption as well? And if so, what were they to be redeemed from?

They were fair questions, but they were not questions for today. Today he had to lead the 102nd against the opposition. Today's question was: Were they, Anders included, up to it?

The company was organized on an Eridani pattern and was equipped with Eridani matériel, but it was not staffed exclusively by Eridani. What in MilForce was, these days? Besides himself, there were only four Eridani, not enough to fill all the noncoms slots. The rest of his noncoms and all of his troopers hailed from various parts of the IDL, which raised the usual integration issues. Nearly a quarter were Lancastrians, most of whom were experienced in war. Half of his blower chiefs were Kansians, who by living up to their national stereotype as mechanically minded were providing the company with a strong asset. They and their fellow nationals were the next largest group. Add in the nearly as numerous Gallentinians, you'd have more than half of the troops. There were also Holsteaders, Nusians, and Grenwolders. The sole Rift's Verger was a fresh-faced kid with high aptitude scores but no seasoning, and though he had a couple of steady veterans in his lone Eustan and only Caledonian, troopers of their competency were in short supply. Far too many of his 'pounders were green, fresh out of PBH advanced training. Even some of his noncoms were new to 'suits.

The troops needed practice, a lot of it, and they needed to get used to doing things the right way, the Eridani way. It was something that he knew from experience could be difficult for folk from some of the League worlds. That same experience told him that it could be done; he had his reformed troublemaker Milano as proof of that. You could get silk from a sow, but you had to work at it.

Aside from the cultural issues, he had the more serious issue of combat effectiveness to consider. Anders had done what he could with the personnel he'd been given, trying to spread the existing expertise around while not diluting it too much. Though he'd hated to do it, he'd broken up the only battle-experienced full squad, Mossberg's Lancastrians, but the transfer gave him a veteran hardsuiter to lead the second squad in that platoon. If it worked out well, newly promoted Sergeant Lerner would turn his batch of greenies into an effective copy of Mossberg's squad.

There had been other tough choices. Each and every one fretted him, but the time to worry about them was not really available. Blowers were on the move. Today would see the 102nd's first test.

Anders brought up his visor's magnification to check on how they were doing. Hewitt's 1st platoon and Mossberg's 3rd platoon were headed across the hardpan, making good time. Somewhere out ahead of them, the single carrier of Vadi's 2nd platoon was waiting, its hardsuited troopers deployed in overwatch. And somewhere ahead of that, Vadi's scout car was probing. Behind them, Anders's command team and Chee's 4th platoon's support vehicles waited. It was almost a textbook deployment. Almost.

"Cable, this is Cutter," he commed. "Your blowers are too close. Min fifty-meter interval. RBA."

It took Sergeant Mossberg twenty seconds to relay his order and execute. That Response By Action was about fifteen seconds slower than standard and the execution left something to be desired. The calibration field on Anders's visor showed the Mk. 3's to be almost exactly fifty meters apart and closing up the distance every time the terrain offered an obstacle. Clumping was a twitch of Mossberg's. She had her troopers do it when they were dismounted too, he recalled. It was a habit that needed breaking.

Anders gave the order to advance so that the command team and 4th platoon wouldn't be left too far behind, and slid down into the body of the command car. As Gordie set the car in motion, Anders patched the feed from the command console into his 'suit. With transponders synched to position satellites that relayed data to command units, the command circuit showed unit positions far better than any one man's eyes.

"Let's close up the distance a bit, Gordie."

"Will do, sir."

Anders studied the display, noting several likely places where an ambushing unit or two could be concealed. Hewitt's platoon was supposed to have swept the area, but they were learning their jobs too, and mistakes got made.

Ten minutes later, they were still well short of the foothills where 2nd platoon was waiting. The lead maneuvering elements were reaching a stretch of broken ground. Sure enough, Mossberg started edging her two carriers closer together.

"Smoke, sir!" Milano announced. "Someone's brewed up."

The updated screen agreed: Mossberg's number two carrier was gone. No telltales came on to show troopers having successfully bailed from their totaled vehicle.

The reason was plain. Two new blips had appeared, glaring in the red of enemy units. The computer identified the newly revealed units as Remor fighting machines of the type called *Skinks*. A GLT Mk. 3 Universal Carrier was armored, but not well enough to stand up to close fire from a single *Skink*. A pair of them had concentrated their fire on number two.

Feeling the need to see with his own eyes, Anders hauled himself back into the gun basket. He didn't need amplification to see the rising smoke, but he did need it to see the action. He called it up as Milano, not needing orders, ducked down to monitor the console.

Mossberg's own blower was catching fire from the enemy. Trailing wisps of black smoke from hits, the carrier tried to dodge. It banked too hard. Dust rose as air spilled from the hovercraft's skirts. The exposure was all the enemy needed to drill the blower. Crippled, it skidded to a halt.

More smoke appeared, intentional smoke. Someone aboard had popped the dispensers. A roiling swirl of chaff, visual and electronic and dispersive, boiled up between the vehicle and its hunters.

"Got three 'pounders, sir," Milano reported. The troopers' lights would be showing on his screen "No, four. One's Sergeant Mossberg."

So far she'd survived her mistake. Half her squad and her number two carrier with all aboard hadn't.

Anders was about to call Vadi, but he was already on the ball. Four vapor trails rippled through the evening air. A moment later two more joined them. It was a sloppy launch but a timely one, and Anders could hear Mossberg's troops cheering on the missiles from Vadi's deployed 'pounders. Three of the birds bore in on *Skink* alpha. One missed, but the other two did what they needed to do.

"Alpha bandit, scratched," reported Milano.

Vadi's trailing missiles also came in on alpha, too late to do more than kill an already dead machine. The lone missile on *Skink* bravo didn't kill it.

"Comp estimates substantial damage on *Skink* bravo."

But not enough to defang it. The enemy's energy weapons raked Mossberg's position as *Skink* bravo advanced toward the grounded troopers.

"Ford's gone. Jabi's wounded."

Milano was getting his data from the status board. Anders could have checked for himself, his 'suit was still in the circuit, but his eyes were elsewhere. There was more cavalry riding to the rescue.

Hewitt's platoon had altered vector almost as soon as the *Skinks* had emerged. The 1st's scout car had been closer and was faster. It came screaming over a low rise, heavy pulse gun blazing.

On the tac channel Anders could hear Hewitt calling for Robson to back off, to wait for support. The scout car commander didn't reply. The car swooped toward the enemy, its weapon hammering out continuous, mostly accurate fire.

"*Skink* bravo taking damage. Shite!"

Anders didn't need to hear Milano's report that the scout car's icon had gone dark. He could see the new ball of expanding smoke.

A missile burned through the cloud to streak past the nearly dead *Skink*. Another blasted in from Vadi's position. That one was on target.

"*Skink* bravo down," Milano said with satisfaction.

Anders wished he could feel any sort of satisfaction. The company had been mauled. Losing one blower to the ambush was, perhaps, unavoidable. Proper interval would have given Mossberg's carrier a chance to get clear. And Robson's car—how did an officer teach his men the difference between rashness and boldness? The latter won battles, the former just filled body bags.

Anders shifted the command team's scout car to replace Hewitt's lost one and had Gordie take the command car into the drifting smoke that masked the confrontation site.

"Bad luck," Mossberg said when the command blower pulled up alongside her smoking carrier. "But we got them."

"We will be discussing it later, Sergeant. For now, you might be interested to know that the referees have declared you and the rest of your 'survivors' to be victims of *Skink* bravo's dissolution."

Remor vehicles deconstructed themselves when destroyed and showed a nasty tendency to do the same to anything else in the vicinity. Mossberg's troops had been within the usual zone of destruction, and had their opponent been a real *Skink,* they would have likely been disabled at the very least.

She started to curse the unfairness of it. Anders cut her off.

"I don't want to hear it. You can start on your report while you sit out the rest of this exercise. I suggest you consider what you might have done differently." Gordie received Anders's private circuit blip and started the blower on its way. "And I want your recommendation for a suitable chastisement for your platoon too."

The roar of the engines swamped her renewed cussing.

The smoke was starting to clear, aided by the passage of the command blower and abetted by the OpFor troopers shutting down the smoke candles that simulated destruction hits. Anders opaqued his visor so he didn't have to show his face to the commanders of the tanks that had played the *Skinks.* With broad "gotcha" grins, they stood on their vehicles and waved as he passed. He waved back, as proper form required.

With the site of the debacle dwindling behind them, Anders opened a link to Sergeant Aurie Fiske, his senior sergeant and second in command. They had served together before, which was one of the reasons Anders had slotted Fiske as senior. That and Fiske's combat experience, good record, and cool head. The fact that he was Eridani didn't hurt either.

"What do you think, Aurie?"

"They did a lot worse than in sim, sir."

"It was a lot more like the real thing out there."

"Truth."

"And the real thing will be worse still."

"They'll get better, sir."

"May St. Michael let it be so."

"Amen to that, sir. Amen to that."

INTERSTELLAR DEFENSE LEAGUE, TARSUS THEATER
TARSUS STATION

Tarsus Station was, like all orbital facilities, limited in space.
Christoph Stone understood the necessity, but that had not
made it any easier to settle his command staff into the compartment that bore the designation *Pacifica Theater Command (temporary)*. The space and accoutrements ought to
have been the equivalent of a sector command headquarters.
Having been a sector commander, he knew they were under-
sized and underequipped. More specifically, having been the
commander at Tarsus Station, he knew the station offered
better than this converted training compartment. He was actually looking forward to transferring his flag to his old ship
Constantine when she arrived on station. The Emperor-class
heavy cruiser wouldn't have more space, but it would be *his*
space, not some begrudging, cast-off-equipped, makeshift
dole from Gleason's toady Schadow, the new master and
commander of Tarsus.

"We all work under constraints. I'm sure you understand,"
Schadow had said when making the assignment.

Stone understood quite well. The allocation of marginal
space was another component of the marginalization strategy of his self-appointed rivals at StratCom. Such morons
were a plague and a threat to the war effort. *Saint Michael*,
Stone had prayed then as he did again now, *save the universe
from such goffs and put their tendentious energy toward
worthwhile tasks.*

So far Saint Michael hadn't listened, and the headaches
continued.

For Stone, headaches came in two varieties: the organic
ones that were too tough for anything short of Doc
Howarth's little black prescription pills and the organizational ones that were a daily part of coordinating his new
command and the "constraints" under which he was being
forced to do his duty. He was quite confident that the latter
form of migraine spawned the former, with deliberate and

malicious aid and abetting on the part of the universe and the devil.

Today, the conspiracy was working overtime.

"Chip! What is this?"

Stone's outburst didn't disrupt the susurrus of chatter from the consoles. Like hive city dwellers, the officers and technicians working in the cramped compartment had learned to ignore anything that did not directly impinge on them. Chip Hollister, hearing his name, paused the scrolling screens at his station and looked up. "Sir?"

Stone highlighted the offending entry, seconded it to the main stage, and stabbed a finger at it.

"Colonel Mainwaring's Expeditionary Force, volunteer auxiliary forces," Chip read aloud. "Just what it says, sir. Our latest assigned unit."

"It has got to be a bad joke. What's it doing on my force list?"

"No joke, sir."

Stone studied his exec's face. Such a joke, even to the denying of it, wasn't beyond Chip, should he consider levity warranted and necessary. Today there wasn't the slightest hint of humor in those blue eyes.

"The assignment's authority triple-checks," Chip added.

If this nonsense wasn't of Chip's instigation, he would have checked on this dubious posting before it ever reached Stone's attention. He wasn't one to pass along other people's humor. His demeanor suggested that he found it no more humorous than did Stone. So if it wasn't a joke . . .

"StratCom can't be this crazy."

Chip shrugged. "StratCom simply forwarded the appointment authorized by PoliStat Bureau."

Whenever the politicians at the Policy and State got involved in force organizations, line commanders wept. Stone's headache grew worse. "What could be going through those politicians' heads? Belay that. I really do know better than to ask unanswerable questions. Let's stick to the concrete. Since we're stuck playing this game, what cards have we been dealt?"

"Unknown at this time, sir. The assignment did not carry a TOPE."

No Table of Organization, Personnel, and Equipment? That was irregular at best, but then the very assignment was irregular. Stone was beginning to scent a very bad odor.

"Do some digging, Chip. Put Olivàres's people on it if you have to." Major Olivàres was the head of Stone's Intel and Recon. She was competent though not brilliant, unlike her predecessor Major Ersch of the infamous Operation Chameleon fiasco. In her favor, she lacked the "any means" attitude of her predecessor. "I want to know everything there is to know about this Expeditionary Force, but most of all, I want to know why we've been given it."

Blessed Saint Michael knew that he needed all the force he could muster, even units that were ill-trained and ill-disciplined, like most of what he'd been given. Guns were guns, and against the Remor numbers counted. But so far, the assembling fleet did not look to have a good chance of surviving contact with the enemy, let alone beating them.

6

RIM WORLDS ECONOMIC UNION (DEFUNCT)
PACIFICA

Awareness comes slowly, blurring through the darkness.
Pressure. On wrists, ankles, chest, head.

Warmth beneath, cupping like a bodysuit. Above, cool air,
roiled by the passage of . . . something

Light, beyond closed eyelids.

A touch, like a prodding finger, pokes and remains. Another. Another. Something walks on his chest, moving toward his neck.

His body does not move. His hand does not rise to sweep
away whatever it is.

What is it?

He opens his eyes and sees the thing walking on him. It is
some kind of ugly alien spider like nothing he has ever seen
before. Or wants to see now. It has a head that looks like
somebody stuck a syringe through a hairy tennis ball. The
insane mosquito head dips down, out of sight.

Pain stabs into his neck.

He screams. His eyes shut, trying to shut out the pain. It
doesn't work.

Cold in his veins.

Pain fades.

Softens.

Dulls.

Drifting away . . .

* * *

He drifted up through the darkness to air that smelled like a bad low tide. But he hadn't fallen asleep on a beach.

He lay on his back on some kind of gelatinous slab, its surface cradling his body the way sand molded itself to sea wrack. He was sunk in it almost up to his ears. That alone would have made it hard for him to move, but he was also bound to the slab at forehead, chest, wrists, and ankles. The ankle bonds held his legs stretched tight, almost to the point of pain, more than enough to keep him from moving legs or hips, save to twist a little.

"What is your name?"

The voice came from outside the pool of snot-green light that bathed him and the imprisoning slab. It was a human voice, dull and a little slurred. He recognized it, having heard it before—when he'd been captured. How long ago was that?

"You are conscious and can speak," the voice said. "What is your name?"

Down in the cellars, somebody had put a name to that voice: Jim Breen. A rival's lieutenant who had gone and gotten himself xombified by the aliens.

He hadn't liked the frickin' jerk when he'd been human. Xombification hadn't improved Breen's charm. "Why're you playing games, you frickin' xombie? You know my name."

"State your name."

He didn't see any point in answering.

"Compulsion can be applied," Breen stated, stepping into the light where he could be seen.

The frickin' xombie had an opaque jar in one hand and a pair of metal tongs in the other. The writhing boneless thing that Breen fished out of the jar was covered in slime and stank of decay. A drop of that slime hit the slab and sizzled. Probably his flesh would have the same reaction. He wasn't a coward, but neither was there any point in getting acquainted with Breen's whatever-it-was over so little a thing.

"Bartie," he said. "Bartie Lars."

Apparently satisfied, the expressionless Breen plopped his oozing ugly back in the jar and stepped away from the slab. Frickin' xombie. Bartie heard jar and tongs meet a table somewhere. Hidden in the darkness, Breen stated, "That is correct."

"Designate Bartie," a new voice said.

The scratchy intonation sounded like a kid's first attempt at a computer-synthesized voice, all awkward and a bit distorted. He couldn't see where the voice came from.

Breen appeared again, reaching toward Bartie. He tried to flinch away, but he had nowhere to go. The xombie touched something on the table, down by Bartie's neck, where he couldn't see.

Cold flowed in his veins. His eyelids fluttered.

Thought mushed.

Drifting away . . .

The slow easy drift through the darkness was interrupted.

"Designate Bartie."

The synthetic voice was cold and brittle. Bartie didn't want to answer. It kept calling, nagging, dragging him away from the quiet, safe nothing.

As he swam up out of the dark, he could feel that he was still bound to the table, or whatever it was. The restraining bands were still in place. The warm, snug grip of the slab remained the same.

He didn't wake happy.

The room was lighter than it had been, but it still stank. His prison slab was no longer isolated in its pool of green light. To either side there were tables covered in what looked like some kind of branching coral, at least it looked sort of like stuff he'd seen in the city aquarium on one of those pointless school field trips he'd had to take when he was a kid. Thick branches and thin. Some long, some short. The tallest reached up and into the darkness shrouding the ceiling.

There were things stuck in the coral, like bugs in a spider's web. Machines, he guessed. Some of them hummed, others had flashing lights, some tubes and articulated levers, others all of the above. Was he somebody's science experiment? Maybe this was the xombification factory. Whatever this place was, whatever they wanted of him, it wasn't likely to be good for Bartie Lars.

"Designate Bartie."

He couldn't see the speaker. In some way he couldn't explain, he knew the speaker was nearby. Maybe it was just that the voice box was nearby, tucked among the machines in the coral web. It had to be one of the frickin' aliens.

"Who the hell are you?" he demanded to know anyway.

"Irrelevant," the voice said. "No question. Designate Bartie will answer."

"Go to hell."

"Unresolvable. No order. Designate Bartie will answer."

Forget that. They wanted him to talk, he wouldn't. He could at least defy what he couldn't hit.

"Compulsion can be applied," the voice reminded him.

The memory of Breen's acid-dripping compeller was compulsion enough. Strapped to the frickin' slab there was nothing he could do but soak up the slime and get burned. Not a lot of point in that. "All right, all right. Whatcha want to know?"

"Deferment. No question. Designate Bartie will answer."

Was he dealing with an idiot? "Yeah, all right. Designate Bartie will answer. So ask your frickin' questions already."

He expected to be grilled about what was going on back in the city or maybe what had been going on before the frickin' aliens showed up, but the voice wanted to know stupid stuff, like his favorite color, the names of animals and everyday things, what media he'd scanned, and the details of every pet he'd ever had as a kid. Stupid stuff. The voice asked questions until the cold began to flow again.

It wasn't like any of it mattered, so Bartie answered until the cold started affecting him. He could hear his words begin to slur, his voice falter.

The quiet dark beckoned.

He started *drifting* . . .

* * *

Drifting . . .

The dream fragmented, curling up and taking away any memory of its content. He was left with a pleasant, fuzzy feeling of the babe that had been taking care of him. It had been good, that was for sure. He was still aroused.

Hell, he was still feeling her. How could that be? He was still strapped to the slab.

He opened his eyes.

Breen stood by the table. Bartie couldn't actually see where the xombie's hand was, but he could feel it. Jerkin' him. Breen's face was blank. Frickin' xombie. He might have been milking a cow.

Bartie could feel the traitor between his legs responding to that touch. Gawd . . .

The cold, when it came, was a welcome relief, taking him away from the stickiness splattered over his belly.

Drifting . . .

"Designate Bartie."

Go to hell.

"Designate Bartie will answer."

The questions again. Some the same, some different. None were important. Bartie was a good little lab rat and answered till the cold came and took the boredom away.

Drifting . . .

"Wake up." Breen's voice. "Time to eat."

The frickin' xombie might call it eating. Hell, maybe he even enjoyed the mush.

Bartie had given up refusing, since all that got him was a tube jammed down his throat. Today the crap tasted like three-day-old fish. Today it was worth spitting some back at Breen.

He tried to put it right in the frickin' xombie's face but he barely managed to hit the jerk's arm. Breen looked down at the mess. No anger. No cursing. Nothing. The frickin' xombie just loaded another spoonful.

Bartie gagged it down, having learned that while he might

not get any visible reaction out of Breen, more than one show of defiance got him the tube.

Stomach sour, he lay waiting for the cold, waiting to go back to the dark where he didn't need to lie on the slab. It was a long time coming, but at least he felt the chill creeping along his veins.

"About frickin' time."

His complaining stomach followed him down into the dark.

Drifting . . .

"Designate Bartie."

"I don't feel like talking." The last thing Breen had fed him had knotted his stomach. It still ached even after however long it had been in the dark.

"Irrelevant. Designate Bartie will answer."

Another round of stupid, pointless questions. Another round of stupid, pointless answers. Sometimes Bartie lied, just to be different. The frickin' alien didn't seem to know or care. Hell, Bartie didn't care either.

Drifting . . .

The rattle was different.

Bartie opened his eyes, trying to see what made the new sound. He got lucky. Breen had rolled a cart up to the slab table. There were half a dozen small pots on it, each with a stick poking up from inside. There was also a glass beaker nearly filled with a colorless liquid, slowly sloshing down to rest.

"Lunchtime?"

Breen ignored him. The frickin' xombie was stretching pale blue gloves onto his hands. What did Breen think he was? A surgeon?

For a horrible moment Bartie thought that maybe that was exactly what the frickin' xombie thought. His fear rose when Breen dipped a sponge into the beaker and started swabbing Bartie's belly. The tang of antiseptic caught in Bartie's nose.

Instead of reaching for a cutter, Breen took the stick out of the first pot. Its end was covered in pink gunk. Breen swabbed the stuff onto Bartie's belly. The gunk was cold, but that was all. Breen put another dab on a different part of Bartie's belly. The third one burned when it was applied, but only at first. The fifth one started an itch. After Breen applied the sixth, he pulled off his gloves and tossed them on the cart. Dragging some kind of device on an articulated arm away from the coral wall, he positioned the thing over Bartie's stomach and fussed with it until he had it exactly where he wanted it. He flipped a switch and a pale violet light bathed Bartie's torso.

As a kid Bartie had had an allergy test. The doctor had applied various substances to Bartie's skin in an effort to see what might be causing the rashes he kept breaking out with, so the doc could treat him. This was kind of like that. Or maybe it wasn't like that at all. The allergy test hadn't involved whatever was hanging over Bartie, shining light. Maybe the frickin' aliens wanted to know what could hurt him.

Only nothing did. Even the itching faded.

He lay on his slab for a long time after Breen left with the cart. Bored. When he started drifting away, he wasn't sure if it was the cold finally come to take him away or if he was just drifting to sleep naturally. Didn't matter. The dark came and that was what was important.

Drifting . . .

"Designate Bartie."

Once more the dark offered him up to the frigid voice. Breen and his cart were present even though Bartie hadn't heard them arrive this time. The cart held a big beaker, filled with liquid and something else: some kind of frilly sea worm that slowly writhed and coiled on itself.

"What is that frickin' thing?"

"For you, Designate Bartie. Recipient Bartie supersedes Designate Bartie."

"The hell!" Just seeing the squirming worm-thing made his blood run cold, and without the ability to escape into the dark. "I don't want to be a frickin' xombie."

"Compuls—"

"You don't need that thing! I'm cooperating, ain't I? I answer your questions, don't I? It's not like I can do a lot for you while I'm strapped to this frickin' table. You want me to help you like Breen does? I would. I swear I would. You want more meat to make frickin' xombies? I'll help you get all you want. You don't need me to be one."

"Designate Bartie offers compliance in recipient acquisition?"

"Will I get you more xombie fodder? Hell, yes. Just don't make me one."

Bartie knew he was pleading. Hell, he could feel tears running down his cheeks. If any of his slugs could see him, he'd never be able to boss them again. But they weren't here. They weren't about to get xombified. To hell with them! Bartie kept pleading.

Something dark shifted in the overhead darkness, moving down among the machines hanging in their coral branches. Articulated arms unfolded from a long narrow cylinder, reaching down. Another machine?

No. Something else.

The arms were legs, and the cylinder wasn't really a cylinder. It was more a pair of unequally sized ovoids, one hinged back from the other. The smaller was topped by a globular mass, studded with lenses and levers. No, not lenses and levers. Bartie saw that what he'd thought had been lenses were eyes, compound and gleaming with a bright iridescent green sheen. The levers were something else: Mandibles? Bartie didn't know.

Hell, the frickin' thing is alive!

It reminded Bartie of a Cawdore mantis, a predatory bug of unusual size that infested the Cawdore Archipelago. A mantis was nearly a meter long. This thing was closer to three.

Its six legs began to move, taking it to the table side with a fluid motion that had all the creepiness of a spider's crawl. The jewel-eyed head rocked to the left, then to the right, staring down at the trapped and trembling Bartie.

A bunch of thin arms unfolded from beneath the thorax.

One reached out toward Bartie's face. He flinched away, as much as he could, still pleading, though he wasn't sure if he was making sense any longer. The bristly tip of the arm touched his cheek. He felt hairs splashing in his tears.

"Recipient Breen," the cold voice spoke. "Animate precision prognosticator."

The voice came from the mantis. This was his frickin' xeno interrogator.

A rustle from out of sight suggested that xombie Breen was following his master's orders. When the xombie reported the precision prognosticator animated, the mantis ordered, "Designate Bartie, repeat."

"Repeat what?" he stammered.

"No question. Restate intention."

Intention? His intention was to survive. What had he said? What had he said that this thing wanted to hear? Oh, yeah. "I'll do what you want. I'll get you all the xombies you want."

"Compliance in alternate activities also offered?"

"Sure. Anything you want."

"Compliance is earnest?"

"Earnest? Yeah, I'm frickin' serious."

The bug eyes stared down at him for a long time. Without any apparent reason, the head cocked to the right, then back again. It nodded jerkily.

"Acceptance conditional. Performance will corroborate. *Gawkhore* will monitor." The mantis's head swiveled to one side. "Recipient Breen, apply *gawkhore*."

The frickin' xombie scurried away and came back cradling something in his hands. It looked like a scrap of wet leather.

"What's that?"

"Yours," Breen said as he placed the thing onto Bartie's neck.

Bartie felt it squirm and knew that it was alive like half the things in this place. The *gawkhore* settled itself in, reaching down and around and wrapping itself about Bartie's throat like a scarf. After a moment, he couldn't feel it at all. Not so bad, he thought.

The mantis nodded again, leaning in until it loomed in Bartie's face. "Designate Bartie will restate intention."

Again? How many times did he have to say it? "I meant what I said. I'll do what you want."

"Designate Bartie will state incorrect personal designator."

You want me to lie to you about who I am? Sure, why not? Gotta be cooperative, don't I? "My name's Breen."

A vise clamped down on his throat, worse than a stranglehold. There was no more air. He could feel his blood struggling to force its way through the constriction, trying to get to his brain. His blood wasn't succeeding. The room started to get dark.

"Designate Bartie will make no incorrect statements," ordered the mantis. A thorax arm reached out and touched the *gawkhore* on Bartie's neck. It relaxed. Air and blood flowed again.

"Yeah, I get the picture," he croaked.

"Satisfactory."

"Recipient Breen, apply *gnass*. Removal."

Hell, now what? What sort of torture beast was the frickin' xombie going to haul out now? The frickin' mantis was still in his face. Waiting for the show?

From the corner of his eye, he could see when Breen came back with a clear box that looked like a kid's terrarium. A half dozen shelled things crawled around inside. Breen used tongs to snatch one up and place it by the side of Bartie's head. He could feel the thing poking him, but the restraining strap kept him from turning to see what it was doing. Breen plopped another down on the other side of Bartie's head.

The sound of chewing came from either side of his head. The gentle pokes continued. He didn't feel any pain. Did these *gnass* excrete an anesthetic like a hairball mosquito did? Were they chewing their way to his brain?

"I thought we had a deal, you frickin' monster!" Bartie

raged. His spittle flecked the mantis's eyes, but it neither blinked nor moved.

"Shut up and lie still," Breen said.

Bartie ignored him and started to struggle. The mantis touched the *gawkhore* at Bartie's throat, causing the thing to contract. Bartie stopped fighting. Better to have an anesthetic bug chewing painlessly into your brain than strangling. Once he lay still, the mantis prodded the *gawkhore* into letting him have air again.

It was hard, lying there, listening to the *gnass* chew, but Bartie managed it. After a couple of decades, he felt something odd. The pressure across his forehead eased. It was like somebody had loosened the strap.

Experimentally he tried lifting his head. He could move it. He could also still hear the *gnass* chewing. Hell, the frickin' *gnass* had been chewing on the strap, not his head.

Using the tongs, Breen picked up what was left of the strap and dropped it into the terrarium. The *gnass* within swarmed it. Breen picked up one of the *gnass* on the table. It squealed in the tongs, protesting. The frickin' xombie set it down next to Bartie's chest strap. The squalling stopped as the *gnass* set to chewing again.

Go, you little monster, Bartie silently ordered. *Eat it all.*

Breen moved the other one down to another strap.

One by one the *gnass* ate their way through the bands holding Bartie down. One by one Breen tossed the leftovers into the box. When the *gnass* were done, the frickin' xombie returned them to the terrarium to join their buddies feasting on cut-off straps. Breen and his chomping pals went away. The mantis remained, hovering over Bartie.

"I can't get up with you standing on top of me."

The mantis backed away.

Bartie pried himself out of the slab. He was no longer restrained. It was progress. He might get out of this yet.

7

INTERSTELLAR DEFENSE LEAGUE, TARSUS THEATER
TARSUS STATION

In what Benton Mainwaring immediately ascribed to rudeness, the well-scrubbed officer meeting them wore only two pips on her collar, which, if memory of IDL rank structure served him correctly, and he was sure it did, meant that she was a lieutenant and therefore she stood almost as low as it was possible to stand on the command ladder. Her cornflower-blue eyes scanned the party debarking from CMEFS *Auditor* and settled on Benton, which was perspicacious of her, since the Combiners were wearing their shipboard casual uniforms—simple, nondescript coveralls without any rank insignia. The lack of markings was according to Coppelstowe's advice for avoiding ill feelings, either through any confusion that Combine insignia might cause or through adopting inappropriate IDL equivalents. Drawing herself to rigid attention, the lieutenant snapped a crisp salute. Benton shoved aside his offended sensibilities, smiled broadly for the young thing, and returned the salute.

When she finished the obviously preplanned formal welcoming statement, he commented, "We had been expecting to be met by Commander Stone."

"Marshal Stone is pressed for time, sir. I'm to escort you to the briefing room at your earliest convenience."

Different customs, he reminded himself. "Ah, well. We didn't come all the way out here to be idle layabouts, now, did we?" While a couple of his officers chuckled, he said to the lieutenant, "Let us be about it, then. And while we walk, you can tell me why you referred to your superior as Marshal Stone."

The poor lieutenant gave Benton a confused look. "That's his rank, sir."

"I was informed that he was a theater commander."

"He is a theater commander, sir. But this is Tarsus Theater, not Pacifica," she responded as though it explained everything.

Coppelstowe, with her habitual efficiency, stepped up to fill Benton's gap of knowledge.

"Within the League military forces, commander is a situational rank, colonel," she clarified. "It is analogous, though not identical, to your rank of colonel-in-command. Your expeditionary force may include other colonels, but none other than yourself may claim the additional 'in command.' To avoid confusion, on any given League vessel or in any given jurisdiction under the administration of League military forces, only the officer in command is properly referred to as commander, which means that General Schadow, though strictly beneath Marshal Stone in the formal rank structure, is the commander here by virtue of his appointment as Tarsus Theater commander. I have not misstated the circumstances, have I, Lieutenant Lucas?"

"No, er"—the lieutenant seemed to grope for a proper response—"ma'am."

"I accept your courtesy," Coppelstowe said. "However, I observe a hesitation that suggests you wish to use the correct courtesies. I inform you that robed initiates of the Alsion Institute are usually addressed as sister, brother, or sibling according to their gender."

"I'm sorry. We don't see many Alsionites around the League."

Coppelstowe nodded. "Thus comprehensive ignorance excuses especial lack of knowledge."

Her pronouncement stifled conversation, but had no effect on the brisk pace maintained by their guide. To Benton, the corridors through which they traveled looked little different from corridors on any number of starships or stations upon which Benton had traveled. Why had he expected otherwise? More importantly, why did he feel disappointed?

At least he was not disappointed in the others sharing the passageways with them. The men and women around them were quite unlike the sort one saw back home in the Combine. There was very little excess poundage to be seen. Save for Coppelstowe, not a single one was in civilian clothing, assuming one could count Coppelstowe's initiate's robes as civilian, though the robes followed as strict a dress code as most military uniforms. But it wasn't clothing that truly arrested Benton's attention.

Sprinkled among the League soldiers were a remarkable number of allotypes. Benton even caught sight of one very wide fellow who had to be a heavysider from Barstowe's Rock or maybe even Tartarus. Intriguing. The Leaguers, so widely portrayed throughout the Pan-Stellar Combine as narrow-minded, were apparently showing a far higher tolerance for allotypical humanity than was common in the Combine.

Most of the allotypes were tall, well-muscled specimens of the sort that Combine media producers presented as ideal soldiers. Unlike such fabricated media-heroes, these people were very real. They could hardly be anything but the famed and supposedly rare Eridani. When he mentioned his observation to Coppelstowe, she explained their abundant presence as "circumstance constrictive confluence."

"Ah, yes. Of course," he replied. Sometimes she forgot that not everyone was as versed in alinear sociodynamics as she. He'd get a real answer later, after they actually met one of the Eridani: Stone himself. Benton was looking forward to it.

Their escort led them to a conference room, well lit but poorly decorated. The lieutenant saw them all seated, then departed, leaving them to contemplate the notable lack of pictures, mementos, or active displays on the walls. It wasn't long before the inner door slid open and a figure of clear Eridani allotype walked through. Benton recognized Stone at once, but he was not prepared for the sheer sense of presence that surrounded the man. Almost as though compelled, Benton drew himself to his feet and saluted. His entourage followed suit.

As Stone acknowledged the military greeting in kind, his eyes flicked briefly over the assembled Combiners before settling on Benton.

"Colonel Mainwaring."

Benton saluted again. "Reporting for duty, Com—Marshal Stone."

"And these people are?"

"My Command Committee, of course. I'd like to introduce them to you.

"This is Master Piet Lugard, guild spacer, my fleet commander and second in command for the expeditionary force," Benton began. Stone nodded to each of the committee as Benton named them. Major Edward Marsh, commander of ground forces. Major Emannuel Thorpe, logistics. Stone actually looked annoyed when Benton presented Jasmine Coppelstowe as his advisor without portfolio. Benton might have taken it for the usual disdain that often greeted the robed initiates, but given Stone's clear dislike for Combine management practices, he suspected that having anyone on his Command Committee in an advisor without portfolio slot would set the fellow off. Benton continued on to introduce each of his ship commanders, careful to name each as captain rather than commander. "And when will we have the honor of meeting your committee?"

"MilForce is not run by committee, Colonel," Stone observed icily.

"I am sure you have your regular procedures and ways of doing business, but—"

"We do indeed have regular procedures. They do not include 'buts.' I suggest you begin learning them." Stone gestured to include the committee, but his eyes remained locked on Benton's. "You and your volunteers have been assigned to my theater. It was not my request, but a good soldier follows orders. My orders are that I make use of you. In Mil-

Force, we follow orders, and regular procedures as well. Do I make myself clear?"

"Not entirely."

Stone's eyes closed for a brief moment, then he touched a control panel inset into the table. "I am summoning Captain Zeke Shaler. He is a member of my staff. I advise you and your people to treat him, and all members of my staff of whatever nominal rank, with the same respect you will show me as theater commander. Captain Shaler will help you acclimate yourselves.

"Colonel Mainwaring, there is a meeting of all force commanders at 0800 Standard tomorrow. I expect you to have a plan for the integration of your force into the theater fleet."

"I'll have Master Lugard start—"

"Did I ask you to detail your procedures, Colonel? *You* will present *your* plan at the meeting tomorrow. Understood?"

"I believe I am beginning to understand."

Stone's curt nod signaled that Benton's response was acceptable. Barely. "Dismissed."

The polite Captain Shaler dutifully led them on a tour of the facilities, which Lugard quietly pointed out did not take them to what he called "sensitive" areas. When they were unshepherded and taking refreshment in the officers' mess, Benton's people talked quietly among themselves, careful to keep from being overheard by the Leaguers around them.

"Stone doesn't seem very welcoming," Thorpe observed.

"You be surprised?" Lugard asked. "Leaguers don't be liking Combiners. They be calling us Pansies when they think we be not listening."

"Pejorative appellation is hardly exclusive to one faction, Master Lugard," Coppelstowe pointed out.

"We are here to do our part," Benton reminded them all. "The marshal's brusque reception is irrelevant. Need I point out that if we were not welcome, we would not have been allowed to join the cause?"

No one answered.

"Quite so, then. We need take no offense, nor shall we give it by letting old habits and attitudes cloud our interactions with the valiant warriors of the League. We shall by our own good manners and cheerful compliance be ambassadors of goodwill. All will be well. You will see. Marshal Stone will warm to us when he sees just how committed we are. How could he not? Are we not the vanguard for a humanity united against the alien threat? In time, all will come to appreciate our importance in the flow of the dynamic. Is that not right, Sister Coppelstowe?"

The Alsion initiate nodded serenely. "Without deep knowledge, time alone reveals the flow of the dynamic."

"Quite right. Now, Master Lugard, about this plan the marshal desires. . . ."

8

As a trooper, Anders had always found intersystem transport to be a time for training, busywork, and boredom in nearly equal parts. Now as an officer, the third partner of that team was dominant, mostly due to General Paperwork.

Paperwork, the ancient term for the tangle of so-called necessary forms demanded by the goffs and their pet desk pilots, didn't involve paper anymore, but it had never given up its hold on the time of people who had more important things to do. As far as Anders was concerned, "more important things" meant "anything else" to do. While he made a point of clearing it out as fast as possible, sometimes, like today, the avalanche was overwhelming. Most of the stupefying pile was due to Colonel Cope's reorganization of Pacifica Theater ground forces that had resulted from the arrival of Colonel Mainwaring's Expeditionary Force.

The 102nd had received a force augmentation from the reorganization: an entire infantry company. It would have been a notable add-on if equipped by MilForce, but this "First Mechanized Dragoons" was a Combine-style company. By body count, they outnumbered the hardsuit troopers of the 102nd by five to one, but their equipment—weapons, suits, *and* vehicles—was well below the state of the art.

When Anders reached the point where he could pass on the details of their new force augmentation to his top sergeant, Aurie Fiske, the veteran took one look and frowned dubiously. "You are gonna change the Pansie rank assignments, aren't you, sir?"

"Does Saint Barbara use gunpowder perfume? Run them through the sims and give them the 32 Fett sequence. That ought to separate the men from the boys. I'll take the platoon kicks' recommendation on who gets to lead this goon squad."

Fiske still looked doubtful. "They're an integral unit by their lights, but you aren't going to leave them whole and on their own, are you, sir?"

"You making a career of questioning my sanity, Aurie?"

"Not a career, sir."

"For now we'll add the unit to Command Team, officially as a reserve. And since you're so worried about them, you can nursemaid them."

"For my sins."

"Exactly."

Fiske departed to run the sims, but he left behind his concerns. With each personnel folder he reviewed, Anders wondered if he was right in ignoring Colonel Cope's integration plan. The colonel recommended sticking with MilForce tradition as the best way to integrate Mainwaring's ground forces, to whit, by salting the new troopers throughout the command's existing formations. Anders's 102nd had gotten its share, but the sheer number of troopers dumped on him was a problem, let alone the issues of equipment compatibility. The 102nd was a lean, Eridani-style company of hardsuiters; its fighting trim could be lost with too many differently equipped newbies getting underfoot. Anders really didn't want to disrupt the platoons he had been working so hard to train.

Fortunately, Cope, passing on the authority delegated to him by Marshal Stone, had left it to the discretion of individual unit commanders how to deal with their new troopers. The colonel had made it clear that he believed that the traditional approach was the best, right down to shifting newbies into established squads, but he had also noted that Stone would back up all unit commanders on whatever decisions they made regarding disposition of the Pansies. The freedom Stone had granted was letting Anders keep the Combiners together under his command while keeping his platoons' fighting balance stable, also under his command.

No method chosen by unit commanders was going to satisfy Mainwaring's chief of ground forces, Major Marsh. The burly major had not taken the breakup of his little army well at all. Too bad. Marsh didn't have experience commanding a company, let alone the nearly full regiment that was on Mainwaring's TOPE, so he had no sympathy among the MilForce officers. Too many good troops had been wasted by well-meaning but incompetent novices over the centuries. No matter how much Marsh complained—and scuttlebutt said the complaints were loud, long, and ongoing—it wasn't going to change; Cope had taken a stand against that sort of disaster.

Anders knew that even with the Pansies isolated within their own subunit, there would be integration problems. The bumps along the way would probably be worse than they'd had absorbing fresh League recruits. And no matter what he did, sooner or later, Major Marsh would be breathing down his neck, especially since the Combine major was billeted aboard *Auditor,* with Anders and the 102nd right under his nose. It would be good to be able to pass the buck up along the chain of command to get the brash Marsh off his back.

Too bad he couldn't ignore General Paperwork as easily.

Anders had just finished his paperwork and was tiredly starting to contemplate just where he'd stow his personal gear when Aurie Fiske showed up at the compartment hatch with the reports from the first sim runs. Despite saying that they had gone well, Fiske was looking uncomfortable. Anders invited him in, letting the door slide shut on the hubbub in the corridor.

"Something is bothering you, Aurie."

"Permission to speak freely, sir."

"Freely given. It's what I expect of you, Aurie, especially when there's nobody else around."

"Thank you, sir." It took Fiske another moment to actually

get out any words with content. "I thought you had some kind of in with the commander."

"What do you mean?"

"I mean, what are we doing aboard this refugee from the breakers? Why are we the ones stuck here?"

The CMEFS *Auditor* wasn't a new ship, but at least she was a real, built-from-the-keel warship rather than a ramshackle retrofit like the other so-called "warship-rated" ships of Mainwaring's fleet. She was what MilForce classed as a cruiser, a big ship, well armed and capable of extended independent operations, but she was not on a par with the most modern of IDL ships. To be honest, from the specs Anders had checked, as a fighting ship *Auditor* wasn't even up to the standards of old classes like the Honorables, but she had served in battle and served well. She was hardly ready for the breakers.

"What's wrong with our new home besides not being an Eridani ship? She's roomier than *Stalwart*." *Stalwart,* an Honorable-class cruiser that had seen better days and smelled of it, had been their last home. Fiske hadn't complained about her. "We've got more bunk space here and the rec facilities are top-notch. And the air filters have been changed this century. Hmmm, it's not the ship, is it?"

Fiske nodded. "It's the Pansies, sir."

"We'll integrate them. At least all of our assignees have infantry experience. We even have three with hardsuit experience. I'd be happier if they were rated on modern battlesuits, but we can bootstrap them if we have to." Anders's babbling, though meant to be reassuring, didn't seem to be having any effect on Fiske. "All right. What's wrong with our greens?"

"It's not *our* greens that bother me, sir. It's the Auditors."

The Auditors? What was wrong with the *Auditor*'s crew? *Auditor* carried the same crew she'd sailed with, Combiners all. As was so often the case, the space forces went about things differently than ground forces. When faced with the influx of new personnel and matériel, Colonel MacAndra had obviously felt that the Combine ships were best handled by Combine personnel and used in conjunction with other Combine ships. Mainwaring's fleet remained intact, and so had the crews of the ships. And with action imminent, Colonel MacAndra might have the right of it. There was a lot more room for mistakes on a planetary surface where the cold hard vacuum of space wasn't waiting to suck you up first chance it got. "Just a moment and you're lost" was an old spacer's saying, meaning that a moment of delay or confusion could cost the life of a crewman, or a ship. *Auditor* would be fighting soon and with MacAndra's dispositions, she'd be fighting with a crew that had trained and served together and, presumably, knew her well. There ought to be fewer opportunities for glitches.

On the whole, Anders preferred his chances on the ground. There wasn't a lot a 'pounder could do while a passenger on a ship. It bred a feeling of impotence, and maybe that was what was troubling Fiske. "Combiners fly as well as anybody else. They'll get us to where we can do our job. They'll fight the ship better for not having tyros in the linkages too."

"I'm not having can shivers, sir," Fiske said, using the slang for the problem Anders thought he had detected. "And it's them, not me. The Pansies have got an attitude thing going, acting like this is some kind of school outing or something."

"It's not uncommon among troops who haven't seen the sharp end."

Fiske shook his head, signifying that Anders was still off the mark. "And they've got no respect for somebody who's been at that end of the stick."

So that was it. The Combiners weren't giving the veteran sergeant his due. "The Combiners are basically civilians at heart. They don't understand respect the way we Eridani do. A flaw in their genes, I expect. It'll take them a while to learn the ways of the real world. Remember what Milano used to be like? In a lot of ways that Lancastrian kid was worse than any Combiners I've met so far, but we got him trained, didn't we? We'll get these pups synched too. Give it a little time, Aurie. Meanwhile, I'll do some talking and see if I can't—how do they phrase it in the Combine?—promote some consciousness."

"Thank you, sir."

Fiske left Anders contemplating just how he was going to effect the promised consciousness promotion. The knotty problem wormed its way through his sluggish brain, competing with the more immediate task of stowing his gear in the unfamiliar arrangement of the compartment. He was just turning down his bunk, a tentative plan of action forming, when the door chimed again.

It was one of the Combiner assignees. Anders recognized the face but had to check the man's name flash.

"Yes, Private Williams, what is it?"

"Just a question about the sims, Captain. I was delegated by the rest of the guys to see if the results were finished. People want to know what their standings are."

"You were delegated by the others?"

Williams shrugged. "Yeah. You know how it is. We figured it would trample on military decorum if we all tromped up here to officer country to get the results, so we caucused and I got elected spokesman and here I am. So what's the deal, Captain?"

"The deal?" Anders suppressed the urge to squeeze the bridge of his nose to cut off the headache he felt starting. "The deal is that you and your fellows are part of a military unit. This is neither a sports team nor a corporation. We do not have performance rankings." Which was not exactly true; every MilForce unit had them, though unofficially. "And we most certainly do not have elected officers. You are not in the Combine anymore."

Williams had the grace to look chagrined, but he didn't take Anders's rebuke quietly. "Hey, Captain, we all know that. We volunteered, remember? It's just that everybody is eager to do their part, you know. There's been a lot of betting that you'd be changing ranks and assignments, which a lot of us think is a good idea 'cause old Major Marsh played favorites. Connections and compensation over competence, you know. Not the way we hear it's done in the League."

Anders held up his hand to cut the man off. "You want to do things the League way?"

"Sure—I mean—yes, sir!"

Williams's salute was sloppy and didn't mollify Anders. "The League way, then, is this. You will leave this compartment now. You will go back to 'the guys' and tell them that they will learn the results when they are told the results. You will suggest to them that they can find details of the chain of command and how it works in their manuals, which they should be reading even as we speak, since little time remains before lights out. And you will hope that by morning I will think this conversation was only a fatigue-induced delusion. Are you receiving, Private Williams?"

The second salute was sharper, as was the "Sir, yes, sir!" and this time Anders was somewhat mollified. Anders returned the salute and dismissed him. The private left without another word.

There might be hope for Williams. Might. Still Anders prayed as he tucked himself into his bunk, "Saint Michael, may it please you and God that at least some of my greens ripen into real soldiers."

One thing real soldiers did was to go to sleep as soon and as often as they could. In that way at least, Anders proved to be as real as they come.

9

RIM WORLDS ECONOMIC UNION (DEFUNCT)
PACIFICA, KILAWA ISLE, PALISANDRA

Two of them were holding her down for Bartie Lars, their
leader. Sue fought them but she was too weak to break their
grips. Their laughing mocked her struggles. Bartie laughed
too as he opened his trousers. He didn't laugh when she
wrenched a foot loose and kicked him. The blow didn't land
where she'd intended, just against his bared hip. He caught
her foot before she could try again. The twist that he gave
her foot dragged a scream from her.

"Not nice," he said, shoving himself between her legs.
"No way to treat somebody who's got something for you."

She writhed in their grip in a futile effort to stop what was
happening. He slapped her hard, stunning her.

"Better," he said, pawing her.

Then came the sound of running feet. "Look out," one of
the flunkies shouted. Bartie's head twisted around, but hands
grabbed his shoulders before he could do more and he was
yanked away from her. As the two men tumbled backward,
she saw her rescuer's face. It was Jacques.

Giatti and the other one let her go and piled into the strug-
gle. She should have run, but she couldn't abandon him.
He'd come for her, knowing he was no match for the jackals.
He was her white knight, her foolish, helpless Quixote.

She ran to help him.

Bartie, somehow free from the fight and on his feet again,
snagged her hair. He hauled her back, stumbling in tears and
pain, and tossed her into Giatti's hands. Clasped to his stink-

ing body, she could only scream her rage. Another two jackals held Jacques helpless on the ground.

"So this one's yours, eh?"

"My husband," she said.

"Wasn't talking to you, sow," he said while he kicked Jacques. "Nothing to say, Mr. Hero?"

He had his flunkies haul Jacques to his feet. He was bleeding, hunched in pain. She wanted to comfort him, but only after she'd hurt those who had hurt him.

The jackals taunted Jacques. They did things to him, terrible things. When they were done, Jacques was beyond all pain. Bartie, grinning and bloody, came to her. He wasn't done with her, not yet, not done at all.

She fought against the hands.

"I'm next," panted the lackey Giatti.

Then another voice spoke, soft and insistent, as a hand covered her mouth. "Nobody's going to hurt you."

It wasn't Bartie's harsh grate. It wasn't Giatti's drooling whine. But did it matter who the liar was? She had already been hurt, beyond pain, beyond bearing. She tried to bite the hand, but it fled, only to come back to stifle her as she drew breath for another scream.

"Sue, you've got to be quiet! Quiet! Do you understand? They're out there!"

The insistence in the voice finally got through to her. The last vestiges of her nightmare slunk away to hide and she came fully awake. It was, she knew, a temporary reprieve. The memories would return another night when no one was watching.

It was no dream that she was being held. The hands belonged to some of her people. She didn't like their hands on her, but she stopped fighting them. They were doing what they had to do: holding her down and keeping her quiet so that her haunted sleep didn't betray them to those who hunted them. They could have abandoned her to her fate. But for reasons Sue didn't fully understand, they risked capture should her thrashings bring down the hunters. She had told them often enough that she didn't want anyone getting hurt for her.

As soon as they saw she was in possession of herself, she told them again. They released her with apologies. She offered an apology of her own, for she saw fresh scratches on Ren's young face that she'd likely put there.

"Sorry about that, Ren," she whispered.

"S'okay." He grinned at her sheepishly. Even softer than she'd spoken, he asked. "You okay?"

"I'm fine," she lied.

"Same one?" asked Doc Shelly. She wasn't a real doctor, let alone a psychiatrist, but she had been a certified medical assistant and was as close to either as they could come these days.

"Yeah."

Shelly nodded in sympathy. She had her own nightmares to live with. She said, "Jesse came in from sentry and said there are xombies working this neighborhood."

"If he's seen them, it's probably too late to move."

"That's what we figured." Ren offered her a flensing pole. When she took it he hefted his rifle. He had strapped a wicked-looking knife to the barrel. "We'll slice 'em if they find us. Quiet and quick so more of 'em don't find us."

The boy's strategy was good, but Sue grieved to hear the callousness in his young voice. The xombies had once been ordinary people like them. It wasn't their fault the aliens had made them their servants.

"They're human beings, Ren. Show some pity," Doc Shelly said.

"They ain't got none for us."

"He's right," Sue said. As far as anyone could tell, the xombies no longer felt any emotions. "We can't afford pity when they're trying to drag us away and make us like them. But we don't kill them just to kill them, only to survive."

Was that a hint of disappointment on Ren's face? She was afraid that it was. The boy was getting wilder all the time. His growing callousness was a concern for another time. Tonight they needed to survive.

"Did Jesse go back to his post?"

Doc Shelly affirmed it, so Sue got a dozen of her best

fighters together, figuring on making them a rear guard to hold off the xombies if they were discovered. If they were lucky, they could buy time for the others to escape and still manage to get away themselves. Xombies were easy enough to fool and almost as easy for a healthy person to outrun.

Her little band of brave souls quietly slipped out of the camp and joined Jesse. Wordlessly he pointed out a dozen xombies poking through the buildings nearby. Sue held her breath whenever one of the aliens' dupes wandered toward them, but none got very close. They did not seem to have figured out that her people were nearby.

It was, she thought, only a matter of time before they were discovered.

Then she saw a man moving through the rubble-strewn street beyond the xombies. She could tell by the way he walked that he wasn't one of the aliens' catspaws. But there was something wrong. He wasn't being stealthy, and he wasn't charging them. In fact, he stepped right up to the first xombie and started to talk to it.

"Bastard," Jesse hissed, loud enough that Sue feared he had inadvertently betrayed them.

But if the strange man heard Jesse's slur, he showed no sign. The man started gathering the xombies in and forming them into an inhumanly precise column. More groups came in and joined them. Moments later, a truck rolled down the street, silent on its electric motor. The caged-in cargo area held captured people, as silent in their sullenness as the vehicle bearing them. The truck stopped briefly and the strange man swung up into the cab. As it rolled away, the xombies fell in behind it.

What kind of man could do that?

A shaft of moonlight illuminated the face of one of the overseers and Sue knew exactly what kind of man.

10

The sharp tang of burning metal filled the bay assigned to the 102nd, defying the overtaxed air purification system. Perversely, Anders was pleased to find that the vaunted cutting-edge comfort systems of the Pan-Stellar Combine did no better than League air cleaners in that regard. Or maybe it was just that the Combine designers hadn't anticipated quite so much activity.

Anders and Sergeant Fiske snaked their way through the maze. Every available space was filled, if not with the 102nd's own Mk. 3 carriers getting overhauled, then with the tuning and conversion work under way on the twenty Combine-built "Dust Badger" carriers belonging to the Expeditionary Force troops under Anders's command. And it looked as though Sergeant Frazier Brizbin, commander of the 102nd's support platoon and the company's chief mechanic, had every member of the 102 ArmInfCo (Reinforced), save Anders and Fiske, hopping to his tune. It was a good show and Anders found a moment between Brizbin's whip-cracking and fussing to let him know so.

"You sure we can't replace these fratchin' Badgers with real blowers, Captain?" Brizbin asked, not for the first time. "They are such pieces of air-cushioned junk that I can't begin to tell you how little they're worth."

Which was not what Brizbin had said in his official report, but then nothing met the mechanic's standards unless it was MilForce spec, and half of that he also characterized as being worthless when not making an official report. Such complaints were just a part of Brizbin's public face, possibly a way to keep his maintenance teams from slacking off. "And you don't want to know what we have to do to get them into a drop pod."

"You're right. I don't want to know." It had still not been decided how the 102nd would go in when they reached Pacifica. If the insertion was hot, all of the unit's vehicles needed to go down in drop pods. If not, they'd go down in shuttles and most of the modifications currently under way would be superfluous. Anders intended the 102nd to be ready for either possibility. "But I do want to know when you'll have them ready for the pods."

"That's hard to say, Captain. With these fumble-"— Brizbin interrupted himself to shout directions at the nearest work team—"fingered Combiners, it'll probably take twice as long as it should. Half of them have no idea where to weld on a strap-down pintle, and the other half don't even know what a fratchin' strap-down pintle is! And the armor reinforces need to be angled just right or the fratchin' Badgers'll catch on the pod doors when they blow, which'll probably rip the panels right off. If it doesn't just scrag the fratchin' blower totally!"

Anders looked to Fiske, who raised an eyebrow.

"So it's under control and on schedule," Fiske observed.

Brizbin shrugged. "Pretty much."

"Captain Seaborg," Colonel Mainwaring's voice boomed out.

"Carry on, Sergeant Brizbin," Anders said before turning to face the approaching Combiner officer.

"Captain Seaborg, you've been avoiding me."

"Not true, sir," Anders lied with a friendly smile. He waved his hand to take in the hubbub around them. "Duty comes first."

"And it looks as though good progress is being made, eh? But that's not what I was referring to. Is it not within your duty to dine with your ship's commander?"

"Not in Eridani service, sir. It's been an Eridani tradition since the foundation of the old Stellar Legion that dinners are social occasions. They are most definitely *not* required duty, especially when superior officers are sending the invitations," Anders said, seeing no need to inform Mainwaring that such invitations were rarely refused.

Mainwaring looked a little taken aback. "I will have a word with Sister Coppelstowe about the thoroughness of her research. I had no intention of offending you."

"An invitation to dine is never an offense, sir."

"But badgering you about it is, eh?"

"I never said that, sir." *I will also never say anything about thinking it.* "It would be my pleasure to dine with you when circumstances are felicitous."

"No hard feelings, then?"

"How could there be, sir?"

"Good man, Seaborg." Mainwaring gave Anders an overly familiar clap on the shoulder. "Well, consider yourself to have a standing invitation to my table. I hope you will avail yourself of it soon. Tonight would not be too early. Truth to tell, I've got something I want to discuss with you. Oh, it's not business. Well, it *is* business, but not our mutual business of dealing with the alien threat, eh?" With a wink, Mainwaring added, "Something more profitable."

Anders hoped his smile remained polite. He had heard about this business, and it was part of why he had been ducking the colonel's invitations. Duty really had kept him from accepting Mainwaring's first invitation and, feeling guilty, he'd sent Fiske in his stead. Fiske had returned to the League quarters appalled. Despite having agreed to "keep it quiet" as the colonel had requested, Fiske had divulged the nature of the colonel's "business." Colonel Mainwaring, it seemed, was in the market for Eridani genetic material; he wanted to purchase some and was willing to pay handsomely for a sampling. Anders had matched Fiske in his revulsion.

"As duty permits, sir," said Anders, keeping his voice as even and neutral as possible. He intended to be sure that duty didn't permit, no matter how much duty he needed to invent.

But just now, he didn't need to invent any. "But I am afraid that duty will not permit me to attend tonight. There are some time-sensitive reports that I need to verify. I expect that resolving the issues will take me well into the night watch."

Mainwaring, frowning, seemed ready to protest, but Anders didn't give him a chance.

"And I had best be about it. However, if you have the time, sir, perhaps you would like to tour the bay with Sergeant Fiske to inspect the work. He can show you how well we're adapting the Dust Badgers you have supplied for your volunteers."

Fiske snapped Anders a "you're calling for action above and beyond the call of duty" look.

"Yes, well. An Eridani must attend to duty, must he not? For if he does not, he is hardly a proper Eridani," said Mainwaring, showing that he did know *something* about Eridani.

"As you say, sir."

"Very well, then. Another time, Captain. Soon, I hope." He gave Anders another wink, then turned to Fiske. "Shall we be about it, Sergeant? I can't say that I'm eager to see what you people have been doing, tearing into those expensive vehicles the way you have been doing, but I suppose I ought to, eh?"

"Right this way, Colonel," Fiske said, stiffly polite. "I am sure we can get Sergeant Brizbin to tell all you want to know about what is necessitating this work."

Anders watched as Fiske led the colonel straight to Brizbin. He felt unhappy about shoving Mainwaring off onto Fiske, but didn't think the duty would be too bad. The colonel was unlikely to raise his "business proposition" again with Fiske as long as he held hopes that Anders might accept. Even if Mainwaring was considering badgering Fiske about it, he was unlikely to raise such a private issue in the very public expanse of the crowded maintenance bay. Now Anders saw that Fiske had implemented his own battle plan as Brizbin's lecture began. Fiske stepped back, then found something to do with the nearest work team. Anders was sure that the sergeant would soon be on the other side of the bay, if not somewhere else entirely.

Somewhere else entirely was where Anders should honestly be, specifically in the hardsuit storage chambers. He had not spoken falsely when saying he had reports to investigate.

Sergeant Greg Robson, in charge of the 102nd's operational security, both in the field and out, had come to Anders with word of an anomalous entry in the access logs for the hardsuit chambers that *Auditor*'s shipboard security hadn't reported. Robson had admitted that the anomaly might possibly be no more than a records glitch and was presumed to be so by the *Auditor*'s security personnel. When Anders had raised the possibility that they might be dealing with espionage, if not sabotage, Robson informed him that the computer records offered no evidence that any suit had been improperly accessed. His conclusion regarding tampering was "inconclusive."

The situation was unclear, but raising false alarms would not improve relations between MilForce and the Mainwaring volunteers. Assuming that they were dealing with a false alarm, however, wasn't a viable option.

Even with humankind in a war for survival against the Remor enemy, not all star nations were fighting that war. Some, it occasionally seemed, were ready to start new wars, intraspecies wars that could gut the effort against the alien invaders. The Pan-Stellar Combine had long been vociferous in condemning "IDL warmongering." Some of their more foolish politicians had gone so far as to claim that the IDL had invented the Remor to serve the League's "imperialist aims."

Whatever those might be.

Anders was well aware that no star nation was a monolithic and absolute collective where every citizen believed and thought the same thing. Such was not human nature.

Mainwaring's people could all be what they appeared. They could be people who had recognized the reality of the dire threat posed by the Remor, dutiful people who were willing to put themselves on the line to stop that threat. However, they, or some among them, could be something else. Problem was that the colonel's force, being volunteers, wasn't a component unit of League MilForce. Further, as they were not government-sponsored, neither were they an allied force. What it boiled down to was that the Combiners' devotion to the cause could not be accepted as total. And given that much of the League equipment aboard was still classified and not for release even to allies, there was room for concern.

The disposition of forces for the Pacifica relief operation had put Anders and the 102nd aboard a ship belonging to Colonel Mainwaring's Expeditionary Force as a gesture toward cooperation and integration of assets, which meant that the 102nd's hardware was aboard as well. That hardware included several classified systems, the prime example being the newest-model hardsuits. Such secrets were certainly not to be handed over to persons of dubious status like Mainwaring's people.

Anders mulled over the conflicting imperatives of cooperation and secrecy all the way to the storage chambers.

Like a lot of the space aboard *Auditor,* that now serving as the hardsuit storage chambers was converted from a previous use. Much of the ship had been repurposed when Mainwaring bought it, but the troop-carrying facilities had not been altered since Mainwaring had recruited a mobile infantry force such as the ship had originally been designed to transport. Trooper country had only been revamped when Anders's unit had been assigned. The drop pod launchers and support facilities had been one major change, the battlesuit maintenance and storage chambers another.

In the interest of expedience, they had adapted one of *Auditor*'s ground vehicle hangars. Although its location was farther from the barracks compartments than Anders liked, the workshops had been suitable and the armory chambers easily modified for 'suit storage slots. The armory's warding had looked to be more than adequate, especially after Robson and other IDL specialists had done some work on the safeguard codes, so that the usual live guard had been deemed unnecessary. The fact that the physical security systems were integrated with *Auditor*'s systems hadn't been considered an issue.

Anders hoped that those presumptions were warranted.

The locks responded to his codes, and the door shushed open to admit him. He didn't call for lights, satisfied to prowl with only the low level of illumination coming from the 'suit cradles.

The battlesuits were arranged in ranks, each platoon's 'suits forming a row. The recharge cradles supporting them shone down soft spotlights onto the helmets. The light offered a constant source of power to the solar cells, and prevented any drain to the power cells, keeping them at full charge and the 'suits at instant readiness. The arrangement had the side effect of making the chamber look somewhat like a museum display of ancient Terran suits of chivalric armor.

Feeling a little self-conscious, Anders went to his own suit first and made sure that it was free from tampering. Satisfied that it was clean, he proceeded on to the other Mark 17 suits. As the most advanced technology, the 17s were entrusted almost exclusively to the Eridani members of the 102nd. They too all appeared secure.

Perhaps it was a false alarm.

He started in on the earlier Mark 'suits. Some were a generation or more behind the advanced Mark 17s, but still better than what most star nations fielded. Certain of their systems and capabilities remained classified. He intended to check them all.

As he worked, Anders slowly became aware that *something* was out of place in the chamber. But what?

He didn't have his 'suit's sensors to call on, but he had his Eridani senses and they gave him advantages over most of humanity. He listened as his eyes roved over the chamber. He sniffed. Stooping, he laid his palm against the deck plate.

Nothing of note, yet he still felt uneasy. It was like being in a dark room and being sure that, although you had not heard or smelled anything, you were not alone. It was the sort of sensation that made a child fearful. It made an Eridani wary.

Silently he moved from row to row. When he reached the last, he saw that his uneasy feeling was justified. He was *not* alone in the dark.

Faintly lit by the spill from a recharge beam was a still figure, sitting wedged between two cradles. Dust motes swirled in the beam, dancing before being caught up in the suction of the ventilating system. Now that he was close, Anders could hear the man's soft breathing over the ship's ambient noise. A whiff of recognizable human scent mixed with the very familiar machine odors told him who it was.

"Williams," Anders said aloud.

The man jumped to his feet like a startled rabbit, head turning as he searched for Anders in the dark. Anders made it easy for him and stepped into the aisle between the cradles. Williams turned in his direction, snapped a salute, and froze at attention. His eyes were wide. Anders noted a slight tremble in the man's hands.

It was good that he was afraid. Anders felt doubly betrayed. It was bad enough that someone had broken into the chamber. It was worse because it was this someone. Despite his rocky start as an "elected spokesman," Williams had done well in the test simulations. He'd done better during three weeks of training, well enough to impress Anders and get himself a promotion to sergeant and a command slot in a Combiner platoon. Even Fiske, who had little charitable to say about any of the Combiners, had passed a positive remark or two about Williams's capabilities as a soldier and potential leader. It had been looking as though the man was worthy of his "election." But now . . .

"I think you have some explaining to do, mister," Anders said, stating the obvious.

Williams stuttered out a response. "Permission to speak freely, sir. It's the only way I can explain."

"Confession is good for the soul, soldier. Sometimes it even brings leniency. You can start with how you got in here."

Williams swallowed. "I, uh, let myself in."

"You overrode the entry code?"

"Yes, sir." He shrugged. "It's a knack I have."

The man *had* scored high on electronics aptitude, though his résumé showed no experience with security systems. "You are not supposed to be here."

"I know that, sir."

"Really? The duty roster puts you in the vehicle bay with everyone else. Did someone change your orders without notifying me?"

Another shrug. "I don't think so, sir. But I got my assignment completed, and I was getting in the way of the welding teams. I thought I'd grab some private time."

"So you came here?"

Nodding, Williams said, "And it's not the first time, sir."

That was an interesting admission. "Explain."

"When I was a kid I used to dream about being a hardsuit trooper. Too many combat vids and games, I guess. Everybody knows the League has the most advanced suits. I, uh . . . this is kind of embarrassing. Right now being in the same room is as close as I get to the cutting edge. Someday that may change, but . . ."

Williams babbled on with such obvious naïveté that Anders started to feel some sympathy. As a child he too had dreamed of being a hardsuit trooper. Were their positions reversed, would Anders have broken the rules to get near the coveted 'suits? The boy he'd been would have done so in a heartbeat. But he was Eridani and it had never been an issue. Besides, that boy was gone. Williams's child self was also long gone. He should have known better, acted more wisely.

Winding down, Williams gave a shrug of defeat. "I'm sorry, sir. I know I shouldn't be here. I made a mistake and I'd like a chance to correct it. I'll show Sergeant Robson the glitch I exploited, if you'd like."

"You'll start with that." Anders used the ship commo to

summon Fiske. "And then you'll get your quiet time in the brig."

"But you'll let me out when we get to Pacifica, won't you, sir?" Williams looked shaken, but more disappointed than worried.

"Why would I?" Anders asked, curious at the man's reaction.

"I know you Leaguers think we're a bunch of Pansies. You don't trust us. Right now I'm sure you *really* don't trust *me*. I understand that, sir. But Sergeant Fiske is right when he says that combat is the true test of a soldier. We'll prove ourselves then. I'm confident that we won't let you down there, sir. Even if we are running second-rate softsuits. I want a chance, sir."

"You had a chance."

Williams flushed. "A second chance, then. You do believe in giving a man a second chance, don't you, sir?"

Anders felt sympathy give him a hard strike below the belt. Thoughtful, he didn't respond and nothing more was said until Fiske showed up. Anders watched Fiske escort Williams down the passageway, then went back and checked the rest of the suits. As far as he could determine, none had been tampered with.

Perhaps innocence was not dead?

Williams wasn't the first man to break the rules and follow his heart. Perhaps Anders ought to do unto others as he had been done unto himself.

Part 2

Intertissued Trajectories

The last transit was almost upon them. The long trip to the Pacifica System was nearly over.

Stone listened to the calm voices throughout the fleet command center. They sounded no different than the voices on the various commo channels of the fleet, but here he could catch the slight tang of nervousness that pervaded the compartment, something electronics could not convey. Even good troops like those around him would have their fears. And who in their right mind would suggest that they should not? Weren't they about to enter a solar system held by the enemy?

But fear could not be allowed to rule. Fear was an enemy worse then the Remor. And though it could never be fully vanquished, it could be controlled. The men and women of the Pacifica Theater Fleet were doing that.

What planning and training could be done were finished. Contingencies had been proposed and prepped. They were as ready as they would be.

He activated the All Fleet icon on his commo panel.

"Attention the fleet. This is Commander Stone. Prepare for transit. All first-wave ships synch transit generators to *Constantine*. Second-wave ships synch to *Auditor. Constantine* and *Auditor* confirm chronometrics."

Elsewhere aboard *Constantine,* on the command bridge, Colonel MacAndra was confirming both the synch and the chronometrics. It was his ship to fly and fight. Stone, in the command center, had a different responsibility. He was to direct the fleet as a whole.

Stone was familiar with the process, but each time it came to the cusp of action, he recalled his days as a ship commander. Were he to confide such reminiscences to another, that person might suggest that he was longing for the lesser responsibility. But that person would be wrong. When lives were in your keeping, numbers neither increased nor decreased your responsibility. The impossible goal was to safeguard each and every one of those lives. Knowing that some could not be saved gave no license to spend any lives carelessly.

So why did he harbor a nostalgia for command of a single ship? Today, as always before, he saw no clear reason. As ever, there was no time for reflection. Duty demanded other things of his mind.

At Chip Hollister's order, the command center crew sealed their vacuum suits. Like the men and women around him and all across the fleet, Stone fastened the seals of his suit. This was the last preparatory task, and it was executed with efficiency and assurance. Fear was fastened down.

Green lights winked on in the holotank beside each ship icon, signaling their readiness for the transit. "All vessels ready," Chip reported as he canceled the acknowledgment display. The green lights vanished, leaving only the blue dots of friendly forces. Expectant faces turned to Stone.

It was time.

"Initiate."

There was a delay, the trifling seconds for Stone's order to be obeyed and to have the readied jump engines goosed to their threshold levels, then the universe collapsed into nothingness for a timeless moment.

No clouded night, no sealed bunker, not even a deep-driven mine could match the darkness that enfolded a soul during transit. Some said it was death that one experienced. Some claimed to have quiet chats with God, others with the devil. Scientists argued that there was no experience at all, just a subjective attempt on the part of an overwhelmed mind to cast the instant of transition across light-years of space into something approaching understandability. Who knew the truth of it?

One truth of transit was that before the engines reached peak field one existed in a certain part of space and time, and afterward one existed in another part of space with, to all appearances, no elapsed time.

Another truth was that neither human nor human-made machine handled transit without complaint.

The stars returned. Their grandeur was as breathtaking as ever, just spinning in a different configuration. By the sounds on commo, several people were greeting them with the remains of their last meals.

The shuddering *Constantine* had its own complaints, an inelegant symphony of metallic moans, hisses, and pings punctuated by the occasional screech. No damage alarms sounded, nor was there a shipwide disaster alarm, so Stone ignored the ship's complaints. If *Constantine* had suffered any significant transition damage, MacAndra would pass the word to the command center.

After transit, ship's sensors always took time to rebuild their picture of surrounding space. *Constantine* and her sisters were doing that. It was a vulnerable time. Stone watched the holotank, willing the process to go faster, to no effect.

Naturally *Constantine* was the first to appear in the tank. Before more than a third of the first wave's ships had reconfirmed themselves, something else appeared: the sullen orange sphere of a high mass unknown.

"We've got a bandit in proximity," Scan Officer Xiang reported, quite reasonably assuming the unknown was hostile.

"Resolve its identity," Stone ordered. "I want weapon threat projections on-screen now."

"In process."

It would take time they might not have.

The unexpected Remor ship was too close. It could not have missed their arrival. Transit had left the ships of the fleet unready to respond. The Remor ship was too big for comfort, probably a dreadnought. It had only surprise to deal with and would surely be preparing to attack.

"Inbound on the bandit!" Xiang announced excitedly.

"Hoo-rah, *Cerval!*" someone cheered.

Stone too realized that the missiles inbound on the enemy ship could have only one source: the lurker-grade vessel *Cerval. Cerval,* after conveying her most recent survey to the fleet, had made transit back to the Pacifica system to watch over the transition point chosen for the invasion. There had been no guarantee that *Cerval* would make it back into the system undetected, no surety that she would be able to remain undetected near the chosen transition point. And, with transition points as diffuse as they were and space as vast as it was, there was certainly no assurance that the lurker would be in a position to do anything about any enemy ship that might be nearby when the fleet came through. But *Cerval* had made it, presumably undetected, and God had placed her in a fortunate position.

The tricks of physics that cloaked a lurker from detection depended on the vessel's limiting emissions of all sorts. With no emissions other than her own heat, a lurker was almost undetectable; stealth was her main protection, since she carried little in the way of armor, shielding, or defensive weaponry. Any weapon use would compromise that stealth. Yet *Cerval* had fired, revealing herself to guard the incoming fleet and to buy them time to ready their own response.

Cerval needed support and would get it.

"Initiate Contingency Charley Solo," Stone ordered on the All Fleet.

The contingency plan for encountering a single capital ship within combat range would go into effect on his order. The fleet's heavy elements would be plotting firing solutions. Small craft would be launching from all of the nearest ships, not to pose a threat but to avoid one. Should the hostile score against one of those ships, the survivability of the smaller craft was higher if they were free in space. Similarly, all vessels were dispersing to limit the chances of proximity kills. The Pacifica Theater Fleet could afford no unnecessary loss of assets.

While the new arrivals made ready their assault, *Cerval* was undoubtedly preparing as fast as she could for a second launch. She was also transmitting current data on in-system conditions. Already the main plot boards were updating.

"Can we bring *Cerval* under the fleet's aegis?" Stone asked.

"We need to reposition some—"

"Do it." Stone opened commo to *Cerval.* "Enough, Commander Rider. You've done your job. Our thanks. Now get under cover."

"Acknowledged," replied Rider.

Rider would move his ship in coordination with the redeploying vessels of the fleet, getting his lurker where the defensive systems of the fleet could provide cover. All that could be done would be done. Stone put *Cerval* from his mind.

Ramses won the race among the first wave's capital ships, achieving first fire with an elegant full spread of a dozen missiles.

"Well done, *Ramses,*" Stone broadcast. "Remaining elements to hold fire for saturation strike."

Acknowledgment lights began to wink on.

"On ready lights?" Chip Hollister asked.

"Neg." Stone's response would keep the barrage from launching as soon as all elements had achieved a solution. "We'll see how *Ramses*' birds fly."

It was a calculated risk. If they had surprised the hostile, *Ramses*' missiles ought to be enough to cripple the enemy vessel, probably destroy it. But if the enemy crew was wary, or just had very good reflexes, their defenses would be more formidable. Their ship would likely survive and continue to be a threat. If all fleet elements launched, the hostile could be eliminated with a virtual certainty. No known enemy vessels of the bandit's mass had the defensive power to stand against such an incoming weight of fire.

But if all elements launched they would be expending precious munitions that might be needed later. They would also be providing information to the enemy about the fleet's capabilities, because sooner or later the enemy would be analyzing the energy signatures released in this skirmish. The longer the enemy could be kept in the dark about the fleet's strengths, the better.

"Bandit reads as a *Gorgon. Cerval*'s ID is 99 plus," Chip reported. The probable fighting statistics of the *Gorgon* appeared in a new window beside the now-red icon.

The Remor destroyer-grade vessels code-named *Gorgon* were not as bad as the dreadnoughts, but they had a heavy throw weight of missiles supplemented by powerful electronic warfare capabilities and backed by batteries of beam weapons for close-in work. God had granted the fleet sufficient grace that the *Gorgon* wasn't close enough to use the latter. But it was still close enough to maul several of the first wave's ships.

"*Gorgon* launching."

"Three birds. Five."

Only five? They must have surprised the Remor.

"First flight on *Cerval*'s position."

"Seven birds."

Still short of a full launch for a *Gorgon*. Good news.

"Second and third flights inbound on fleet."

The first to resolve would be *Cerval*'s missiles. Their tracks had nearly intersected the *Gorgon*'s position in the holotank. Stone dialed a higher resolution. The apparent distance increased, but the missiles still closed on the Remor ship. One went dark, but the other bored in.

"*Cerval* has scored. One hit amidships."

"Secondary radiation sources. It's a good hit."

But not enough to take out a *Gorgon*.

Ramses' flight appeared at the fringes of the expanded display. The capital ship's missiles were a good deal heavier than any carried by a lurker. They were true ship killers. Since the *Gorgon* had displayed limited anti-missile capacity against *Cerval*'s birds, there was a good chance *Ramses*' missiles would do what needed to be done.

"One minute to mark."

The enemy launched countermeasures at the approaching death. Half of *Ramses'* birds fell to the anti-missiles. Another four were lost to the enemy's defensive fire. Two got through. The *Gorgon* launched six new missiles before the impact from *Ramses'* birds, but they were no threat. The expanding fireball that had been the Remor warship devoured them before they could blast clear.

There were cheers on fleet commo, but none filled the command center. Everyone in the center was a veteran, and they all knew that the engagement wasn't over. The *Gorgon* might be atoms on the solar wind, but it had left a very solid legacy. The enemy's earlier missiles were still in flight.

"Three minutes to outer intercept zone."

It was not known whether the Remor used live gunners to telemetrically adjust missiles' courses after launch. Humans did. It made the missiles' courses harder to predict and thus more difficult to intercept. Battle reports suggested that Remor missiles were easier to intercept after the launching vessel was destroyed, but probability curves hinted that successful intercepts were not quite as frequent as they would be for human missiles relying on their internal computers. The common wisdom was that the Remor just had better guidance and control systems. Lord knew their warfighting technology was superior to human in other ways.

The tracks Stone studied in the plot tank were no statistical averages. They were real live missiles. Any failure of the fleet's interception systems would likely mean real casualties. Human skill and human technological capabilities would decide the outcome of this singular event today, not probability.

Though—*thank you, Saint Michael*—probability favored them today, for there were only seven missiles coming their way and those enemy birds were far outnumbered by ships ready to vaporize them.

Time crawled.

The missiles drew closer.

"One minute to outer interception zone."

Chip looked up from his station. "Commander, we can get a probability of ninety-nine to three places with only *Constantine, Fearless,* and *Stalwart* firing."

Stone dropped his eyes from the plot to his own screen, tapped a few icons, and pondered the results. Allowing the cruiser *Fearless* to hold her guns while patrollers *Bayard, Reginald Cobham,* and *Rickenbaker* fired offered a two-place solution. Not as strong, but better for concealing the fleet's strength.

"Revised solution," he said, sending it to Chip's station. "Make it so."

Would the difference make a difference? Would he pay for his hopes with the lives of men and women under his command? It wasn't likely, but war was full of improbability.

"Thirty seconds to outer interception zone."

It was a glacial thirty seconds, until Scan Officer Xiang reported, "Enemy missiles destroyed."

Stone relaxed, releasing his grip on the arms of his command chair. The engagement was over. No other enemy ships were in range.

"Attention the fleet. Secure from action stations. Shape course for the inner system."

They had drawn first blood, but the fight to retake Pacifica System had only begun.

12

The 102nd was rigged for hot assault. The blowers were secured in their drop pods. The troops were in their suits and crammed into assault capsules where they were experiencing more than a touch of can shivers, especially among the Combiners.

Anders checked the chronometer. Not long now. He hurried to complete his circuit of checks to ensure that everyone was snugged in and locked down. He could have done it electronically, but he felt better putting eyes on each and every capsule. The fact that the dispositions were precautionary didn't seem to ease his anxiety.

Assault wasn't imminent. *Auditor* was part of the second wave going into the Pacifica System, the bulk of the fleet having already gone in. How they had fared was unknown as yet. The second wave could be getting ready to emerge into a battle, thus the troops were put into their most survivable positions.

No message torp had come back with a change of plan. Of course, that could mean that no human ship had survived long enough to send such a torp, and that they were heading into oblivion. There was nothing he could do to change things if it were so. Anders shoved the thought away with a prayer that it might not be so.

As he reached the capsule assigned to his team and swung himself into his seat, the transit alert sounded. Gordie and

Milano made jokes about somebody always being the last to the party as he strapped down.

The disorientation of transit spun him into the dark place, then wrenched him back. Nothing looked different, but he knew they were elsewhere. His stomach insisted that it was still back in interstellar space. While Anders waited for it to catch up, he wondered what would happen next.

The *Transit Complete* bell rang, signaling a successful, and safe, transition.

Anders was already climbing out of the assault capsule when the unit chatter started. He left Fiske to deal with it and headed for the operations control station in the launch bay. The ship's technicians manning it made way for the bulk of his armored body.

Updates were no doubt flooding the bridge. He expected that it would take a few moments to filter down to this console, but he keyed in his authorization and requested a status update. It took more time than it should have for the data to be sent. Either the Combine computers were slow or someone was filtering the data before it passed to him. That, he decided, was something he would look into.

Through his helmet's peripheral monitors he could see the troops clambering out of their capsules. A number were headed for him. Fiske and the other noncoms were soon clustered around. The hardsuits worn by Leaguers were almost enough to totally displace all of the Auditors that ought to be manning the station. Mainwaring's people in their soft-suits finished the job.

"What's to tell, Captain?" asked Sergeant Williams.

Williams's eager question came before Anders was ready to speak, as the Combiner's questions so often did. But what would have been on the edge of impertinence for a ranker was allowable from an NCO, and Williams wore a sergeant's triple bars as commander of 1st platoon, reserve company.

"Still sorting it out, Williams."

The newly minted sergeant nodded, accepting. Anders was pleased. Williams's cheerful acceptance of discipline after his unauthorized entry into the 'suit storage chambers had scored points among the Eridani within the 102nd. His voluntary exposure of the security glitch he'd utilized, as well as a couple more, had only improved his score. Even Fiske had commented on the man's good attitude. Since nothing had turned up wrong with the 'suits and Williams had tested out well in the sims, Anders had not been able to justify leaving him as an ordinary ranker. It was an Eridani sin to waste resources, so Anders had included Williams among those who got their rank "adjusted." So far Williams had done nothing to make him regret it. In fact, the popular Williams was proving valuable in bettering the morale and discipline of the Combiner troops.

The news trickled in and the situation looked good. The fleet was moving into the system. The first engagement with the *Gorgon* had gone well and the surprised enemy warship had been utterly destroyed. The first wave had encountered several more Remor vessels, including a dreadnought-mass *Rukh,* and destroyed them as well. Fleet casualties were light and ship losses nonexistent. But their good fortune couldn't last forever. Other enemy ships were out there, and not just lightly armed stuff either. And though scattered, the enemy was starting to react and coalesce into clusters.

"The vacuum-heads aren't doing half bad," Robson opined.

"Let's hope they keep doing it," said Fiske. "I don't really want any xeno ships hanging around to chew our arses when we drop."

"Amen to that," chorused several others.

"The real fight's gonna be on the ground," Williams declared.

Anders agreed. "Spoken like a true 'pounder."

13

"I'm sorry, Commander Stone," finished Mainwaring.

The second wave had transitioned into Pacifica space, but would be delayed in proceeding in-system as some of the ships had suffered damage from the transition. The Second Wing of the Pacifica Theater Fleet was mostly the ships of Colonel Mainwaring's Expeditionary Force. Nearly all of the Combiner vessels were refitted commercial ships and, though intended for frontier service where the beacons that eased interstellar transits throughout human space were rare, they were not as resilient in making unaided transitions as warships. First Wing had transitioned and engaged in combat as soon as they hit normal space and had not lost a single ship. Second had lost four ships without a shot fired. Repairs would put them back into service, but repairs would take time. The fleet's timetable was the unrecoverable casualty. While it was not welcome news, it was not exactly surprising.

"Understood," Stone replied. "Maintain cohesion and keep us apprised. You'll get an update on orders when we've integrated this new wrinkle into the operational timetable."

There was a few seconds' pause before Mainwaring acknowledged the orders. Time lag was already beginning to become noticeable in the transmission.

"Perhaps we should view it as a silver lining," Colonel MacAndra suggested as the compressed technical data from Second Wing unspooled into the command center's main display.

Stone was not happy about the repair estimates that were appearing. "If you see something good here, Craig, I'd be happy to hear it."

"Well, it's obvious that we won't be able to break atmosphere as quickly as we'd hoped, but that may not be so bad. Opposition is not as strong as we feared and there are few Remor fleet elements well positioned to oppose a landing on Pacifica. The orbital high ground is ours for the taking—"

"There are those two *Rukhs* lurking out by the second moon," Chip Hollister pointed out.

MacAndra nodded. "I haven't forgotten them. But they are pretty much all the enemy has to put in immediate opposition. If we don't have to cover the advance of our transport ships, I believe we can go after them, maybe even flash them both."

"I'm not so sure of that," Chip said, voicing Stone's concern.

"We ought to be able to force a withdrawal at least." MacAndra focused on Stone. "We do that and Second Wing can come in clean and safe."

"I, for one, wouldn't mind a delay in the landings, Commander," said Colonel Cope, commander of the ground forces. "It would give us time to improve the resolution of our reconnaissance. I'd feel better if we had more to go on than *Cerval*'s long-distance scans."

"We'd all feel better about that," Stone agreed.

"And we ought to be able to soften up the landing zones better once we take care of those *Rukhs*," said MacAndra.

"I know a lot of hardshells who would be thankful of that," Cope said in support.

"I smell a plan cooking," observed Stone. "All right. How long for something to sink teeth into, Craig?"

MacAndra glanced over to his staff and must have seen what he wanted among their thoughtful faces. "We can have a draft plan on screen in two hours."

"Very well. Meantime, First Wing continues to advance on our original vector."

PACIFICA
KILAWA, PALISADRAN ENCLAVE

Working for the frickin' xeno-mantises turned out to be better than Bartie had anticipated. There was a decent place to doss down, all the food he could eat, and he even got to play a little with the female xombie candidates he hauled in. Hell, he even had a new gang of slugs to boss around. The only important thing missing was some decent booze.

The big problem was that he had to jump when they told him to. *That* he didn't like. Not at all. But a guy had to be practical. As long as the frickin' xenos were in charge, the best a guy could do was get himself a slot as their muscle. *That* he'd done. And he was starting to figure out how to minimize his efforts for his frickin' bug masters, so his world was getting better. If this new guy Hernandez managed to get his still working, life would be even better, a hell of a lot better than grubbing in the ruins of Palisandra and playing robber baron against what was an obviously diminishing flock of peasant sheep.

A dozen of the xeno-mantises came boiling out of the bug house and dispersed in a dozen different directions across the Lair.

"Who kicked over the anthill?" Hernandez asked, looking up from the coils of copper tubing he was sorting through.

"Dunno." But Bartie figured he could ask. Sometimes one of the frickin xenos deigned to answer his questions. The clipped and cryptic answers weren't much, but he was smart enough to make some sense of them. Usually.

This time the frickin' xenos couldn't be bothered to even notice him when he tried to talk to them. They were strutting around doing whatever it was they were doing. They didn't even stop when he tried to flag them down, and he was nearly run down by a squad of their fighting machines hustling out of the Lair to who knew where.

Except when those machines went out on escort for a food bug run, he hadn't seen them for months. Overhead he could see nearly a dozen of their flying machines and, higher up, a handful of contrails. He hadn't seen so much frickin' xeno activity since the first months of the conquest.

Something was up.

Damn frickin' xenos.

Least they could do was tell their number-one boy what the frickin' hell was going on.

14

PACIFICA THEATER FLEET
CMEFS *AUDITOR*

"The fleet has had their moment," said Colonel Cope, concluding his speech to the ground forces. "Ours is upon us. May God go with you all."

Amen, Anders prayed silently.

The fleet had cleared space around Pacifica of Remor ships and allowed the additional reconnaissance that Colonel Cope had wanted. Unfortunately, something the enemy was doing continued to interfere with the satellites and drones collecting that intelligence—a problem fleet was still working on. Nevertheless, enough data had been gathered that the original plan for assaulting the planet had been altered.

Pacifica was a planet of oceans, and had very little land surface: one small continent and a brace of continent wannabes. The rest of the land made up island chains of varying size. The human population had been concentrated in cities dotted around the coasts of the three major island-continents. Intel reported that most of those cities appeared to be mainly intact, something not seen previously on Remor-occupied worlds. In fact, it had been *Cerval*'s report of their survival that had prompted this reclamation expedition.

Now, however, visions of an embattled, still-resisting human population had been replaced by a mystery. The cities, ringed by apparent defensive barriers, were devoid of any signs of power sources or industry, and there were no traces of military hardware. Yet signs of Remor presence were scattered all over the land surfaces and on the oceans as well. Everywhere, in fact, but in the cities. There, humans were living; not as they once had, certainly, but surviving, even farming, on an enemy-occupied planet.

A puzzle.

Naturally Colonel Cope had wanted more reconnaissance, but Commander Stone had insisted on having boots on the ground as soon as possible. It was apparent that the fleet's arrival had caught the enemy off guard. The on-planet Remor were every bit as scattered as their ships had been. But that was changing, and no one wanted to assault a prepared enemy. Delay would also squander the strategic surprise they had achieved, and surprise was a force multiplier that no soldier ever gave up willingly.

Anders's unit would be going down hot and hard.

The scattered enemy meant there was no obvious target for assault, so the plan was to drop fast and establish a beachhead on Kilawa, the largest of the island-continents. From there, the ground forces would expand, dealing with enemy forces as they were encountered and moving to make contact with the cities, one by one. Since there appeared to be no strong points or enemy troop concentrations, a serious orbital bombardment had been ruled out. Stone refused to allow such a diversion of resources with Remor ships still active in space. Logically, Anders knew it was a good decision, but the groundpounder in him was starting to feel a little naked. Fleet would supply interface and air cover but, as always, resources were limited. There would surely be some point when things got hot and the poor bloody infantry would be on their own.

"Ten minutes to insertion," announced assault command.

They would be long minutes, longer because there wasn't much left to do.

The blowers were in their drop pods. He'd checked. The support pods were crammed with their designated loads. He'd checked. The matrix autopilots for all the pods were loaded with the proper coordinates for the primary landing zone and all three alternates. He'd checked. The troopers were all suited with full loads and all systems green. He'd checked. All were snugged in their assault capsules. Each blower team was in its assigned capsule, linked to coordinate with the drop pod carrying its ride, to avoid scatter in the drop. No one had managed to strap into the wrong slot. He'd checked. He'd done all his unit commander's tasks.

His personal gear was all nominal. As familiar as the 'suit he was wearing felt, it wasn't the simple trooper's 'suit he wished he was wearing. This rig was light on weapons and heavy on communications and command circuitry. Where his troopers carried ammunition cells and tactical devices in their external stowage points, he was packing electronic black boxes and reconnaissance devices. All very valuable. Saint Michael knew he'd always been glad when his unit commander had deployed such things to his unit's advantage. But despite all the training he still felt more comfortable handling a Mark 22 Individual Energy Weapon and its accessories. Lack of comfort had not kept him from running all the checks and getting stowed away all Brisholt fashion.

The only thing left to do was to get his butt into the assault capsule and strap in.

" 'Bout time," Milano commented as he crammed himself through the hatch.

"As if you ladies were going anywhere without me," Anders replied. "Who'd tell you where to find your tool when it was time to piss?"

"Got that right, Captain," Gordon said. "We're total babies without you. Say, Milano, what do the regs say about dealing with a delusional officer?"

Milano started listing several definitely nonregulation solutions. While his blower crew bantered on, Anders strapped in, then brought up his link into fleet interface operations channel. The link to the 102nd command team's assault capsule was a privilege of his rank and position, as had been made clear to the Second Wave commander's staff.

"Five minutes to insertion."

The guardian interface craft would soon hit atmosphere.

Anders confirmed their deployment by calling up the near-space display. They were on track and on time. Behind them came the transport ships, including *Auditor*. A few red dots appeared, indicating Remor atmospheric craft rising to meet them. They came from different places and followed different tracks. The coordinated human ships disposed of them relatively easily. The transport ship tracks began to diverge as each headed for its designated unloading point. Farther up the gravity well were the landers, waiting. They would descend as soon as the landing zones were clear and unleash the armored formations. It looked as if everything was going according to plan.

"Captain Seaborg." Colonel Cope's face displaced the vector tracks on Anders's screen. "I am very sorry to do this to you, but we're changing your drop zone. Please key open your computers for an update on parameters."

Anders did so. Weren't plans supposed to go belly-up after contact with the enemy? Did the piddling skirmish with the interceptors count?

"What's to tell, Colonel?"

"It looks like we've got enemy forces starting to concentrate near Palisandra. That's one of the cities where we have confirmation of survivors. The enemy focal point is too distant to reach from the planned beachhead and we need a blocking force, so we're diverting your force to intercept. You are going to prevent a massacre of civilians."

That was easy for the colonel to say. "What will we be facing, sir?"

"Nothing you can't handle. Intel's report is included in your download, along with the details of your force group attachments. You are now in command of Task Group Seaborg. Sorry for the short notice, Captain. I know it's not going to be easy, but this is not the occasion to let the daunting make us pause."

Cope wasn't Eridani, but he knew something about them. "The impossible will just slow us down, sir."

"I'm counting on that, Captain. So is Commander Stone. Cope out."

The vector tracks reappeared on Anders's screen. Nothing looked different, save that all vessels had moved a little farther. Yet Anders knew things had changed. The question was: How much?

Anders warned Fiske, then dumped data on him. He'd have to do the best he could to bring the other noncoms up to speed. Anders opened the situation download and tried to fit his mind around the new data.

"Two minutes to insertion." The flight operations officer's voice might have belonged to the ship herself for all the humanity in it.

Normally the last seconds before insertion were a time for worry. Today there was no time. Anders shoved his concerns aside and burrowed deeper into the download. He barely felt the launch as the assault capsules and drop pods hurtled free from *Auditor*.

A hot planetfall from orbit was fast, as far as moving mass from orbit to the ground went, but it could still take upward of fifteen Standard minutes. Heat concerns and orbital mechanics could not be ignored. Their fast descent was scheduled to take twelve Standard from launch, giving him about ten minutes to absorb data before the immediacy of landing became paramount.

Unfortunately, the need to know what was going on around them intruded. Anders checked the near-space display. All of the 102nd's pods and capsules had launched clean and were steady on their planned tracks. Several more tracks seemed to be converging on theirs, heading for the same destination. They were all blue. Friendlies. They would be his force additions. As yet no red tracks were angling toward them.

The capsule started to shake as the atmosphere grew thicker around them and resistance to its passage increased. The outer hull was heating but the compartment's insulation was still handling it.

As far as Anders could see, there were no enemy interface strikers headed for them. The few on-screen were giving their attention to the heavy transports, trying to break through the fighter screen and get at them.

The ride got rougher as turbulence increased. They were well into the atmosphere now. The ablatives on the capsule's hull would be gone, burned away. She was still hot enough for the insulation to be struggling. He, of course, couldn't feel the temperatures, as his 'suit was protecting him.

The escort commander reported no signs of enemy aircraft rising to challenge their intrusion into the airspace over Pacifica. A few seconds later he was back on the line to wish them good luck. His flight had been redirected to assist in covering the main landing.

At one minute to set-down, Milano said. "Looking like we've got a free ride."

To put the lie to his words, small red dots appeared on the screen, coming from somewhere south of the drop point. Warning alarms sounded. There were surface-to-air missiles inbound on them.

PACIFICA
KILAWA, PALISANDRA

Sue abandoned her ghost-haunted sleep and rolled off the hard mattress, dragging her blanket with her. Wrapped in its enfolding embrace, she left the room she had called home for the last week and wandered the corridors of what had been the Landorf Luxury Suites Hotel. No one else seemed afflicted. Snoring emanated from some of the rooms she passed, the urgent sounds of lovemaking from others. She hurried past those rooms, not wanting the memories the sounds stirred.

It was her problem, she knew. Her people needed to take what comfort they could. She could not fault them for that. More, she was glad for them. But that sort of escape was not for her, no matter how briefly. For her, that path was closed.

Floor by floor she made her way upward, away from the

levels occupied by her diminished band. Eventually she found herself taking the last, cold stairs to the roof.

The air was clean, chill but welcome. The dead city around them was quiet, but the solitude she sought was denied her. There was someone else already on the roof.

Young Ren stood by one of the defunct air-conditioning units, staring up at the night sky. He seemed relaxed and still. She'd often seen him that way when he lay in ambush, practicing the sniper skills he seemed too young to own, but there was something different about his stillness tonight. His young face, bathed in the wan starlight, was intent, his attention totally ensnared by the sky.

She almost turned around, abandoning her quest for a quiet place to someone who had already found his. Almost. His calmness hinted at a balm for her own disquiet. Could she allow herself to soak it in?

No.

She needed to go before she disturbed him. Anyone who had found a moment of peace in their mad world deserved to savor it.

As she turned to go, he revealed that he was not quite as absorbed as he appeared. He knew she was there.

"Can you see them?" he asked.

His voice was troubled, perplexing her. Without putting her own eyes on the traitor stars, she asked, "What are you looking at?"

"I don't know."

"I bet Professor Murch could tell you which constellation was which, but I don't think he'd appreciate getting woken up."

Sue knew very well that he wouldn't. She didn't know the pattern of the night sky very well, but she decided to do what she could for the boy. Reluctantly she raised her eyes to the heavens. She swallowed hard and dry when she saw the fire there.

Tiny motes of light danced among the steady glitter of the stars. Some vied in brilliance with them, flaring briefly, then fading to nothingness. Meteoric flames flickered to life and streaked downward.

She had seen this when the Remor had come, when they had destroyed the poor souls who had tried to defend Pacifica. That fight was long over and the defenders long gone. The Remor ruled the heavens now, just as they ruled the earth.

So what was happening up there?

15

PACIFICA
OVER KILAWA ISLE

With speed no human could match, the matrix autopilot cut in evasion routines for Anders's assault capsule. No time was lost between the sounding of the missile warnings and the start of electronic spoofing. Decoys deployed. Across the sky, assault capsules and drop pods alike began to pitch, yaw, and roll as part of the effort to throw the ascending enemy missiles off target.

Anders had experienced rough rides before, but familiarity with the gyrations only took a man so far. The human body had limits of tolerance for such abuse. The hardsuit's shock gel liners minimized the inevitable bruising, but nothing could be done to quell the nausea arising from the abuse administered by the pitching capsule. He managed to get the barf tube into his mouth before he needed it.

Detonations further rocked the capsule. Something blasted a hole in the hull beside his head and smashed its way out the opposite side. The lights winked out. A wave of heat rolled through that Anders felt through his 'suit. The lights flickered back on.

"Everybody all right?"

Milano and Gordon gave thumbs-up. Milano looked noticeably pale, but Anders's squad monitor didn't show any damage to the trooper. They had all survived the barrage intact. The capsule was still descending. The autopilot signaled a low-level deployment of the drogue chute, warning them of a hard impact to come.

But what was true for Anders's capsule wasn't true for the rest of the task group. Four elements had disappeared from the tracking screen, all troop carriers. Three were from the reserve company and the fourth was from 3rd platoon. Sergeant Selma Mossberg and her Lancastrian veterans were gone. At least a dozen more icons were flashing to indicate that they had taken damage. Most of those were also assault capsules. He'd get the casualty reports on the ground. The remaining two were the drop pod carrying the 1st platoon's scout car and one of the task group's add-ons. Anders had to query to find out what had been lost. He didn't like the answer he got—it had carried the equipment of the 334 DistOpSdrn. The squadron's rigs had been intended to provide improved reconnaissance capability as well as mobile close support fire for the task group as it operated away from the main force's assets. Task Group Seaborg had lost its distance vision and long reach.

The assault capsule shivered as the protective panels for the landing rockets blew clear. They lit up. Deceleration, sudden and implacable, shoved the passengers back with a force that would have been dangerous had they not been in hardsuits. Then it was gone. A second later the capsule crumped to the ground.

Gordon popped the hatch and Milano, weapon ready, shouldered Anders aside to go through first. Gordon slipped into the opening, blocking it as he covered Milano's dash for cover. Once Milano signaled all clear, Gordon stepped aside. Neither of them asked Anders's opinion about their unscheduled change in debarkation procedure.

Balanced imperatives, Anders told himself, deciding to let it slide. Eridani had a tradition of leading from the front, but they also had a tradition of respecting those around them. His team was only trying to keep him safe, doing what it could to ensure that the task group retained its leadership. And there truly were times when a leader, even an Eridani, needed to let his men go first. It was a lesson some higher-ranking Eridani had trouble keeping in mind.

Saint Michael, guard me from becoming one of them.

As he hit the ground, Fiske appeared. He had been aboard a small, fast, two-man capsule, but there had to have been a notable variance between their capsules' matrix autopilots' evasion routines for him to have reached the ground with enough time to be now trotting toward Anders's capsule.

"That was a rough one," the sergeant observed.

"We took hits."

"I know. My blower's a wreck. I think the rockets didn't fire. But the command car made it. Price is bringing her up now."

"Good." The sooner they could establish the unit's commo net, the sooner they'd know how bad the ride down had been and what they had left to accomplish their mission.

Fiske led them toward where the command car had come down. They were moving through open grasslands dotted with copses of trees. Anders guessed that it had once been agricultural land, as was much of Pacifica's restricted land surface, although clearly there had been little agricultural activity since the Remor invasion. Visibility was good. He could see the expected steam rising from several touchdown points. Unfortunately, he could also see several darker smoke plumes where damaged or wrecked transports had plowed in. A grass fire had started from one and was spreading to the west.

"We'll shift to Rally Point Barley," he announced. "Get the word out."

"Will do, boss," Milano acknowledged. "Soon as I get commo access."

The rising roar of turbine fans suggested that it wouldn't be long. The command blower, with Private Price at the controls, came skating out from behind a dense clump of jewel-leaf trees and cut a track through the swaying wild grain directly toward them.

"Command post reporting for duty, sir," Price joked as he spun the Mark 8 into a stop that offered its rear access point to the four soldiers.

Anders acknowledged as Milano scrambled aboard to

bring up the equipment. Within thirty seconds he got the word out on the change in rally points and started the unit check-in process. Fiske stepped in to help Anders bring the rest of the command car's management systems up.

While they worked, Anders could hear Gordon berating Price about the lack of care and respect he'd shown the vehicle. Price called the command car's blower chief "a fussy old woman" and got called "a reckless baboon" in return. Any bemusement Anders felt at the argument drained away as the status reports started coming in.

The 334 DistOpSdrn had lost people as well as all of their equipment. Caldwell's engineers had come through without a scratch, but Medical Detachment Powell, while still in good shape, hadn't been so lucky. The 102nd's reserve company was still sorting out their situation. Mainwaring's force had lost three assault capsules, including the command team's. No one was quite sure who was in charge.

Anders had Milano direct-copy all of the check-ins for the 102nd itself through his circuit. It was unfair of him—as task group commander, his responsibility was to the group as a whole—but having seen the loss of half a platoon on the ride in, he felt a strong need to hear of any more losses first-hand, so he did it anyway. To his relief, there were only minor casualties, just two troopers taken off active duty. Then the commo circuit crackled with an unexpected voice.

"Cable One to Com One, all present and accounted for. We're down and open for business. Anyone know where our blower came down?"

That was Mossberg. How? Anders cut into the channel. "Com One. Your capsule was flashed. You're supposed to be dead, Sergeant."

"News to me, boss. Good news, though. Since we're dead we don't have to play in this fratching fustercluck."

"Sorry, Sergeant. Nobody's excused yet."

"I live in hope, boss."

"You live, Sergeant. That's the important part."

"Roger, boss."

Obviously their capsule had been damaged badly enough to destroy its autoresponders. It was a miracle that they had all survived as Mossberg had reported. As happy as he was to hear it, Anders couldn't quite believe it. "You sure you don't need medical?"

"Affirm. Just cuts and bruises. Find us our ride and we're ready to lay down some paybac—"

Something loud and piercing overrode Mossberg's response.

"—nemy aircraft!" she was shouting when the channel cleared. "Inbound on your position, Com One!"

Mossberg's warning wasn't timely enough.

A flight of four *Hawks* ripped through the air above the staging area, their shrieking wails blanketing the commo channels. The sleek delta-shaped Remor craft were fast and agile. They'd been given their code name for their ability to swoop down and rake ground targets with deadly kinetic and explosive weapons. Devastation ran in their wake. Acker platoon's scout blower exploded. A boiling black cloud erupted from it and clawed at the sky.

That was all Anders saw before the world blanked around him. In the dark, a giant's hand smashed him against the coaming of the command car. Implacable fingers crushed down on him.

PACIFICA ORBIT
CMEFS *AUDITOR*

Benton Mainwaring admitted to himself that he really didn't know what he had been expecting when the Pacifica Theater Fleet started its invasion of the planet, but staring at the assorted command and control monitors and hearing all the battle reports, he was reasonably sure that what he was seeing and experiencing wasn't it.

Fleet intelligence had predicted minimal enemy opposition at the interface and in atmosphere. They'd been right about the first, but badly mistaken about the second. First there had been those flights of missiles that had come from Alsion knew where. Now there were reports coming in that the freshly landed troops were under attack by ground attack aircraft. Aircraft! The modern battlefield was rife with weapons systems that made their use effectively suicidal. How was this happening?

"Coppelstowe, where did these enemy forces come from? Why didn't you know they were there? How were you wrong about the dynamic flow?"

The Alsion initiate's expression was bland, unperturbed.

"The dynamic is perfect," she intoned, sounding aggrieved. "Humans are not. Our understanding of events is constrained by our information and our interpretation of the data. No matter how great the latter, it is a slave to the former. I have never presented my interpretation of the dynamic as flawless. Hence, to encounter an unexpected turn in the flow of events is not to experience a diminution of the power of alinear sociodynamics."

Benton waved a hand to take in the displays of the command center. "These reversals must have an explanation."

"I could assimilate the new data into my calculations. Perhaps a superior clarity will emerge."

"Yes. Do that," he said, rather more harshly than he intended.

She nodded acquiescence and returned her attention to her console.

Benton Mainwaring was no one's fool, although he did have to reluctantly admit that he was, like everyone else, sometimes made the butt of the universe's jokes. Alinear sociodynamics was supposed to put a man in a position where the universe couldn't manipulate him. It had done so for Ambrose Alsion, and it had made him the richest man in known space. Clearly the science worked. Coppelstowe was supposed to be putting it to work for Benton. And it ought to work for him, oughtn't it? Alsion had told him that he was a butterfly, a linchpin in the flow of events.

Clearly something wasn't right.

Were his actions or inaction somehow at fault? Or maybe

it was simply that he was in the wrong place. Must not a pivot point be at the crucial point to work effectively? Yes, that must be it. He ought to be at the heart of the action. Instead he was sitting here, safe in orbit, doing essentially nothing. Down below, in all levels of the atmosphere and on the planet's surface, men and women were dying. Something needed to be done.

But what?

16

PACIFICA
KILAWA ISLE

Voices came into Anders's darkness. Some were angry, some frightened. Many were excited, a few were calm. None made much sense. He was still dazed. It took him a while to figure out that the voices and other sounds weren't coming over his commo circuits.

The important thing was that they were real voices, and that meant he wasn't dead. It also meant that at least some of his command had survived the attack of the enemy aircraft.

He forced his eyes open to check his 'suit diagnostics. Among other things, his commo circuits were badly compromised. The damage assessment circuits were requesting replacement units. He was out of touch with command until they were repaired.

Slowly he realized that he wasn't doing any work to keep himself in the awkward position in which he lay. Something was jammed against his 'suit and holding him in place. When he tried to move, he found he couldn't. A check of his medical status screen showed him to be intact, so the fault lay outside.

The augmented strength provided by his hardsuit should have been enough to tear himself free, but he had no leverage. All his struggling did was make the unyielding metal groan and set up a serious throbbing in the back of his skull.

He tried again, working until his head was pounding. All he could manage was to work one arm free. He could find nothing to grip that made any difference to his entrapment. He'd have to wait till someone could pry him out.

He didn't have much of a view, just a section of the command car's interior, mostly his command station. Alone among the monitors, the unit status board remained intact. He almost wished it wasn't, for it showed bad news. The monitor lights for Sergeant Vadi and his entire platoon were red. They were all dead. There were other casualties as well.

His audio pickups made it clear that the attack was being renewed. It sounded as though a second flight of four *Hawks* had joined the first. His unit was under attack and he, the commander, couldn't communicate with it.

And there was nothing he could do about it.

Or was there?

With his free arm outstretched he could reach a small section of the command console. He was just able to reach the controls to select alternate feeds for the status monitor. As he worked, new red and amber lights lit up to record additional carnage. He blanked the screen. His first attempts at getting new input got nothing. Sensors were down. Circuits were broken. At last he acquired one of the visual sensors on the outside of the command car. The view was skewed since the car now apparently lay on its side, but a portion of the rally point clearing was visible.

Disruptive screeching announced the return of the *Hawks*. More explosions tracked their route. People scattered as the enemy aircraft swooped in. Desperate, they dove for whatever cover could be found. Some lay tumbled and broken. Others just vanished under the impact of enemy ordnance.

Anders caught sight of Fiske crouched on a scout car. It wasn't his, but that didn't matter. He had his hands on the controls of the heavy pulse gun and was swinging it toward the *Hawks*. Eye-searing cyan pulses lit the clearing as he poured fire at the swooping enemy.

Corporal Jem Chee had her support platform in action. The 200mm launcher aboard pumped ASDC shells into the path of the *Hawks*. Exploding like fireworks, each Air Space Denial Cluster shell exploded into dozens of mini-bombs that filled an even larger volume of the sky before detonating and creating a lethal kinetic kill zone. One *Hawk* wasn't nimble enough to avoid Chee's deadly curtains. It plowed through in a firecracker blaze and emerged looking more like a Swiss cheese than a fighting craft. Greasy smoke trailed from it. As usual, Remor disintegration worked to claim the dying bird. The *Hawk* crumpled in on itself like a burning wad of paper and spiraled toward the ground. Nothing but a rain of dissolving components pattered on the vegetation.

Sergeant Brizbin of Dog platoon moved into the pickup's range. He was hustling Lazuki, the gunner for the platoon's other support platform, toward his machine. Corporal Sakamoto, the blower commander, should have been getting that weapon system in gear, but he was nowhere to be seen. Brizbin was picking up the slack.

High in the sky the *Hawks* banked, turning for another pass.

Four smoky trails rose from near where Anders remembered 1st platoon gathering. Sergeant Hewitt's people had gotten off anti-air missiles.

The *Hawks* split formation. Their flight paths corkscrewed as they tried to avoid the incoming missiles. Most of them succeeded.

As the enemy aircraft reformed for their attack run, another volley from 1st platoon streaked up. Six more missiles rose from positions scattered around the task group's position. The *Hawks* scrambled to avoid the fire. But with nearly a dozen missiles boring in on them and clouds of the ASDC shells rolling into their paths, they didn't have enough room. A thunderstorm of destruction boomed through the sky. The lone surviving *Hawk* fled the field.

The task group's response had been late, but well done.

It was a quarter of an hour before Anders could tell anyone that. It took that long before Fiske and Milano showed up to pry him free.

"Took you gentlemen a while," Anders said when he was back on his feet.

"We got distracted," Fiske replied.

They dragged the unconscious Gordon from the blower's control seat, then with the help of three other hardsuit troopers got the vehicle righted. Milano starting checking systems while Fiske helped Anders replace the flashed units in his battlesuit's commo systems.

"Shouldn't have been caught like that," Fiske said gloomily.

Anders knew that. "If I had—"

"Not what I meant, sir. The first flight caught us fair and square, but I should've gotten missiles on that second flight before it made its first pass."

"But you did get missiles on them and we're still here. Our responses are not always what we want them to be, Aurie. Mistakes get made. If we don't get killed making them, we learn from them and carry on." Anders realized that the same applied to himself. "Time to move on. Let's leave the blame-placing to the goffs, shall we?"

"Like we could stop them." Fiske shrugged. "As you say, sir, we're still here, and we've still got a job to do."

"You got that right, soldier."

But before they could do the job, they needed to know what they had to do it with.

Beyond the loss of Barley platoon's infantry carrier and her crew, casualties among the 102nd proper turned out to be light. Anders shifted Barley's scout car and crew to Acker platoon to replace Robson's wrecked vehicle. Robson himself was one of their invalids, so Anders shifted his driver over to Sergeant Lerner's infantry squad to replace the company's other invalided trooper. Nobody else had taken enough damage to get any time off, not even the slightly concussed Gordon, who was nursing a pair of blackening eyes.

The situation was worse among Mainwaring's people, in part because their softsuits were not as damage-resistant as hardsuits. Between losses in the drop and the *Hawk* attack, they were down to fifty percent effective. Lieutenant Hassan and his entire command section were among the dead, lost when *Hawk* munitions had found their blower and sent it to oblivion. Sergeant Williams reported that they were reorganizing squads to suit their still-mobile vehicles.

"You're in charge," Anders told Williams.

"But—"

"You questioning orders, soldier?"

"No, sir!"

"Good. You'll do till you're dead or I find someone better. Now get those people organized and ready to move."

"Will do, sir!"

Anders felt reasonably confident that Williams could do the job. He'd said he wanted a chance to prove himself. Well, he was getting it. Anders had other things he needed to worry about.

The task group's attached elements had suffered as well. The 334th had soaked up a half dozen hits and Caldwell's engineers had lost three troopers and a supply vehicle. Even the medical detachment had taken casualties, though not many. One nurse was invalided by ASDC fallout and two orderlies from contact with dissolving Remor fragments. The doctors had come through safe, which was good news for everyone, though the news would have been better if the *Hawks* hadn't taken out the surgery blower and two of the ambulances.

It was taking longer than Anders wanted, but the task group was pulling itself together. He had launched a spread of "watchers" to help protect them against any more surprises. The little surveillance drones didn't have a great deal of range, nor were they equipped with an extensive suite of sensors, but they were the best available, since the 334th's equipment hadn't made it down.

He'd also put Cable platoon on dispersed perimeter guard in an arc between the rally point and the last reported concentration of Remor. He was hoping the enemy hadn't altered their position. He didn't know because his main link to the fleet had been damaged when his command blower had flipped. When Milano got it working again, or rather when the diagnostics *said* it was working, the channel was filled with static. He was unable to get the intelligence updates he desperately wanted.

Unfortunately, it wasn't long before Mossberg reported enemy action.

"We've got movement in sector, Com One."

Anders vectored a watcher in that direction as he checked the crippled feed to the command car's sensors. He still had no feed from the recon satellites. Archived maps and company status links let him see how Cable platoon was situated. As far as he could tell, Mossberg had her troops well deployed. He brought his watcher's data onto the main screen and sent another one swinging wide toward a defile the enemy might use to achieve a flanking position.

The watcher's eyes were trained down and forward, allowing it to follow terrain and avoid obstacles. Its other sensors ranged ahead, first confirming Mossberg's position, then starting to pick up enemy vehicles moving toward those positions.

Anders sent the watcher high and wide, trying to get a visual on the enemy. It looked as though there were a half dozen Remor machines in the lead element. When he finally got a visual lock, the computer identified all of the enemy vehicles as *Caymans*.

No one had any idea what the Remor called their machines. No one even knew how they categorized them. Mil-Force needed a handle for them, and so Intel grouped the various types into categories according to their overall configurations and apparent capabilities. Most of the land-bound Remor machines operated on legs, mechanical imitations of animal locomotion, rather than treads or ground-effect, or even wheels. Hence most categories were given animal names. Remor ground-bound fighting machines were given reptilian code names.

A *Cayman* was a medium-sized machine, the equivalent of a human tank. It strode the battlefield on two legs like some antediluvian predatory monster. Ancient Terran carnivorous dinosaurs might have matched a *Cayman*'s 4.5-meter height, but no carnosaur was ever so well armored, nor was one ever equipped with powerful energy weapons and missiles. That didn't keep some soldiers from likening fighting the monstrous machines to hunting dinosaurs or even dragons.

Anders had fought this type before, once with nothing more powerful than a hot-wired pulse rifle. Today, he was much better equipped for the hunt.

He opened the link to Dog platoon. "Sergeant Brizbin, prep your gun platforms, please. Dispersed Anti-Armor rounds for both guns. Three volleys, ten-second spacing. Coordinates to follow."

"Will do."

Anders checked on Mossberg. Both squads were still in position. They seemed to still be undetected by the enemy. Good. Anders ordered Acker platoon to an intermediate position, ready to support Mossberg or to cover her retreat.

"Com One, Dog is ready," Brizbin reported. "Initial flight time sixty-two seconds."

"Stand by, Dog."

Sergeant Hewitt signaled that Acker platoon was in position.

"Com One to all Cable. Cable One gets first tag, Cable Two does the second tag. Nose and tail. Prep KMK defense. You will tag on dispersal of Dog's DAA."

Mossberg and Lerner acknowledged.

Anders checked the topographic screen again. The *Caymans* were closing on Mossberg, moving past.

"Com One to Dog One, proceed with fire mission."

"Proceed, aye."

Away to the right, out of sight of the command car, Dog platoon's support platforms fired with a sound like a gigantic lion's hunting cough. Sixty seconds later, high over the *Caymans*, the incoming rounds of the first volley burst to release their Dispersed Anti-Armor submunitions. The individual warheads scattered as the targeting beams from the troops lit up the designated first and last *Caymans*.

They could have tagged the whole enemy formation, but the dispersal of the munitions would have been wider and the chance of a solid takedown lower. Any tagged survivor would have a far better chance of backtracking the targeting beams to the troops who used them. Also, the more beams on a target, the more of the submunitions from DAA shell would get good locks. The kills were surer that way.

The submunitions picked up their beckoning tags. They swarmed in. The targeted *Caymans* erupted in smoke and flame. The leader toppled over with half its torso gone. The hindmost simply ceased to exist.

As the leader's wreck began to dissolve, the surviving *Caymans* shifted into defensive mode. Weapons and sensors appeared from beneath their carapaces. Seeing them through his watcher's eyes, Anders thought that they didn't seem to have a good idea of where their ambushers were. Good.

One *Cayman* tried an anti-personnel missile launch anyway. It looked headed in the general direction of Mossberg's position.

"Hold KMK," Anders ordered, seeing that the enemy's shot was not very close on target. Defensive fire would be protective, especially if Anders had misjudged the missile's track, but it would give away their position.

"Tell the rubes," Mossberg responded.

Dog platoon's second volley was inbound. Anders looked for any reason to change the plan. He didn't see any.

The second pair of shells burst above the enemy position. Lerner's squad lit up two of the *Caymans*. The Dispersed Anti-Armor submunitions found their tags and dropped on the scrambling machines.

This time the enemy managed a bit of defensive fire, taking out some of the incoming rounds through sheer kinetic or explosive force. They didn't have enough of either to save themselves. A third *Cayman* crashed to the ground with a thoroughly cratered carapace. The greasy black smoke of Remor dissolution began to rise from it. The other target was mauled, but it didn't go down.

The wounded Remor reacted. Missiles arced from it. On pillars of flame they screamed toward Lerner's position.

This time the KMK was needed. Anders's orders were not. Lerner's squad fired.

Kinetic Missile Kill shells were designed to release a blizzard of totally dumb spheres into the path of an incoming missile. Combat missiles moved too fast to target individually at most ranges, so the theory was that blasting enough junk into their paths would kill the missile, either through sheer impact or through premature detonation. If that didn't happen, there was a good chance that a collision would knock the missile sufficiently off course that it would miss its target. The defense was a good bet when used by a hardsuit trooper and nearly as good for a vehicle; unprotected troops usually needed a wider miss to escape the effects of a warhead.

Most of the Remor missiles were picked up by the KMK. The remainder rocked the countryside as they exploded all over Lerner's position. The hardsuited troopers came through without a loss.

By then the third volley had come on target. Both of Cable platoon's squads lit up the three surviving *Caymans*.

Maybe the troopers didn't get a good targeting spread. Maybe the Remor defensive fire was particularly good. Whatever the reason, the DAA shells didn't do the job. The previously wounded *Cayman* died, but the others survived. They were badly damaged, to be sure, but they still fought. They launched missiles apparently at random as they strafed the brush with beam weapons.

Anders's watcher got caught in the fire and went down.

"All squads, take them down," he ordered. "Fire at will."

In less than a minute Mossberg reported, "Hostiles flashed."

The immediate threat was over, but those six *Caymans* were only a part of the Remor force he knew was out there. Somewhere.

Task Group Seaborg didn't have the reconnaissance assets it ought to. The enemy had demonstrated that they possessed fast-moving ground attack aircraft as well as the more usual ground forces. His force was under continuing threat of attack and they were practically blind. Unless . . .

Most of the surviving vehicles had most of their integral watchers. There were too many for the damaged command car to control, but working together they could provide perimeter security.

"All units, this is Com One. Launch all watchers and reroute their feed on repeat to this station. Private Milano will coordinate a perimeter orbit sequence."

Milano gave him a "you could have mentioned this to me first" look. Anders ignored him for the moment as he double-checked some calculations and scanned inventory. Yes, it could work.

"What exactly am I supposed to be doing here?" Milano asked.

"We need to get the watchers out a klick or so from the column. Individual vehicles will control their own watchers' motion according to directions from you. Get them spaced evenly around our perimeter. When the feeds start coming in, composite them in the command car's comp. That'll give us an overall view of our position."

"Your own sky-eyes are supposed to be doing that."

"I've got other things for them to do."

His command hardsuit could handle several watchers at once, though not with the facility that the command car's systems offered. He redirected his active watchers and sent the rest out as well, sending them in widening spirals around the task group's position. They were a poor substitute for the 334th's lost eyes, but they'd have to do. With luck he'd improve his knowledge of what lay ahead of them and, more importantly, where the enemy was.

Luck proved fickle. Anders did discover several enemy forces. The problem was that, in total, they looked to be more than strong enough to destroy Task Group Seaborg.

17

Fortunately, the destruction of the *Cayman* patrol seemed to cool immediate Remor interest in Task Group Seaborg. No probes followed the first. No further flights of *Hawks* came to harass them. Anders used the respite to get the task group on the move. They left the relatively clear area of the landing zone, taking a path through the more closed-in terrain of a forested belt.

As soon as the task group got under way, Anders had Milano reduce the number of watchers on perimeter circuit to a third. The recalled machines started recharging. Half, when ready, would replace those on patrol, swapping places to keep up the guard. The other half would be a reserve, to be put to work should any trouble be spotted. Milano began to draw up a rotation schedule for the human operators so they could get some rest too.

The plan didn't provide sufficient coverage to make Anders comfortable, but it was sustainable. With fleet communications still out, he needed to think about making the task group as self-contained and self-sustaining as possible.

To Anders's surprise a faint, garbled voice crackled through on the ground forces tactical channel.

"Say again," he requested, not sure that he'd really heard it.

For a moment Anders thought he'd been right to dismiss the sounds as a trick of the static, but then the voice came again, growing stronger.

"—ay again. Com One Tee-Gee Seaborg, this is Com One

Ay-Gee Armstrong. We are in your vacinity and we have assets with extra eggs."

"Rog," Anders acknowledged. "We won't say no, Armstrong, but I have to ask how we got so lucky."

"Main force is down and taking names. Colonel Cope saw what you guys caught on the way down and thought you might need this stuff more than he did."

"We'll take what you can give us, Armstrong."

Group Armstrong was aerospace assets assigned to force protection. He hadn't expected to have such heavy assets trickle down to his sideshow, but since the opportunity had arisen . . .

Armstrong's available ordnance popped up in a window on his screen as he checked his watchers. Finding the enemy wasn't the problem. Finding the best use of Armstrong's offered munitions was only a minor one. It didn't take Anders long to determine a fit.

"Still with us, Armstrong?"

"Rog, Seaborg."

"Good. I've got you a place to make omelets. Ready for feed?"

"Aye. Send feed."

"Will do." Anders forwarded the selected targets. "Feed on trans."

"Seaborg, we have your targeting data." A brief pause. "Ordnance on delivery."

Over the horizon, in the direction of the biggest enemy concentration, the sky lit up.

Anders allowed himself a grim smile. That ought to more than even the odds. He'd send a watcher in to check once the smoke died down. "Many thanks, Armstrong."

"Glad to be of service."

"Speaking of service, what's the word from the fleet?"

"No word," the flight leader reported without surprising Anders. "But I intend to find out. Now that we're not carrying extra ballast, we're going up to see. No rest for the worthy."

"Never. Well, good luck to you."

"I'd rather not need it." Armstong's voice was fading into the static. Anders barely heard his "Armstrong out."

Long-distance commo was totally fritzed. Short-distance stuff was doing better. Robson might have been able to do a work-around, but he was laid up in a medical van. Anders wished he could call on the electronics whiz's expertise to help them break through the junk. But wishes might as well be a damned sinner's prayers.

The task group moved on. What else were they to do?

Traveling through enemy territory was never fast, not when you did what you could to be sure you made it through alive. Two hours later, they were still moving through the forest when Sergeant Fiske's voice scratched through the static.

"Com One, this is Acker Two."

With satellites not available, Anders couldn't use the unit plot to see where his lead scouts were. But experience let him estimate how much distance they'd covered, and the map on his console showed him that they ought to have reached what mission planners had dubbed the "barrier rings," the enigmatic dark lines that orbital recon pictures had shown surrounding the city of Palisandra, and that Intel supposed were part of the city's defenses. He asked for grid reference to verify the scouts' position.

Fiske confirmed, then added, "Got a surprise for you, sir. Intel is a little confused. I think you'll want your own eye-balls on this."

"Will do, Acker Two."

Anders trusted the sergeant's judgment, and sent target coordinates to Gordon. He'd pick the best route, leaving Anders to fret over what he'd find.

Acker Two was currently Corporal Medrano's scout car, formerly of Barley platoon. Barley's troop carrier was gone, as was the scout blower from Acker. Anders had combined the two platoons, and before sending the scout car out on forward patrol, he'd added Sergeant Fiske as a supplement.

Acker Two had one drone on overwatch. Anders picked up the watcher's feed, but left it under their control. He wanted some idea of what his scouts had found, but he didn't want to compromise their security.

Though the imagery shifted constantly as the watcher moved about, Anders soon had a good idea of the local scene. Acker Two was at the edge of the forest belt hard by the outskirts of Palisandra. The archive map gave the name of the suburb they had reached as Halcione. It had been a sizable town once. Now young forest encroached against its outer fringes. Beyond the main built-up area, what had once been agricultural land was little more than pocked and cratered earth. The town was in no better shape than its farms. The shattered remnants of homes, shops, religious houses, businesses, and factories lay in mute evidence of the enemy's destructive capability. Heaps of broken and twisted vehicles of all descriptions lay in drifts against the hard bones of the buildings, making it look like some kind of bizarre, wrack-strewn reef between a leafy green ocean and a desert island beach.

In the distance, beyond the cratered strip, he could see what looked like a hedge. It was tall, but in the far distance beyond it, he could see the broken towers of what was likely the city center of Palisandra. The wall of plants curved away out of immediate sight in either direction. Anders didn't need to send the watcher up for a high view. This "hedge," sixty or so meters wide, encircled the city of Palisandra. There would be another dead zone, several hundred meters wide, immediately on the other side, whose far "shore" would gradually blend with the outskirts of Palisandra proper, their destination.

Somewhere over there were the humans they had come to save.

Fiske waved the command blower into a preselected spot about twenty meters from where Acker Two's blower was parked. Anders had a good view of the blasted strip.

"What's the problem?" he asked as Sergeant Fiske and Corporal Medrano walked up. "Mines?"

"Not that we can detect, Captain," Medrano replied.

"Scope out the hedge," Fiske suggested.

Dialing up the magnification on his visor, Anders did so. There was a variety of plants. Some had dark glossy leaves, others were shaggy and variegated. All had a strange oily glint to them. Most of them had spikes, lots of sharp and viscous spikes. Many were heavy with pustulent fruits or slimy seedpods. Only a few looked anything like what they had seen in the forest or on the plain where they'd landed.

"We didn't think it looked native," said Medrano.

"Most of it isn't," Anders agreed. "Remor imports."

"Gotta be," said Fiske.

"And there's things living in it," Medrano added.

"Remor critters?"

"Not clear," stated Fiske.

"Whatever they are, they're relatively small and fast. Remor rats, maybe, or whatever it is that they have that passes for rats."

Fiske shook his head in disagreement. "Too big for rats."

"Dangerous?" Anders asked.

Medrano rapped his carapace. "Not to 'suits. I won't vouch for how well those Pansie softies will shrug them off, though."

"So we may have a wildlife issue. Other than that, is it passable?"

"It'll take a direct recon to be sure," Fiske said.

Medrano was more positive. "Don't see why not. It'll take a little chopping. A lot of chopping if you want to take vehicles through."

They would need the vehicles through sooner or later. "Let's start small."

"Will do, sir." Fiske started forward.

Medrano managed to get in his way, bringing him to a halt. "When did you get your last scout rating, Sarge?"

"Now, don't tell me," Fiske said warily. "You're not only more current but you got a higher efficiency too."

While Anders checked the records, Medrano said, "Not a brag, Sarge. Just a fact."

"Medrano's right, Aurie. We ought to go with expertise here." He didn't add that if there was a problem, the sergeant would be the one to take the fall, and Anders wasn't about to risk his valuable expertise when there was someone else who could do the job.

"Two sets of eyes would be better," Fiske protested.

"There'll be more than two, Sarge," Private Holden chimed in the circuit. Sitting atop her scout car, she was pointing at a watcher drone newly released from its carrying cradle and hovering above the vehicle. "Overhead Angel will be there. She's my special baby, really good sensors, and she's got more eyes than a double-stalked Mimak."

"Holden can outhunt your average Eridani with that toy," Medrano said by way of support for his blower chief. "So if we don't have to go through any more *metoo*, I'll get started. That a will-do, Captain?"

Anders understood that Medrano's "any more *metoo*" was directed at him. They were all Eridani, and Eridani wanted to be where the action was, whether their rank and responsibilities were appropriate for it or not. He chuckled. "Aye, soldier. Sergeant Fiske and I await your report. It's a little late, isn't it?"

It was Medrano's turn to chuckle as he saluted. "Just making sure it's done right, sir."

Medrano shifted his hardsuit camo to match the blasted rock of the open zone before he reached the edge of the trees. Fiske, camouflaged for the forest edge, took up a position to cover the advancing scout. Holden was ready by the heavy pulse gun of the scout car, but her attention was on the drone she was guiding on a parallel course to Medrano's zigzagging passage.

Nothing disturbed the quiet save an occasional distant screech from somewhere within the hedge.

Upon reaching the edge of the wall of unnatural vegetation, Medrano readjusted his camo. With visor magnification dialed down, Anders lost him against the murky gaps in the plants until Overhead Angel swooped down to join him.

Man and machine disappeared into the shadows of the vegetation. The drone occasionally popped up above the canopy for fast scans but otherwise stayed down among the higher reaches of the plants, effortlessly sliding past branches and other obstacles.

It was down close to Medrano when he triggered something. The drone's video feed showed a spiky vine whipping out across the path Medrano was walking. Spikes big and small snapped against his armor, and a cloud of small spikes whipped away, peppering the undergrowth. The force of the strike staggered him.

"Medrano!" Holden shouted.

"Izokay, Mike. Just winded," he replied. "Wouldn't have wanted to take that outside of my shell."

Even over the drone link Anders could see how likely such a trap would be to incapacitate or kill an unarmored person. Humans built deadfall traps with similar effects, but this thing was alive. He watched as the main trunk slowly twitched its way back toward where it had come from. His last doubts that this barrier had been put into place by the Remor were gone.

Ten minutes later, Overhead Angel, dipping back down from a pop-up, hit something. It wasn't Holden's fault, for the obstacle had jumped into the drone's path of its own volition. The collision knocked the creature free from the branches. It scrabbled as it plummeted in a vain effort to arrest its fall. Medrano flashed the critter with a low-power pulse and it hit the ground still and crispy.

The dead animal bore a vague resemblance to a Terran badger. It was little more than a meter long, including its naked blue tail. The body and all six limbs were armored in a hide of iridescent scales that blended well with the oily sheen of the vegetation.

"One of your rats?" Anders asked.

"Whatever it is, it's a dead one now," Medrano replied.

Within seconds a dozen more of the species—live ones—came leaping through the branches. Medrano flashed three or four. Overhead Angel rammed another, snapping its spine. The rest descended on Medrano like a swarm of gladiator ants after an intruder.

With the creatures clinging to him in a whirlwind of teeth and claws, Medrano couldn't bring his weapon to bear. He didn't need to. One by one he snatched the animals, crushing them in his armored fists before tossing them away. As he had predicted, his hardsuit was impervious to their attacks. He crushed the last one underfoot.

"Disagreeable critters," he commented.

"Bet the locals don't play with them," Fiske commented.

"Bet you're right, Sarge."

"Bet they're too dumb to stop trying to gnaw on a hard-shell too."

"Still not betting against you, Sarge."

Despite their foreboding, no more of the animals came near Medrano as he continued across the hedge. As he reported the vegetation thinning, Holden cut in.

"Hold up, Medrano. Angel's just picked up some movement out there. I've got a dozen marks moving on the far side of the dead zone. Ninety-percent prob they're humans. No weapon sigs, but I think they're carrying something."

"Welcoming signs?" Fiske wondered.

"Who knows?" Medrano answered.

"You will be the first, Corporal. Push on and find out," Anders ordered.

"Will do, Captain."

"Holden, see if you can get us some more data on those marks."

"Will do, sir."

Holden's drone lifted above the canopy and started out across the barren strip. Still in the hedge, Medrano moved forward. By Anders's calculations, Medrano was nearing the far edge when his screams filled the unit commo. For a horrifying ten seconds, the scout corporal's tortured cries echoed in their ears, then Medrano's circuit went dead.

Without orders, Holden reversed course on Overhead Angel. A glint in the sun caught her attention and she angled the drone in toward that spot, zooming the magnification as she did.

Medrano's Mk. 22 IEW filled the screen. The pulse rifle lay abandoned amid a patch of spiky thorns. Anders thought he saw something else deeper in the shadowy hedge.

Holden cursed.

"Keep it off the commo," Anders ordered. He launched one of his own drones and sent it homing on the signal from Overhead Angel. He did not have Holden move her drone in closer. "Holden, when my watcher reaches station, I want you to get your bird into Palisandra. Get me full data on the area opposite us."

"Aye, sir." Her voice was shaky.

It took almost two minutes to get Anders's watcher to the other drone. During that time he talked to Holden, detailing what he wanted to know. It wasn't anything special. It was the sort of reconnaissance that Holden did all the time. By belaboring the routine, Anders was helping her focus and keep her mind off the fate of her partner. Holden was responding almost normally when, through DistOp eyes, he watched Overhead Angel rise into the sunlight and set off.

Almost immediately, Holden reported that her scanners showed that the humans were scattering back into the depths of the city.

"Pursue, sir?"

"Neg. Let them go. Concentrate on topo. But if you see anything nonhuman out there, anything that looks like it came from this vege-hell, anything that you don't like the color of, you dump the data to me. I'm going to be making a list."

"Will do, sir."

He turned his attention to the grisly scene. The dark shape he had noticed still lay where he'd first seen it. He maneuvered the watcher to put a beam of light on it. A battlesuit glove. Rising from where the arm should have been, a tendril of greasy smoke rose lazily.

Beyond the glove was nothing but a man-shaped pile of goo soaking into the loam.

Anders dropped a transponder to mark Medrano's remains. Damping down his reaction, he guided the watcher through a thorough recording of the site.

The hedge was a living death trap, a killing zone where even a hardsuit trooper wasn't immune to its hazards. It was a wall, apparently for keeping the surviving humans penned inside Palisandra. No doubt it did its job well.

He recalled his watcher.

"You ready for a little hedge-clipping, Aurie?"

"More than, sir."

18

"Designate Bartie!"

Damn frickin' xenos.

Months of working with the frickin' xeno-mantises and Bartie still couldn't tell one from another, but he knew a summons when they issued one. He gulped down the last of the fiery swill that Hernandez called his "fine southern-style mash" and tossed his mug onto the table. If he had left any, it sure as heck wouldn't be there when he got back.

The numbness that came from sufficient application of Hernandez's swill didn't take away the stench of xeno-mantis, but it did make a guy care less that he was rolling in it. Bartie's fast application hadn't kicked in by the time he entered the Bug Palace, the place where the master bugs held audience for their minion humans.

The Bug Palace, like all the recent structures in the Lair, was some kind of excreted hut that the frickin' xenos had built. On the outside it didn't look like much more than something a Kilawan mud nester might build. The inside was stocked with high-tech stuff, not that you could tell much about it, since the only light inside came from various screens and lights on those devices. Bartie left the door open when he entered because it made for more light and kept him from tripping over the cables that snaked across the floor or, worse, over the vermin that seemed to infest the place. The damn bugs never complained about his busting up their darkness, but he hoped that it annoyed them at least a little.

As usual, the frickin' xeno didn't waste any time on pleasantries.

"Macerias," it rasped out.

That was what the damn bugs called the vegetation barrier they'd built surrounding the city. Everybody Bartie knew called it the Wall.

The screen behind the boss bug lit up with a map of a nearby part of Palisandra. It was human cartography, likely filched from some human database somewhere, but it was covered in squirmy characters that only meant something to the frickin' xenos. A highlight drew Bartie's attention to a portion of the Wall nearest the old Sturkhe Brewery.

Damn shame the damn bugs had dusted the place.

Insensitive to Bartie's mourning, the frickin' xeno continued its clipped briefing.

"Contrary entity intrudes."

He figured he knew what the frickin' xeno wanted, but he was gonna make the damn bug spell it out, at least as much as the bugs ever made things clear. Clear orders were easier to find ways around than assumed orders.

"How nice," he said. "It's not like I'm some kinda forest ranger border guard. Whatcha want me to do about it?"

The damn bug ignored his sarcasm. "Be unseen. Observe. Deny entrance. Report. No interchange with contrary entity."

Damn, that was detailed for a frickin' xeno order. Maybe they were catching on to him. "You gonna tell me exactly what I need to observe and deny entrance to?"

"Contrary entity."

Big help.

"Vehicle waits. Go now," it ordered.

Bartie left the Bug Palace quickly, less out of eagerness to be about the damn bug's business than to get back out in the fresh air.

"All right, you slugs," he called as he entered his own lair. "Get your guns. We got some work."

He had to kick Goss's feet off the furniture, reclaim his mug from Hernandez, and roll Sheriden out of his bunk to get his slugs moving. Sometimes they showed less initiative than first-generation xombies.

"What's up, Bartie?" Sheriden groaned from the floor.

"Somebody's trying the Wall from the other side. The bug wants us to go take a look-see."

"Waste a time," Aziz announced. The burly Muslim was the laziest bastard Bartie had ever known, but he was a hellion in a dust-up. "Nobody makes it through the Wall but bugs."

"Right," Bartie agreed. "And all of us here know it. 'Cept the damn bugs. The frickin' boss bug ain't got no faith in its own death traps, so we get to be the bouncers. Got it?"

"We ain't got to go up against bugs, do we?" asked Hernandez. The former Pacifica Defense Force trooper had bad memories of when the frickin' xenos had blitzed his unit and wiped the floor with them.

"This ain't a damn bug," Bartie assured him.

"Going through the Wall?" Sheriden snorted. "Gotta be a bug."

"I said it ain't a bug."

"Well, if it ain't a bug, what is it, then?" whined Goss. Goss always whined.

"Goss, you get to be any more of a pain and I'll send you on a stroll through the Wall to find out. Don't want to go by yourself? Fine. Grab your piece and fall in.

"Listen, you slugs, the damn bugs call our uninvited guest a 'contrary entity.' I don't know what that means,'cept that it ain't one of theirs, and our boss bug don't want any 'contrary entities' crashing its party here. We good little minions get to go pop us a trespasser. Ain't something you slugs ain't good at."

"I still say it's a waste of time," Aziz drawled. "The Wall will eat anybody trying to get through it."

Bartie thought so too, but the big damn bug wanted action. The big damn bug was gonna get it. "Yeah. Okay. You stay,

Aziz, we'll go waste our time. When the boss bug comes out to see why you're still here, you tell him that you got better things to do than run his damn errands."

Aziz, like Bartie and the rest of the guys, had a *gawkhore* nestling around his throat. He fingered it with a thoughtful look on his face. Could he give the damn big bug a story that wouldn't set the thing off and strangle him? Bartie doubted it.

"You coming along or not?"

"Yeah." Aziz slouched to the arms rack and grabbed his assault rifle. "Yeah. But I don't have to like it."

He detailed his dislike as they boarded the truck that the frickin' xenos allowed them to use. The surly driver wasn't one of Bartie's slugs; he belonged to a different press gang. But he wasn't too bad a guy because right away he told Aziz to shut up. That started an argument over whose was bigger. Bartie let it go, since the driver seemed capable of driving and haranguing Aziz at the same time. He got into his own shouting match with the driver when the slug pulled up a good kilometer short of the Sturkhe Brewery. The truck jockey pulled out the usual "bug's orders," which Bartie couldn't contradict.

They started humping.

The day was hotter than usual for the time of year, something that seemed more and more common. Bartie didn't like it. He didn't like having to move around in the heat. He didn't like sweating. He didn't like being out doing the frickin' xenos' dirty work while the frickin' xenos sat back in their shady holes. But he shoveled all those dislikes under his biggest one. Most of all, Bartie didn't like not being alive. To stay alive, Bartie needed to play along with the damn bugs. At least till a better opportunity presented itself. Bartie might not be some kind of university genius, but he wasn't stupid. He could act stupid when it paid, but the way he figured things, it was never worthwhile actually being stupid.

By way of not being stupid, he sent Hernandez and Goss

on ahead. The one because he was their best scout and would find a decent place to watch the Wall. The other just to get his annoying whining out of earshot.

It worked.

When Bartie and the gang caught up, Hernandez had himself a nice sheltered spot where he was scoping out the Wall with a set of oculars. Goss, rifle cradled in his arms like a teddy bear, was sacked out.

"The guy who wakes Goss up early gets to be his partner for a month," Bartie told the gang. "Spread out and find yourself a place to set up."

His guys were real quiet as they moved to do what he told them. Bartie went over to Hernandez to find out what he'd seen. Turned out it was nothing so far. Nothing for sure, anyway.

"I thought I saw something pop up over the Wall, but it dropped back in before I could focus on it."

Could have just been one of the things that lived in the Wall. "Some kinda hopping bug?"

"I think it was a machine."

Bartie mulled that over. A machine? Given that they used living things the way people used machines, maybe the bugs couldn't tell the difference between a machine and a being. Maybe Bartie had been sent to take down an automated probe?

Or was it something else?

"Keep looking."

They did. With only one set of oculars, it wasn't all that easy, but once whatever it was reached the dead zone that lay between the Wall and the verge of the city proper, whatever it was would be easy to spot.

Watching the Wall was dull. Neither Bartie nor Hernandez caught sight of the scout's maybe machine. Nobody else reported anything either. The afternoon heat was like a drug. Pretty soon, Goss wasn't the only one sacked out. Bartie himself was drifting when Hernandez suddenly swore loudly, ending everyone's naps.

"That's a guy in a battlesuit," he announced.

"Gimme that!" Bartie snatched at the oculars. It took him a couple of seconds to fumble the focus into clarity and a couple more to locate the figure nearing the edge of the Wall. The camouflage it was wearing made it hard to pick out. If it hadn't been moving Bartie figured he'd never have seen it.

Whatever was moving out there was humanoid, all right, but big and blocky. A squarish helmet sat on its shoulders. Light and color played across the armored surface, making it really hard to see. Hot and cold spots randomly flickered on its surface too, and broke up the infrared image in the oculars. Bartie was sure the figure was carrying a weapon, but other details were just too hard to confirm. Hernandez was ex-military, so he was probably right about it being a battlesuit. The good news there was that they were looking at a human and not some new kind of frickin' xeno.

"It's just one guy." At least Bartie thought it was just one. The boss bug hadn't said 'contrary entities.' "You think he's some kinda vid hero or something?"

The fear in Hernandez's eyes wasn't reserved for Bartie today.

"He's wearing a fricking battlesuit, Bartie! He doesn't have to be a hero to make paste outta all of us!" Hernandez's gaze flicked out across the dead zone. "Crap!"

He lit out.

Bartie turned to see what had pushed the man to rabbit. Something small had cleared the Wall's vegetation. It wasn't big. A glint like metal sparked off it as it flew pretty much directly toward them.

Aziz and Goss followed Hernandez's example. The rest of his slugs exchanged glances and did the same.

Bartie laid the oculars on the thing flying toward them and got a better look. It was moving too slow to be a missile, but it had stuff poking out that could be weapons. He knew armies had war machines that could be run at a distance and had heard that some could be pretty small. The battlesuit had been bad enough. He didn't like the idea of tangling with the combination. Not with just an assault rifle.

He lit out after his gang.

This "contrary entity" was something that the frickin' xenos would just have to handle for themselves.

19

Stone didn't need to turn around to know what was happening at the hatch. It had opened to admit a crew member on legitimate business and given Benton Mainwaring his chance. The colonel, who had been cooling his heels for far too long by his lights, had jumped at the chance to infiltrate the command center. The smack of flesh against hardsuit said that Mainwaring had run into the sentries as they did their job and got in the Combiner's way.

"Commander Stone!" Mainwaring shouted. Stone could hear him swatting at the hardsuited guards. "Get out of my way, you oafs. Have you any idea who—I say, take your hand off me. I will have—"

Stone closed his eyes and settled back into his seat, sighing, "At ease, soldiers. Colonel Mainwaring may pass."

"Quite right," the Combiner officer huffed. He made his way to Stone's command chair. "Commander Stone, I have been waiting in that corridor—"

"Exactly." Stone spun his seat to face Mainwaring. Though Stone remained seated, the slight elevation of the command chair put him eye to eye with the tall Combiner. "By all that is right, you should have been in the brig. By what authority did you leave your command?"

"You were not answering any of my communiqués, Commander. I thought that if I came in person to—"

"Thought. I doubt you really thought, Colonel. We are still

in a combat zone, and a dangerous one. You did notice that our communications with the surface are currently nonexistent and even in orbit we only have intermittent commo, didn't you?"

"Quite so. Which is why I shuttled over here."

"Was your ship receiving status updates?"

Mainwaring looked perplexed. "Yes."

"So what made you think that I could not respond?"

"You didn't, so I assumed that—"

"Bad assumption, Colonel. Your operational concerns were addressed along the chain of operational communications. They continue to be coordinated with your ship commander, Major Lugard. I appreciate your concerns regarding the strategic situation, but each and every one of them was addressed in our planning sessions. Circumstances remain fluid. As long as they do, there is no point in reopening such discussions. Thus, you got no responses."

"But—"

"I have more to do than hold your hand, Colonel. That we are having this conversation is but the latest in a series of allowances—generous allowances—that I have made for the fact that you are operating in an environment quite obviously different from what you are used to. Colonel Mainwaring, my patience is running thin. This is an hour in which I expect, and must have, professionalism and competence from my officers."

In point of fact, the current diatribe was evidence that Stone's patience had run out rather than thin. Had it not, he wouldn't be breaking his personal rules. The dressing down he was giving Mainwaring was not the sort of thing he did in public, even when the public was only Stone's own close-knit command center team. But the assault had begun. . . .

"You have fears," he continued in a more conciliatory tone, "justifiable fears that the Remor may be motivated by our assault to finally begin their massacre of the civilians below. The final assault plan took those fears into careful account."

"But the situation is not what we expected, Commander."

"And it never is, once you contact the enemy. We cannot afford to flail about without direction."

Mainwaring furrowed his brow. "But we must adapt. You said so yourself."

"I did say so. We do adapt. Did you not get Colonel Cope's update on the disposition changes to ground forces before insertion?"

"The formation of Task Group Seaborg? Yes, of course, but we've lost communication—"

"Exactly. And until we regain communication, until we get some idea of how what we did plan is working, it would be insane to change things. An army is not a *tetsuhara* master who can strike on target despite being blindfolded."

Mainwaring looked ready to launch into more objections when a series of staccato announcements from the consoles cut into their conversation.

"Commander, we've got ships breaking interface."

"We've got transponder signal. They're ours, sir!' "

"It's Aerosupport Group Armstrong, sir."

Stone didn't need any more. He picked the group's channel and snapped, "Armstrong, report."

"Commander Stone?" Armstrong sounded surprised.

"We're cutting out the middlemen on this one, Captain. Dump us all the data you have while you give me your assessment of things planetside."

"Aye, sir. Will do, sir."

Armstrong didn't have the whole picture, but Stone didn't expect him to. He did, however, have an encouraging report. There had been some surprises, which in itself was no surprise, but on the whole the parts of the operation that Armstrong had seen seemed to be going well enough. The flight leader also had his commo records, and with them dumped to the central computers additional details emerged.

Perhaps more important, a copy of those records passed on to the electronic warfare department gave those baffled eggheads more insight into the bizarre interference that the fleet was experiencing. They began to locate something they dubbed null nodes in the orbital debris fields. Investigation was in order.

"The *Stanley* used to be an explorer ship, Commander. She still has all her survey equipment aboard. I think she would be admirably suited for this hunt."

Stone had not forgotten that Mainwaring was still present, but he had put the Combiner colonel from his immediate awareness. The suggestion, therefore, came as a slight surprise, the more so because it was a good one. Stone gave the orders, making sure there was some MilForce muscle to support the Combiner ship.

Mainwaring seemed pleased to be of help. "And when these nodes are neutralized, communications will normalize?"

"We can hope so."

"Then we can turn our attention to protecting the civilian population on the planet."

Stone had to admire the man's persistence. And he did. Only a little bit more than he despised the man's presumption.

"Colonel Mainwaring, we both have jobs to do. Mine is here. Yours is not. Are we communicating?"

"For the moment, Commander."

Insufferable. "Dismissed."

Mainwaring snapped a salute that would have done an officers' academy plebe proud and departed. Stone returned his full attention to the real problem: the Remor.

20

The sun was moving down, kissing the trees of the forest under which Anders's troops were sheltering as Gordon again brought the command car to a halt near the impromptu command post set up by Captain Caldwell's engineers. For the third time, Anders hopped down and strode through the settling dust to confront the chief engineer. Caldwell made a sloppy salute as Anders started in on him.

"You seem to be making decisions for me, mister. I have the entire task group waiting on your people."

"Can't be helped," said Caldwell.

"That's not the answer I want to hear."

"Sorry, sir, but it's the answer I've got. Look. You set the parameters, Commander Seaborg. I'm just working on follow-through here."

"Follow-through? I expected the troops to be following you through that barrier by now, Captain."

Caldwell shrugged and continued on as if Anders hadn't interrupted him. "You've got three factors all trading off against each other when you're breaching an enemy barrier. You've got width, speed, and safety. Multiple avenues, you said. Safe passage, you said. That only leaves speed to give way. I've got to take time if I'm going to give you safe, multiple avenues."

Anders's frustration boiled over. "You have run out of time, mister. You *will* make a lane. You will make *multiple* lanes. And you will make them *safe*. Now!"

"It's just not—"

"This is not a debate, Captain. Either you execute your orders—now—or I will find someone with some competence in combat engineering to do so."

Caldwell's eyes narrowed and bored into Anders's. The older man clearly resented the tone Anders was taking. Too bad. Anders was commander here.

The troops needed to be moving, and this little standoff wasn't helping anything. Anders broke off the staring contest. He caught a glimpse of satisfaction flare in Caldwell's eyes as his own swept across the gathered engineers. He found what he was looking for: a lieutenant, presumably Caldwell's second in command. The nameplate read *Howell*.

"Lieutenant Howell, how long until you will have my lanes cleared?"

Her eyes snapped over Anders's shoulder, seeking her superior. With a barked "Lieutenant" Anders reminded her who was addressing her. Caught in the sudden crossfire, the lieutenant gobbled unintelligibly.

From behind Anders, Caldwell's small voice said, "Fifteen Standard."

Anders didn't turn. "What?"

"I said fifteen Standard minutes. It'll take that long to charge the glazers. Even orders can't change the laws of physics."

"Get it done. The blowers roll in fifteen minutes and thirty seconds. I expect Caldwell's engineers will be out of the way by then."

"Will do, sir," Caldwell responded.

Eight minutes after the contretemps, ribbons of demolix were arcing over the vegetation wall. They detonated twenty-two seconds later, scything trees and pseudotrees alike as they cut swaths through the hostile growth. Here and there fire took hold, adding to the smoldering clouds rising from the explosions.

At the twelve-minute mark, more streamers followed the paths of the first. These dispersed aerosol incendiary, heavier than the air and smoke so that it would drift down until ignited by an electrical charge coursing through the carrier line. Cleansing flame erupted to incinerate any plant or animal along the intended pathways. Boiling clouds of sooty darkness swelled into the sky and tumbled out onto the seared plain to either side of the ravaged barrier.

Forty-nine seconds later the CEVs of Caldwell's engineer company were rolling forward. They disappeared into the roiling clouds. Hellish light lit the lowering darkness from within as the glazers ignited. The energy bombardment vaporized organic matter, and fused mineral matter into a glassy substrate, a crude but effective highway through the barrier.

At seventeen minutes and twenty-two seconds, Caldwell announced that they had exited the far side. Late, but sufficient. While Caldwell complained that his CEVs had been overtaxed and would be useless to support the advance, Anders ordered his troops forward.

Whatever had gotten Medrano would not be a problem, at least not within the lanes. Likely there were other problems and threats out there. They'd deal with them when they had to.

The 102nd rolled through the barrier and across the open space without a hitch. They moved into the outskirts of Palisandra. They had reached their objective.

"So where are the civvies?" Fiske asked over the command circuit.

"You were expecting cheering civilians to greet us?"

"Would have been nice."

"You mean it would have made our lives easier. You know better than to expect easy, Aurie."

"Sorry, sir. Don't know where that optimism came from."

"Now's not the time to look into it. It's not just our wayward sheep out there. There are hostiles too. Keep your eyes peeled."

"Will do."

Anders followed his own advice, with his natural eyes, with the command car's sensors, and with every drone-carried viewer he could muster. Despite his bantering comment to Fiske, he was bothered that they had not been met by "cheering crowds." This was a liberation. So where were those they were supposed to be liberating?

In hiding, apparently. From time to time, he noted shadows drifting among the buildings and flitting through the overgrown parks. Occasionally one would stray into the sunlight long enough for Anders to see with his Mark 1 eyeballs what he knew they were: people. Ragged scarecrows of people.

Very wary people.

His rearguard drones picked up some fleeing down the glassy lanes they had opened into wilderness. He sent a patrol to contact them, but the people fled into the surviving vegetation barrier rather than speak to his troops. Anders had little doubt that the Remor-spawned terrors were still out there beyond the ravaged edges of the lanes, and those people were likely going to their deaths. Though it hurt, he refused to grant the patrol leader's request to follow them; the depths of the Remor barrier were too dangerous.

Clearly the people of Palisandra didn't see Anders's people as rescuers. Something had to be done about that, but there was no vid system left to tap into to broadband their message of salvation at hand. Setting one up would take too much time and he doubted that there were any operable receivers out there anyway. They'd have to do it the old-fashioned way. Trying to sound as friendly and reassuring as he could, he recorded a message announcing who they were and why they had come. Dispatching it to his vehicles and suits, he gave orders for it to be played on all external speakers.

It still took several hours before he got a report from Mossberg of a gathering of locals who did not immediately disperse as the troopers approached. He told Mossberg to hold back and wait for him, not believing the gruff Lancastrian to be his best politician.

Naturally Fiske managed to reach the area first and scope it out. He reported, "We've got a sniper."

"Show me."

A highlight appeared in Anders's heads-up display. He looked through the glowing mark to the target, zooming to get a closer look at the potential threat. "It's a kid."

"With a big gun. I make it a Landzinger target rifle. Twelve-millimeter. Not much of a threat to a 'suit's armor."

"Think he knows that?"

"Maybe. Might be a problem if he targeted a joint. Want to bet the kid can make such a mark?"

"If I were a betting man, I'd bet he could, But I'd also bet he wouldn't. Not with you on him, Aurie."

Anders hoped it wouldn't be necessary, but he knew Aurie could take out the young marksman before the lad got off more than one shot, probably even sooner.

Gordon halted the blower and Anders dismounted, his 'suit set to parade colors. Signaling an end to the local loud-speaker announcements, he strode forward alone.

Watching from what she hoped was a good hiding place, Sue wanted it not to be a trick. A lot of people had gathered here, more than she'd seen in one place for well over a year. Most were her own people, but there were solos and people from other groups as well. The strangers' promise of hope had put aside caution and distrust.

Some of the gathered Palisandrans were discussing the possibility that these strangers might really be offering liber-ation, but there was a lot of fear that this was just another trick. Her heart shivered at the hope she heard in their voices when they spoke of liberation. Did they dare nurture that hope?

The newcomers were near. She could hear their vehicles. Big throbbing engines of the sort she hadn't heard for years.

Soon she'd see them for herself.

She heard the vehicles easily, but it was people on foot, moving ahead of the vehicles, that she saw first. Armored men. At least she assumed they were men. There might be women among them, but the suits hid gender as easily as the visored helmets hid the faces of these strangers.

They were armed, as she had been told, with modern weapons. The aliens ruthlessly destroyed such things, along with anyone daring to wield them. So how were these strangers able to walk freely about with such weapons?

Was it a trick? They didn't look like the collectors, but that didn't mean a lot. The aliens could give their pets anything, including battle armor and modern vehicles.

Could the xenos be gone? Could they have been defeated by these newcomers?

No one had seen any sign of the food bugs in days. Nor their xeno masters either. Even collector and xombie patrols had just about stopped. All since the fire in the sky.

For no reason that she could see, the advancing strangers stopped. Their vehicles throttled down, returning the dead city to something like its usual silence. But only something. The recorded voice went on, announcing who these strangers were and claiming liberation, over and over.

If these people from the Interstellar Defense League were friendly, why did they wear battle armor and hold their guns ready?

Professor Murch and Doc Shelly tried to ask questions, but Sue shushed them to silence. This wasn't the time for talk. Too much was unknown. "We watch for now," she hissed at them.

Time passed.

Another of the hovercraft arrived and pulled up near the leading vehicle. One of the armored strangers got down off this hovercraft and stepped forward. He didn't carry a weapon that she could see, but Jesse had warned her that battle armor often had built-in weapons. A sign of peaceful intent or a deception?

Unlike the others, his battle armor was colored the black of deep space. He was a giant, and cut a menacing figure like some deadly black knight in an adventure story. Sue knew the armor was enhancing his stature, and she hoped that his menacing appearance was also something of a sham. Was it foolish to hope that?

He looked directly toward their hiding place and a voice, a natural voice, spoke.

"Is there someone in charge here?"

Sue recognized the voice as the one in the recorded announcement. If this man wasn't their leader, he was at least their spokesman.

Sue looked to Doc Shelly. To Jesse. They were both staring at her. All of her people were staring at her. Some of the solos and outsiders too.

The stranger seemed to notice, as if he could see them where they hid. Maybe he could.

With a snap his visor retracted, revealing his face. It was a gesture of trust that she doubted a collector, once gifted with the protection of battle armor, would ever make. His pale blue eyes settled on her.

"My name is Anders Seaborg, ma'am. My troops and I are part of an expeditionary force from the Interstellar Defense League. We've come to help."

Sue had never heard of the Interstellar Defense League that the broadcast announcements had been going on about. She had no idea if they could help at all. No one did. But everyone in Palisandra was running out of food and, therefore, options. She looked into the eyes of this Anders Seaborg and couldn't see any deception.

It was time to take some chances.

Signing the others to stay put, she got up and emerged from hiding.

"My name is Sue. I'm not in charge, but some of the people around here listen to me. We've got questions."

"Ask what you like."

"Have you beaten the aliens?"

"I wish I could say we had, ma'am. We're fighting them for sure. And winning, I think. At least here on Pacifica we are."

Not the sort of completely soothing answer a collector might give. She felt hope pounding on the shell she had built around her heart.

She asked more questions. He answered. He didn't make

wild assertions and he tempered all his hope-inducing claims. She began to believe in his honesty.

She also began to believe that there might be a chance that she could get her people out of this hell that had been their home.

21

Stone sat in his cabin, lights low. He was supposed to be sleeping, something he was never very good at while operations were ongoing. It was always worse when the situation remained unresolved, as it did in the Pacifica system. His console glowed. Studying situation reports gave his racing mind something practical to do.

All in all, things were not going too badly. In three days, they had taken the space immediately surrounding the planet, but enemy space forces remained and their local superiority remained just that, local. With significant elements of the Remor fleet at large in the system, the enemy was still a threat. He couldn't afford to split the fleet to chase each of those enemy forces as long as the ground attacks were still meeting significant opposition, and they were. The on-planet operation was behind schedule due to an unexpectedly high level of enemy resistance and the continuing communications problems. And though the latter were slowly being dealt with, he continued to worry that some new wrinkle might shift the situation down below from disappointing to dangerous. Until things stabilized on the planet, he was constrained in dealing with the enemy space forces. And until that was done, the system would remain unsecured.

The best news so far was that they had not detected the awful commo screech that the Remor used to summon reinforcements.

The door chime interrupted his cogitation. He admitted Chip Hollister, who should have been getting some sack time of his own. Normally only an emergency warranted an intrusion on the commander's downtime, but there had been no call from the bridge and Chip's face showed no sign of distress.

"I can see it's not an emergency," Stone said affably. "What brings you by to disturb my so-called rest?"

"Is there ever any for the worthy? I figured you wouldn't be doing what you are supposed to be doing," Chip said, chiding in a way unacceptable for anyone other than his long-standing executive. "The latest report from *Stanley* just came in. Our people are looking it over, but I thought you might want to scan the raw stuff."

Stanley was Colonel Mainwaring's electronic warfare ship that had once been an explorer. He'd said they still had a lot of survey equipment aboard and promised it would be useful in tackling the commo problem. Apparently it had proven so. Chip would, of course, have already looked through the report himself. "Good news or bad?"

"Good, I think."

"Let's have a look."

Chip keyed the data up onto Stone's console. Though encouraged that Mainwaring's people had done some useful work, Stone soon found his well-disposed attitude marred. The *Stanley* material was indeed "raw stuff"—nearly pure technical biology, chemistry, and electronics—and well beyond Stone's limited expertise in those fields.

"What's this thing that looks like a jellyfish? They seem to be spending a lot of time on it. More Remor biotechnology?"

"Most likely, since there's no record of the phenomenon before the Remor invasion. It's one of the biggest culprits in our commo fritz: a life-form with a natural gas bag that deposits various minerals in its cells. They're natural electromagnetic scatterers. They form a layer that bounces most forms of commo and garbles the rest. There's even a variant that partially reflects and scatters lased energy. All together they work something like an ocean's deep scattering layer that fouls up sonar scans, except these things are airborne rather than plankton in a sea. *Stanley*'s team is calling the phenomenon an Atmospheric Scattering Sheath. ASS for short."

"Wait a minute. What about ground-to-ground? Bounce-back should be helpful, like using the ionosphere."

"The ASSes have got cousins infesting the lower reaches of the atmosphere."

"I haven't seen any of these things in the combat vids."

"Check the scale on the little gas bag again. They're practically the size of pollen grains. At best they show up as haze."

Stone shook his head ruefully. "Smoke and mirrors."

Chip looked perplexed.

"It's an old phrase for obfuscation. Doesn't matter. What's the solution?"

"*Stanley*'s people have got a few suggestions, but they're still testing. They've identified channels where we get clear commo, lanes swept by the passage of transatmospheric craft, but they don't stay open. They tested a few additives to shuttle and aircraft fuels and we're getting clear commo in several zones."

"We can't keep punching holes in these just to send orders. It'd be like using the pony express."

"Or normal interstellar communication," Chip pointed out wryly.

"But we're not dealing with interstellar distances here." The whole setup bothered Stone. It surely played havoc with coordinating the invasion, but why set it up in the first place? It couldn't have been emplaced overnight, and they had surprised the Remor when they arrived. And even the Remor used EM to communicate. They ought to be suffering communications problems too. "So how do the enemy get around it?"

"Keremeyer on *Stanley* doesn't think they do. Given the greater-than-usual lack of coordination among enemy planetary forces and between their ground and space forces, I think she may be right."

"So why did they breed their ASSes?"

Chip didn't have an answer. Neither did Stone. Hours of poring over the *Stanley* report revealed that the science boys and girls had no idea either.

22

Anders had his people distribute their rations among Sue's civilians. It would put them low till the next supply drop, but the humanitarian imperative had precedence. Watching the way that the civilians devoured what he knew wasn't exactly haute cuisine told him a lot about how bad conditions had been in Palisandra. He watched the delight flash in Sue's face as she discovered the tiny square of chocolate included in the rations pack. How long had it been since she'd tasted any such? He waited until he was sure it had melted away in her mouth, and then, reluctant to chase away the enraptured peace he saw on her face, waited a little bit more. Crouching down beside her, he asked, "Do you know of other internees?"

She pushed a hand through her short-cropped brown locks, looking puzzled.

"Sorry," he said. She probably didn't think of her fellow civilians that way. "What about other civilians? Other people the Remor walled in here. Could you help us call them in?"

She made a sound halfway between a snort and sob. "They won't listen to me."

Rivalries, he guessed. He understood something of what happened in internment camps. And he'd read about the horrors of Blockade Times during the Access War. If Eridani could turn on each other, what would less disciplined folk do?

"It's been hard since the aliens came," she understated. "People looked out for their friends."

"I understand."

Doubt filled her face, but she shook it away. "I think you'll get more people to at least talk to you if you tell them about the food and medicine you've got. Liberation doesn't fill bellies or stop an infection."

"I'll keep that in mind."

"Be careful, though. Some of the people you attract might not be exactly people anymore."

"We won't tolerate feral behavior." They couldn't afford it. Having taken back even a part of the planet from the Remor, MilForce was now in charge of the liberated sections. Authority brought responsibility, but there were not enough troopers on-planet to fight the Remor while acting as a police force, even for this city alone. "This is a martial law situation. We can't do anything about what's happened before, but hereafter it's a different story. We will have order. We will not tolerate stealing or looting. There can be no hoarding and no black marketeering."

"How will you stop it?"

"The uniform code of martial justice sets the penalty for transgression as death."

Her eyes went cold, her face still as stone. "I thought you came here to rescue us."

"We did. But we are seeking the greatest good for the greatest number. Selfish and greedy individuals threaten everyone. War rules are a temporary necessity. I hope it won't be for long. Once proper authority is established and we get proper lines of supply running, things will be different."

A bitter, wild smile twitched across her lips. "Do you think I disagree?"

For some reason it bothered Anders to see such naked bloodthirstiness on display in this woman. It was plain from her face, from the way she held her body, that she had suffered, so he could guess where the attitude was coming from. The universe should not be so cruel, though he knew it often was. *God's plan,* he told himself. *There are always reasons for the way He tests His children.*

Sue was searching his face, looking for something. She didn't look very sure about what she was finding. When their eyes met, he got the momentary impression of something deep-seated snarling like a rabbit before a fox, then shutters came down. Her face closed down with the speed of a starship's emergency vacuum seals. The stoic expression she resumed was as secure as that of a good Eridani officer.

"I've got a guess," she said. "You're only thinking about the jackals. There's worse than them here."

"What do you mean?"

"The xombies and the collectors. People who work for the aliens."

Belligerence and revulsion welled up, and he felt a little slip past his own mask. "We will have no truck with species traitors."

This time they shared a savage smile.

Two days after Commander Seaborg gave her the chocolate, Sue watched his soldiers move through the crowd. A crowd! Could you believe it? She thought she'd never see the like again.

Under the protection of the League soldiers, one part of Palisandra was beginning to look and act like a town again. A shantytown to be sure, but something more than the shifting mosaic of hardscrabble farming communes and nomad scavenger camps that they had endured these last years. Of course people still were sticking with those they had grouped with to survive, but now the groupings more resembled neighborhood cliques than rival tribes.

She thought she'd given up believing in armored knights coming to the rescue of the downtrodden. Then this. She still had trouble believing it was real.

The soldiers still wore their battlesuits, but had opened their helmets and shouldered their weapons. They made it clear to any who asked that there was still fighting going on, but here, at least, there was peace.

Their progress through the crowd was slow. Their leader, Seaborg, who she had learned was one of the fabled Eridani super-soldiers, wasn't acting very soldierly just now. He stopped every few steps to talk to someone or to answer a question. He even tapped into his battle armor's systems to give water to any in need. Rations he would not hand out, reminding those who asked that they had to wait for the distribution time. He did make sure that his subordinate cut ration chits for any who hadn't gotten theirs yet.

Those chits were a reminder that the technology the Palisandrans had lost was still out there in the universe. A promise that they could have it again. And something else Sue didn't dare let herself think too much about. Not yet. No, not yet.

While Sue was wondering what had prompted this tour by the League commander, she realized that he was heading directly for the awning where she was helping Doc Shelly make good use of League medical supplies. When they got close enough for conversation, Seaborg greeted her politely and said, "I wanted to come by and say thank you, ma'am."

Sue was confused. *He* was the one who had come to *their* rescue. "For what?"

"For your advice. I thought you'd like to know that we're getting more and more civilians responding to our loudspeaker calls."

She smiled at his oblivious naïveté. Couldn't he see that she didn't need to be told that it was working? He didn't even have to use his eyes. Anyone could smell the people, and the noise was inescapable. The evidence was all around them. Her sprite of mischievousness, whom she'd thought dead and buried, prodded her to make a sarcastic reply. She said, "Good. Still telling them all the rules?"

"All the rules." He went on to tell her that they'd had a few run-ins with what he called "hostiles" but that they had taken no casualties. The hostiles hadn't fared nearly as well. He told her too that a new food drop was scheduled and that a water distillation unit was nearly set up, no little thanks to her friend Professor Murch. She found herself bemused by his attitude. This giant of a soldier was acting more than a little like a schoolboy trying to impress.

"I want you to know I am glad of the news, Commander Seaborg, but I was wondering if you could answer a specific question for me."

"Surely, ma'am."

"Why do you keep calling me 'ma'am'?"

He blinked. "I don't know your last name."

Her amusement evaporated. She'd had a last name once. She'd gotten it from her husband. She'd put it aside since it had ceased to matter, but she supposed she could have it again. What else did she have that was his?

"Merrick," she said. "My name is Sue Merrick."

"Very good. Gordie, I want you to escort Ms. Merrick to the command tent for the meeting."

He gave her a time, not thinking that she had no way of telling when that might be, and went about his business. Sue, in a more sober state, went back to helping Doc Shelly, who wisely kept the conversation to practical matters. Private Gordon tried to help out as well, until Doc Shelly politely but firmly suggested he take his clumsy armored hands elsewhere. He did not go away, but he did stop trying to be helpful. Some time later he said, "Ms. Merrick, we ought to move out now."

Maybe Seaborg had not been unthinking when he stated the time of the meeting. After all, he'd left her someone who did have a timepiece. She finished what she was doing and let Private Gordon lead her.

On entering the command tent, Sue saw that most of the League officers and noncoms had already gathered. She was still learning their names and ranks. She also saw that she wasn't the only group leader to be invited to share the soldiers' council. Sheldon was there, and the Ali brothers, as well as several others whose faces she recognized but for whom she had no names. One face stopped her in her tracks, a face from her nightmares. She felt her knees go traitor. Standing there, calm as could be, was Giatti.

"You all right, ma'am?" whispered Private Gordon.

The smell of the soldier's sun-heated armor plate brought her back from the bad place into which she'd tumbled, back to the present.

"I'll be fine," she replied, willing it to be so.

She was safe here among the soldiers. Safe. Wasn't she? Just then Seaborg noticed her and gave her a smile of welcome. She took it as a promise of strength and justice.

His voice cut through the conversations and demanded the attention of everyone in the tent.

"All right, gentlefolk. There's no time to waste here, so I am going to cut right to the heart of our problem. Due to increasing enemy activity, we can no longer consider this portion of Palisandra to be a safe locale," he said. "We may not be able to consider any part of the city safe. Fleet command has decided that evacuation is the most suitable course of action. We have therefore been ordered to move all rescued civilians south to the plains for a dust-off. Unfortunately, fleet command seems to be ignoring the fact that we have inadequate transport for the civilians currently under our care. I called this conference for ideas on how to accomplish our mission. Let me hear them, people."

"Relays?" Sergeant Fiske suggested readily.

"And who guards the civilians while we shuttle back and forth?" a captain countered. He was an older man who seemed to have a habitually sour expression on his face.

"How about this, Caldwell?" Fiske offered. "We set up fire bases, here and at the dust-off site. Minimal staffing. We keep all civilians inside the berm. You can build us a suitable berm, can't you, Caldwell?"

"Might work," Caldwell conceded. "But what happens when the xenos hit both locations at once?"

"We don't know they can do that," said Fiske.

"We don't know they can't," pointed out another sergeant. This one, though big and broad-shouldered, was not an Eridani. His name flash read *Brizbin*.

Lieutenant Powell, the head of the medical detachment, was shaking his head. "Even with all the healthy civilians walking, there just aren't enough blowers to move all the sick and wounded at once."

Sue heard Giatti mumble, "Who cares?" Aloud he said, "Shouldn't we get out who we can? Greatest good for the greatest number, right?"

"That is our goal, Mr. Giatti," Seaborg said. "I do not plan on leaving anyone behind. We need a solution, people."

"What about wagons?" Sue asked.

Seaborg looked at her. "We haven't got any, Ms. Merrick."

"Jan Spicer's group used to have horses and wagons; if we can get them in it'll help. My people have some handcarts. They can carry kids. Martin Ramierez's people have a few bigger things. Maybe some of the other groups can contribute."

"Can you give me numbers?" Seaborg asked.

She told him what she knew. Sheldon had some more information. Powell shook his head again. "We can cover my patients with those, but we'll lose kids and elderly on the march."

A sergeant standing in the back of the room cleared his throat. Sue recognized him as leader of the less-well-armored soldiers, who were apparently from the Pan-Stellar Combine. He had a ready smile and was beaming it now.

"I bet I know where we can get some more wagons," he said. "That junk pile back in Halcione. A lot of that stuff was totaled, but I bet there are enough hulks with good wheels that we can gut till they're just shells. Pull them with the blowers."

"Sounds good, Sergeant Williams," said Seaborg.

"Not by my math," said Powell. "Assuming each blower pulls two wagons, and assuming each blower load is the equivalent of a city bus, I'd guess that we'd still have a hundred or so people who can't take the march."

"A hundred people?" Seaborg clearly didn't like the accounting.

Williams shrugged, but his eager smile never wavered.

"That's like, what, two more buses? A squad of battlesuited troopers have the muscle to haul that."

The soldiers all turned to look at their companion. He wilted a little under the attention.

"They do, don't they?" he asked a bit shakily.

Slowly Seaborg nodded. "I expect they do."

There was a lot more talking about details. A task force of soldiers and civilians was put together to make the trip to Halcione and conduct the salvage operation. Sue, still shaky from her near encounter with Giatti, slipped out of the tent.

While the meeting had been going on, one of the military hovercraft assigned to rations distribution had moved nearby and started handing out the day's allotment. They had gotten very good at it. The line was nearly gone and most people were hurrying back to their safe places before consuming theirs. She understood the impulse, having so long lived as they had.

She started toward the vehicle automatically. The draw to a known food source was so great.

But she only took a few steps.

Giatti.

Why now?

She wasn't hungry. She hadn't been hungry then. She hadn't wanted to eat for days after—

The past, she told herself. *You no longer live there, girl.*

She didn't believe what she told herself. The past was there, before her eyes. Giatti.

Sue stood in the middle of the street, hugging her arms tight to her body. She knew she was on the verge of tears that she didn't want to shed. Rage and revulsion wrecked her. She just stood there, watching the soldiers finish their distribution.

"Aw, crap, we missed them," a voice whined behind her.

A hand gripped her shoulder and spun her roughly around. She stared, stricken, into Giatti's petulant face. Several of his lackeys hulked behind him.

"Come on, girlie. Hand over your goodies," he ordered. "This hungry man's got more call for them than you."

Sue shrank away from his touch. He grinned wickedly at her, reveling in his power.

His piggy eyes showed no recognition.

You're nothing. Used. Abused. Discarded.

Giatti's face scrunched into a scowl when he saw she had nothing.

"Aw, crap, she blew it too." He turned away as if she were invisible. "Come on, boys. I see some pickings that ain't so slow and stupid. Let's get us some eats."

Giatti led his jackals toward the last people to draw their rations, an older couple. Sue could see they understood what was to come. The man tried to put himself between the woman and the scavengers and hurry her away, but the jackals were too quick for them. Cut off, the couple was backed into a corner.

It's only trouble for you, girl.

Sue stood frozen, hating him, hating herself.

Giatti and his bullies started roughing up the couple, cats to their mice. Sue tried to scream out for them to stop, but nothing came from her throat. She knew too well that these monsters savaged whatever hindered them. She could make herself their victim again and still accomplish nothing to help that unfortunate couple.

Where is the knight-errant when he's needed?

There. Sue stared at the battlesuited Eridani soldier walking toward the tableaux. *Where he's needed.*

It was Commander Seaborg. His armored footfalls must have hammered into Giatti's skull even through the jackal's predatory haze. Giatti turned to face what Sue prayed was justice.

"Hey, Commander," Giatti fawned. "I thought you'd be busy getting important stuff organized."

Seaborg ignored the comment. "Are you having trouble remembering the rules, Mr. Giatti?"

"No, sir, Commander Seaborg."

"Each and every one?"

"Sure thing, Commander. I'm your man."

"Very well, Mr. Giatti."

Seaborg turned away and walked off. Sue wanted to run after him to put herself in his shadow, but Giatti was watching the Eridani soldier closely. He'd see her, know she was vulnerable.

When Seaborg was far enough away, Giatti began to mock him. His jackals laughed at their master's cruel humor. Then they turned back to their crueler game. Giatti finally snatched away the ration packs. First the woman's, then the man's.

If Sue had not already been looking, if she had not been positioned where she could see Giatti robbing his victims and the retreating soldier at the same time, she would have missed at least part of what happened.

Seaborg didn't stop walking. His right arm swung up and pointed behind him. A panel popped open on his gauntlet and something emerged. A beam flicked from that something, a brief pulse of light that speared through Giatti's skull. Only when the monster's body hit the ground did Seaborg turn. His weapon disappeared back into his gauntlet as his amplified voice boomed out from within the helmet.

"Mr. Giatti, having affirmed his understanding of his position under the uniform code of martial justice, has violated that code's strictures 7.32 and 7.33 within the sight of an officer of that code during a state of martial law. Accordingly, the mandatory sentence of death has been executed by said officer of the code."

Seaborg marched back to the body of the executed man. Bending down, he retrieved the ration packs Giatti had stolen and returned them to the man's victims. He turned to the stunned remnants of Giatti's pack.

"Have you gentlemen learned a lesson today?"

They scattered like whipped dogs.

23

The place had been a park with a full suite of recreational fields. Those fields were now part of a young forest and haunted by alien critters as well as remnants of the local wildlife, all working out the new food chain. People avoided it because of those foreign critters, but they didn't scare Bartie. Not anymore. Not since he'd started dealing with their masters.

He sat in the shade of a big old adapted maple, munching his way through a ration pack and wondering how bright it was for him to be doing this spy stuff. The bugs wanted more info on the contrary entities and they'd told him to get it for them. He could have sent some of his slugs. It would have been safer. But not very smart. His slugs were good enough in a brawl, but none of them, not a one, had any sort of finesse.

Sometimes a guy had to take care of business himself, even the tricky stuff. Sometimes especially the tricky stuff.

Not that it was hard to penetrate the perimeter of these off-worlder troublemakers from the Interstellar Defense League.

Gawd, what a mouthful of a name. As arrogant as they are.

Anyway, it wasn't hard to get inside their camp. They were passing any human who didn't have a controller on his back, which meant that they knew something about xombies. But they hadn't checked his throat, so they didn't know about the frickin' *gawkhores*. He'd had a story ready to explain the thing wrapped around his throat. Just as well. It hadn't been that good a story, and he'd never been sure he'd have been able to sell it.

So he got in. Of course, once in, he'd had to say he'd follow their damned, nancy, no-fun rules. Bartie could deal with that for a couple of days. It wasn't like he was going to make a habit of it.

From what he'd heard, the offworlders were serious about their rules. The sheep were all talking about what had happened to Pig-face Giatti. Way Bartie figured it, the stupid git had gotten what he'd asked for—he'd broken one of the soldier boys' rules and been sloppy enough to get caught at it. Giatti had never been one of Bartie's smartest boys. Hell, he'd proven that when he went out on his own instead of sticking with Bartie. Truth be told, Bartie was surprised Giatti had lasted long enough to run afoul of these League soldiers. Well, old Pig-face wouldn't be stupid anymore. Hard to be stupid when your brain is cored and cooked. Bartie chortled at the thought of it

Wish I could have seen the look on Giatti's piggy face.

The soldiers had given Bartie a chip when they logged him in to their rationing system. It used biometrics as a certification. They said it was to make sure that everyone got their fair share. Maybe so. But it also meant they had a tag on him. It was the sort of thing that could have gotten him into trouble in the old days, but these guys' computers had no link to the old databases. They couldn't tell Bartie from the law-abiding sheep. That could change if they stayed, but Bartie wasn't too worried about them staying. Not with what he'd seen and heard here. Not with what he'd seen in the Bug Palace.

The bugs held the real power on Pacifica and they weren't about to surrender it to any contrary entities. They had power and resources they had yet to put into play. They were going to make their occupation stick. Who was going to tell them otherwise? The high and mighty Interstellar Defense League? Hell, the bugs had *plants* that could eat these League soldiers, battlesuits and all.

And it was looking like the soldier boys had figured out they were outclassed. Everywhere Bartie looked he could see the signs. He didn't need to hear the sheep talking about it.

As if some of them could keep from bleating everything they thought they knew about it.

Evacuation, the sheep called it. Running away was a better phrase.

He tossed away the empty ration pack.

For a moment, he considered running with them—they were escaping the bugs, after all.

But for how long?

They were probably just running to their own destruction. If he went with them, he'd probably just die with them. Besides, the little present the bugs had given him probably had some kind of self-destruct trigger. That'd be just like them.

As far as he could see, his best course still lay with the bugs. When it came down to it, Bartie preferred living, even if it meant taking orders from some frickin' xeno-mantis.

Speaking of which, the old bug was probably starting to get twitchy waiting for Bartie to report back. Not that he cared if it had a hissy fit, but it might decide to send one of the boys after him and that could just screw things up.

He heaved himself to his feet. He could do a little more snooping, but why bother? He had enough to give something to the old bug.

He was amused at how simple it was for him, a spy in the employ of their sworn enemy, to walk away from the Interstellar Defense League and its soldiers. He practically laughed all the way back to the Bug Palace.

An aerial drone running perimeter patrol near what the locals called the Lair, the reported central position of Remor forces within the Palisandra perimeter, went dead with no indication of attack. It didn't worry Anders especially. Such things happened. Technology never worked as well in the field as it did in practice or simulation, but when its replacement did the same thing, he began to be concerned.

The drone losses could be coincidental techno glitches. It

might be due to interference from a local pocket of ASSes.
Or it could be the first sign of the enemy offensive that fleet
Intel was predicting.

Most of his combat troops were at the Gramerton base
camp. But with work crews in Halcione prepping the transport wagons and half of Caldwell's engineers widening the
lanes through the vegetative barrier and making them as safe
as possible, his forces were dangerously spread. Not that
they wouldn't be able to defend themselves; they could. It
was the civilians that were the problem. Protecting them was
his job and his response time to any threat wasn't going to be
good.

He doubled the drone and foot patrols moving through the
city. It was a screen between the clustered civilians and the
enemy, but it was a porous screen, and without a lot more
troops and drones at his disposal it would remain that way.
He could only hope that his scouts would spot any trouble
before it got too close.

As a further precaution, he got Sergeant Brizbin on the
link. The support platoon commander was in Halcione,
helping with the work there. "Sergeant, I'm taking you out
of the motor pool."

"What's up, boss?" Brizbin sounded justifiably puzzled.
They both knew that work was going slowly there, and they
needed all the hands they could get. "Are the hostiles stirring?"

"Not sure. I hope it's just paranoia, but I want your platoon in ready mode."

"You got it, sir. Where away?"

"Pick your spot. Keep a watch on all the probable lines of
attack, but I especially want you able to support a withdrawal from the city."

"Will do."

There wasn't a lot more to do but keep watch, which he did.

All that afternoon, the patrols contacted probes from Remor forces. It was all light stuff, no more than four machines
at a time. Support from Brizbin's Dog platoon put them all
away without more than a few light casualties that Powell's

medical people patched up and sent back to duty. Remor losses were notable and the destroyed machines dissolved away as usual, leaving scorched real estate and slag pools as the only signs of the actions. The only permanent loss to Anders's force was expended ammunition and a dozen more drones. Three of those were not obviously destroyed in combat—apparent victims of additional technical glitches.

Anders's concerns deepened. He pulled Caldwell's people from their work on the Wall and sent them to expedite the work in Halcione. If the lanes weren't wide and safe enough, it wouldn't matter if they didn't have the transport to roll through them.

More civilians came in to swell the refugee ranks. It was going to magnify the transport problem, but Anders couldn't turn them away. He continued to see others on his drones' cameras, but they remained aloof from the Leaguers. All he had to do was count heads in the refugee camp to know that they had only collected a fraction of the local population. The rest were apparently more willing to take their chances creeping through the Remor-infested ruins of greater Palisandra than to try and get free of the prison the enemy had made of their city. Anders couldn't force them to accept the League's helping hand, and apparently he couldn't coax them. What more could he do?

He didn't have a good answer. He was a soldier, not a diplomat. He had made the effort, so he told himself to be content with the ones he was saving now. Only problem was, he hadn't actually saved anyone yet.

And he might not.

He linked to the team at Halcione to chivy them along. Caldwell replied. The engineer officer actually sounded happy.

"I was just going to commo you, sir. We're organizing to pull out now."

"You got everything you went after?"

"Yes, sir. We even acquired two spare transport rigs. And Sergeant Williams also has a surprise for you."

"A what?"

"A surprise, sir. He told me it was a thank-you present. Something about having faith in him." Something akin to a stifled snicker came from Caldwell. He continued, "I didn't press him any further. It sounded personal."

Anders shook his head. Why couldn't the engineer have been an Eridani? Otherworlders picked such odd times to display their senses of humor. How had Williams conned him into this silly conspiracy? Anders considered diverting a drone to spy out this "surprise," but not for long. Operational security couldn't be compromised for a commander's idle curiosity.

The sun was setting over the Sturkhe Brewery when the returning convoy passed the base camp's perimeter. By then Anders figured he'd seen the surprise through the eyes of the sentry drones. Williams confirmed it on arrival. The Combiner had managed to scrounge or patch up several dozen functional vehicles. It was an eclectic mix, ranging from a two-seater recreational hovercraft to a tandem passenger bus. Quite the ragtag fleet for the fugitives, but it was barely enough extra capacity to handle the new arrivals. Even then, Anders figured he'd have to assign eight more battlesuited troopers than he'd planned on, to tow those wagons the extra vehicles couldn't haul.

"I figured we might need more capacity," Williams said.

"You figured right," Anders told him. Once again giving the Combiner a second chance had proven to be wise. "Well done. Now let's put them to use."

The civilians griped about setting out. Too many seemed to think it would be a good idea to wait for morning. Anders disabused them of that foolish notion. Yes, they would have a hard time seeing, but Anders's people didn't have that problem. They had enough spare night-eyes for the civilian drivers. What more was needed? It was not like those few healthy folks walking or biking alongside the vehicles were going to get lost.

No one knew how good Remor night-vision capabilities were, but they were likely more limited than their daytime capacity, same as for humans. Saint Michael knew they could see well enough in the daytime. So it made sense to use the night. He told them that, unwilling to reveal that his real reason was his growing concern that they might not have until morning before things got hot.

It took hours just to get everybody loaded up. Then another two to get the vehicles sorted out into a caravan. They'd lost half the night before they managed to get rolling.

Passage through the Wall was thankfully free of incident, though Anders couldn't tell if the engineers had done their job well or if the convoy was just lucky. They rolled on.

Progress was frustratingly slow. Without the wagons they'd have been moving even slower, so Anders figured he ought to be grateful. Still, it seemed to him that an arthritic Malaxian two-legged tortoise could outpace them to the dust-off site.

They crossed the barren zone and passed through Halcione and into the woods on the far side. Gauging their progress, he guessed that they would take three or four days to reach the place where Fleet considered it safe enough to bring down the transports. They might do it faster if things didn't get too disorganized when they took the necessary breaks, but he didn't have a lot of faith they would. The figurative cats he was herding would have too many ways to snarl things up.

He passed up and down the column, urging people on. He didn't speak of the reports from the rear guard to anyone but his unit commanders. They needed to share his concerns and know that the enemy was probing into the vacated Gramerton base camp.

Would the Remor pursue? Or would they be content to let the League make off with some of their captives? And if they were, would the column run into random patrols? There were too many possibilities, too many ways for them to find they had jumped into the fire.

The simultaneous loss of four scout drones announced the materialization of Anders's fears.

Ambush!

Energy beams crackled through the trees, frying vegetation along with those unfortunates who happened to be in their path. Shells and rockets roared through the woods.

A tree that had stood for hundreds of years was scythed mercilessly. It fell, toppling its neighbors and bringing the whole mass crashing down onto Acker platoon's carrier. The blower slammed into the earth, buried under the fallen canopy.

In the center of the column, the tandem bus caught a missile. The front half exploded in a glowing ball that hurled debris for a hundred meters.

Anders tried to get a response going, but he wasn't moving fast enough. The enemy had another volley incoming.

All around him soldiers and civilians were screaming and dying.

24

Colonel Craig MacAndra looked pleased as he entered the fleet command battle center. He had just returned from a tour of the fleet, inspecting the combat readiness of their vessels. Stone concluded that progress in dealing with their accumulated battle damage was satisfactory.

"Everything we can fix this side of a space dock is fixed, Commander," MacAndra reported.

"Good news," Stone agreed. "And timely."

MacAndra nodded. "I've been following the plots."

As had Stone. Isolated Remor fleet elements were no longer isolated. Single ships were joining others, and small groups were forming into large ones. "What do you make of it?"

"Looks like they are getting organized to deal with us. I assume we will start dealing with them first."

"Naturally. With repairs completed, we're as strong as we're going to get. I don't intend to let them consolidate."

Chip Hollister broke in. "Excuse me, Commander. I've got the revised battle plan contingencies. Also current enemy positions. Would you and the colonel care to review them?"

Chip's timing was, as usual, excellent. "A good idea."

MacAndra's more immediate knowledge of the fleet's current capabilities informed their review of the plans to deal with the enemy's remaining space forces. The newly reported enemy movements called for changes, and they made several obvious force adjustments. The real problem remained: They needed a way to defeat an enemy that matched them in tonnage but was faster and, kilogram for kilogram, tougher. Defeat in detail was the only way to deal with the enemy. They had to catch them to do that, and catch them before the Remor commander gathered his forces together.

"I like the opening of contingency C, sir," MacAndra opined.

That plan called for an orbital control detachment, mostly Colonel Mainwaring's volunteer ships, to remain close to Pacifica in support of ground operations while the rest of the fleet moved out into the system to engage Remor space forces.

"I think the enemy will take the bait," he continued. "With them holding in near space waiting for their chance to pounce on the detachment, we ought to be able to shift the main fleet's vectors and englobe them before they catch on that we're not immediately going after their more formidable elements. Given the support of our orbital detachment, we ought to have a short, decisive engagement."

"I concur," said Stone. "And then?"

"Then I think we ought to shift to contingency G and take on enemy groups beta and epsilon as we pass between them. We don't need to annihilate them, just maul them enough to scatter them. We have the strength to do it with minimal losses. But we have to press on and go after the dreadnought's group. Again while we have the strength to do it."

"A good basis, but I do not wish to see any survivors from beta and epsilon groups."

"It'll slow us down in meeting the dreadnought group. The threat any stragglers pose will be minimal."

"In-system, yes. But we cannot afford them running to get help from elsewhere."

"Good point," MacAndra conceded. "They just might start thinking we've gotten the upper hand too early. And we can't have that, can we?"

"Exactly." Stone closed down the plot sims. "Let's get the fleet ready, Colonel. We've got a war to fight."

PACIFICA THEATER, PACIFICA ORBIT
CMEFS *AUDITOR*

Benton Mainwaring killed the comm channel to the flagship before letting himself frown. He looked around at his bridge crew. The loyal and hardworking people were busying themselves at their usual tasks, pretending that they hadn't heard. Piet Lugard, his fleet captain, who ought to be as outraged at the slight as Benton, went on reviewing station-keeping reports. Even Coppelstowe, his patient advisor, sat quietly in the VIP-couch. Her eyes were closed, her expression calm and meditative.

Didn't they understand the inequity of it all? Benton couldn't stand it. It just wasn't fair! "Once again we are left behind while the League ships go off to do the real fighting."

A few eyes turned to him, but flicked back as rapidly to their work. Was that a smirk lurking on Lugard's face?

"We came to fight the enemy. Why won't Stone let us?" He turned to Coppelstowe and she opened her eyes, knowing he wanted her attention. "I—we have a part to play here. Alsion said so. We can't allow Stone to thwart the dynamic flow of events, can we?"

"Commander Stone is not an initiate," she said serenely. "His decisions are made in ignorance of the dynamic."

"So he's wrong."

"Perhaps. Perhaps not. The complexity of the intertissued trajectories makes predictive accuracy in these circumstances most unreliable. The commander is making the decisions he thinks appropriate."

"Are you saying he's *right*? That this is how it *must* be?"

"This is how it is. The commander's rightness is as irrelevant as his understanding of the dynamic. All flows. We cannot change the dynamic, for we are a part of it. Time will reveal much to the clouded vision."

"You make it sound like predestination," Benton observed gloomily.

"The differences are subtle and deep."

"It be deep, all right," Lugard commented. His quiet

words were pitched a smidgen louder than a comment truly intended for himself alone. If Coppelstowe heard him, she gave no sign.

"You have something to say, Master Lugard?"

"You be asking, I will be speaking," he replied. "Question be, will the good sir be listening to a plain simple man speaking plain simple truth?"

"So you have the truth, Master Lugard," Benton said a trifle more sarcastically than he intended. "I would love to hear the truth."

"Truth be, Stone be thinking we not be fighting in the space battle as good as them. Truth be, Stone be right."

"Gad, even my own officers have no faith in us."

Lugard shrugged. "Faith be not in it. I be practical and honest."

"The League hasn't cornered the market on courage and conviction, Master Lugard. Our people are their match there. You cannot tell me otherwise."

"I be not. But I be sure that our ships be not the match of theirs, and their ships be not the match of the Remor's. Commander Stone, he be making the choice I would be making in his place."

"You are not being shut out from events, Colonel Mainwaring," Coppelstowe said consolingly. "You have been given the responsibility of ensuring continued success on the planet."

"It's a nursemaid's job." This wasn't at all what he'd expected. Alsion had promised him he was going to be an important part of what was happening.

"A nursemaid's job?" Copplestowe mused. "A curious perspective. This responsibility could as easily be likened to a sentry's or a protector's. It is no less serious however it is viewed."

Protector? That did make the task sound more . . . important. Perhaps he had let a little too much ego shade his judgment. The role he'd been assigned was not really an unimportant one.

As if on cue, the signals officer shouted, "Colonel Mainwaring, we've got an emergency distress call from the surface!"

Sue huddled next to the overturned Palisandra Tourist Board jitney she'd been riding in when the Remor attacked. It wasn't a safe place, but she couldn't see a better one. And running around in the open was just a way to die.

She wasn't the only one sheltering in the shadow of the vehicle. Everyone aboard who could get out or be pulled out was there. Some were dead now, some dying. Ren was among the latter. The boy had taken a meter-long splinter from an exploding tree through his belly.

Their situation was far from unique. The screams and moans of the wounded and dying seemed to come from everywhere around them. Sue could not see much from her refuge, just enough to know that she was not as inured to violence as she thought she'd become. But then this wasn't the sort of fight she'd survived so often in the ruins of Palisandra. Never before had she faced the unleashed fury of the aliens' weaponry.

Now and again she caught glimpses of Remor fighting machines stalking through the woods. They prowled about the convoy, unleashing blasts that could splinter the largest of the forest giants or mangle one of the soldiers' armored vehicles. What they could do to a human being, even a battle-armored soldier, was best not thought about.

She supposed it was only a matter of time until one of those blasts found them where they cowered, helpless against the violence erupting around them.

For some of us, she thought, cradling the mortally injured Ren in her arms, *it might be a mercy.*

The boy moaned, as if sensing her thoughts. His face was wizened by the agony that was wracking his body. Doc Shelly might have had something to ease his pain, but she had been in another vehicle. Who knew where she was now? Or whether she was alive or dead?

Ren's eyes fluttered, then opened. They didn't focus on her. His hand clutched weakly at hers. She sat there, cradling him close to her like a baby. He had always claimed to hate it when she'd tried to comfort him before. It had been a young man's bravado then. There was no complaint now, for he was past all bravado.

"Mom?"

His voice was breathy and weak. Recognizing how near death was, she lied to ease him. "I'm here, Ren."

"It hurts."

"I know, darling."

He never said anything else. He just stopped breathing and was gone. In a world gone strangely distant, she closed his eyes.

Some time later Professor Murch eased Ren from her arms and helped her lay the boy down. Murch met her eyes and an understanding passed between them. He did what she couldn't and pulled the lethal splinter out. Removing the violator did nothing for Ren, but it made his mortality, and all of theirs, a little less conspicuous.

The universe never paused to note the passing of anyone, not even a boy who, if there was justice, would not be lying bloody and dead in the shadow of a mangled tour bus. Their hiding place was abruptly invaded by a dozen or so soldiers. They came tumbling in, roughing people up as they collapsed or threw themselves down.

Of them all, only Ren made no complaint.

These soldiers were the lighter-armored troops, not the battlesuited soldiers, but even so the shadow of the jitney was instantly overcrowded. Sue found herself oddly disappointed that Commander Seaborg wasn't among them.

"Oh, shite," exclaimed one of the soldiers.

Sue thought she recognized his voice. Williams. The sergeant who had gotten the extra transport vehicles.

"What are you people doing here?" he asked.

Wasn't that obvious? Professor Murch answered for her.

"Trying to stay out of trouble."

"Good instincts. Unfortunately, this is now officially a bad place to do that. We've got at least three *Caymans* headed this way. They catch you here, you're dead. Frankly, I don't fancy our own chances." He raised his voice. "All right, people, listen up! We've got to get these civilians to safety. Brent, you lead them out. Everybody else, cover fire on my mark."

He turned to Sue. "Ms. Merrick, isn't it? Think you can get these people moving? There's an old streambed back a ways to the east. It's got good cover and it's within the perimeter. Brent knows the way. You'll be safer there than here."

She nodded.

"Here," he said, snatching up Ren's rifle and thrusting it at her. "You know how to use this? Yeah. Good. Won't be much use against the machines, but it's better than nothing, eh?"

She took the rifle, almost dropping it. It was slick with Ren's blood.

"Hey!"

She started at his voice, but kept looking down at the bloody rifle.

"Talk to me," he ordered. "I know you're alive. I need you to know it too. Answer me, ma'am. Can you take these people to safety?"

Her voice was a squeak. "Show me where."

"You heard the lady, Brent."

"Yes, sir." Crouching low, Brent made his way over. "Ma'am, I ain't stopping till we're fifty meters from here. Maybe not then."

Sue had been grateful to escape the burden of responsibility when Anders Seaborg and his League soldiers had come and taken charge. She'd thought herself released from obligations for their safety. Now she glanced around at the people looking to her for leadership. Most had been her people before. Some had not. They were all hers now. She couldn't let them down.

"You heard Private Brent," she said, putting steel she

didn't feel into her voice. "We can't stop for anybody. You all have to run as hard as you can. We'll rest when we reach the stream. I know you all can do it."

The last, she feared, was a lie.

"That's the spirit," Williams commended her. Then he shouted, "Let 'em have it, troops!"

Brent was up and sprinting. Sue was up too, running hard. In moments some of the people passed her. Was that all of them? She didn't look. She ran. She could hear more footfalls behind her in the occasional lulls in the battle's frenzy. Behind them Williams was shouting, "Disperse!" His troopers kept up their firing. An explosion from farther away suggested that they were having some effect. But the enemy weren't deterred. Alien fire raked the trees and demolished vehicles that weren't already wrecked. Sometimes a beam whooshed over Sue's head. Severed branches and crisped wildlife rained down on them, but they kept running.

"Disperse! Grab cover!"

One of the troopers didn't make it. Sue didn't need to look. She'd come to recognize the sound of a death scream. It was the last human sound she heard from the battle.

But Brent needed to see. At least he stopped and turned around. Then Sue noticed he was holding a hand to the side of his helmet, like a person listening to something.

Sue ran toward him and the other, faster refugees, who were already standing around the soldier looking worried. More of her people were catching up. She could see others stumbling through the brush. They were wounded and exhausted and probably couldn't go farther. At least not at a soldier's pace.

"Change of plans, ma'am," Brent announced as she reached him.

"We're not going back," she told him.

He pulled back as if she were going to bite him and quickly said, "No one's asking you to. We just got a new rally point."

"Safer than your streambed?"

"I don't know."

"It had better be."

"Yes, ma'am."

A mighty roar came and went back in the direction of the wrecked tour bus as they waited for the slowest refugees to catch up. Sue was sure that they couldn't afford to linger long. Brent wanted to get moving after ten minutes. Sue made him wait another five. It didn't make any difference. No one else emerged to join them. Four people she'd seen at the bus, not counting Ren, were no longer with them.

"All right," she conceded. "Let's get going."

Brent brought them to a shaded glade, almost obscene in its peacefulness. This was not a day of peace.

The impression only lasted until Sue's eyes fell upon the League armored vehicle hidden in the deep shadows along one edge. Its guns were silent. Its engines idling. Its crew quietly, calmly sitting in their places.

No machine of war deserved to be at peace on this day.

The hovercraft was one of the command vehicles. Sue could see Commander Seaborg sitting in its main compartment, working at a console. Reflected light played off the deep black of his armor. That armor looked unscuffed, unsullied by the carnage.

As if nothing were wrong.

As if no one had died today.

So very wrong.

Filled by a sudden towering rage, she stormed up to the hovercraft. She reached across the coaming and slapped at him, shrilling, "Why aren't you out there fighting?"

The helmeted head turned in her direction and lingered for a moment. She couldn't see his face behind the visor, couldn't see what expression her outburst had put there, but she thought he might be about to address her. Then the moment passed, and his attention was back on his consoles.

"Get her out of here," Private Milano commanded from his place beside Seaborg.

Brent appeared at her side. He took her gently by the arms. "Come away, ma'am. The commander is awful busy right now."

The soldier's words lanced into her brain, shattering the grief-fueled fog in her head. Seaborg *was* fighting. He was fighting the way a commander ought to fight. It was his job to coordinate his people. Hadn't she done the same?

There were still people out there fighting for their lives. His people. Her people. They needed protection and coordination. His consoles gave him tools to do that job in ways she barely understood. If the defense that he was running didn't hold, everyone would die.

He was doing what he needed to do.

His silent, faceless rebuke now made her feel foolish. More than foolish. Her gut twisted. Had she taken his attention just when someone else truly needed it? What if someone had died because she hadn't been able to contain her rage and frustration and had poured it out on a man just trying to do what she was incapable of?

She twisted away from Brent's guiding hands and slumped to the ground. She let the long-dammed tears take her.

25

It wasn't often that Stone got to move through space and see it with his own eyes as he was doing now. It wasn't proper protocol for someone of his rank. A shame, really. Screens and holotanks just couldn't convey the majesty of the real thing.

Of course, it was that same stifling rank that was allowing him to sit in the copilot's seat of the transfer shuttle. With great power came many ways to abuse it, large and small. He tried to confine his vices to the small.

The expressions on the faces of the shuttle's rocket jockeys had been priceless when he'd announced his intention to "travel over up front." You would have thought he'd asked them to hand over their firstborn for his dinner. Once he'd made it clear he wasn't intending to fly the craft himself, the pilot had relaxed and her obvious relief was entertaining by itself. He'd actually had to order her to can the chatter.

With all that was in the offing, there were precious few minutes left when he'd get something resembling solitude. This was one place he could justify snatching a few of them, and he wanted to savor the last bits of calm.

Some might suggest he was being derelict in his duty, with the fleet nearly ready to start what ought to be its most significant operation against the enemy in the Pacifica System, but they would be wrong. Chip was handling the preparations just fine, like the good executive officer he was.

Stone had no worries in that regard, just his usual frustrations in not having his fingers on the pulse of things. An officer who couldn't delegate, as much as it might pain him, had no business holding a higher command billet.

Some things could be trusted to subordinates, others needed the personal touch. Since he was leaving Colonel Mainwaring in charge of the still very important operations that were ongoing on the planet, Stone felt he needed to do whatever he could to ensure that Mainwaring understood his role and that he would play that role like a League officer. Given Mainwaring's temperament, no one other than Stone was likely to have the proper effect on the Combiner. A linked conference with the man would have been easier, faster, and done less to distract Stone from fleet preparations, but a face-to-face was more likely to yield the results he wanted. Since the best use of resources required leaving Mainwaring essentially unsupervised, Stone wanted—no, needed—to be as assured as possible that the man understood what was required of him.

He felt sure he'd be back aboard *Constantine* in plenty of time to oversee the last of the necessary preparations. He had the time to enjoy a small interval among the stars.

"We're nearly there, Commander," the pilot announced all too soon. "Shall I request a boarding clearance, or would you like to do it yourself?"

"And spoil the surprise?"

She smiled. "Understood, sir."

As the pilot reached to open the commo channel, Stone noticed something unusual about Mainwaring's *Auditor.* His hand forestalled the pilot's.

"Take a look at *Auditor,*" he said

The pilot stared, then adjusted her heads-up display. Schematics and scan results of the ship appeared.

"Her launching bays are open," she said, voicing Stone's own conclusion. "She's launching assault shuttles!"

"Link me to their bridge," Stone ordered.

Mainwaring, you maniac, what in the name of Saint Michael and all the angels are you doing now?

PACIFICA THEATER, PACIFICA ORBIT
IDL ASSAULT SHUTTLE *LISA*
(SECONDED TO CMEFS *AUDITOR*)

"Atmospheric insertion in three," announced Flight Commander Charron. "We don't have any sign of enemy moving to intercept, but we will be hitting some turbulence. It's going to get hot and more than the usual bumpy, people. So strap down and enjoy the ride."

Benton found the flight commander's cheerful enjoinder just a little out of place.

He was already strapped in, but he checked the fastenings of his shock rig just the same. Both the seat and the rig were intended for IDL infantrymen. The Combine hardsuit he wore wasn't as big or as bulky as their battlesuits and it didn't have bumps in all the same places. The seat's cushioning was supposed to be conformable, but there hadn't been time to reset it. Despite Major Marsh's assurances, Benton wasn't entirely convinced that the disparity wasn't going to be important. He'd seen the results of harness failure in the training sims he had endured along with his recruits. Those graphic aids had incorporated cabin monitor records of actual disasters. Thus he really, truly had no desire to become educational material for the next generation as an example of such dangers.

Nearly all of the trained infantry he'd brought along were already engaged on the planet's surface. So for this rescue mission he'd had to bulk out what was left with mechanics, shipboard ratings, logistics specialists, and support personnel. If he hadn't prudently doubled the number of spares and replacements Major Marsh had requested for the expeditionary force, there would have been no way to equip them. It really was too bad they didn't have time to assemble any vehicles from the spare parts they carried.

His newly formed infantry task group wouldn't be a very effective force. Few of them had as much experience with battlesuits as he had, and he'd done no more than take the training sims. But desperate times demanded desperate measures, and it was clear that Task Group Seaborg needed all the help it could get. Benton hoped his makeshift relief force would be up to the job.

And why wouldn't they be? They were good people. Throughout history, hadn't determined people defied the odds and stood in desperate defenses? Hadn't those been the moments of heroism, the times when the true spirit of humankind shone forth, and very often the turning points of history?

And here he was, soon to be a part of history.

For what else could this be than the moment Alsion had promised him? The butterfly was emerging from its cocoon, entering the flow of the dynamic at a decision point and about to shape the future. Though he knew that any true Alsionite would scoff, he could not help but think that his moment of destiny was upon him.

The shuttle shuddered as it encountered the first vestiges of the atmosphere.

"Here we go," the flight commander announced cheerily.

Benton found himself wondering what his mother would think if she could see him now.

PACIFICA THEATER, PACIFICA
KILAWA ISLE, SOUTH OF PALISANDRA

Like the attack by the enemy *Hawks* when they'd landed, this ambush had caught Anders with his pants down. This time, however, he wasn't trapped.

Time to pull the pants back up.

Without orders from him, his command car team went into action. Milano put out a squawk for help and started launching extra drones. Gordon cut loose the wagon they were towing and got the command car into motion. That was good. It left Anders free to concentrate on coordinating the troops and getting a handle on just what had hit them. Before getting serious about that, Anders transferred a pair of drones to his driver's control and left him to find a really secure location to park while Anders directed the task group's response. Dodging enemy fire didn't make operating command commo any easier.

Things were bad, but not as bad as he'd feared.

The blowers of the 102nd were all free, having jettisoned their wagons at the first sign of trouble, and were laying down fire. Brizbin's support platforms were pumping smoke shells along the flanks of the column to provide a screen. His troopers had shredded their towing harness and were taking cover. Powell's medical people were working at the crushed blower, pulling out survivors. Some of the Combiners were helping them—it had been one of their vehicles—while most of the rest were going to ground. Some were firing wildly into the trees. One group led by Williams was rousting the civilians out of the transports, which were far too fat and tempting as targets.

The enemy wasn't sitting still. Remor machines scooted through the woods, shifting positions constantly and keeping up a steady fire. Their missiles roared through the smoke. The screening fog decreased their accuracy, but that didn't matter to the unfortunates who happened to be near where they hit. The Remor energy weapons were still reaping victims. Too many of them were powerful enough to punch through the dispersives in the smoke. Ravening beams cut swaths, oblivious to whether it was trees or humans dying in their paths. Their kinetic weapons were deadly where they had a clear line of sight, but Brizbin's smoke shells were starting to close down those places.

"More smoke," Anders told Brizbin, and sent him a map highlighting where coverage was thin. A higher density of dispersives would further weaken the beams.

"The damn trees are catching our shells," the artillery officer complained.

"Then blow them down and drop smoke as follow-on. I won't have people dying because some tree has too many branches."

"Will do."

Using his sensors, drones, and feeds from trooper helmets, Anders started to put together a picture of what they were facing. *Caymans*, mostly, but there were other machines out there as well. Some were combat models but most were smaller noncombat machines. One Anders recognized from personal experience on Grenwold. The computer called it a *Shepherd* and insisted it was not a combat machine. It might be intended to be some kind of working machine, but he knew too well that it could fight.

"Aurie, take a team here." Anders sent him the coordinates. "There are three *Caymans* on converging courses near there. Take them down."

"Will do."

And he too was as good as his word, ambushing the ambushers as they tried for a better angle to increase their slaughter.

Whatever the enemy was using to knock out his drones was still operating. He lost a dozen before he got a handle on how close he could get them to enemy positions. He probably shouldn't have lost more than eight, but he was distracted by keeping the task group's actions coordinated, a more important priority. But drone inventory was dropping too fast. They would be at a disadvantage in another encounter or ambush.

Worries about future disadvantages, he realized wryly, were a good thing. It meant that the situation had shifted enough that it no longer looked like their only fate was annihilation. They might get out of this mess. Though not soon. And not easily. They were still in the woods—literally—which wasn't the best of places for them.

He considered making a run for Palisandra. For whatever reason, enemy forces were practically nonexistent along that axis. Once out on the plain, Brizbin's artillery would be able to make short work of the small numbers of the enemy that they had engaged so far. Unfortunately, the enemy weaponry would also be more effective. It wouldn't be so bad for his hardshells, but the Combiner troopers would suffer, and the casualties among civilians would be unacceptable.

He needed a better idea.

For a start he sent Mossberg's Lancastrians to sweep up what they could of those light forces, to give them something close to a secure rear. Hoping his confidence in Mossberg's people was justified, he sent out several rally points in the zone and started trying to get the civilians moving in that direction. Without direct communications with them, he needed to do it through his troops. By preference he used the Combiners, keeping his 102nd troopers as a shield for them.

The deadly dance in the woods went on.

Motion unexpectedly registered on his peripheral screen. Since his 'suit wasn't warning him of enemy in proximity, he ignored it until something light impacted on his armor.

A woman's hand?

For a moment he was disoriented. Gordon had clearly found a safe spot and the blower was idling, but settled. Sue Merrick was standing before him, clearly distraught. She had shouted something at him.

But there was more shouting on the unit link. The enemy was making a push against the left flank where coverage was weakest. If they broke through . . .

He swiveled back to his boards.

Merrick fled from his awareness as he dealt with the threat.

26

PACIFICA THEATER, PACIFICA ORBIT
CMEFS *AUDITOR*

Stone stormed past the greeting party, still assembling outside the docking bay. He didn't know the exact details of *Auditor*'s layout, but he knew her general conformation. Somewhere ahead of him would be an accessway that would lead to the bridge.

Footfalls followed him, closing. Stone let the fellow come up alongside him. It was the same person who had been trying to straighten out the greeting detail. He wore a Combiner uniform, complete with rank insignia. As a part of the Pacifica fleet, he should have replaced the rank marking with his assigned League rank. Doubtless Colonel Mainwaring still considered the ship Combine territory.

Stone didn't know Combiner insignia well enough to recognize the rank, but this fellow's atttiude suggested that he was a junior officer. Stone observed the obvious terror at having failed to complete orders and equally obvious, painful uncertainty of trying to deal with an invading and errant hostile officer. Stone had been a junior officer in the distant past, and memories of that trying time raised a hint of sympathy. He glanced down for a name tag and found it: *Mikawa.*

"Mikawa," he said to the puffing Combiner at his side, babbling an incoherent combination of welcome and apology. "Did Colonel Mainwaring send you to intercept me?"

"Uh, no, sir."

"Really?"

Another black mark for Mainwaring.

Stone halted. Mikawa stumbled on for a couple of paces. As he turned, Stone indicated the passage at his left.

"This is the way to the bridge, isn't it?"

"Y-yes, sir," Mikawa stammered.

"Lead or follow, son."

"Yes, sir."

To his credit, Mikawa jumped to it, leading Stone directly to the bridge. There were no marines on station by the hatch.

The hole's getting deeper, Mainwaring.

Mikawa opened the hatch and Stone swept past him. His eyes surveyed *Auditor*'s bridge. He disregarded the inefficient layout. He disdained the overall sloppiness of the crew at their stations. Most of all, he ignored the totally unmilitary Alsionite seated in a priority position in a special couch near the empty commander's post.

Mainwaring was nowhere to be seen.

There was, however, a command-grade officer present. Stone was almost surprised.

"Lugard, isn't it? I will see Colonel Mainwaring right now."

"With respect, Commander, you'll not be doing that for some time yet."

"Explain yourself, mister."

Stone got what he asked for, and he didn't like it.

What in God's name does Mainwaring think he's doing? He has no business leading a landing party. Saint Michael, what is going on in that man's head?

"Does the man think he's the hero in some kind of entertainment sim?"

He apparently spoke aloud, for Lugard responded. "I couldn't be saying, Commander."

"Get him on the link."

"Again, with respect, you'll not be doing that either for some time. We be monitoring increasing atmospheric scatterers across the hemisphere, and the colonel's flight be just passed into a sheathed zone. We be not even able to tell him you be here."

Wonderful.

"I certainly am here," Stone stated, sitting himself down in the command couch.

Lugard's expression pursed. He presumably considered the seat to be his just now. Perhaps he harbored hopes that his commander would not return from his ill-considered adventure and the chair would truly become his. Right now, it was all irrelevant.

"Right now, Mister Lugard, since I am here, you will give me a full status report on this vessel. You will also get me a report on each and every vessel in this command. I want to know what kind of mess Mainwaring left up here so he could go haring off down there to make what is most likely to be a bigger mess. And while you're doing that, I want a secure link to *Constantine*."

He needed to talk to Chip Hollister, not just for the necessary military reasons, but to hear a sane voice.

PACIFICA THEATER, PACIFICA
KILAWA ISLE, SOUTH OF PALISANDRA

When they lost the link with *Auditor* just after entering the atmosphere, Benton queried the flight commander about the situation. He'd expected to hear that it was just a normal part of the entry, but the pilot had told him otherwise. The enemy, it seemed, had released new swarms of their disruptive organisms, multiplying the effectiveness of their Atmospheric Scattering Sheath. Even had Benton not been a student of alinear sociodynamics, he wouldn't have thought it a coincidence.

It made sense, really. The Remor were attacking Task Group Seaborg and would wish to hide that as much as possible from Seaborg's allies. Did the enemy know that Seaborg had gotten out a distress call? Did they know that, as the horrendous jostling he was receiving proved, help was on the way? And if they did, what might they do about it?

The flight commander was full of bravado, assuring Benton that they'd reach the ground safely. Benton suspected that the man was working from incomplete data. Perhaps perilously incomplete. None of Benton's experts had predicted a resurgence in the ASS. Could the flight commander, experienced in combat operations though he might be, reliably predict the Remor response to their incursion?

Benton had neither the requisite background nor the immediate data to second-guess the man. He could only hold on and hope. He could also worry, which he did a bit—perhaps more than a bit.

To distract himself he reviewed the plan that he and Major Marsh had concocted. Already it had been compromised, or would be if the ASS prevented them from coordinating with Seaborg. Was the plan robust enough to survive? Perhaps.

What are you making of this new wrinkle in the flow, Sister Coppelstowe? Are you seeing what I'm seeing?

Fortune, it was said, favored the bold, but he knew better. Fortune was nothing more than circumstantial happenstance coupled with assertive agency.

Timing, it was also said, is everything, and that he knew to be a crude but correct expression of a truth. Assertion under the wrong circumstances was doomed to failure at best, disaster at worst, and the difference lay in the individual's perception of the dynamic.

Was he perceiving the true flow? Alsion would know, though he doubted that the enigmatic master would either confirm or deny Benton's certainty. Coppelstowe, for all her protestations of incomplete understanding, would also probably know. She at least might tell him he was on the right track. But neither was available. In fact, there was no one with whom he could consult who had even his limited exposure to alinear sociodynamics.

He linked to the flight commander. "My good man, I believe it is time for us to adapt."

"It's getting bad out there," Aurie Fiske reported. The left arm of his battlesuit was frozen under a lumpy mass of expanded foam, the result of a malfunctioning medical system that had been trying to immobilize his injured arm. Fiske had fought on, as the burn marks on the foam attested. The injury was not preventing him from field-stripping and cleaning his Mark 22 IEW.

"Hand me the lube," Anders requested, needing it for his own weapon, "and tell me something I don't know."

Fiske did, filling him in on details of the sergeant's last engagement with the Remor forces steadily constricting their defensive perimeter. There were a lot of details Anders had missed with his few remaining drones.

"We must have taken down a dozen *Caymans* since this mess started. Four in the last scrap alone," Fiske concluded.

"Sixteen all told," Anders corrected. "You've done well, Aurie. Everyone has, even the Combiners."

The bloody nose that Fiske had just given the enemy had taken the pressure off for the moment, but it wasn't enough. The two surviving *Caymans* had pulled back and joined four more before beginning a circle that would take them around to join another four fighting machines lurking on the task group's left flank. Anders had seen that much before the enemy had swatted his spying drone from the sky. The Remor would renew the assault soon and, with both of the support platforms knocked out, there wasn't enough heavy firepower to stop them. One or more of the enemy fighting machines was going to break through what was left of the infantry screen and get to the civilians.

Fiske seemed to be having the same pessimistic thoughts. "We're going to lose this one, aren't we?" he whispered as he finished reassembling his weapon.

"They just keep coming, Aurie. And there's only so many of us."

Fiske gave a resigned sigh and blew an invisible speck of dirt from his Mark 22. "We few, we happy few."

There was more to be said, but Anders just couldn't think of the words. Milano shattered the moment with a shout from the command car.

"Hey, boss! We got incoming from orbit."

"Put it on the main."

Anders sprinted to the car. Fleet commo had been down since Milano had squawked his call for help. Could this be the answer? He vaulted the coaming and his boots slammed the deck as Milano finished the linkage transfer to the main console.

A flight of assault shuttles was coming down. At least the computer thought they were assault shuttles. Eighty-five percent prob. It was good enough for Anders. Even with the Remor's commo busters going full blast, he doubted the comp couldn't tell a xeno ship from a human one.

There was still no fleet commo and everything from the incoming ships was garbled. Anders needed to know what was going on. He prodded the computer and it refined its identification, MilForce model IIC-10L20. It was the model that Fleet had seconded to the Combiner ships with League infantry aboard.

Their track, adjusted for IDL evasion doctrine, put them down somewhere in a ten-kilometer area roughly centered on the original ambush site. That could put them down right on top of the rally point. They could just as readily come down on top of the enemy's heaviest concentration. Wherever they came down, they were going to be part of this fight.

Of course, the enemy was probably making the same calculations. Fiske, perched on the coaming, said as much.

"Infantry load-out," he suggested.

Anders's evaluation of the shuttles' flight profile was the same. They were laden, though not heavily. Not vehicles. Not freight. It probably was infantry, but from where? The fleet wasn't carrying any reserves of 'pounders.

Anders checked on the enemy positions. The *Caymans* hadn't joined up yet. There might be time.

"Aurie, take every other trooper from the right flank and form a mission squad."

"Reserves?"

"Distraction. We need to give those guys a chance to get down."

Fiske nodded. "Hit the xenos before they hit us and keep them looking the wrong way."

"Exactly."

"And if they've got something to hit us on the left while we're shifting to the right?"

"We're screwed."

"No change there."

Anders outlined his thoughts for hitting the *Caymans* before they consolidated. Fiske listened. He had some suggestions. Fiske had been on the ground out there, Anders hadn't. He modified the plan to reflect Fiske's insights.

"It'll cost," Fiske said.

"I know. Try to keep the bill low."

"Will do."

"And, Aurie, keep your head down."

"Always do," Fiske lied.

Anders set drones prowling to scope out good positions and routes for Fiske's people. He kept an eye on the *Caymans,* afraid they'd shift unexpectedly and negate his plan. For once the enemy cooperated. The fighting machines continued on track but slowly. Anders directed Fiske to take advantage of them.

The violence erupted while the uncommunicative shuttles were still five minutes out. Almost immediately Anders's linkage with the mission squad broke up. For some reason Anders still had linkage with his drones, though he was unable to use them as a relay link to reach Fiske. He suspected that meant that Fiske wasn't receiving anything from them. Fiske would be practically blind. Anders vectored as many of his drones as he dared into close proximity. They went with orders to slave to Fiske's command. Anders hoped they'd help, prayed that Fiske would be able to use them. He was gratified to see that all but one sent a command shift notice to his boards before he lost linkage with them. The other one got flashed by the Remor.

He had kept one for himself and put it in distant orbit of the action. Its sky monitor caught the flash of shuttles streaking overhead. He queried the computer on trajectory and saw that the landing zone was a couple of hundred meters outside the immediate zone of the firefight. Very close.

Much closer than Anders would have wanted to come down. He was afraid that the Remor would rush the site, trying to hit the debarking infantry at their most vulnerable.

But Fiske must have caught the implications of the landing position too. His troopers increased the pressure on the enemy, working to give them too much trouble to risk breaking off. It worked too well. The second group of *Caymans* joined the fray. The Remor concentrated a savage weight of fire on Fiske's positions.

Fiske began a withdrawal.

The Remor had forced him back far enough that Mossberg's platoon in the main right flank line started adding supporting fire. Anders did what he could to direct Mossberg in her efforts. It wasn't enough. The defensive line started to crack.

Saint Michael, this is a good time for a miracle.

Apparently Saint Michael agreed.

A timely salvo of infantry missiles heralded the arrival of a howling, wildly firing horde of men and women in Combine-style battlesuits. A *Cayman* exploded. Already dissolving, its debris caught the foremost ranks of the newcomers. Six went down, dead or dying. Anders's drone didn't pick up their screams amid the battle noise, but he could imagine them. He'd heard those caught by Remor dissolution fragments before.

Anders could tell that, despite their battlesuits, these were not trained groundpounders. But there were quite a few of them, and a surprising number of them were actually firing their weapons in the direction of the enemy.

In moments the momentum shifted. Hit from two sides, the Remor began to withdraw. Sometimes weight of fire could compensate for lack of training. This appeared to be one of those times. Leaving the rapidly dissolving wrecks of their fallen comrades behind, the last two *Caymans* fled the field.

Beeps from the console announced the return of Anders's drones to his control. Fiske had released them. Anders sent them scouting to be sure that the enemy had disengaged. The miracle was continuing to unfold. All hostiles he could spot were in retreat.

Fiske and his survivors led the newcomers into the rally point. Anders recognized the hardsuited officer at Fiske's side. It was easy, the man had doffed his helmet like a true goff. Colonel Mainwaring.

He walked straight to Anders and stuck out his hand. Anders saluted. Mainwaring, obviously recollecting himself, did so too, then said, "Captain Seaborg, I'm glad to see you made it through."

"Thank you, Colonel. You made a timely appearance, but I have to ask what you're doing here."

"Rescuing you, of course." Mainwaring was grinning wide enough to split his skull. "You called for a rescue, yes? We were the nearest, so we took up the task. My expeditionary force didn't come all the way out here to stand around on our hands, and Commander Stone didn't seem to have anything better for us to do."

Sue was a little surprised at the deference the League soldiers showed to the newly arrived Colonel Mainwaring. He did not have the same soldierly air as the Eridani troopers, and somehow watching Commander Seaborg act subordinate to the man just seemed wrong.

Mainwaring doffed his armor as soon as Seaborg confirmed that all known Remor forces had withdrawn from the area. His uniform carried the same sort of insignia as Seaborg's, allowing for a difference in rank, but his accent made him out to be from the Pan-Stellar Combine like Williams and the bulk of the League soldiers. Hadn't someone said that the Combine wasn't a member of the League? Why would one of their officers be in charge of League soldiers?

There was an awful lot about militaries that Sue didn't know. She had neither need nor desire before the aliens came. Those halcyon days were long gone. And, she feared, unlikely to come again anytime soon.

In a scene that incongruously reminded Sue of a politician

working a crowd, Mainwaring was passing among the Palisandrans. The colonel was smiling at everyone, asking questions and looking concerned at the appropriate times, and passing out assurances like candy. People seemed to be cheered by him. Commander Seaborg, still armored although he did have his visor open, followed in the colonel's wake.

As the foreign military men approached her group, Sue didn't wait for Mainwaring's cordial routine to start rolling. She tendered an immediate question of her own.

"Will they be back? The aliens."

He looked at her as if surprised by her temerity. Seaborg answered for him. "Probably."

She nodded, appreciative of his blunt honesty. "There will be more of them next time."

"Most likely," he agreed.

In his eyes she could see his bleak evaluation of their chances, even with the addition of Mainwaring's troops. "Then we need to get everyone out of here now, while we can."

"That, my good woman, was the plan," said Mainwaring. "We'll be flying you over to Colonel Cope's bailiwick. They've done quite a good job in securing the western reaches of Kilawa. I'm sure there will be plenty of room there. Doctors too. I understand the western beaches were quite the vacation spot."

"No one here is expecting a vacation, Colonel," Sue told him. She didn't think it suitable to say that all they wanted was to get through it alive.

"Nevertheless. Our destination is western Kilawa near, oh, what was the name of the place? Kenshan City. Yes, that was it."

"Is Kenshan City the colonel's intended destination?" asked Seaborg.

Mainwaring nodded. "Why not? When we departed *Auditor* everything seemed fine. Has the situation changed?"

"Colonel, from the snatches of commo we've been getting, it looks like things are getting hot for the rest of our forces on-planet. Colonel Cope's troops are engaged with the enemy in several places, and Kenshan City was mentioned. I don't think it would be prudent to try to shift the civilians there. It might not be prudent to shift them anywhere on the surface just now."

"Hmmm." Mainwaring looked thoughtful. "You really think so? Ought we to take these people up to my ships? You know, Flight Commander Charron made the same suggestion earlier. Of course, his argument was something about optimal use of his assault shuttles. A lot of chatter about unstable intra-atmospheric flight profiles and threat vulnerabilities. I'd assumed he was just being a—what is it you groundpounders call them?—ah, yes, a vaccuum-head. Yearning for the great cold black—"

"Colonel," Seaborg interrupted.

"Eh? Rambling, was I? I must confess I am a bit rattled by all the excitement. Or by something, anyway." He winked and leaned confidentially closer to Sue. "You might not be so keen to cross the atmosphere with Flight Commander Charron if you had done it as I have. Quite the thrill ride, I must say. Still, if there's really trouble at Kenshan City, we'd best not drop ourselves into the middle of it, eh? Don't want to go from the frying pan to the burner, do we, now? I'll wager old Charron has already got a return flight plan readied on his ship's computer. Shall we put it to use, then? Will that suit you, Captain Seaborg?"

"Affirmative."

Mainwaring turned back to Sue. "And what about you, my dear?"

"I hope so."

"Quite. Soon everything will be, well, right as summer waves, as you Pacificans say. Good news, what?"

As far as Sue knew the aphorism had never been popular outside the Kilawan surfing culture, and only on Kessawanno Islet at that. She mumbled something positive, but Mainwaring didn't seem to care, he was already on his way to another group to bring them his "good news."

Seaborg started to follow him. Sue began to reach out a hand to restrain him, but found she couldn't bring herself to actually touch him. She spoke instead.

"Commander Seaborg?"

"It's Captain Seaborg while the colonel is here, ma'am. He's now the commander hereabouts."

"Odd thing, to be shifting ranks around."

"Not to me, ma'am. Just standard military protocol."

"You didn't address Colonel Mainwaring as commander."

He looked at her, his expression blank. She'd noticed that this cold and stony look took over his face when he was evaluating something. "My mistake, ma'am. You're very perceptive for a civilian."

"Thank you, I think. Is this shifting commander thing a League practice or just an Eridani thing? I'm guessing it's not standard for the Combine."

"It's Eridani practice, ma'am. MilForce adopted it. But I don't think you stopped me for a lesson in military protocol," he said wryly. His chilly professionalism had gone back to wherever it had come from and a warm smile had taken its place. "Was there something you needed?"

"A question, Com—Captain."

"I'll answer if I can, ma'am."

She almost told him to forget it. She'd spent years now hiding her fears, and expressing them didn't come easy. But there was seductive optimism in him that called to her and made her want his reassurance. Something about him made her feel that she could allow herself to be vulnerable around him.

Or was she just kidding herself and getting swept up in that whole knight-errant thing? She knew better than that, didn't she?

It's not about you, she told herself. *You need to know for the people who depend on you. That's why you have to ask.*

Right. Sure it is, another voice said.

She shushed that sardonic voice and, armoring herself in conviction and responsibility, put her question.

"Will we be safer up there? Aren't you still fighting the aliens in space?"

"We are still engaged with enemy, ma'am." Again he showed no hesitancy in giving the truth even when it had to be painfully obvious that it wasn't the answer she wanted to hear. "But local space is clear of threatening forces. At least it was when I last had access to fleet commo. Commander Stone won't let anything through."

"Commander Stone? He outranks Colonel Mainwaring?"

"Definitely, ma'am. He's the theater commander. He outranks everyone in-system."

"You say he'll protect us."

"If it's humanly possible, Commander Stone will do it."

"I think Colonel Mainwaring wouldn't have added that caveat about being humanly possible."

He quickly glanced away in Mainwaring's direction, then said softly with a hint of shared conspiracy, "Between you and me, ma'am, I think you're right."

She felt something she vaguely recognized as amusement. It had been so long that she was not sure she identified it correctly, but the odd sensation emboldened her.

"One more thing, Captain?"

"Yes, ma'am?"

"Could you stop calling me 'ma'am'? It makes me feel matronly."

"I'm sorry if I offended. You've done as good a job holding your people together as any Eridani would have. That deserves respect."

As good a job as any Eridani? From him, that was a strong compliment. And the look in his eyes was . . . what, exactly?

The waters were getting strange and deep.

"I've got to get my people ready," she told him, and hurried off to lose herself in that work.

Part 3

Constrictive Confluence

27

Stone watched the return of the assault shuttles carrying the remains of Task Group Seaborg, refugees from the planet, and Mainwaring's unauthorized, ill-advised, but fortunately for everyone successful rescue force. With fine precision, he gauged his timing and swiveled the command couch to face the newly arrived Mainwaring as the Combiner entered the bridge.

Mainwaring didn't look the least surprised to find Stone sitting on his bridge, in his chair. Doubtless someone had informed him. It might have been the Alsionite Coppelstowe, who stood in her customary place behind Mainwaring's left shoulder. It might have been Mikawa, being a better guide to his own officer than he had been to Stone. It could have been any one of the crew trying to be loyal to their commander.

"Loyalty is an admirable trait, Mainwaring. I speak of true loyalty, not fear of retribution or blind allegiance to authority or even the motivated self-interest that is often mistaken for it. True loyalty requires merit to inspire it. Sometimes, however, loyalty is given where it is not deserved. One can hardly fault those who give such loyalty, save perhaps for their naïveté, but those who accept and squander it? Those must be dealt with. Wouldn't you agree, Mainwaring?"

From the look on Mainwaring's face, the point was obviously escaping him.

"I found an empty chair when I came aboard," Stone

stated to clarify. "I don't recall approving any leaves of absence."

"What are you—" Mainwaring interrupted himself to master his misplaced indignation. "I did not neglect my responsibilities. I left Master Lugard in command."

"So he told me. I expect that he will stay in command unless I hear something to convince me otherwise."

What he heard, however, was the ship's klaxon sounding general quarters, then Chip Hollister's voice on the secure link to *Constantine*.

"Commander, enemy group alpha has emerged from behind the moons. They're ramping steep acceleration toward the planet. I have elements moving to engage, but we are badly positioned to intercept. I don't think we can stop them all. Plot updates on feed."

Stone acknowledged as he scanned the feed. It was group alpha all right. Both *Garpikes* and their twelve interface strikers were all there, boosting hard for the planet. He hadn't anticipated their moving at this stage and fleet positioning was indeed poor.

Trust the Remor to pick a bad time to demonstrate their unpredictability.

"*Auditor* doesn't have the facilities for me to run things, Chip, so this one is up to you. I'll do what I can here with the orbital squadron."

"Affirmative. You can count on us, Commander. Shall I send a ship in for you after we see this batch off?"

"Negative. With all this local activity, I don't think the other Remor groups will be sitting idle. Letting them consolidate could cost us everything. Don't miss a chance to pick off the serious threats to deal with this diversion by alpha group."

Assuming that alpha group's movement was a diversion. Even with the Remor tendency to erratic and odd behavior, it was reasonable. Alpha group didn't have the force to deal with Stone's orbital squadron and the elements of the main fleet that were moving into launch position. Having already limited the distraction value of the enemy maneuver, Stone set about seeing that the Remor paid a high price. He alerted the orbital squadron and set its gunners to computing solutions at maximum range.

Mainwaring tried to interrupt, wanting to return to what he inanely referred to as their "conversation." Stone shut him down.

"I've no time to waste just now. You can keep quiet and remain at liberty, or you can be locked down in your cabin. Either way, you will not cause me any more concern for the duration of this situation. Is that clear?"

Glaring defiantly, Mainwaring saluted.

Stone put the troublesome Combiner from his mind and returned to studying the tactical situation. With each update, his sense of unease grew. Something wasn't right.

Chip was sending occasional updates on the strategic situation. The other Remor groups were indeed moving on their predicted paths toward consolidation. There was no apparent shift in either their rendezvous point or the speed at which they were approaching it. Their maneuvers should have altered somehow in conjunction with the diversionary action on alpha's part. Had they realized that their distraction wasn't having the desired effect and abandoned whatever plan they had begun?

If they had, wouldn't alpha group then have altered its flight path? Why were they pressing on?

Then Stone saw something else that didn't make sense. Patrollers *Gawaine* and *Von Richtofen*, the elements Chip had sent to deal with alpha, had moved within the missile envelope of the *Garpikes*, but the Remor had not opened fire. They were letting the human ships get close enough to fire their own missiles without taking any preemptive actions.

There! *Gawaine* and *Von Richtofen* launched. The Remor did not reply, but bore on. The outer edges of their engagement envelopes would soon reach *Cerulean Cygnet*, the nearest element of the orbital squadron.

"Why be they not evading?" Lugard asked.

"What?"

"The Remor ships. They be not taking any evasive maneuvers."

It was true.

Remor could sometimes be very persistent, one might say single-minded. Could they be so eager to engage the orbital squadron that they were willing to take hits from the patrollers rather than accept the delay that evasion would entail?

Two of the enemy interface strikers went down to the patrollers' missiles. The enemy ships pressed on. *Cerulean Cygnet* fell into their attack zone and still they refrained from launching.

More missiles leaped from the League ships. *Cygnet* launched shortly thereafter. Neither provoked a response from the Remor. Even when those birds struck home, the Remor didn't lash out at their attackers.

Madness.

Or some plan that made sense to an alien mind.

In the holotank, the extension of the flight paths of the Remor ships had remained steady. Stone had stopped paying attention when they'd forgone evasive maneuvers, focusing on the mystery of their intentions. He had been so intent on dealing with the enemy before they reached the heart of the orbital squadron that he had missed something. The Remor formation's path remained where it had been from the beginning. They were on an intercept path with *Auditor*.

Someone else with lesser restraint noticed as well, blurting out, "Ohmigod, they're coming for us!"

Quite possibly. But why? The ill-disciplined bridge crew began babbling the same question.

Coppelstowe had a theory for them, addressing it to him. "Commander Stone, it is conceivable the Remor have been monitoring the amount of communications traffic going in and out of *Auditor*. They may have used the anomalous levels to deduce that you are aboard."

"Decapitation strikes are not Remor style," he informed her.

"They are enigmatic and unpredictable. Perhaps this is a change in style."

Stone had been fighting Remor for over a decade. Yes, they were enigmatic, but their unpredictability lay more in strategic matters than tactical. Most people, even many military commanders, misunderstood that salient fact.

"What if the attack be not an attack?" asked Lugard, joining in as if they were all part of some debating society.

Stone was more than willing to accept speculation from trained officers, but these Combiners were of dubious quality. Still, Lugard was an experienced spacer. "Elaborate."

"What if they be accelerating to be using the planet's gravity well as a slingshot to hustle themselves out to rejoin their fleet?" Lugard threw up a plot to make his point.

Stone had already dismissed that possibility. "Militarily untenable. They'll take too many losses on such a run to preserve squadron integrity."

But Lugard's question stuck in his mind. What if the attack *was* only incidental? He looked again at Lugard's plot and noted that the Remor would have to make a course correction to follow it.

He queried the computer to predict the path without that course correction. Their unmodified course wouldn't skip them off the atmosphere and send them around the planet. It would take them past *Auditor* and straight down into the atmosphere.

Suicidal.

Then Stone perceived the terminus of that suicidal path. Those ships would be coming down on the heads of Colonel Cope's largest concentration of ground forces on Kilawa Isle. The plunging ships wouldn't be moving at planet-busting speeds, but their impact would still be equivalent to massive nuclear strikes. This Remor squadron *was* being suicidal. They were kamikazes.

Sue heard the footfalls outside the cabin door. They were a man's, steady and measured and not at all like the scurrying, frenzied ones immediately following the warning alarm. Her first thought was that she had made a mistake in asking Seaborg to override the door controls to keep it from seal-ing. But then she never would have heard this set slow down and stop outside the door.

Whoever he was out there, he was hesitating. Looking at a door slightly ajar? Wouldn't an honest man, seeing what looked like a violation of ship's procedures, call out?

She remembered the madness that had followed the last alarms on Pacifica. Seaborg had told her that her concerns about feeling locked up had been foolish. Had they really? Just now, a locked door might be a very good thing.

There weren't many places to hide in the small cabin.

The door shifted. Light from the corridor stabbed a blade of red-tinged emergency light into the darkened space. Involuntarily she cringed and tugged her exposed feet back into the shadows.

From her position tucked under the cabin's table she could only see boots as the door slid open. The man said nothing as he stepped into the cabin. Silhouetted against the light, he was a dark, muscular shadow as he hunched down at the table edge.

"Ms. Merrick?"

It was Seaborg.

She jerked away when he reached for her. Not out of fear, but simple ingrained reaction. He drew his hand back, but continued to speak to her, more gently now.

"Please, Ms. Merrick, it's really important that you get out from under there and get into the couch. The ship will be maneuvering soon. That's going to be bad enough. But we might take damage and the centrifuge might fail. Bad things happen when centrifuges fail, and hiding under a table won't be good enough."

"You're up," she snapped, anger at herself slipping into her words.

"I shouldn't be," he said softly. "And I won't be for long. I came to make sure you were squared away. I'll need to secure the door too."

"Go ahead."

He blinked, surprised, but only for a moment. "Very well. But first you need to get into the couch and get the safety restraints rigged. It's just to keep you from getting hurt, that's all. Let me show you how easy it is to operate the quick release."

She edged to the corner of the table and watched as he did.

Safety restraints, she repeated to herself. *Emphasis on the* safety, *you silly girl. You want to be safe, don't you?*

She did.

She levered herself up off the floor. He gave her a smile, a warm, encouraging smile. To her relief, she could find no hint of condescension or pity in it.

So why do you care?

Why, indeed.

He stood to one side as she approached the couch, letting her take her time getting settled. His instructions guided her to arrange the harness properly. Only when she had finished did he step forward and, with an apology, check the tension in the system.

"Where are you going to be?" she asked.

"I'll be in one of the training sim tanks. All the regular couches are occupied."

"That's not as safe, is it?"

"Not as, but it will serve. Don't worry."

"All right," she agreed, and realized that she was lying.

Anders had left his cabin, where he had installed Sue Merrick, as the last checkpoint on his rounds. He'd expected to find her all snugged down and ready to argue with him about securing the door. Finding her hiding under the table had been a surprise. Despite the competence she normally displayed, she had episodes of extreme vulnerability, brought on most likely by whatever she had suffered since the Remor took her planet. He was sure she had the inner strength to get better, with time and care. He hoped she would get them.

His hope, he realized, was something more than professional concern for a charge. He truly admired the Sue Merrick who, with nearly Eridani steadfastness, had managed to keep a survivor band together through the rigors of the Remor invasion and the trials that had followed.

He tried to give her as much of the moment as possible, working to be patient with her weakness. It wasn't easy, but he coaxed her out from her hiding place and got her snugged in.

As safe as he could make her.

"All right," she told him when he urged her not to worry.

As he turned to go, the collision alarms began to sound.

They were out of time. No time to secure the door. No time for him to reach safety restraints. He had arranged for Sue Merrick to have his cabin as a courtesy and a thank-you. Unlike duty stations, the cabin had no emergency restraints, just the one couch. He hoped he wouldn't be paying too high a price for his chivalry.

He crammed himself into Sue Merrick's abandoned hiding place and wrapped his arms around the stanchions. He filled it far more full than she had and it offered him a certain amount of bracing. Still, it was a truly terrible substitute for a proper safety harness.

Auditor shuddered.

Not too bad.

Then she shook like a dog after a dowsing.

Something hard hit the side of Anders's head and he lost interest in the struggle.

28

When the Remor ships finally opened fire, *Auditor* alone was their target. It was not as bad as it could have been. Sustained fire from the pursuing League patrollers and *Auditor*'s attendant ships had taken a toll. By the time *Auditor* came within the enemy's range, both *Garpikes* were balls of vapor and debris expanding in space. Only one of the *Typhoons* survived among the oncoming interface strikers.

With the aid of her escorts, *Auditor* managed to knock down all but one of the first enemy missile salvos. That one bird, of course, had struck home. *Auditor* took the hit better than her crew did. The internal commo channels were deluged with dangerous clogging chatter that threatened the proper fighting of the ship. Stone wasted precious time restoring order.

The enemy ships were moving fast now, so fast that *Auditor* was able to launch before the interface strikers got off a second salvo. *Achilles, Cerulean Cygnet,* and *Buena Vista* also had birds in space. It wasn't a precise salvo, but it did mean that Remor defenses would be dealing with a lot of incoming. Interface strikers didn't have anything like the defenses of deep space ships such as the *Garpikes*.

Von Richtofen, the smallest and fastest patroller in the fleet, was hard on their tails as well. Unfortunately, that meant all her missiles were playing catch-up, but every bit of fire was welcome. It was unfortunate that *Gawaine,* the patroller's companion, had been coming in on a different vector and was now out of engagement range and moving too fast to return while it mattered.

Only four hostiles made it through their attack, but those ships launched missiles of their own.

Auditor shook from the nearby concussions as the enemy missiles were stopped at the last possible moments by anti-missiles and defensive beam fire. Stone thanked Saint Michael that the defensive gunners had known and done their job.

Even without actual impacts, *Auditor* was suffering from the enemy attack. Stone could hear the crashes of unsecured equipment and bodies. The ship was hurt more than it ought to have been, because the Combiner crew was so inexperienced in battle.

His squadron's salvo had also had unfortunate consequences. One of *Auditor*'s missiles, spoofed by the Remor, had gone wild and, ignoring all destruct codes, had piled into *Cerulean Cygnet*. *Cygnet* was now limping out of the engagement zone, having taken the missile amidships. Mainwaring had called her a fighting transport, but she was no true warship, just a converted frontier hauler. She had never been meant to survive a hit from a high-yield missile. That she had was a tribute to the work done by the Combine engineers who had retrofitted her.

Too bad those engineers had not done a comparably good job on the missiles they had provided for the Combine ships. *Cygnet* should never have been threatened by a friendly missile.

Cerulean Cygnet and her problems passed out of Stone's consciousness. The battle was all that mattered.

The closing range left only *Auditor* and two others of the orbital squadron able to engage. Fortunately they were good ships. One was *Achilles*, a refitted FSN hull and a true, if obsolete, warship. The other was *Jack Aubrey*, an IDL Captain-class patroller attached to the squadron.

All three ships pumped fire into the oncoming enemy, taking out the last *Typhoon*.

Lugard's gloomy voice undercut the bridge crew's cheers.

"Commander Stone," he said, "we be needing to move the ship."

Stone looked to see what had prompted Lugard's suggestion. Save for the reduction in numbers, nothing appeared changed on the plot. The track predicted for the surviving Remor ships still intersected with *Auditor*'s position, the uncertainty gone now. That track still continued down to Pacifica, right onto Colonel Cope's command area. The mass of even one interface striker, moving at the speed they had achieved by eschewing any defensive maneuvers, would be sufficient to vaporize the two thousand ground troops within the blast radius.

Even with the recovered troops of Seaborg's task group and the civilians brought aboard with them, *Auditor* was carrying something under a thousand.

It was a simple, two-for-one equation.

"Maintain fire," he ordered.

Missiles were next to useless now. The interface strikers were too close for *Auditor*'s birds to conduct proper maneuvers, but the missiles' presence created a zone akin to a minefield. And there remained a chance that *Auditor*'s concentrated beam fire would take out the hostiles.

One more enemy died.

The Remor craft continued closing. Their beams lanced out, seeking and finding *Auditor*. Stone closed his mind to the damage.

"*Jack Aubrey, Achilles,* concentrate fire on hostiles approaching *Auditor*. All other ships maintain targets."

"We can't," the *Achilles'* commander objected. "You're too close!"

"Use your best solutions, *Achilles*. We need your fire."

Auditor was being flayed.

"Maintain fire," Stone reiterated.

"You be killing us all!" Lugard shouted. "We must be moving the ship!"

"We will maintain position and continue firing."

Achilles was making the mistake of restricting herself to "safe" shots. Stone began to wonder if it would make any difference had she been firing full out. The last remaining Remor seemed impervious to everything thrown at them.

Closer.

The outrider of the Remor ships began to break up, savaged by fire from *Achilles* and *Jack Aubrey*. The energies of its overloaded drive broke free and devoured it in an incandescent ball of expanding plasma.

But the last two came on.

Closer.

"My God, man, they'll ram us!" Mainwaring screamed, stating the obvious. "Lugard, I order you to get us out of their way."

"Captain Lugard, you will ignore that illegal order," Stone snapped. "Colonel Mainwaring, you will refrain from giving orders on my bridge."

"Your bri—" Mainwaring sputtered. "Master Lugard, you will move this ship and you will move it now!"

"It be too late," pronounced Lugard. "The drive's gone."

Stone watched the screens as beam after beam faltered. *Auditor* had run out of strength.

The last two interface strikers were visible without magnification. One of them was without a drive now too, but it still moved ballistically on its deadly course. Its companion was drawing away from it, closer to *Auditor* with each breath.

Stone saw that he had lost the gamble. The leading striker would take out *Auditor* and clear the way for its crippled companion. It looked like debris and relative positioning would likely shield that last Remor for what little of its course still lay within range of either *Achilles* or *Jack Aubrey*. The enemy had won. They would get his ship. Only luck or a miracle could save the ground troops.

With nothing else to do, he prayed for that miracle.

Screens overloaded with a light like a star being born. Intense electromagnetic radiation pulsed through *Auditor*, frying even hardened systems. Scanners failed, but not before Stone saw that the nearest Remor ship had come apart in what must have been a catastrophic drive failure. A moment's glimpse was enough for his professional eye to gauge that the fragments of the dead craft were too small to survive reentry. It was also long enough for him to know that those same fragments were still big enough to threaten anything in space that got in their way.

Auditor was still in their way.

Could she survive them? Would there be enough of *Auditor* left to destroy or deflect the last Remor?

They had done all that mortals could do. Their fate was in God's hands.

Auditor rocked under multiple impacts. Something smashed its way through the bridge bulkhead in a cloud of fragments that blasted across the compartment like shrapnel. Stone went down into bone-searing darkness, still wondering if his prayers were being answered.

29

PACIFICA THEATER, PACIFICA ORBIT
CMEFS *AUDITOR*

Anders didn't remember lying down, but there was no doubt he had. He was supine on the deck. How?

Hadn't the collision alarm sounded?

Reclining on the deck, unsecured, was not a good place to be.

He had not intended to be in such a position. The ship had been hit; he remembered feeling it. He'd been hit too, and knocked out, obviously.

Feeling was coming back into his limbs. Other sensations were returning as well. Pain, for one, but pain was only a signifier. In this case, the signal proclaimed a battered and bruised body, nothing worse. He felt something else as well: a gentle hand on his head.

Time to open his eyes.

Sue Merrick was kneeling by his side, frowning with concern. As he stirred, she spoke. "Can you hear me? Are you all right?"

"Survived worse." Stupidly stating the obvious, he added, "It's dark."

"The power's gone," Sue told him.

"Not entirely. We still have gravity, so there's power somewhere." Which meant *Auditor* wasn't dead, not completely.

Fumbling in the dark, he got to his feet. She helped, her aversion to touching apparently held in check when she initiated the contact.

He glanced around, trying to reorient himself. His Eridani eyes were better than hers, but even he didn't have enough light to see by. His hand found the hatchway frame. The hatch was stuck, partially closed. The corridor was as dark as his cabin.

By feel he located his cabin's commo panel. When he slid back the collision cover, the faint glow of its emergency light brought welcome illumination. He tried the unit linkage and got no response. He tried a direct link to the bridge with no better result.

Not good.

Outside in the corridor they could hear people stumbling about in the darkness. Not all of them were quiet about it. There was some panicky shouting about abandoning the ship.

"Maybe we should get to a lifeboat," Sue suggested with a hint of that same panic in her voice.

"This is no inner-systems liner. There won't be enough life pods for everyone." He didn't think he needed to add, *assuming everyone survived.*

"What about using the assault shuttles?"

"A possibility," he admitted. He rummaged through his kit until he found a hand light, gave it to her. "Let's see if we can find Flight Commander Charron and get him working on it."

She flicked on the lamp. "Not much, is it?"

He showed her how to dial a beam more suitable for her eyes.

"Better. Let's get going."

The hatch had lodged partially closed, but Sue slipped through the opening. Anders needed to force the door back to get clearance. By the time he was through, a half dozen survivors, all Pacificans, had gathered to the light like moths. There were lots of questions. Anders told them to head for the launch bay.

"Shouldn't we be trying to fix the ship instead of abandoning it?" one of them asked.

"Fixing the ship is a job for the ship's crew. We need to be ready if they can't do it."

"We can't launch without power," wailed one. "We need the power back!"

"It won't come back without somebody fixing it," Anders told her. "So unless someone among you is secretly a systems tech or knows one nearby, we need to find somebody to fix it. No techs?" Anders wasn't really surprised. "All right, then. You all move to the launch bay. Ms. Merrick here will lead you with the light. I'll see if I can do something about the power."

"But you're not a tech either."

"True enough, but I expect I will find some on the engineering decks."

"The ship's damage control systems have everything beyond frame eighty-seven sealed off," said a voice out of the dark. "You can't get to them."

The first thing Benton Mainwaring noticed when he stopped screaming was that he was covered in blood. After a moment of panic, his probing fingers told him that it was not his own. His skin and the suit he wore were intact. So whose blood was it?

He blinked, trying to hurry his eyes' adjustment to the emergency lighting. His efforts didn't do much good. The smoke that defied the ventilation system wasn't helping.

In the near-darkness, he could see at once that the bridge was a mess. There were too many candidates for the source of the blood. Nearly everyone he could see was wounded.

All around him he could hear moans and whimpers of pain from the survivors. No one seemed to be paying attention to their consoles. It was as though the ship no longer mattered in the worlds of distress and grief through which they moved.

Why hadn't Stone taken charge? Why wasn't he barking orders?

Benton, lying as he was in what should have been Coppelstowe's couch, realized that Stone's usurped couch should have been in plain sight. It was not. He craned around and saw the stumps of its moorings. Something had torn it loose from the deck plates and smashed it across the compartment. He could see Stone hanging limp in the restraining harness. Was he breathing? Benton couldn't tell. Dead or alive, he wouldn't be giving orders anytime soon.

Which meant that Benton was in command again.

What should have been a satisfying thought was far from it. Though unhurt, he'd been shaken up by the ordeal he'd just endured, and the horrid stench and unnerving sounds all around him weren't making it any easier for him to compose himself.

Like Stone's couch, Benton's console had been ripped away and doubtless was now a part of the wreckage along the port bulkhead. How was he supposed to get information?

The ship was badly damaged. That much was obvious from what he could see. But how badly? Fatally? In his imagination he saw the bridge adrift and spinning slowly away from the wreckage of the rest of *Auditor*. It seemed all too possible.

Or was this just the moment of respite before the last Remor ship plowed into them and sent them all into oblivion?

No, it couldn't be that. It had been too long. Hadn't it?

He lay back. The last ship had been less than a minute behind the first. He waited for what he thought was a minute. Then waited through another. Nothing came smashing through the bridge. Nothing rattled *Auditor*. All the carnage and destruction was over. They really had survived.

There was no guarantee that they would continue to do so.

Something needed to be done, and lying strapped down in an unlinked couch wasn't going to get it done. Benton hit the strap release and hauled himself up.

A wave of relief rolled over him as he saw Lugard still at his post. The man was a treasure!

Speaking of treasures . . . where was Sister Coppelstowe?

She wasn't in the emergency couch she'd taken when the shooting started. The couch was there, though, so that meant she hadn't suffered Stone's fate. But where—ah, there. His faithful advisor, though spattered in blood, was apparently little harmed. Coppelstowe sat alert at the communications console. He could hear her trying to contact the rest of the fleet, although it didn't sound as though she was getting any response. If anyone could get through, she could.

Relying on her, he moved to the main console. Lugard acknowledged his presence with a noise that could only charitably be called a grunt.

"How is my ship?" Benton asked anxiously.

"Still alive. Main backup be off-line. Emergency systems be at only sixty percent."

"Are we going to get hit again?"

"I be having no idea."

A lot of the main console was dark. Benton pointed to the dysfunctional proximity and long-range scan screens. "What's wrong with the scanners? I need answers. I need to know what's going on out there."

"If you be shutting up, I might be finding out," Lugard snapped.

Benton knew how to make allowances for employees under stress; but later, when things were stabilized, they would be having a talk. He backed off to let Lugard do his job. It was, after all, the sensible thing to do. Lugard was a guild spacer and a master of his profession. He had far more experience with these things than Benton did.

It seemed there really was nothing for him to do but let his professionals get on with their jobs. Painful though it was to wait, unknowing, Benton steeled himself to the task. Time seemed to stretch interminably long. At last, Lugard deigned to make a report.

"I not be knowing how or why the last Remor ship missed us, but it did. Things be bad, but *Auditor* be not breaking up. Engineering thinks we can be making enough repairs to keep her in orbit. That be true and we be getting some parts from stores, we be able to make her spaceworthy enough to be making the trip home. It be taking time, though."

"We may not have time," Coppelstowe said. "I have managed to contact *Achilles*. Captain Crais is relaying new reports of enemy ships rising from the south polar ocean at escape velocity."

* * *

The voice from the dark turned out to be Sergeant Williams, leading a large group of League soldiers. Sue was appalled to see how many of them were wounded. Their section of the ship must have suffered heavier damage.

"The healthy help the wounded, then fight on," Williams said as he saluted Captain Seaborg.

"You're too short to be spouting Eridani proverbs, Sergeant," Seaborg said. "But I'm glad to see you living them."

Seaborg questioned him closely on his information and how he had gotten it. Then he asked after the rest of his soldiers, listening gravely as Williams told him who had died. There were some soldiers whose fate remained unknown.

"We took a lot of hits around the barracks compartments. There's a lot of sealed hatches down that way. We had to cut through one to get out. Some of the troops could be trapped by malfing hatches like we were."

"Pray to Saint Michael and Saint Jude that it is so," Seaborg said.

The Eridani commander's remark wasn't an order but it might as well have been, given the way that the rest of the Eridani started to mumble under their breaths. Sue was not given to religious entreaties, but she did hope that the missing troopers were alive and safe.

"All right,'pounders," Seaborg shouted. "We don't get paid to stand around."

"Actually, we usually do," Williams commented, not quite to himself.

Sue felt sure that Seaborg heard him too, but the Eridani said nothing. He continued to exhort the troops to get moving toward the landing bay, getting the group sorted out and on their way.

As they went, they gathered in other survivors. Everyone seemed glad to have someone taking charge. Sue was glad it was Seaborg, considering that it could have been Mainwaring.

Some parts of the ship had emergency lighting. As Sue

was boosted up the access tube to the deck on which the landing bay was located, she saw that the bay was so blessed. The faint, lurid light spilled from the open access to the landing bay to shine on a crowd of Pacificans and ship crew pushing into the bay in a disorderly line. Once all the wounded were lifted up and the last stragglers got themselves up, Seaborg led the League soldiers and their charges into the press. Sue put herself behind Seaborg's mass, following in the relative calm of his wake.

Inside the landing bay the scene was chaotic. It reminded Sue of the day they had first discovered that the eggs laid by the xeno carriers were full of food and medical supplies. The difference was that these people weren't struggling for sustenance, but for escape.

Fists flew as bodies struggled to jam into the escape pods along the bay walls. Weapons, blunt and sharp, flashed in the light and not all of the red glints on the metal came from the tint of the illumination.

"They are only rated for five, you idiots," Seaborg roared as he charged the nearest pod.

Sue had seen at least seven cram themselves aboard. Who knew how many had crawled inside before they entered the bay?

Seaborg waded into the struggling group, using his strength to make an impression where his words failed. Any weapon that came his way seemed to jump from the wielder's hand and fly toward the other Eridani soldiers where they stood as a bulwark for the wounded from the surging tide of panicking people. Sue flinched at the first one, but Sergeant Fiske caught it with his good hand. All the others were caught in a similar fashion. After the third, Sue started to enjoy the show.

Sue didn't know if it was good sense or simply self-preservation, but the people who had been trying to cram into the pod finally started to back away, clearing the way for Seaborg to reach it. He grabbed the nearest limb, hauled out one of the excess passengers, and tossed her, limbs flailing, into the crowd that was starting to press toward the pod again. The door on the pod started to close, but Seaborg's arm flashed out and he stopped it.

"You're making a bad decision here," he told the people aboard the pod. "You don't know if there's anyone out there near enough to pick you up. You won't have much time if the pod is overloaded."

"To hell with you," snarled the man wearing ship's uniform, swinging a wrench hard at Seaborg's hand. The Eridani snatched his hand away from the smashing impact. Without his restraint, the door swished closed. The prelaunch warning sounded.

Sue felt the vibration in the deck as the pod launched. Across the bay, another pod launched. Sue could only guess how overloaded that one was. As Seaborg rejoined the group, Fiske said, "That didn't go very well."

"And it's not likely to get better."

"So what do we do?"

"Keep warning them," Seaborg told him. "But nobody gets hurt trying to stop them, got that?"

Fiske nodded.

Sue guessed that "nobody" actually meant "none of Seaborg's people." Since those people seemed to include those of her own she had gathered up, she approved the sentiment.

"Aurie, you take charge here. Milano, find Charron or whoever is now in charge of the shuttle squadron. Have the vaccuum-heads get the shuttles prepped."

"What about the mob?" Fiske asked. "They see us prepping transport, they'll try to board."

"Most of the craziest ones are already busy killing themselves on overloaded pods. If there are any left, we will not let them drag us down as well. Use whatever force is necessary. Those shuttles may be our only ticket off this hulk, and I don't mean to lose it."

"Understood."

Seaborg and Fiske exchanged curt nods. The Eridani commander turned to Williams and ordered him to take a team forward to see if they could make it to the bridge.

Williams didn't ask why, or what he ought to do if he got there, but he did ask, "What are you going to be doing, sir?"

"I'm going aft and see what state engineering is in."

How could he do that? "But aren't the hatches all sealed?"

"There's an airlock over there, Ms. Merrick. Without power, we'll have to manually cycle it, but I see more than enough hands to do the job."

Sue didn't know a lot about spacecraft, but it was plain he meant to go outside the vessel and move along the hull. She assumed there would be another airlock there that he could use to reenter the ship.

"Be careful," she told him. "If there is still shooting out there . . ."

"If there is, as you say, still shooting out there, I'll be as safe out there as you will be in here."

There was a twitch in his face as he said that, and for the first time Sue suspected he was lying to her.

"Don't worry," he told her. "The enemy squadron that attacked us is either destroyed or moved on to other things. The worst thing I'll have to dodge is debris."

30

Try as he might, Benton Mainwaring could not make sense of the raw data flow emerging from the console. The main holotank that normally interpreted the data into comprehensible form was destroyed. The navigational console attempting to stand in for the tank didn't have access to the ship's network, also destroyed or at least taken down—techs were trying to determine which. Without that access there was no way to second the interpretive software to the console and so all they had was the raw feed from the few remaining sensors left to *Auditor*. It was said that master spacers of the guild, like Piet Lugard, could read the raw stuff nearly as well as computer-interpreted plots, and indeed, Lugard's face was furrowed in concentration as he stared at the console.

Coppelstowe responded to Benton's quizzical look with a slight shrug. She was a trained interpreter of the dynamic, but this flow of data was as beyond her as it was outside Benton's ken. *Ah, well, Lugard will tell us when he's ready.*

"Sister Coppelstowe, any improvements on communications?"

"Some. Ship-to-ship and surface contact remains interdicted by the scattering effect, and, though I believe our transmitters have enough strength to cut through for local communications, no one is responding to our calls, which suggests that there is no one near enough to render assistance. The intraship network continues to malfunction. Most decks are blacked out, but we have intermittent connections with engineering, three weapons barbettes, and the galley. Lieutenant Gutermann in engineering reports work parties engaged in damage control."

"Gutermann?" Kirkpatrick was in charge down there. "What about Jill Kirkpatrick?"

"I lost the linkage before I could inquire. Judging by Gutermann's attitude and choice of language, I believe it likely that Kirkpatrick is a casualty, and the lieutenant is senior among the surviving departmental staff."

"Let's hope not. Jill is a very good engineer, and we'll need every one we can get to put *Auditor* back together."

Coppelstowe began to fill him in on the reports from the weapons stations but was interrupted by the loud arrival of some of the ship's complement of infantry. Their leader's face was familiar to Benton.

"Williams, isn't it?"

"Yes, sir."

According to Williams, they had been sent to contact the bridge and ascertain conditions for Captain Seaborg. Apparently the Eridani was taking charge in the midsections of the ship. That was fine as far as it went, but it did raise the question again of the status of the nominal superior in the section. What had happened to Major Marsh? Williams had no idea.

As Benton questioned him about what he did know, the soldiers he had brought with him moved about the compartment. Using field medical kits, some attended the injuries of the stalwart crew at their stations. Others sorted the dead from the wounded, something the reduced command crew had yet to deal with. To Benton's surprise, it turned out that Stone was still alive, doubtless due to his superior Eridani physique.

"We must get the wounded down to sick bay," he mused aloud.

"Won't do any good," Williams told him. "Sick bay is trashed, sir."

"What are you talking about? We haven't had any damage reports from the medical team."

"We passed by on the way here from the boat deck, sir. You won't be getting any reports from the medical team, except maybe their casualties."

"This is bad."

"Agreed. Captain Seaborg has ordered the assault shuttles prepped for evacuation. I recommend we get as many of the wounded down to the boat deck as we can. We ought to get them aboard some other ship that can do something for them."

As Benton started to agree with Williams, Lugard spoke up.

"Near space be empty of ships. If we be lucky, the other ships of the fleet be too busy to be helping us just now, but for all that we be knowing they be destroyed already and we be on our own."

"Perhaps there are no ships near enough to help," Coppel-stowe said, "but *Cerulean Cygnet* was moving just beyond *Auditor*'s short sensor range when we were hit. She is most likely still out there. The assault shuttles could reach her."

It would give the wounded a better chance. *Cerulean Cygnet* had good medical facilities, assuming they hadn't suffered as *Auditor*'s had. "What do you think, Master Lugard?"

"It could be so. I could be piloting one of those shuttles."

What was the man thinking? "*Auditor* still needs her captain."

Lugard sneered. "This ship be needing its chief engineer more than its captain. And you be needing a good pilot to be getting you through the junk outside to a live ship, Commander."

Was he suggesting what it appeared? "*Auditor* is not yet dead. It would be dishonorable to abandon her."

"Dis—" Lugard rolled his eyes. "This be not a matter of blind-eyed honor but of practicality. *Auditor* may not be dead, but she be dead in space. Until she be under way again, she be not part of the fleet, and you made me your fleet captain. The fleet be out *there*! I be no use here!" A short pause. A narrowing of his eyes. "Neither be you!"

There was some sense to what Lugard was saying.

"And practically speaking, I be the best pilot to get anybody anywhere," said Lugard. "I can be giving the wounded their best chance to make it to another ship."

He was probably right about that. Did it make sense to abandon *Auditor*? As Benton pondered the question, Williams asked him to move. Annoyed, he snapped at the soldier, "Williams, what are you doing?"

"Pulling the emergency power cells from this unit," the soldier responded nonchalantly. He already had three more cells lined up at his feet.

"But these systems won't work without those cells until we get the main engines back on line."

"That's right," Williams agreed. "But do you really need science stations right now? Didn't think so. These cells might come in handy to power up some systems on the landing deck."

"Or other systems that could tell us something," Coppelstowe observed. "Excellent. Give me one."

"Get your own, Sister," Williams suggested with more than a hint of rudeness.

Were all his people going rebellious?

"Give her one," Benton ordered.

Williams looked suspiciously at Benton, but then held out one of the power cells to Coppelstowe. "Hope you can do something useful with it, Sister."

"As the dynamic allows, Sergeant."

"Right," said Williams, eyeing her dubiously. He got back about his business. Before long he and his soldiers departed, taking with them the wounded. The dead they left in bags for later attention. Though the bags seemed invisible to the bridge crew as they continued on with their own work, Benton found his gaze drifting toward them far too often. The edging from the chaos of the attack and its aftermath toward normalcy made their presence an intrusive discrepancy. He had never fooled himself into believing that there would be no casualties in this adventure, but sitting, nearly idle, among them had not been part of his imaginings.

He had always believed that he was very good at selecting personnel for their good qualities. Today he wondered if he was too good at it. Quiet or cussing, his people were doing what needed to be done. No one seemed in need of his direction. No one offered him a distraction.

When Coppelstowe called for his attention with a slight hint of concern in her voice, he was up and at her side in a moment. "Yes, Sister, what is it?"

"The signal is corrupted, but I believe that I am seeing ships on approach."

"Let me see," Lugard said, shoving Benton aside to get to the screen.

Benton could see that Lugard was studying the readings carefully, though what he was seeing Benton could only guess. To him, it looked like nothing more than static.

"Not ships. One vessel," Lugard concluded. "A small craft. It be a Remor interface striker and we be doomed."

"Have we any weapons we can bring to bear?" Benton asked.

Lugard gave the orders. Then whispered to Benton, "It might be best to consider transferring the flag, Commander."

What would the dead say to that?

"Is there some way we can tell if they truly are hostile?" he asked. He didn't want to face another attack.

"Be you not listening when I be telling you that *Auditor* is useless?"

"Not entirely useless," Coppelstowe countered. "I believe I have revived one of the astrogational telescopes with the emergency power cell. Do you think Sergeant Williams would consider achieving a visual on the approaching ship to be something useful?"

"To the deeps with Williams," Lugard exclaimed. "*I* be needing to see that ship. It could be the death of us."

Coppelstowe made room for him at the console screen,

noting, "Your concern is understandable but unnecessary. The approaching vessel is of human origin, not Remor."

Human? Dread drained from Benton. Could it be a relief ship from the fleet?

"Human it be," Lugard stated. "But it be not one of ours."

Benton assumed he meant it was not a Combine ship. "What does it matter if it's a League ship? We are all allies in this adventure. Our allies will surely render whatever aid they—"

"It be not a League ship," Lugard said ominously.

"What?" If not a Combine ship and not a League ship, whose could it be? "It is a human ship, though, isn't it?"

"Aye."

"Well then, let's talk to them. Sister Coppelstowe, we can talk to them, can't we?"

"I am working on—ah, there."

The face of a man appeared on Benton's console screen. He wore a uniform that had clearly seen better days, and with his pouchy, debauched eyes, broken nose, and assorted scars, he looked more the type one expected to find in a dark alley than at the helm of a ship. His thick lips parted in a broad smile.

"Sir, I am Provisional Captain Leon Bartosiewicz of the reconstituted Pacifica Defense Force. The force doesn't have the weapons to help you in the fight for our liberation, but we do have people with expertise. I have techs and medical personnel aboard ready to do what we can to help restore your ship and take care of your crew."

That explained much. "Captain, you are a most welcome sight. Your offer of help is even more welcome."

They exchanged a few pleasantries before Benton offered a berth on the boat deck to Bartosiewicz. "It's much easier than a lock-to-lock docking. Let me get you an approach vector."

"This ship is a little cranky after being mothballed so long. Best we pick our own approach. Just be sure your gunners don't decide we're the bad guys."

"Don't give it a thought, old man. We'll be talking face-to-face shortly."

Off circuit, Benton told Coppelstowe to be sure their three operation weapon stations got the word. Then he spoke aloud for the benefit of the whole bridge crew. "The flow seems to favor us again, my friends. A node facilitates and is facilitated, eh, Sister Coppelstowe?"

"The flow *is* inexorable."

"And it buoys us back toward its crest." Benton felt almost giddy in his renewed confidence in the rightness of events. "I think we should go meet our new friends."

"I be staying here," Lugard announced sullenly.

"I disagree," Benton told him. "Didn't you imply there was nothing worthwhile for you to do here until *Auditor* is spaceworthy again? Well, I have thought of something for you. You can come along and see that these volunteers are put to the best use. The least you can do is be polite to Captain Bartosiewicz and his noble people."

Dodging debris proved to be less difficult than Anders had feared when he conceived of his extravehicular trek. Periodic checks for inbound fragments were the key. The emergency evacuation suit that he was wearing didn't have a proximity detector like his hardsuit, but so far his Mark 1 eyeballs had been up to the task. If, as he hoped, he could access the armory from the lower decks, he'd have that 'suit for the trip back.

Reaching an apparently intact airlock, he made a last safety scan. A dark shadow against the stars caught his attention. It seemed to be heading for *Auditor*. For a moment he thought it might be a chunk of dead ship, one big enough to cause *Auditor* mischief should they collide. Studying the shape a little longer, he realized that it was a live ship, decelerating and matching orbit with *Auditor*.

Not being a vaccuum-head, he didn't have space vessel silhouettes committed to memory. He didn't have access to his hardsuit's computer to query the data banks, but he didn't need that access to know it wasn't a Remor design. In this region of space, that alone made it a friendly.

Hand-waving from the hull wasn't going to be terribly effective, so he decided to leave the meet-and-greet to *Auditor*'s regular crew and got on with the business of working his way through the airlock into the engineering section.

31

The situation in the docking bay was much calmer by the time Williams and his men returned. No more overloaded escape pods were launching, but that was because there were no more to launch. After a demonstration of resolve from the soldiers guarding access to the assault shuttles, the most frantic people had fled the bay to look for pods in other parts of the ship. The rest milled about, casting anxious glances past the perimeter maintained by Sergeant Fiske's men and women. Sue, safe within that perimeter, wondered how long the situation would remain calm, especially now that Williams had returned with more casualties.

Williams led the wedge that cut through the crowd. In his wake came soldiers and wounded crew members, carrying other wounded too badly hurt to walk. Sue observed the soldiers taking special care with one of the stretchers. That one, after Williams had a brief word with Fiske and Flight Captain Charron, went straight to a shuttle and aboard. Charron himself scurried aboard seconds later.

"Who was that?" she asked Fiske.

"Commander Stone, ma'am. He took a hard hit up on the bridge. Soon as we can get the doors open, we'll be trying to get him back to Fleet."

Sue could see technicians making what she presumed were final preflight checks on all of the shuttles. Wounded were being conveyed aboard all of them as well. "You're sending all the ships?"

"Better security, ma'am."

"Did Captain Seaborg order this?"

"He didn't need to, ma'am. Some situations take priority."

"Has this launch been cleared?" shouted one of *Auditor*'s crew.

Fiske ignored the man and continued speaking to Sue. "You should get on board, ma'am."

"Why?" she asked.

"Captain Seaborg told me to see you safe, ma'am."

"There are still wounded in need of medical attention that this ship cannot supply. They ought to go before me, don't you think? What happened to 'the healthy help the injured, then fight on'?"

"That's a combat priority, ma'am. We do not seem to be in combat at the moment."

"I don't think I should take the place of one of the injured."

"We'll be taking as many aboard as practical. The shuttles will be a little overloaded, but it's not as bad for them as it is for escape pods. You're a light load and won't make much difference."

The offer of a flight to safety was as seductive as it had been when Seaborg had offered one from Pacifica. But Sue had already made one flight from pan to fire. Would this one be any different? Would it be more successful?

The crowd outside the perimeter was growing more restive. Some of them were recognizing what the soldiers' activity presaged. They too wanted a flight to safety. Who could blame them?

Why should she get what they so obviously would not? What had she done to deserve it more than any of them?

Fiske seemed to sense her uncertainty. "Ma'am, you'll be safe on one of the shuttles. It would be best if you got aboard before things get ugly."

Ugly? Yes, it would likely get quite ugly. The crowd was sure to panic again when the soldiers tried to clear the bay, as they must to launch. Every one of those people would see that they were not being allowed places on the departing

ships, and desperation would set in. As Sue knew all too
well, desperation easily overtook intelligence. No one would
remember that *Auditor* was not in flames when the soldiers
cleared the bay, that there was no pressing need for them to
leave the ship. They would fight the soldiers, ineffectually,
she expected. She had little doubt the soldiers would accomplish their mission, no matter how "ugly" it got.

"You say I'll be safe. But I heard recently that we're not in
combat, so my safety shouldn't be a current issue."

"Ma'am, I—"

"You're wounded yourself, Sergeant. Shouldn't you be
aboard one of the shuttles?"

"I will be, ma'am."

"Even if it means not seeing me 'safe'?"

"Even so." Fiske looked genuinely pained, as if gored by
a horned dilemma. "Balanced imperatives, ma'am."

"I can't say I understand your reasoning, Sergeant, but I
do understand that you have to follow your conscience. Allow me to do the same."

The Eridani sergeant didn't say anything to that. He just
took a step back and saluted awkwardly with his injured
hand. Sue felt a little foolish, unsure whether she should return the gesture, and if so, how. Before she could settle it in
her mind, Fiske spun on his heels and headed for a knot of
soldiers.

They would be discussing their next step. Ugliness. Sue
thought it best to be elsewhere. She passed beyond their
safety perimeter and pushed her way through the restive
crowd. She managed to reach the flight control deck before
the ugliness began.

As he led his little procession of welcomers through the
decks toward the boat bay, Benton observed that *Auditor* in
her damaged state was much quieter than normal.

Quiet like a grave, he thought gloomily.

Yet the hush offered a certain tranquillity, a soothing to
jangled nerves and stressed senses.

The stillness was also the reason he heard the raised

voices ahead of them in the corridors as well as the other faint sound beneath the hubbub.

"Isn't that the launch warning for the boat deck?"

"It be that," Lugard confirmed.

Suddenly the anger and confusion he heard in the shouts ahead made sense.

"Williams!" He recalled the sergeant's suggestion on the bridge. And that Williams had left before they had learned of the inbound aid ship from the Pacifica Defense Force. "They don't know about Captain Bartosiewicz's ship. They're launching the shuttles."

Lugard cursed with a fluency that made Benton envious.

With the Pacifican ship on approach, there was the danger of a fatal collision. Worse, there was the chance that the nervous captain of the ship might construe the launch of armed ships as a threat. Worse still, trigger-happy soldiers aboard the shuttles, finding an unexpected ship in their path, might shoot before asking questions. Such a misunderstanding could be more fatal than collision.

"We've got to stop them."

"If they be launching, the flight deck be open to space," Lugard warned.

"The flight control deck is the center of a launching event," Coppelstowe noted.

"Then that's where we need to be. Come on!"

Their path took them along an observation corridor. Benton could see that the boat deck was empty of ships and open to space. Through the yawning port he could just make out the flare of exhaust from the departed shuttles.

"What's going on here, Sergeant?" he demanded of Williams as he burst into the flight control compartment.

"The shuttles have just left on medevac, sir."

"Idiot! Do you have any idea what you have just done?"

32

When Anders reached the main engineering section, he found crews hard at work on restoring ship systems. Lieutenant Gutermann, the senior surviving officer, told him that until the main power was restored and enough wreckage was cleared so that power conduits could be checked, repaired, or rerouted, *Auditor* would be surviving on emergency power. Systems would work when and where they worked.

Gutermann also had news, thanks to engineering's intermittent commo channel to the bridge. The worst of it was that Commander Stone had been seriously wounded. More welcome was the word that Williams's team had evacuated the wounded, Stone included, to the boat deck.

Anders was confident that the IDL regulars wouldn't wait on orders from him. They would launch the shuttles as soon as they could if they thought there was a chance of saving the commander. They wouldn't wait for anyone, certainly not for Anders.

Of course, they would also carry as many of the casualties as possible, but there were too many Combiners and Pacificans gathered at the boat deck to fit aboard the shuttles without the craft suffering as badly as the overloaded escape pods and risking every life aboard beyond acceptable limits. Aurie would see to it that loading was controlled. Brutally, if he had to. Anders feared that it would come to that. He'd seen how even *Auditor*'s crew had panicked earlier.

Explanations would be needed. Not everyone understood

the imperatives at work here. The cold logic of transport equations and the hot demands of loyalty made a combination difficult for civilians to understand. Anders prayed that Commander Stone might recover and give those explanations, so that he didn't have to.

A quick calculation of elapsed time matched against his understanding of his troops' capabilities suggested that the launch might happen in time to possibly interfere with the approach of the vessel he'd seen. As far as he knew, his people hadn't gotten word of the stranger. He was sure that his people would not fire on a strange human ship, but he was less sure of this reconstituted Pacifica Defense Force. A flight of assault shuttles launching into your face was unnerving.

He tried to signal the bridge so that someone up there could try to warn the incoming ship, but Murphy frowned on his efforts. Commo was down.

It was looking like he knew where the next crisis was going to be. And where he ought to be.

He reminded Gutermann that, since *Auditor*'s orbit was stable for the time being, there were higher priorities than machines. The medics aboard the incoming ship were going to need to get to the casualties in the downspin and aft portions of the ship. And there were other sections needing to be checked for survivors. He directed Gutermann to refocus his people's efforts. Getting through to still-isolated portions of the ship was a priority. Time could save lives.

Unhappily, Anders left them to it and started to suit up again for the extravehicular trek back to the boat deck. He had wanted to know what had happened to his missing people, but he would have to live with unconfirmed worries for a while longer. He had a more pressing imperative.

Sue, sitting unnoticed in a corner of the flight control compartment, got to hear every bit of the foolishness Mainwaring spouted at Williams. The most ludicrous part was the bit about his irresponsible and illegal theft of power cells.

Those scavenged power cells had enabled systems vital to

the launch procedures. They had allowed Williams to seal
the access hatches to the deck once Fiske's soldiers had
pushed the would-be escapers off the flight deck, and
thereby put a life-saving wall between the two factions. Another cell had been attached to what the soldiers had called a
"booby bunker," a safety measure for any personnel without
suits who got caught on the flight deck after depressuriza-
tion started. That bunker was currently sheltering those unfortunates that the soldiers had incapacitated when they
cleared the flight deck of people. Finally, those cells had allowed the launching bay doors to be opened so that the shuttles could carry their loads of injured away, presumably to
Cerulean Cygnet, where they could get help.

Hardly irresponsible actions, legal or not.

Launching into the path of an incoming ship would have
been irresponsible—had anyone on the flight deck been
aware of the situation. It seemed to her that the irresponsi-
bility lay elsewhere on that one.

Mainwaring's tirade washed across Williams with little
apparent effect. The sergeant was a Combiner, so maybe
Mainwaring's bluster was commonplace to him, or maybe
he just saw through it. In any case, he moved into a pause in
the malediction and pointed out, "We haven't felt any nearby
explosions, so it would seem there haven't been any problems."

"A notable observation," said the calm-voiced, slender
woman in the robes of an Alsion initiate.

Mainwaring seemed to pay more attention to her second-
ing than Williams's original conclusion. He visibly recom-
posed himself, then offered an apology for his abusive
comments. "The heat of the moment," he said, as if that explained everything and excused his excesses. "We've got a
clean bottom line and that's what is important. Now, is there
some way we can check on Captain Bartosiewicz's approach?"

"We haven't got the power to bring up the flight operations systems, so we're stuck with visual scanning. It'll be
tricky," Williams told him, then promptly proved his evalua-

tion overly pessimistic by spotting the incoming ship. "There they are, coming around from the left. Odd approach."

"Prudent, I'd guess," Mainwaring said. "They probably had to shift to avoid your hasty shuttles."

"Could be." Williams didn't sound entirely convinced.

As they watched the ship draw closer, Mainwaring lectured them on its nature and how they ought to respond to this aid from the "reconstituted Pacifica Defense Force." Sue thought he was mostly working out his own response out loud.

Sue had never heard about any reconstitution of any of Pacifica's institutions, let alone the military forces. Still, she had been confined to Palisandra for years, living in a tightly confined nightmare. It was possible that other Pacificans had done better. Certainly the vessel easing onto the flight deck looked like ships she'd seen when visiting Kilawa's main spaceport.

The giant launching bay doors slid shut behind the arriving ship as it settled to the deck. Only now did its size become apparent. It was big, with two or three times the bulk of an assault shuttle. Had it been here earlier, there would have been no need to fight for space on the departing shuttles. But if it had been here earlier, it wouldn't have fit.

"Guess it's a good thing we made some room, eh, sir?" Williams remarked.

Mainwaring scowled at him.

As repressurization began, two of the men who had come with Mainwaring slipped out of the flight control compartment. Sue could see them heading down to the main access hatch to the flight deck. Mainwaring, seemingly unconcerned, leaned over the console and studied the new arrival. He and the Alsion initiate discussed whether the aid they anticipated was going to be paid for by Mainwaring or by the League.

Sue wondered who on her poor ravaged planet was in a position to offer anyone aid. Someone apparently was. The first half dozen men who emerged from the craft wore uniforms that looked something like Pacifica Defense Force uniforms. Not that Sue would have known if they were forgeries or simply poor copies made by people who couldn't do any better. They carried slung or holstered weapons, which twitched her reflexes.

Why was she reacting? Since the aliens had come, a Pacifican without a weapon of some sort was a far less ordinary sight than one with a weapon. Maybe it was because the strangers were carrying obviously modern weapons.

Did it matter? They were here to help.

More uniformed people started to exit the ship. The main access hatch to the deck opened, and some of *Auditor*'s personnel and passengers started moving to meet the newcomers. The two in ship's uniform who had arrived with Mainwaring were among them.

"Looks like Lugard's gotten the jump on us, Sister," Mainwaring commented. "We'll sort the financial details out later. Right now we ought to get ourselves down there."

Details.

The word rattled about in Sue's head. Something about the details wasn't right.

"Sergeant Williams, is there a more direct way to the deck?" Mainwaring asked. "We mustn't be slow in greeting our new friends."

Slow.

Yes, that was it. Some of the newcomers were moving slowly. Awkwardly. Like . . .

Why hadn't she seen it sooner? Because they didn't belong here. In a fair universe, they rightfully didn't belong here.

Sue pushed past Mainwaring, shouldering him aside in her rush for the console. Her hand flashed in front of the startled Williams and stabbed the activation switch for the loudspeaker system.

"Xombies! They've got xombies!" she screamed. "They're collectors! Get away! Get away!"

33

Bartie cursed as the loudspeaker shrieked out its warning. Someone had twigged to their ruse. One of the sheep that had bugged out with the soldier boys, probably. Didn't really matter how.

"Let 'em have it," he shouted.

His own weapon was out. Flipping the selector to full, he started pumping out bursts and dropping targets. He did his best to make sure that nobody was left standing anywhere near the hatch controls.

It didn't take long for his hand to start going numb from discharge leakage. But he wasn't no nancy. He kept firing and taking down the shipboard sheep. There were a lot of them running around and bleating.

The frickin' curdler wasn't his idea of a *real* weapon, but the frickin' bugs wanted him to use it. They wanted as many breathing bodies as possible. Bartie didn't really care about whether they got their lab specimens or not. He did, however, have a healthy concern about puncturing the hull of a space vessel he was aboard. He hoped the morons who had let him aboard this tin can felt the same way.

It looked that way from how they had armed their muscle. Nobody had opened on them with anything more than light pistols. His slugs gave any frisky fellow who tried shooting at them some serious tickling.

Did these stooges really think they could kick down Bartie and his gang without some serious weaponry?

Maybe he'd ask a few of them before the bugs xombified them.

The sudden chaos erupting below them on the flight deck horrified Benton Mainwaring. It wasn't just the sight of his people falling before the guns of the invaders. That was bad enough. But if what the Pacifican woman was shouting was true, Benton himself had facilitated the murderous agenda of this Captain Bartosiewicz and his fellow species traitors.

"Get down!" Williams shouted, emphasizing his order with a rough shove that sent Benton reeling into Coppel-stowe. He knocked the wind out of the unfortunate woman when he fell on her.

A bone-chilling howl racketed through the chamber as something struck the observation window, then struck it again. Benton felt as if someone had dragged icy talons along his spine. Whatever the invaders had fired at, the chamber seemed to want to crawl into his nervous system and shake it apart.

Thank goodness the beams didn't seem able to penetrate the observation window.

"Looks like we've got some protection against whatever it is those pirates are using," Williams observed rather calmly. "At least until they haul out something nastier. I recommend staying down so we don't tempt them to try."

He promptly disobeyed his own suggestion and snatched a glimpse below.

"We can't just sit around doing nothing," Benton protested.

"You sure of that, sir?" asked Williams, hauling out his pistol. "There's limited access to this booth. We can hold them off for a good while."

"They've got more xombies than you've got bullets, Sergeant," the Pacifican woman pointed out. "They always do."

Benton still couldn't remember her name. He took his petty amnesia as a sign of how rattled he was.

Williams shrugged off her remark. "They won't have as

many as they started with by the time they get around to us. Could be I will have enough."

"Why does that matter?" asked Coppelstowe. "Should they not care to risk themselves, we are trapped here. They need only starve us out."

Benton had seen the same problem, but he hadn't wanted to be negative. "They have to win down there first."

Williams had been sneaking peeks at the combat below. "They're doing a pretty good job of that. They're taking losses, but most of my men are down. I'd say it's only a matter of time till the bad guys secure the landing deck."

Very well, then, Benton conceded to himself. *We are cornered.*

It was his fault that they had gotten into this predicament. Before long Bartosiewicz's interlopers would be pouring onto his bridge, taking over his ship. If only he'd listened to Lugard, and let him remain on the bridge. At least then there would be a last stand, a last chance to defy the invaders. Lugard would . . .

"Where's Lugard?" he asked, suddenly aware that the guild spacer was no longer present.

"He went with Sanchez to the flight deck entrance before the fighting started," Coppelstowe told him.

Prescience, coincidence, or a shift in the dynamic? Whatever it was, it seemed Lugard had made the right move. If only they had gone with him, they wouldn't be trapped now.

Benton risked a look to see whether he could spot the fallen body of his second in command. There were a lot of bodies sprawled on the decks. Far, far too many were wearing expeditionary force uniforms, but he failed to spot Lugard.

Had he made his escape from the ambush? Was he now headed for the bridge to defend *Auditor* to the last? Was he riding the crest of the event wave sweeping them along, as Benton ought to be doing?

Ambrose Alsion once said, *We build our own walls out of bricks only we can see.* Benton had done just that, assuming they were already trapped. If Lugard could make it past the deadly melee at the flight deck access, so could they.

"Sergeant Williams, we need to get out of here while we still can. There are more important places to defend than this useless control booth. We are going to the bridge. This is my ship, and if I must die defending it, I shall do so in my proper place."

Sue sat where she was when the others got themselves up and moved to the control booth hatchway, ignoring Mainwaring's "Come along now."

Mainwaring and the others were heading into the mess below. It was not, to her mind, a good choice. But the only other way she knew out of the control booth was the maintenance accessway she'd used to get to it. Unfortunately that passage opened onto the flight deck itself, also not a good choice.

Or was it as bad as it first appeared?

The control booth's observation window had resisted the collectors' weapons and they had not immediately tried anything stronger. Sue guessed they either had nothing better, or had other reasons not to employ such weapons. There was, therefore, no real risk in checking out the flight deck below.

It appeared that, having made their unsuccessful attempt on the people in the control booth, the collectors had focused their attention on more accessible targets. Partially screened by the bulk of the collectors' ship, the maintenance accessway's hatch on the flight deck looked isolated and ignored.

Of course it was on the outer hull, near the airlock through which Seaborg had left. Anyone emerging there would have to cross the flight deck and fight their way through the collectors and their xombies if they wanted to get to *Auditor*'s bridge. There were, however, other options. There had been more emergency space suits in the locker where Seaborg had gotten his. And the airlock was very near. A quick dash and a grab, then skin into the suit and duck into the airlock. It could work.

Sue ducked back down to tell the others what she had learned, but they were gone. From the door she could see them moving down the main corridor. She was not about to chase them.

The control booth would eventually become a trap, and Sue was, if anything, less happy about being trapped than Mainwaring. It was time to move. If Mainwaring's party did cause a ruckus when they attempted to make their way through the fighting around the flight deck's main access hatch, they would only focus more attention that way and away from where she would be.

She went down the maintenance access as quickly and as quietly as she could. Cautiously, she peered from the hatch. She could see nothing to suggest that the invaders knew it was there and that she was using it.

So far, so good.

Creeping to the locker from which Seaborg had gotten his emergency escape suit, she snatched one for herself and started pulling it on. The fight on the other side of the flight deck raged on. If Mainwaring's party had reached it or had had any effect on its course, she couldn't tell.

She also couldn't tell if she was donning the suit properly. While she had watched with fascination when Seaborg had gotten into his, she found getting into one herself was somehow very different. She did the best she could. At least when she pulled down the helmet-hood and activated it, the plastics assumed their proper shape and air started flowing. The little status display panel just above her eye line showed all green, which was good, since she had no idea what she would have done if it hadn't.

Reaching the airlock door, she was relieved to see that she wouldn't have to operate the lock system manually. Williams had set one of his scavenged power cells to run it. Still, she winced at the humming whine it gave out when she started it.

She looked back over her shoulder to see if anyone had noticed and immediately wished she hadn't.

The thing watching her was an insect out of a nightmare. Its body was the size of the old Motorways Minor two-seater groundcar she used for commuting before the invasion. It stood on six spiny legs and had four more writhing and clutching beneath its thorax. A half dozen glittering jewels of faceted eyes sparkled between two large luminous orbs.

There was no doubt that inhuman gaze was fixed upon her.

She stumbled backward into the airlock as the thing started toward her.

34

PACIFICA THEATER, PACIFICA ORBIT
CMEFS AUDITOR

As Anders was coming up on the flight deck airlock he saw that the cycling lights were lit. Someone was coming out. He had no reason to be cautious, but he couldn't think why anyone would be coming through that lock.

To everything there is a season, his basal development instructor had often said. *A time to be bold and a time to be cautious. A prudent soldier is cautious when he has no effing idea what's going on.*

Anders considered himself a prudent soldier.

Auditor's hull, like that of any warship, was far from a smooth featureless expanse. Battle damage only added to the landscape. Anders ducked behind a nearby antenna array, now broken and dangling, whose distressed status provided more cover than it would have otherwise. From there he watched as a suited female figure emerged.

Emergency suits, unless deliberately opaqued, were see-through so that casualty assessment might be made more easily. It was a side benefit that familiar people could be recognized through the suit. Thus he knew at once that his new companion on the hull was Sue Merrick.

By Saint Joseph of Copertino, what has gotten into her head?

He stepped out where she could see him and waved to attract her attention.

At once she tried to run to him. It became painfully—dangerously—clear that she had no extravehicular experience. Her attempt to run without activating the gecko soles of her suit's boots launched her free from the hull and into a tumbling spin destined to take her into the deeps.

Anders rolled his own feet free, using the momentum to twist to a suitable attitude. Satisfied with the angle, he used a short burst from his backpack thrusters to set himself on an intercept course.

The catch went smoothly. From the first touch, he could feel that she was trembling from fright. He guessed that it wasn't from her inadvertent launch into space. She needed reassurance, but these suits had no commo. Knowing that they could talk by touching helmets together and relying on conduction, he pulled hers to his to get started.

"It's all right," he told her. "I'll get you back to the ship."

"No!" She started babbling about an attack. There was something about a monster in there too.

Clearly something had driven her from *Auditor,* but drifting farther from the ship wasn't going to help them. After a couple of maneuvering bursts to realign, he sent them back toward the hull.

Her increasing struggles required Anders to stay focused on keeping them on course. Only after they regained the hull was he able to calm her down and get a more coherent story from her.

The ship he'd seen approaching had been a Trojan horse, fooling Mainwaring into admitting forces working with the enemy. Sue also described something that sounded a lot like an *Ora*-type Remor fighting machine, which meant that some Remor had accompanied their flunkies on this mission.

But what was their mission? Destruction of *Auditor* from within? Seizure of the ship? Probably the latter. A few well-placed charges in the boat bay could break *Auditor*'s spine. The enemy could have done that and been away by now. But what did they think they were going to do with *Auditor* once they held her?

He was glad that his people had been able to get Commander Stone away before things dropped in the pot. According to Sue, all the troopers save for a squad or two of Williams's reserve company had gone aboard the shuttles, which raised its own issues. There was a serious lack of combat-trained effectives aboard *Auditor,* and cut off from the armory, they wouldn't have much in the way of equipment to deal with the raiders. Resistance would be limited.

So were their options.

He scanned nearby space as best he could, looking for enemy reinforcements or, less likely, for friendly support. He could detect neither. When he felt the vibration of the evacuating pumps, he knew that the airlock was cycling again.

The issue was being forced.

It might not be the enemy coming through, but Anders didn't want to take chances. As quickly as he could he tried to explain the operation of the gecko soles to her. He gave her as stern a warning as he could not to use the thruster unit. "You don't have the necessary training and you'll just send yourself into the sun." She promised that she'd stick to running and headed out, haltingly, toward the collapsed weapons blister he pointed out as cover. He headed for the damaged antenna and wrenched a segment free. It made a crude spear, flimsy, but good enough for at least one good thrust.

It was better than nothing.

Concentrating on using the gecko soles properly, Sue didn't realize immediately that Seaborg wasn't accompanying her on the flight away from the airlock. Once she did, she looked back to see him attacking some kind of aerial cluster. He pulled and pried at it until he had freed a two-meter piece of slender metal.

Light glittered on the rod, making it seem some kind of shining spear. Even though he wasn't wearing his battle armor, she suddenly saw him as a knight-errant awaiting his confrontation with the dragon. In the stories, the knight always won. But Sue knew too well that life wasn't like the stories.

"Run!" she shouted. "Run while you can!"

It was useless, she knew; he couldn't hear her. Moreover, she felt in her heart that he wouldn't have listened if he could. He believed more of the stories than she did.

Don't be foolish, girl.

She hadn't been for years. She started for the pitiful refuge he'd pointed out for her. But after only a half dozen steps, she stopped again.

She didn't need to let him be foolish either. She could go back and drag him along with her. Turning to do so, she saw it was too late.

The airlock's outer hatch was opening.

Anders's faint hope that he would be dealing with the species traitors of the boarding party popped like a child's balloon as a multi-jointed, spiny leg emerged and groped for purchase on the hull. Limb after limb, the insectoid monstrosity pulled itself out of the confines of the lock.

Sue's description had led him to expect a machine, but if this thing really was a Remor fighting machine, someone had gone to a lot of work making it look organic. Not impossible, but that approach was nothing he'd ever seen in an Intel briefing on the Remor.

The upper quadrant of the body was coated in some sort of gelid slime that foamed as if burning off in the fierce glare of unstinting sunlight. More of the stuff bubbled at all of its joints. The hard parts looked coated with a more stable, reflecting coating. With each movement the monster glittered like a mobile ice sculpture. Sue hadn't mentioned that conspicuous effect, so Anders figured it was a change, something special for its foray outside the ship, possibly its equivalent of a space suit.

But machines didn't need space suits.

Saint Michael, could this be a Remor in the flesh?

Whatever it was, it had come for a purpose. It shuffled, shifting position as if searching. Eyespots dulled by their mask of bubbling goo swept across Anders's position. Either it couldn't detect him amid the tangle, or he was not what it sought. It stopped its transit where he feared it would, aimed at Sue.

With a rhythm Anders recognized from Remor machines, the monster's legs began to move. Its stride was steady and it held to the hull as though it had its own gecko soles. Its speed was not great but more than sufficient to overtake Sue as she struggled awkwardly to cover ground without losing her grip on the hull.

He could not let the monster catch her.

He started forward, studying his target, trying to locate weak spots. Had he been wearing his hardsuit, the whole issue would be simple, but all he had was his makeshift spear.

The upper, slime-covered area looked to be his best target. Since the protective gunk there was similar to the necessarily flexible and probably softer leg joints, it stood to reason that any part with the bubbling gunk was soft, or at least softer than the exoskeleton.

Saint Eustace, help this hunter.

His prayer was at least partially answered. The thing showed no sign of noticing his approach.

He closed the distance.

Dodging a scissoring leg, he jabbed at his chosen spot. His weapon's point drove deep into the gel until he felt the tip catch on something. Bone? Armor? He jerked the spear to recover it for another try. It came away, dragging something with it.

First blood to me?

No. There was no blood, nor even any apparently equivalent body fluid. Nothing spurted forth to boil away in the solar wind as Anders had hoped. But there was something caught on the tip of his weapon. It seemed he had snagged some sort of equipage worn by his opponent. He flicked the spear, freeing the object to tumble away into the deeps.

The thing had stopped its forward progress, but it didn't turn to confront him. Maybe it was confused or in shock. Too bad for it. Anders plunged forward with his makeshift spear again.

A leg moved, intercepting his attack. The spear point skittered along bumpy carapace before sliding through bubbling gel and into a joint. The wounded leg spasmed, ripping the spear from Anders's grasp.

He had to dodge under the belly of the beast to avoid the suddenly thrashing legs. A short, thick spine offered a convenient handhold and he grabbed it. He might have been a rat in a terrier's jaws. Muscles straining, he kept his grip. Barely. Opportunity offered him another spine. He snatched at it. He got it on the second try.

Hand over hand he hauled himself up the side of the bucking beast. The smaller gripping limbs stretched back, claws snapping in vain attempts to snare him. He couldn't move forward without falling afoul of their undoubtedly suit-destroying clutches.

His position was precarious. He jammed his feet against the down curve in the beast's abdomen, letting his gecko soles do some of the work of keeping him aboard. His unwilling mount bucked and heaved beneath him. He knew he was in trouble. Even if he could maintain his grip, the rough surfaces of its armor would soon abrade through his suit.

He didn't have a lot of time, and he was weaponless.

No, young idiot, came his old instructor's voice. *You are not weaponless. You are never unarmed. Think about it. You can think, can't you?*

It had been a *tetsuharan* riddle to test his understanding of the true nature of a warrior. It had jarred him all those long years ago. It jarred him now into doing what he had to do.

He didn't have a lot of options, but as the *tetsuharan* adepts were wont to say, *Imminent death offers refreshing clarity.* There might be a way to deal with this monster. It was a potentially costly way, but if successful it would save Sue from the beast.

He set about it.

Wishing he had gecko palms on his gloves, he let go his right-hand grip. He needed a free hand to work. As carefully as he could he unsnapped the harness to his backpack. The monster's gyrations nearly knocked the unit from his grip as

Anders tried to maneuver it around in front of himself. At last he managed to get the pack wedged on edge between his belly and the beast. Then he managed to dig out a suit repair patch. He slapped it against the inside of the backpack and jammed the unit down onto the creature while the sealant was still foaming.

His backpack was now attached in a position that the monster couldn't reach. If it could have, it would have, using its flailing limbs to tear Anders away.

Time to commit.

He aligned the pack's maneuver nozzles for linear thrust and triggered them.

He could feel the heat, and so could the beast. It lifted two of its legs away from the flesh-melting flame. That was enough. The thrust ripped its others free from the hull.

He cut his connection to the backpack, canceled the gecko function, and kicked away. He felt the searing heat of the thruster jets wash over him. His suit didn't blow out; he'd gotten far enough from them that his suit didn't melt away.

The creature tumbled away into space.

Taking his oxygen supply with it and leaving him drifting on a long slow course away from *Auditor*.

35

Sue watched Seaborg's battle with the spidery alien with a mixture of awe and dread. The end had come unexpectedly and was unexpectedly happy. She truly had not anticipated he would survive his Quixotic heroism.

The rush of elation evaporated like a wave splashing against a hot volcanic shore as she realized that his oxygen supply had been housed in the backpack unit he had just sent blasting away. How much time did he have before he suffocated?

He was floating free in space, unable to change his course. She didn't know if he had planned it or not—though she suspected that he just might have—but he was moving on a trajectory parallel to the ship's hull. As he passed near an antenna, he reached out to grab it but missed. As he sailed on, she realized that he couldn't alter his path. That path was rising slightly, taking him away from the hull. Soon he would be the one starting the long journey into the sun.

If she could catch him, though . . .

She set out. Heading straight for him wouldn't do; he'd be gone before she got to him. She hurried along at an angle to his path.

Her breath echoed in her ears. It was hard keeping to the rhythm that let the gecko soles do the vital work of keeping her attached to the hull.

As she closed with Seaborg, she saw that she didn't have

the angle right. She was going to get to the intersection point too late.

On planetside, she could have just jumped and caught him, but here she didn't dare risk a jump. That would only launch her into space, and if she didn't catch him, she would just keep going. She might try using the maneuvering unit, but she was sure that she would, as he had warned her, just send herself into the sun.

Running faster to catch him was the only option.

Harder! Concentrate harder, girl! Make the feet do their work.

She was panting, hot and clammy within the suit. She got nearer. Her outstretched hand almost close enough.

Just. A. Bit. More.

Her fingers brushed against his leg. She tried, but she couldn't get a grip. She felt her hand sliding down along his boot.

She was losing him.

But when her palm slid off his heel and onto the sole of his boot, it stuck as though it had been glued.

He's got the fratching gecko thing going!

Then the shock hit her as his momentum stretched her body out. She cried in pain as her joints protested under the shock. One of her boots came unstuck, but only one.

She'd done it! She could hardly credit the fact, but it was plainly true.

Given an anchor point, he was no longer helpless. He jackknifed his body, getting a hand on her wrist as he released his foot's gecko grip. With a gymnast's grace, he vaulted over her to land with both feet on the hull. He touched their helmets together and spoke.

"You, Sue Merrick, are a lifesaver."

His jaunty tone perversely drove the joy at his safety out of her head. "The alien. What kind of a crazy stunt was that?"

"A successful one, apparently. At least so far. We need to get me back inside soon, as I've not much air left."

The only airlock she knew about was one she didn't think was wise to use. "Not onto the flight deck."

"I concur." He separated their helmets and craned his around. Making contact again, he said, "There ought to be another lock in that direction, just around the curve. Are you ready to hike?"

"What the hell is that?"

Williams was the rear guard and his exclamation made Benton look back. He didn't need to ask what Williams was referring to. Looming dark and monstrous at the far entry to the galley, beyond the position where the enemy humans were beginning to probe the darkened compartment, was a giant, insectlike creature. At least he assumed it was a creature, since it didn't have the metallic sheen of a machine.

"Some sort of Remor hunter beast sent along to help the collectors?"

"Maybe the masters don't trust the slaves."

Was Williams suggesting that it might actually be a Remor? "It can't be."

"I'm going to pretend it is."

Williams slid a flattened rod from his holster and gave it a snap, shaking the memory plastic into its expanded shape: a rifle stock. He rubbed his thumb against the joining point to activate the adhesive before pressing it against the butt of his pistol. Raising the modified weapon to his shoulder, he settled against the bulkhead and took aim.

"Is this wise?" Benton asked.

Williams's answer was to squeeze off a shot. Chunks of matter exploded from one of the joints on the thing's middle left leg. It screamed.

Men started shouting, scrambling for cover. No fire came toward the hiding Combiners, so Benton guessed they hadn't been spotted. That good luck wouldn't last long. He started shouting too, urging the others to get moving and away from the attention Williams had drawn.

Williams fired again, taking the left rear leg, in a different joint. The insect thing collapsed, shrieking.

"Whatever it is it can be hurt," he said, sounding very satisfied.

Then he shrieked himself as one of the enemy weapons caught him. His pistol spun away as he fell back under cover of the bulkhead. His right arm was hanging limp at his side.

"You can be hurt too," Benton pointed out unnecessarily. "Is it bad?"

"Hurts like hell. Thanks for asking."

Benton pulled the man to his feet and gave him a shove to send him stumbling after the rest. He looked for Williams's pistol and spotted it lying in the open. It had lost its shoulder stock, but it was their only weapon.

Crouching low, he went after it. As he snatched it up, the shiver-inducing chill of near-misses from the collectors' weapons sent him scrambling back under cover.

He knew they had nearly gotten him, but he had done what he intended. He had the pistol. Blindly pointing it around the bulkhead, he snapped off a couple shots in the hope that he might convince the collectors to keep their heads down.

He ran as hard as he could, following his retreating companions. They had already passed the next bulkhead and found temporary safety. It wasn't far, but for him it might be a goal never reached.

When no shots immediately sought him out, he started to believe he would make it.

"Let 'em go, you slugs," Bartie ordered. "They ain't got nowhere to run that we can't find 'em. Hernandez, you keep an eye out and make sure they don't double back."

Those two wild shots showed that the rabbits were panicking now. The last curdler volley had probably taken down the damned sniper of a soldier who had pumped two rounds—two frickin' rounds—and taken down one of the frickin' bugs.

The stinking xeno-mantis wasn't dead, but it was moaning like it wished it was. Bartie thought it just might be worthwhile taking a break and watching the thing kick. If it did, he would have a second thing to thank that damned sniper soldier for. The first had been in their last encounter when soldier boy had popped Goss and put a permanent end to the whining.

It sure looked like the thing was dying. Its legs were getting slower and less coordinated as they pushed the body around in a circle. And the puddle of ichor in which it wallowed was growing. It looked like just a matter of time.

Bartie fingered the *gawkhore* at his throat.

Can you make your little convincer work when you're dead, bug?

He didn't think so.

Even if this frickin' xeno-mantis kicked, it wouldn't mean freedom unless he got lucky and the soldier boys took out the other two bugs that they'd had to bring along. Hell, he'd do it himself if he thought he could get away with it. But he didn't, so he would just have to enjoy this little bit of vicarious payback.

The idea that the soldier boys and the bugs might do for each other filled his head. Even if one side just mauled the other badly enough, Bartie and his slugs could mop up the "victor." Then Bartie would be in charge aboard this starship. And damn for sure it wouldn't be going where the frickin' xenos wanted it to go; it'd be going where *Bartie* wanted it to go.

"Designate Bartie."

The cold, demanding bug voice cut through moans, shattering his dreams of freedom. How in hell could the frickin' xeno-mantis talk like nothing was wrong? It was dying! Almost dead! The alien didn't seem to realize that, for its voice was as calm and steady as ever.

"Designate Bartie, construct conveyance. Construct now."

It wasn't fair! It was supposed to be dead, not giving orders. Why couldn't the frickin' thing die like a real organism? Was it some kind of frickin' immortal?

"Conveyance?" He tried to sound dumb while he got his thoughts together. "What kind of conveyance?"

"Carry."

It had to be kidding. "You saying you want a stretcher? It'd take half the xombies I've got here to lift your ugly butt and haul it around. Call one of your buddy bugs to come haul you around."

"Suggestion unexecutable. Construct conveyance."

Its orders were punctuated by a sucking, squelching noise that came from somewhere near its bug head.

Bartie took a step back.

Something was happening to the fallen xeno-mantis. The thing looked like it was splitting apart, like some kind of caterpillar cracking open to let a butterfly out. Pale tentacles appeared between the dimmed lamp eyes and beneath the jewel-eyed bug head. They writhed like an obscene living beard. The tentacles stretched out, finding grips. They tugged. With a sound like pulling a boot from mud, a slug-like shape emerged and slither-flopped to the deck. Small flakes of carapace dropped away. But the slug with the xeno-mantis head didn't just lie there naked and ugly and gross. Dripping slime, it extended its tentacles, hauling itself away from the spider body and toward Bartie.

"Conveyance," it reiterated in that familiar, demanding xeno-mantis voice. "Effort not unexecutable."

One tentacle snaked back and slithered along a line of pouches along its flank. It burrowed into one and emerged wrapped around something metallic. The bug-slug pointed its find at the spider body. There was a flash of light. The body twitched a couple of times and slumped, finally unmoving, to the deck.

Wisps of stinking smoke started to rise from the corpse. It started collapsing like some nature program's fast vid of decay. Within moments it was little more than a puddle with slowly sinking islands of resistant carapace and dense masses of tissue. Another minute and even those were gone and there was just a pit in the floor.

Bartie had heard about Remor machines dissolving when

they got trashed. Just like this. It looked like the spider body was just another machine to this thing that had pulled itself from the wreckage of its organic chassis.

Bartie stared down at the thing he had feared for so long. This was it? This bug head on a slug the size of the bitch that had been the very first thing he had ever killed with his own hands?

He felt his blood simmering up to a boil. He'd never been the kind of guy to knuckle under to a man half his mass. Why in all the hells should he let some frickin', stinking, alien slug half his mass bugger him eight ways to Sunday?

The xeno-slug craned its bug head up at him. The glittering jewels of its eyes were cold and implacable. "Designate Bartie, commence action. Inaction brings punishment."

He'd heard that before and knew the stall was over. He watched the bug-slug put away the zapper it had used to make a puddle of the spider body. Frickin' overconfident xeno.

And maybe that was the answer.

"Okay, boss," he said obediently. "Aziz, get your butt over here. Gimme your gun. You got work to do."

Aziz handed over his rifle-sized curdler as he griped, "Why me?"

"Because I said so, moron." Keeping his back to the bug-slug, Bartie started giving Aziz detailed orders about how to make a nice big stretcher for their bug boss. While he was doing it, he handed Aziz his own curdler. The pistol might not have enough juice.

It had to be quick, clean.

He turned fast, dropping his aim onto the bug-slug, and pulled the trigger as soon as he got the muzzle on line. Leakage numbed his hands, but he didn't care. He'd caught the bug-slug off guard.

The xeno didn't crumple like a human, but it thrashed. Lordie, how it thrashed. He kept on pulling the trigger. Laughing as he watched the bug-slug squirm.

Aziz caught on and gave the xeno a few tickles of his own.

"Good boy," Bartie told him, but he really didn't care

what Aziz or any of the others did right now. Opportunity had opened its legs for him and he was taking it, hard and fast the way he liked it.

"How do you like it, you frickin' xeno? Huh? You like it when I 'bring punishment'? No? Tough. Suck it up, bug-slug."

Its thrashing eventually slowed, then stopped. Bartie lit it up again, but it didn't twitch. Was it dead so soon?

That was no fun.

He shot it again to be sure.

"Nothing more to say, bug-slug?"

Nothing. He kicked it. It just rolled over on its back, flaccid tentacles sprawling around like limp white worms.

It really was dead.

Something popped beneath it. Startled, Bartie jumped back.

What the hell new kind of trick was this?

When the wisps of stinking smoke started to rise, he sussed it. It was the puddle-of-goo trick again. In moments the bug-slug was no more recognizable than the spider body.

That was fine by him. It was gone, and nobody would ever know it was Bartie who made it dead. The big scary Remor weren't so scary anymore. If one frickin' xeno could be made dead . . .

Possibilities flickered through his mind as he fingered the *gawkhore* at his throat. The right time. The right place. That was all he needed.

The game had just gotten itself some new rules.

36

Anders's vision was graying when Sue's helmet slipped up against his. Her voice came from very far away.

"I've found one," she said.

One what?

"Hold on, Seaborg, hold on. We're almost there."

Oh, good.

He'd always liked being there.

There where?

Unexpectedly there was a dark hole in front of him. He fell into it. He fell a long, long way. Somewhere along the line he stopped falling. Sometime after that he opened his wretched, itching eyes and came back to himself inside a head that throbbed like the crescendo of the Heritage Assembly Taiko Drum Festival.

He was inside a cramped airlock, sitting with his back against the outer hatch. He was still wearing the emergency escape suit. He reached up to release his suit's helmet but found that it had already been done.

Should have noticed that right away.

There were a lot of things he should have noticed. Blaming it all on his grogginess, while accurate, wasn't acceptable.

A uniformed body, female, lay across his legs. He didn't recognize the uniform. The woman was breathing but apparently unconscious. Sue Merrick was there too. She had shucked her suit.

"Welcome back," she said. "I was afraid you weren't going to make it."

"We Eridani are hard to kill."

"Seems so."

He pointed to the unknown woman. "Who's this?

"A xombie. They're hard to kill too."

Anders caught the scent of blood and, belatedly, noticed a dribble of blood crawling out from beneath the hair on the woman's left temple. Recent damage. Had Sue tried to kill this woman?

He asked.

She told him how she had encountered the xombie after she had gotten him safely back inside *Auditor* and had left the airlock to scout around. They had scuffled, and Sue had managed to knock the woman out.

"I couldn't very well leave her lying around outside where somebody might find her and start looking for whoever had conked her. Getting found before you woke up didn't seem like a good idea."

"I concur. So what's the situation out there?"

"Hard to say. I didn't go very far."

She gave him what details she could. He questioned her closely on what she'd seen and heard and on what had happened before she fled out onto the hull. She was a good observer, but she wasn't a trained military observer. Anders was left with a lot of questions.

"Maybe she can tell us something about our enemy," he said, pointing at the woman still draped over his legs.

"I doubt it."

"It can't hurt to try."

"Suit yourself."

It took some contortions, but they managed to rearrange themselves within the lock. When they were done, Anders was mobile and standing and the woman reclined where he had been. Sue crammed herself into a corner as far away from the woman as possible.

Anders started by searching the woman. She had no obvious identification tags, but he did confiscate some useful items from her pockets and belt pouches. He handed two of the ration bars he found to Sue. Her dislike of the xombie didn't prevent her from wolfing them down. Anders did the same for the rest of the bars.

"Didn't she have a weapon?"

"Club," Sue said around a mouthful of ration bar. She hefted said item. There was a smear of blood on it. "Mine now."

He started to probe certain pressure points in an effort to speed the woman's return to consciousness. As he reached around her neck, his fingers brushed against something that squirmed. Investigating, he found a thing that looked a lot like a Chugeni multipede nestled on the back of her neck. No, *nestled* wasn't the right word, not the right word at all. Each of this thing's legs was buried in the woman's flesh.

"Before you can cut it out, it'll kill her," Sue said.

"What is it?"

Sue shrugged. "The aliens gave it to her. Doc Shelly thought it might be what makes them xombies."

"Some sort of parasitic bioform controlling device, then?"

Well, devices could be removed. So could parasites. And there were other options besides knives, which they didn't have anyway. Using some of the things he'd taken from the woman's belt and the backpack from Sue's suit, he started preparing one.

He had to concede that his idea was risky, but the woman might have valuable information. And if they couldn't get this woman back to normal, they couldn't afford to leave her behind either. They were in hostile territory and their safety lay in remaining invisible and unknown to the enemy. It came down to a brutal either-or. Either he brought this woman back to the light or he sent her down into the final dark.

His mood was gloomy when he finished his tinkering, but his resolve had hardened.

"What are you going to do?" Sue asked.

"I've built a heating element. If we're lucky, it will cause the parasite to voluntarily withdraw. It's her best chance."

"Maybe you should just kill her now."

The hardness in her voice chilled him. He had thought he was the brutal one.

It is her best chance, he told himself. It was her only chance for life. Were he the one infected, he would have wanted someone to give him the chance.

He rolled the woman over so he could get at the thing holding her in thrall. "God be with you," he whispered to her as he applied the glowing element to the alien parasite.

The woman's screams reverberated within the airlock.

Anders nearly took Sue's advice. He was ready to toss away the heat element and kill the woman when he realized that his scheme was working. The parasite was wriggling, starting to withdraw from her.

As its last tendrils came free, Anders swatted it to the deck and instantly squashed it with his boot. He expected the smeary mess to dissolve away, and possibly take his boot with it, but nothing of the sort happened. Was that it, then? Was it really dead? Was it that easy?

The woman started going into convulsions.

He killed the power to the heater and did his best to stretch her out. A quick gag prevented her from swallowing her tongue. The discarded emergency suits offered padding to help keep her from injuring herself, but there wasn't much else to do but wait out the storm. When at last the spasms faded, Anders cradled her head. He massaged her temples until she opened her eyes.

"You're safe now. Free again," he told her. "What's your name?"

The answer was long in coming.

"Shayla."

"We need your help, Shayla. We're fighting the people who enslaved you. We need your help to do that."

"Where's the music?" she asked. "Can you hear it?"

"What?"

"The music's gone," she sobbed. "Gone. Gone."

Her bizarre fascination with the "music" made his questioning difficult. All the more so as her answers became less and less coherent. It became plain that, as a xombie, she had been happy doing whatever she was ordered to do. She'd never had the tiniest thought of escape from Remor domination. Ominously, he learned that she had been ordered to capture any humans she encountered, not kill them.

"The choirmasters want them," she said.

"Why?"

Her answer was unintelligible. She was slipping away. Anders pressed for details about the enemy. How many? What weapons? The insectoid creatures—were they really Remor?

"Three choirmasters," she said.

"What do you mean? Were there only three of the Remor?"

"The music's gone," she said one last time, and was gone herself.

Anders sighed, looking at the still body of the woman who had been named Shayla by her parents, had lost herself through no fault of her own, and had at the last, by the grace of God, become again Shayla.

"May you rest in peace."

Sue frowned down on him. "Was that of any real use?"

"It's clear the raiders want the crew of *Auditor* at least as much as they want the ship.'

"More xombies for them," Sue said.

"But why do they want xombies at all?"

Sue shrugged. "Does it matter? Once they get you, you're as good as dead."

"Worse than dead," he said, inwardly shuddering at the thought of surrendering all will to the enemy and becoming their tool. What then would happen to your soul?

An enemy that sought your life was one thing. The Remor, it seemed, wanted more. He stood up, filled with grim resolve. "We are not going to let them have this ship."

Despite the fact that he had managed to get nearly twenty people safely back into the compartments surrounding the bridge, Benton Mainwaring wasn't pleased. Twenty was far,

far too few. There might be more out there, hiding where they could, but he couldn't know.

And if he did know, what could he do about it? Williams's pistol was the only ranged weapon they had among them and it was down to four rounds. Their few knives and some makeshift clubs might get them past the xombies, but the collectors with their guns? Never. And should there be another of those spidery aliens—well, the thought didn't bear thinking.

At least they had reached the bridge, denying it to the enemy. And Coppelstowe had managed to link to engineering and warn them about the boarding. The good news there was that she had connected before Gutermann managed to open a passage through the most heavily damaged portion of the ship, a task to which Captain Seaborg had set him. Had the engineers been successful, they would have run straight into the boarders. The engineers were as poorly armed as Benton's pitiful remnant. How could they fight the collectors?

For the moment at least everyone below frame 87 was safe. The flip side was that the engineering crew was of little help to those under siege in the forward sections. But if the dynamic flowed in their favor, that would change. Benton had refocused Gutermann on securing access to the armory, assuming it still existed. With weapons in the engineers' hands, all the equations changed. Without them, Benton didn't need to solve any sociodynamics equations to see that the outlook was nothing but grim.

The question was: Did they have enough time?

It had been over an hour since any xombies had come to test the rough barricade they had erected in a frozen-open hatchway. It was a flimsy barrier. Again Benton considered abandoning the compartment, but nothing had changed. It still offered access to vital environmental controls for the bridge. To lose it was to lose the bridge itself.

"It's been quiet for a while," Coppelstowe said. The worry in her voice sounded strange in Benton's ears.

"What do you think they're up to?"

"I could only guess. They are too strange to analyze. If I had better parameters, perhaps . . ."

Her voice trailed off into doubt. She was as adrift as he.

"Don't let it worry you, Sister. No one is blaming you."

"Perhaps this is the chrysalis."

The nexus in the dynamic that Alsion had said lay here in the Pacifica system? Did she really think it was still in the offing? *Been and gone, most likely.*

"I don't need my morale boosted, Sister," he lied. "Would you go check on Williams for me? I'll feel better if he's starting to get some feeling back in that arm."

"Of course."

He watched her go. He suspected she knew the errand was false, just an excuse to end the conversation. She was too good an initiate for him to fool her unless she wanted him to.

Why had she reminded him of the chrysalis? Did he dare think that current events might indeed be the chrysalis from which the butterfly would emerge? That this was all part of the path that Alsion had foreseen? That he, Benton Mainwaring, could still be the one to make the difference in the war with the Remor? Was he carrying on because of that hope?

Or was it just because he really, really hated losing?

And that, it seemed, was what he was fated to do.

Sullen and dispirited, he kept watch. He wasn't sure why he bothered. What kept him standing here, waiting for whatever would come out of the darkness? Was it a sense of duty? Hope in Alsion's promise? Stubbornness? Or did he just have nothing better to do?

The doubt-filled tedium was broken when a soft voice called from the darkness on the other side of the barrier. It sounded like Lugard's voice.

"Can you be hearing me in there? They be gone now. Off hunting the others. But they be coming back soon, I think. Be letting me through before they do."

Benton bent to one of the loopholes and looked through. It *was* Lugard. The guild spacer stood shifting nervously in the cone of light from the last surviving fixture out there. The man kept apprehensively looking over his shoulder, back down the corridor.

"Be hurrying."

"What happened? I thought we lost you when they boarded."

"Bad time, that. I been hiding. I heard them say you were heading for the bridge, so I came as soon as I could. How many made it?"

"Not a lot. We've got less than twenty people here."

"Twenty? Did you say twenty?" Lugard shook his head. "So few."

There were indeed too few, and despite his sometimes fractious personality Lugard was a guild spacer. His expertise might be useful in tipping the balance.

"I be another if you hurry. Otherwise they be catching me too."

That was likely true. Benton shifted the main brace to open a way for him. It took another few moments to clear a passage.

"I'm glad you made it, Master Lugard," he said, stepping back so the man could enter. "We can use every loyal hand."

The guild spacer slipped through the narrow opening, saying, "And I be glad you opened up."

Lugard's smile was almost feral as he produced a weapon from behind his back and leveled it in Benton's face.

37

The first sign Anders observed of the enemy was a faint, familiar odor. The corroded spot in the deck and the slag-edged hole above confirmed it.

"There was a Remor meltdown up there in the galley."

"Another of those things that look like Cawdore mantises?" Sue asked, shuddering.

"Couldn't say, but whatever it was, it's not part of our problem anymore."

Anders couldn't see any active dissolution, and a hand held near the hole's edge didn't detect any heat. Gingerly he touched a fingernail to the porous metal. The only effect was a bit of the metal crumbling away.

Good. The reaction was complete.

Gripping the edge with both hands, he hauled his head up through the hole. Nobody shot it off.

Also good.

Looking around, he couldn't see anything dangerous.

Better.

He levered himself up and over the edge. He still felt uneasy. The ghost-town atmosphere of the ship was unsettling. But stretch his senses as he might, he couldn't detect any sign of trouble.

Don't be foolish. There's a lot more to worry about than ghosts.

He knelt by the hole's edge and reached a hand down to

Sue to haul her up to join him. As he set her down, she asked, "It's not lunchtime, is it?"

"You're not still hungry?" The ration bars she'd eaten should have been enough to keep a soldier going for a day.

"I'm more worried about running into the lunchtime crowd."

"Just us for now."

"Good."

Auditor's galley, like those on a lot of deep space ships, was equipped to provide one of the only real and visceral luxuries aboard a tin can sailing among the stars: decent meals. Doing that meant decent cooks, and decent cooks demanded good equipment, and good equipment to a cook meant good knives.

Good equipment to a soldier could mean good knives too. Anders helped himself to a selection.

Sue, seeing what he was about, picked a knife out for herself. She lashed it to a mop handle, improvising a spear. It wasn't a bad idea. Anders copied her.

As he was finishing his lashing, he heard the indistinct sound of collectors' weapons firing. At least that's what he assumed it was; the banshee groaning matched Sue's description. The action was quite a distance away, but the hollow, haunted corridors let it echo and travel.

"What now?" Sue asked.

"Trouble."

Time to march to the sound of the guns.

Bartie, waiting in the shadows with his slugs, watched the newly recruited Combiner spaceman talk his way through the barrier like he said he could. It was a good trick, but it would have been a better one if his mark hadn't been that gullible idiot running this lunatic ship.

Bartie had the angle to see. Lugard stopped moving just inside the narrow bit.

Keep moving, you slug. Clear the entry.

Lugard, it seemed, had other things on his mind.

"You be paying one last bill, Mainwaring. You be paying my way out."

The buzz of curdler fire cut the air.

Damn Lugard for jumping the gun! He was supposed to get clear through before dumping anybody.

"Move, you slugs!" Bartie ordered.

Hernandez led the charge, butting Lugard out of the way. The other guys swarmed after him, passing Mainwaring's fallen body as they headed for the soft chewy center before Combiner holdouts figured out that they'd been breached.

Bartie called for the xombies to come up from around the bend where they'd been staying out of sight. A good general kept himself a reserve. Walking up to Lugard, he held his left hand out. Lugard looked down at the waiting palm, then up at the xombies backing Bartie. The spaceman handed over the curdler pistol Bartie had loaned him.

"These things fry synapses that close," Bartie observed. "Boils a man's brain."

"Being too bad."

My, my, how bitter. Looked like Lugard had some kind of score to settle with Mainwaring that he hadn't bothered to mention to his new friend Bartie. Bartie looked down at Mainwaring's body. The man had died with a look of surprise on his face.

Looked like Mainwaring hadn't figured it out either. What a stooge.

"What you wanted be done. You be taking the bridge. Now you be seeing that you can be trusting me."

"Oh, I be trusting you, Master Lugard. I be trusting you very much."

He put the curdler to Lugard's temple and pulled the trigger.

"You think I'd trust somebody who fries his old boss's brains?" he asked the corpse. "Well, actually I would. I'd absolutely trust him to fry his new boss's brains given the chance. But then I'm smarter than some bosses."

Bartie looked down at the two bodies. Bookend expressions. Kind of poetic, really.

38

The corridors remained deserted as Anders and Sue made their way toward the bridge. The firing had stopped some time ago. Whatever action had been under way had been decided.

The section through which they passed had taken significant combat damage. Panels hung from the ceiling on half-cut wires, and debris was littered everywhere. The fitful lighting didn't make it easy to avoid the hazards. For reasons of safety and stealth, Anders slowed their pace.

As they crept closer to the bridge Anders found he could just make out voices. They were discussing what to do with "the meat" and the best way to get the xombies to move it. Obviously the collectors had won the skirmish.

They drew closer, until the next bend in the corridor was likely all that separated them from the talkers. Dropping to the deck, Anders crept forward to take a peek.

Around the corner, the length of corridor was short and lit by a single fixture. It led to a partially blocked hatchway. Beyond that lay another short stretch of corridor that Anders recognized as the last before the bridge complex.

A dozen xombies were working at removing a barricade from the hatchway. Beyond that failed defense, Anders could see the three collectors whose conversation he had overheard. All were armed with unfamiliar guns, presumably the energy weapons whose discharges he'd heard. One of the collectors was fondling a projectile pistol, a custom job that

Anders recognized as having belonged to Larsen Williams. None of the xombies seemed to be carrying anything more advanced than Shayla's club.

As Anders was evaluating his tactical options, the collector with the pistol, presumably the leader, sent the others to "organize the meat."

Anders made his decision.

He eased back from the corner. Safely screened, he rose and returned to Sue.

"Wait here," he whispered into her ear.

Her glare was full of insubordination, but she didn't object. He was grateful for that. It was going to be tricky and he didn't need any distractions.

He calmed his breathing, settling mind and body. He drifted down into the still place and was ready. He walked around the corner.

His approach went unnoticed until he threw the knife. It passed through the midst of the xombies, touching not a one, and slammed home into his intended target: the collector leader still standing near the hatchway. Unfortunately, Anders's aim was not perfect. The knife caught the man in the shoulder. It ravaged muscle and buried itself against bone, but not fatally. The man screeched and went down.

Anders was close enough now to the xombies. The knife-spear licked out and the first went down. He took the second on recovery of his initial thrust, the third with an overhead strike, and the fourth with a reversal. He pressed on. He had eight down before they started to react to him.

He fought on.

Whenever possible he made his strike against the parasite, but he didn't hold back if a different target offered him the opportunity to take down one of them.

Their strikes were slow and clumsy. He avoided them.

As he closed on the hatchway he could see that a collector had been attracted to the fight. The man was readying his weapon. A well-placed kick launched a xombie into the line of fire. The weapon made its banshee wail, but the beam only caught the flailing xombie.

Anders put a knife into the collector's heart.

More collectors were coming.

He dispatched the last two xombies and rolled sideways away from the hungry wailing beams that sought him. Taking up a position in the dark near the hatch, he waited.

A muzzle poked into sight. The man carrying the weapon remained crouching in the hatchway. The muzzle drifted left and right, seeking him.

Anders waited.

When the hand holding the weapon's forestock came into sight, he struck upward against the wrist. The weapon clattered to the deck. The collector's hand fell with it.

Anders faded deeper into the darkness to await the next phase.

Pain blew Bartie to the floor, searing from his shoulder to explode in his head. He'd been bushwhacked. There was a frickin' knife sticking in him. He wrenched it free and nearly passed out from the surge of agony.

Actually, he did pass out. Either that or Hernandez had learned how to teleport. The ex-soldier was standing over him, looking out at the fight in the corridor.

"Damn, it's one of the Eridani," Hernandez said as he raised his curdler to fire.

"Damn." His shot had hit a xombie.

"Damn," he gasped, staring down at the knife that had sprouted in his chest.

Hernandez collapsed bonelessly, a very ex, ex-soldier.

What in hell's name is happening?

Through the hatchway Bartie could see a big man ripping his xombies apart. Just one. Just one frickin' guy!

Footfalls and excited chatter behind him announced the arrivals of his slugs. Four of them anyway. Sheriden, Aziz, and two of the new guys.

Now we see how soldier boy does against real guys.

"Shoot," he told them, and they did.

"I don't see him," Sheriden said. "Did we get him?"

Bartie could see downed and dismembered xombies littering the hallway. He didn't see any lump large enough to be the Eridani.

Sheriden moved forward warily, stopping just shy of the threshold. He scanned the corridor, then took another step forward. A blade flashed out. Sheriden's weapon went one way and his left hand another. He fell back, screaming like a woman.

Curdler fire blasted the entrance. Nothing. Sheriden kept screaming. Bartie's slugs stopped firing but kept their weapons trained on the hatchway. Sheriden just kept on screaming.

"Shut up!" Bartie screamed back at him. "I can't think!"

Sheriden just shrieked louder.

Bartie scrambled over to his fallen curdler. It was awkward in his left hand, but he didn't care. He shot frickin' Sheriden and shut him up.

"Good move," Aziz commented. "Who the hell is that out there?"

"Dunno. Hernandez said it was one of them Eridani super soldiers."

"Shite, I ain't fighting no Eridani," one of the new guys said.

"You ain't got no choice," Bartie told him. "Besides, he ain't so super. He had a chance to take me down and he couldn't do it. Had surprise on his side too. He couldn't do it. You hear me? He couldn't do it.

"Somebody get me a bandage," he said as the wooziness tried to take him. "But keep the frickin' door covered."

Kade, the guy whose name Bartie hadn't remembered, dug out a medkit and did the dirty work. If the coward thought his ministrations were earning him back ground, he didn't know Bartie. Through the whole thing, Bartie kept talking, as much to keep himself from slipping away as to buck up the slugs.

"Listen up, you slugs. Surprise was Mr. Hero's big card and he's played it. The cards are gonna fall our way from here on 'cause there's just one of him. We're gonna get ourselves some reinforcements. With the rest of the xombies for a meat shield, it'll be easy to push him in a corner. Then it gets even easier. A curdler will take him down. It'd take a *real* superman to fight with his nerves scrambled. That guy out there ain't superman, he's just an Eridani. He'll bleed as easy as anybody. And you can bet he'll bleed if I have anything to say about it.

"And now that I ain't bleeding all over myself, we can get started."

"What are we gonna do about the meat?" Aziz asked. "The bugs ain't gonna be happy we just let them go."

"Kade, you go back and get the other guys to lay 'em out, but not too close. We don't want to damage the merchandise. We'll pick 'em up when we come back. Oh, yeah, and save one out. We'll need a shield."

It was breakout time.

Sue didn't obey Seaborg. She crept forward as he had and watched in awe as he demolished the force of xombies. She'd learned her spear-fighting the hard way in the rough-and-tumble of survival in the streets of occupied Palisandra. He handled the weapon like a martial artist. Whirling and twirling, striking with blade or butt. Strike and thrust. Rarely more than one strike to a foe and never more than two.

He thwarted the first shot the collectors attempted and dodged the rest. Then he cut off the hand of their boldest. Their panicky firing made it clear he had put the fear of retribution into them.

She expected Seaborg to charge in and finish them, but instead he drifted back into the corridor's darkness. She assumed he knew what he was doing. She certainly didn't.

One of the xombies moaned, but otherwise the corridor was quiet. The one the collector had shot, she guessed. She doubted any of the ones that Seaborg had targeted would be in any shape to moan.

Something was going on with the collectors. She could hear them talking, but she couldn't make out the words. She did, however, recognize the rhythms of a pep talk. Someone over there had a plan.

It became clear when a half dozen collectors emerged, pushing the captured Alsionite before them. They were counting on Seaborg not striking an innocent. He didn't.

They all got through the hatchway and looked nervously around. After they shuffled a few meters without being attacked, the bandaged man who must be their leader said, "Dump her."

At his order, the hulking brute who had been manhandling the bound Alsionite shoved her down. One of the others raised his weapon to shoot her. Instead of pulling the trigger, he fell over backward, a knife in his chest.

The collectors broke and ran, firing wildly behind them.

Time for her to move.

Sue scuttled back, looking to get out of their way. She had barely taken up a position behind some shielding debris when they rounded the corner, still running hard. Obviously they hadn't spotted her, because they weren't shooting at her. She waited, intending to take their leader down and stall them for Seaborg to finish.

The leader's face was illuminated by the flickering light.

Bartie!

Sue's mind froze. She wasn't on *Auditor* anymore. She couldn't breathe. Her hands shook against the spear that she knew, really knew she didn't have. Then the moment was past.

And so was he.

A second collector flashed past her hiding place. Then a third.

You're a pitiful wretch, girl!

Shame powered the thrust she finally made. She took the last of the five in the armpit.

The shock threw her back, slamming her head into the wall. She fought unconsciousness, afraid that she hadn't finished her man and fearful of what would happen if she hadn't.

A hand reached for her and she slapped it away.

She went for her knife, but the man standing over her didn't move. His hand was still outstretched.

What kind of—

Seaborg.

She let the knife slip back against its magnetic hold plate and took his offered hand. Steady as a rock, he hauled her to her feet.

He had one of the collectors' guns under his arm and another slung on his back. He handed her the one that had belonged to the man lying at her feet with the broken haft of her spear sticking out of his torso.

Seaborg was smiling.

"I think we may have started to turn things around."

39

Bartie figured it was safe to take a breather when they reached the galley, where he'd put down the frickin' xeno, without more trouble. He needed it. He was panting like a geriatric hound and his shoulder was throbbing like a junque-beat drummer solo. To make matters more fun, the frickin' wound had started to bleed again.

His little band of merry men was hurting bad. Only four of them had gotten away from the frickin' Eridani. Just him, Aziz, and two of the new guys. None of the xombies, but that didn't matter.

"We made it," Kade said, grinning.

Then a curdler wailed and Kade went down.

Bartie was off like a rabbit, with Carmody, the last of the new guys, right behind. Aziz snapped off a shot of his own, then started dodging among the pots and pans himself.

Frickin' Eridani! He should have figured the soldier boy would arm himself from one of the guys he had taken down. Bad. Bad. Bad.

The Eridani's curdler shrilled again and hell's own world of pain exploded next to Bartie's left ear. Something bashed him in the back of his knees. He went down. Hard.

To his surprise, he wasn't a board. The shot had missed. It had come close, though. His head, neck, and shoulder felt on fire. Even the frickin' *gawkhore* around his throat was squirming in pain.

Aziz had found himself some cover and was pumping shots across the galley. Carmody was down, groaning.

"You functional?" Bartie asked.

"Yeah, I'm okay. Just tripped."

That explained why the frickin' Eridani's shot hadn't gotten one of them. Soldier boy must have been aiming at Carmody when the oaf fell. As it was, the shot nearly clipped Bartie.

He slapped the idiot.

On the ear? He been aiming for the shoulder. Damn. The near-miss had screwed up his coordination.

He owed soldier boy. First he'd lost use of his frickin' right arm to the frickin' Eridani's knife, now his frickin' left arm was on the fritz.

He had to get serious about shutting down soldier boy, and lying sprawled on the galley floor wasn't going to do it. And from their performance so far, his guys weren't going to do it either. Best thing to do was let the frickin' xenos settle soldier boy's hash.

"Aziz, keep that bastard's head down. We're going to the next hatch. We'll cover you from there."

Anders suspected that the leader of the collectors wasn't accounting for his superior hearing. To be sure, he waited until he heard Aziz start to move, then showed himself briefly. The curdler fire that sought him missed, but it made it plain that the leader hadn't just been deserting his comrade. The prey in this hunt had just gotten a little smarter.

He wished he knew more about how the collector leader thought, but he only had what he had observed so far and what Sue had told him. She had given the collector leader a name, Bartie. She'd said that the renegade had been a brutal faction leader in Palisandra with whom she'd had to contend. Anders had sensed there was something more between them as well but Sue's clinically cold accounting had warned him not to press. It was plain that Bartie had been one of the bad guys even before he'd turned species traitor.

But bad didn't mean stupid, as Bartie was demonstrating. He had some tactical acumen. His new bounding overwatch tactic made Anders's pursuit-sniping riskier.

"What now?" Sue asked.

"We adapt."

One advantage they had over the raiders was that they knew *Auditor.* The general trend of the collectors' path was back toward the flight deck, which matched well with what he'd overheard as they were planning their breakout from the bridge. There were several likely points where the fleeing collectors might be cut off.

A handful of xombies delayed them from reaching the first one in time.

Without direction the xombies were a minimal threat, not worth expending a weapons charge on. Anders and Sue dealt with them and moved on.

At the second point, Anders was able to take down the one called Aziz.

And then there were only two.

Bartie and Carmody were able to shoot their way out of the soldier boy's ambush, but the frickin' Eridani nearly put paid to them all. Bartie would miss Aziz. Hell, not really. But he *would* miss another gun against the frickin' Eridani.

The soldier boy was waiting for them near the docking bay too. He got Carmody that time. But Bartie managed to make it through the access hatch and, despite his curdler-screwed coordination, get the frickin' thing closed before the frickin' Eridani, running faster than he'd ever seen anyone run, made it through.

Bartie laughed till he was out of breath over that. He had a few witty remarks too, but there wasn't anybody around to appreciate them.

Nobody in here but me, some sleeping meat, and my frickin' alien overlords.

Speaking of the frickin' bugs, he could only see one of them. It was busy playing its games with the meat. The other had to be inside the ship, doing whatever it was the frickin' bugs did by themselves. The one on deck left off what it was doing and turned to him.

"Designate Bartie, explain force depletion."

A little chill went through him as, for just a moment, he thought he was looking at the one he'd wasted, reincarnated somehow. He knew it wasn't, but the frickin' things sounded so much alike.

"The bad guys got lucky," he told it. It was a small lie, but the *gawkhore* picked up on it and constricted against his throat. "All right, all right. We screwed up and got caught with our pants down."

His face burned with the admission, but the *gawkhore* didn't care. It kept its grip, annoying but not deadly. Frickin' thing must have gotten damaged in the near-miss.

Bartie told the frickin' bug about how he'd captured the bridge like they wanted and then about how they'd had it taken away from them in a counterattack. It had been an epic gun battle, the way he told it, even if he just never got around to mentioning the odds they'd fought against. He did make sure not to actually lie. Omissions, he'd already learned, didn't rouse the frickin' *gawkhore,* and he took advantage of that. He didn't omit being attacked by Eridani. He made a big deal about that, trying to impress on the frickin' xeno-mantis that it wasn't Bartie's fault. Which it wasn't, but the frickin' bug wouldn't understand that. Then, to make it look good, he mentioned that there was only one Eridani left out there. Just one.

"If I hadn't been wounded, I might have taken him, but you needed to know what happened."

The frickin' bug just stared at him. It might have been evaluating his report, or it might have just been thinking its frickin' buggy thoughts. He hoped it wasn't figuring out inconsistencies in his story. Those compound eyes gave the alien a killer poker face.

Finally it made a long, chittering noise.

"Wait," it told him, and scuttled inside the ship, leaving Bartie to cool his heels on the deck.

Bartie did what he was told, figuring it was the safest course under the circumstances. All around him on the deck lay the unconscious bodies of the League ship's crew and the Palisandran refugees they'd brought aboard. Bartie and his guys had laid out most of them. The xombies had taken down some, but their clubs had done a messier job than the curdlers. The most harshly handled ones were in their own pile, some breathing, some not. Bartie figured those poor bastards might ultimately be the lucky ones. The frickin' xenos didn't seem to be interested in them.

When the frickin' bug came back out, its manipulator arms were stretched around a case that looked a lot like the one the curdlers had come out of.

"Minimal assistance eventuates," it stated. "Maximum local force expedient. Designate Bartie will arm recipients."

What recipients? "We haven't got any frickin' xombies in here with us."

"New recipients eventuate. Bonding transpires. Designate Bartie will arm new recipients."

Bartie started to get it. The frickin' bug had been busy making a new army of xombies. That was fine by Bartie, very fine. He watched as the xeno-mantis opened the case. Inside were shiny new curdlers, enough for even xombies to put down one frickin' Eridani.

Hear that, soldier boy? The tide is about to turn.

Sue caught up to Seaborg just as he launched his charge toward the entrance of the boat bay. The bodies she had seen lying everywhere were gone, but the blood wasn't. Seaborg skidded to a stop just as the hatch slid shut in front of him. He slapped the unyielding metal with an ineffectual hand.

"He's sealed it," he told her as she joined him.

"It's not the only way in." Sue told him about the maintenance accessway she had used.

"A possibility, but the control center may offer us other options."

Sue led the way. They found the flight control center

darker than Sue remembered. Someone had opaqued the windows to the flight deck and the only lighting was the lurid emergency spots. It wasn't so dark, however, that she couldn't see the xombies poking and prying at the center's consoles.

She hesitated in the doorway. Seaborg didn't. He fired his curdler over her shoulder. Even though it was not aimed at her, she felt her skin start a tingling dance. Shocked from her inaction, she shot one of the xombies herself. Seaborg's previous proscription against using curdlers on xombies to maintain the element of surprise was obviously lifted.

With the last xombie down, Seaborg walked to the main console. Staring down at the ravaged mess, he shook his head.

"They've sabotaged all the commo and control functions. They ripped the safety overrides as well, everything from fire control to decontamination."

"So we can't just open the bay to space and flush them out."

"Wouldn't have been an option anyway. There are ship's personnel in there and some of your fellow Palisandrans. Unprotected as they are, they'd die along with the alien and its minions."

The way he said it made Sue a little ashamed to have made the suggestion, but not entirely. "Sometimes sacrifices have to be made."

"I concur. But only when necessary. Direct action is a better option."

"Isn't going in shooting just as bad?"

"Collateral casualties are not as certain, and the greatest risk will be borne by the one taking it on knowingly."

By the *one*? "You're thinking about going in there by yourself, aren't you?"

He didn't answer, but she knew he was.

"We control the accessway here," she pointed out. "We can watch the main hatchway. Why not just wait? The survivors from engineering will get here sooner or later, and then we'll have more than enough people to take them out."

"I doubt we have the time. The Remor was doing something to the captives."

Sue shuddered. "Making xombies?"

"Possibly. If so, even with the people from engineering, we may not have numbers on our side in the end. A swarm of jackyldaws can pull down the biggest lionater, or even a pride of them. Our best bet is to hit the enemy fast, before they are ready."

"I'm going with you," she said, hating the idea even as she spoke it. It had to be done.

"No, you are not," he said.

"Yes, I am."

"Think, Sue. If we both go in and fail, there will be no one to contain the Remor. Sister Coppelstowe can't do it, you can. If the enemy isn't stopped here and now, it will have a new horde of minions ready and waiting for the engineers when they break through. You have to be the second line of defense."

"I don't wan—"

"It was *your* plan to bottle them up and wait."

Sue could see where the argument was going. Nothing she said was going to change his mind, so she said nothing. He accepted her acquiescence and asked to be shown the maintenance accessway. She did so. It was a close fit for a man of his size.

"I couldn't be doing this in my hardsuit. I'd be too fat and stiff," he said, clearly to lighten the mood.

"If you'd had your 'suit, you wouldn't *have* to be doing this."

"I concur. But wishing won't make it so."

"Hopeless wishes separate people from fishes," she said.

He looked into her eyes. There was nothing of his soldier's mask in his expression.

"It will all be over soon, God willing," he said quietly. "It wouldn't hurt if you asked Saint Michael for a little help too.

He's a soldier's saint and surely couldn't refuse a lady like you."

Then he was gone, making his way down the accessway as silently as a ghost.

"Be careful," she whispered, suddenly afraid she'd seen the last of him.

40

PACIFICA THEATER, PACIFICA ORBIT
CMEFS *AUDITOR*

The maintenance accessway between the flight control booth and the boat bay was one of the few such on the ship. In most parts of the ship, space could not be spared for dedicated crawl spaces; there were just hatches along the walls in the corridors for repair crews to work through. On the flight deck things were different, because repairs might be necessary while the boat bay was open to space. Crews in environment suits could do them, but working in a suit was slow and awkward. Sometimes speed and precision were premiums. Thus the environmentally enclosed passage.

To serve properly, the passage had tool lockers and a diagnostic station designed to operate on its own emergency power supply. Anders knew the designers hadn't put those things there for him, and he guessed they would be appalled at the use he hoped to put them to.

By way of actual weapons he had the curdler he had liberated from the collectors and Williams's pistol that he had recovered from where Bartie had dropped it outside the bridge. The latter was likely his best weapon against the Remor, since he doubted the aliens would have given their minions the curdlers if the weapons were truly dangerous to them. Unfortunately he had only four rounds. A single round could be enough against a human, but against a species whose vital points were unknown, a dozen could be too few. The net result was that he was feeling rather underequipped for the task ahead.

He wasn't especially worried about facing the wounded collector. Although if not dealt with expeditiously, Bartie could shift the odds at a bad time, and so could not be ignored. The curdler would take him down.

The real threat was the Remor. Its size and strength were formidable, difficult to deal with equipped as he was. A greater danger lay in the fact that the alien's resources were unknown. Did it carry weapons? Was it a warrior among its species? There was too much he didn't know.

He was not fooled by his success on the hull against the other one. That had been as much to do with luck and their environment as with his skills, and inside *Auditor* he didn't have all of space as a deep well into which to toss his opponent. He knew that he needed an edge, and he looked to the maintenance station to provide it.

The anticipated breather mask was present in the tool locker, but the hoped-for night-vision goggles were not. A demolition ax offered him the close combat weapon he sought as a backup. He knew special-purpose applications for a lot more items, but nothing else seemed to offer a good combination of utility and versatility. He turned his attention to the console.

Through its diagnostics he got a good sense of the status of the flight deck's systems. There wasn't much on line beyond the lights. The console offered him control of even fewer systems. One of those was the backup decontamination system. Having been through emergency decons, he knew that what the steam blasts and chemical sprays did to visibility was something he could use. He made a quick study of the nozzle layout, trying to memorize positions, then programmed a random sequence of starts and stops.

Out there on the deck, the Remor was undoubtedly still working on the captives. He might have prepared more mischief using the maintenance console, but anything he tried would take time. Time, he reckoned, favored the Remor.

He triggered his program and emerged from the accessway under the growing cover of his improvised smoke-screen.

Silhouetted in the thickening clouds, the bulk of the alien's body was immediately visible. Not clear enough for a good pistol target, but the curdler was a less discriminating weapon. There was a chance that the stunning beam might affect the Remor, and if it did, it could yield an immediate takedown. Thinking it worth the chance, Anders fired with the curdler and scored a clean hit on the Remor's side. The thing made a shrill ticking noise and scuttled backward into the rising clouds and out of sight.

Unfortunately, he'd been right about the curdlers not being very effective against the Remor. Still, the shot *had* gotten a reaction. Perhaps he could drive it with curdler hits.

Silent beams of lambent light flickered in the mist, boring through the space he'd fired from.

Obviously, the Remor *was* armed.

He moved cautiously, listening between steps. He'd caught the soft scrape of chitin on metal when the alien had fled from his curdler shot. Knowing from that the noise it made when moving, he listened hard for the sound as he slipped through the roiling clouds.

The susurrus of chemical jets made it hard to hear. So hard that the Remor was nearly upon him before he knew it. He threw himself into a roll to escape the oncoming alien. Rolling away, he cleared its path, only to come up short against a human, upright and mobile.

It could only be a hostile.

Anders slammed the butt of the curdler into a knee. The scream of pain he elicited belonged to Bartie.

Springing to his feet as the collector fell to the floor, he followed up with a swift kick to the side of Bartie's head and laid the man out.

This time he heard the clatter of chitin. With no time to waste, he sidestepped away from the fallen collector, keeping low.

Good thing.

A beam from the alien's weapon flashed over his back so close he felt the heat. There were other beams too, but none as close.

His smokescreen was affecting the Remor senses at least as much as a human's.

Thank you, Saint Michael.

Between the spurts of jets, he could hear the alien taking tentative steps. It didn't seem to be moving, just shuffling in place.

"Designate Bartie, respond."

The cold, detached voice could only belong to the Remor. Anders stalked toward it, pistol ready.

A gap in the drifting vapors revealed the alien. From his experience on the hull Anders knew that the upper back and the leg joints were weak points in the chitin armor. The alien's position didn't offer the more choice upper target, so Anders aimed the pistol for a leg joint.

He fired.

The shot went wide. Anders was amazed to have missed at that range, but he did not let surprise slow him. He dived back into the covering mist. Beam after beam sought him out. He dodged and dived and rolled. Heat seared his left thigh. Another beam crackled past his head, burning flesh and hair.

The Remor was getting his range.

Sue guessed Anders had started his attack when something started spraying against the opaque observation window. For an absurd moment she envisioned him as having concocted some kind of bug spray, then the sound resolved into something more reminiscent of a lawn sprinkler striking a pane of glass. Had he set off the fire-suppression system?

She wished she could see what was happening on the flight deck. Her eyes strayed to the accessway.

There was one certain way.

No, girl. He left you with a job to do.

While he went to fight for both their lives.

She was no soldier. What could she reasonably expect to do to help him? He needed help; that was for sure. Who wouldn't? She knew it. He knew it.

If he fell, did she really think that she could take on the alien alone?

The engineers would never arm themselves and break through to this part of the ship in time. How could they? It was all going to be over soon.

She was useless sitting and waiting in the control booth! Useless!

She felt the curdler heavy in her hands, and remembered someone else, long ago, charging in to the rescue. Some things just had to be done.

What was it Sergeant Fiske had said?

Balanced imperatives.

PACIFICA THEATER, PACIFICA ORBIT
CMEFS *AUDITOR*

Hoping he was screened by the fog, Anders made a sudden change of direction. The hungry energy beams chewed off away from him.

He calmed his breathing, giving thanks for his escape. With his wind back, he took advantage of that escape and slipped away across the bay. As soon as he found some hard cover, he stopped to examine the pistol. It didn't take long for his exploring fingers to detect a slight bend in the forward sight. It might have happened when Bartie dropped it. It might have happened when Williams lost it. How and when didn't matter; what mattered was that he needed to compensate for it or the weapon was next to useless.

He moved toward the far side of the flight deck, stopping when he reached the wall. He backed up until he was at the distance, given the cloaking effects of the swirling decon mists, that he expected to engage the Remor, then he drew a bead, fired, and immediately dodged away.

No beams sought him this time.

He didn't know what the alien made of his random shot, but he was sure it would add to the confusion of the situation. For that alone, one of his meager few rounds was too high a price, but the expenditure had given him important information that he needed. He now knew the deviation to expect from the pistol.

Pain from his leg reminded him with every step of the

shot he'd taken. His head throbbed from the shot that had nearly decapitated him. He was Eridani. Pain was only an inconvenience. He put it from his mind and concentrated on stalking his prey.

Checking the time, he confirmed that a brief slowdown in the decon cycle was due. He'd programmed such lulls to give him chances to assess the battlefield. For safety, he'd need cover when the sprayers went dormant. He slipped back to the raider ship for his refuge.

As the mist gradually died down to the deck, he scanned the bay for his enemy. The Remor was nowhere to be seen. A few of the captives were moaning and twitching in their curdler-induced unconsciousness, but otherwise the bay was quiet.

Where had it gone? The main hatch and airlock were still closed, automatically locked down during decontamination, and the alien wouldn't fit through the maintenance accessway, so it hadn't left the bay. Was it in one of the booby bunkers?

A soft scrape from above gave him his answer. It had gone aboard the ship. Now it was creeping forth again. Hunting for him, no doubt. He repositioned himself beneath the ramp to await it.

The Remor was cautious, moving slowly and as silently as it could. From his vantage, Anders could see that the manipulator claws beneath its glittering jewels of eyes were holding a baroque-looking thing of metal. It might be the energy weapon the Remor had been using against him, but it could just as well be a tracking device, for all he could tell.

He had a shot at the alien's head, but there were chitin plates making armored rosettes around those eyes. If the pistol round didn't penetrate, the alien would likely retreat into the ship. It would be very hard to deal with inside. Anders let it creep farther out.

Unfortunately, as it did, it shifted toward the far side of the ramp. His head shot vanished.

He was still being offered his original target: leg joints.

From experience with Remor legged fighting machines, he knew he would need to disable at least two on one side to cripple the thing. He waited, letting it get a little farther out.

The decon cycle started up again. Apparently spooked by the new clouds of chemical fog, the Remor began to back up.

Anders fired.

The shot was clean and good, blowing out the upper joint of the alien's right front leg just as it was about to put weight on that limb. Screaming its pain, the alien tilted forward, its balance precarious.

Anders's second shot was a graze, clipping the exposed part of the lower joint in the middle right leg. The alien staggered forward, then lost its balance completely and toppled from the ramp.

Right in front of Anders.

A flailing limb cracked him in the chest and sent him sprawling. Spears of fire lanced him. He guessed broken ribs.

He could not stop now. The alien was struggling to regain its feet. Manipulator limbs scrabbled for its dropped weapon. He didn't have much time.

He tossed the pistol ahead of him as a distraction. It caromed off one of the glowing eyespots on what he thought of as the alien's shoulders. The Remor squalled.

Then he was on the alien with the demolition ax. He hewed as he closed. His hands numbed under the shock of metal against chitin. One spined leg swept toward him, and though he leaped to dodge it, the spines snagged his trousers and pulled him off balance.

He landed badly, twisting his ankle. He dropped to one knee as another leg whooshed over his head.

The alien was scrabbling frantically, trying to get to its feet. One pumping leg just brushed against him and sent him stumbling within reach of the manipulator limbs. He struck to his left, severing a grasping claw just as another speared into his shoulder.

He added his scream to the cacophony coming from the Remor.

The upper body drew away from him. What seemed at first to be a relief, he soon saw was a threat. The alien had gotten its feet under itself and was rising. It would soon have a clear angle to drive those sledgehammer limbs down onto him.

He dove in, rolling beneath it. His goal was its rear right leg. If he could disable it, the alien would go down again. Then it wouldn't be going anywhere. The cripple would be the prelude to the kill.

He nearly fell as he came to his feet, almost swamped in the pain flaring through his body. His vision was centered on the limb joint before him. For a moment, nothing else existed in the universe. Wounds screaming their protests, he swung.

The blade skipped off a spine.

Instead of a clean sever, the monomolecular edge dug into the alien's leg armor and lodged there. Some of the softer flesh of the joint was damaged, but the joint wasn't crippled.

The leg lifted, threatening to tear the ax from Anders's hands. He managed to hold on and was lifted from the deck and shaken till his bones rattled for his pains.

And pains he had. His head echoed with the ululating shrieks of agony from the Remor that could as easily have been his own.

A wail like a banshee joined the chorus. Shrill ticking erupted all around him. The Remor stumbled sideways. It slammed down the leg from which Anders dangled. The shock nearly dislodged him.

Let go and you die.

He had no intention of dying.

The banshee howled again. The strident ticking filled Anders's head. Like a bomb, ticking off the last seconds.

And there were only seconds. Anders was near the end of his strength. But his enemy still fought.

Could an Eridani do less?

He got a foot braced on the upper part of the limb. Putting his back into it, he wrenched hard with the ax. The tool was intended for ripping open metal and ceramic debris, and it worked well against chitin and flesh. The exoskeleton of the Remor's leg split open, tearing muscles. Blood spurted as raw inner skeleton was exposed.

Anders never saw the alien fall. Neither did he feel himself hit the deck. He awoke, knowing he had passed out. Everything was blurred, actually doubled in the center of his visual field. The demolition ax was still clamped in the cramped fingers of his right hand. He hurt everywhere.

But he was alive.

As he rolled onto his side he could see that he hadn't been out for long. The alien was writhing on the deck. It seemed to be reaching for him, pulling itself apart in its eagerness to see him dead.

Somewhere a woman was shouting, warning him. As if he needed a warning? He could see the danger, clear and plain. Two of it, in fact.

The sparking compound eyes of the alien glittered at him like a constellation of hate. Closer. A handful of jewels against a night of chitin. Coming for him.

He heaved himself up with strength that came from he knew not where and buried the ax head in the center of those jewels. Armor that could deflect or withstand the soft, relatively broad impact of a pistol round parted before the more-than-razor-sharp hard edge of the blade. Fluid spurted.

His numb hands lost their grip as the Remor spasmed. The ax handle flailed around, nearly as dangerous as the alien's stomping legs had been.

A loud pop heralded a scent that Anders's fuzzed brain recognized even through the miasma of blood and gore and the haze of near-unconsciousness. Remor dissolvers.

Hands gripped his arm. He cried out in pain. Those uncaring hands mauled him, hauling on his arm. Dragging him into new pain.

But away from the dissolvers.

Away from certain death.

"Thank you," he said, not sure the words were spoken aloud.

"You did it," said an angel.

As he eased into the soft, quiet dark, he wondered why the angel sounded like Sue Merrick.

42

PACIFICA THEATER, PACIFICA ORBIT
CMEFS *AUDITOR*

Bartie awakened to find a harsh-faced woman pointing a curdler at him. The woman was a Palisandran. He'd seen her hanging around the soldiers, and maybe somewhere before that. She had a cold, hard voice that rang faint bells.

"Still alive?" she asked.

"Yeah. No thanks to you and your soldier boy."

Bartie shifted his aching head around to see where the frickin' Eridani was. The bastard had to be alive or this woman wouldn't be in here. Ah, there he was, lying next to a puddle of goo that had to be what was left of one of the frickin' bugs. He looked worse than Bartie felt.

Bartie looked for signs that the frickin' Eridani had managed a miracle and gotten the other xeno too, but he couldn't see any. Good. He grinned up at the smug little bitch.

"It ain't over, missy, and the soldier boy is on the ropes. And you ain't got enough juice. It ain't over at all."

"What do you mean?" she asked.

"There's another frickin' xeno. I don't think your boy has got enough left to take it."

"Another?"

Why didn't she look scared? "Yeah. As big and mean as the last one."

"The third of three?"

"Yeah, the third one. It's gonna kick your collective asses."

"Don't think so. Seaborg killed it outside on the hull before we came and kicked *your* collective asses."

"You're lying!"

She *had* to be lying! Didn't she? She gave him a brittle smile that said she wasn't. Hell, he was well and truly buggered. Or maybe not.

"God, it would be good if they were all dead," he said to test the water. "If they're all dead, then maybe I'm free. They were gonna take the ship and run away, you know. They knew the game was up on Pacifica, and they were gonna go someplace else and take over more people. Tell me you stopped them all. Tell me it's true."

The crack in her self-satisfied expression told him he had a chance.

"This thing around my throat. They called it a *gawkhore* when they put it on me. It's like the xombie worms. It's a control thing. You gotta get it off me."

"Don't see why," the suspicious bitch said. "You're someone who needs to be controlled. Besides, it would probably kill you if I took it off. The xombies die when their controllers come off."

"This thing ain't the same."

"I'd guessed that. You aren't changed at all, Bartie."

The bitch kept talking like she knew him. Where was she getting that?

"All right, so you know I worked for the frickin' xenos. You probably think I'm some kind of traitor or something. You think I wanted to work for them? It's this *gawkhore* thing. It's not like I want to do the frickin' aliens' dirty work. This thing makes me do what they want." The *gawkhore* spasmed, tightening its hold. He coughed to hide his gasp. "There's something wrong with it now, though. Maybe 'cause the soldier boy killed the frickin' bug. It's trying to strangle me. If you don't get it off, it's gonna kill me anyway."

"Really? I could cut it off," she suggested, pulling a knife. "Or maybe I'll cut something else off."

Stupid bitch! "Look, lady. I'm telling you, anything I did to you was because of the frickin' aliens." A squeeze on his throat. There wasn't much air coming through. He had to convince her. "They mind-controlled me. Made me do it."

The *gawkhore* tightened hard.

"Ya gotta help me," he gasped.

"What a filthy, pathetic liar you are," she snarled.

"I am not."

The *gawkhore* clamped down hard. His lungs fought to suck down something he could live on. Panicked, he reached for her, trying to get the knife. His shattered knee collapsed beneath him. The pain exploded, but he crawled after her. If she wouldn't do it, he'd cut the frickin' thing off himself. Once he got it off, he'd show her.

He wasn't sure how, but he managed to get a hand clamped onto her wrist.

"Gimme knife," he croaked. "Won't hurt you."

The *gawkhore* clenched harder. His lungs sucked without joy. No. Air. At. All. He let her go to claw at the thing strangling him. His prying fingers couldn't get a grip. He needed the frickin' knife. He lunged at her again, trying to grab it, but she dodged him easily. He collapsed on the deck, awash in pain.

Air. He needed air. Just air.

None.

His fingers slowed their scratching at the frickin' *gawkhore*. Leaden, his good arm fell, useless as the one that had taken the soldier boy's knife. He lay there. It was too hard to move. The edges of the world were cracking apart.

No air.

The colors were dying. All he could do was watch the world narrow down.

Then boots shuffled into his diminishing vision.

"What's going on here?" the frickin' Eridani's voice asked from very far away.

The bitch answered him. "Poetic justice."

He saw her face, dirt- and tear-stained beneath him. All full of hate. Now he remembered her. He heard his laughter.

He couldn't laugh anymore.

And all the world went finally dark.

PACIFICA THEATER, PACIFICA ORBIT
CMEFS *AUDITOR*

Sue watched Bartie's departure from the universe, knowing a chapter in her life had finally closed. She'd expected to feel something more from the conclusion than the exhaustion saturating her. Maybe she would. Later.

At her side, Anders Seaborg started to collapse. She didn't have the strength to ease him down to the deck, but she did manage to keep him from cracking open his skull.

Hard to believe as it was, Seaborg had done it. He had beaten the Remor. Yes, she had helped, but he was the one who had killed the alien, nearly dying for his heroism. She was proud of him.

And she told him so during several of his lucid periods.

He kept trying to get up again when he was awake, not seeming to believe her when she assured him that the enemy was dead and that they had won. But his fabled Eridani strength had fled and she was able to hold him down. He was so very badly injured that she feared any movement would aggravate his wounds.

When he drifted off, she tried to cancel the cycle of decontamination procedures he had used to add fog to his war. Fortunately he had left the console active, because she had no access clearance for anything aboard *Auditor*. It took a little bit of figuring, but she managed to shut the cycle down.

Once she had done that, she was able to open the main hatch and let the ship's air recycling system start to deal with the stenches clogging the flight deck.

Minutes later, the Alsionite arrived, breathless. She must have run all the way from the bridge where they'd left her.

"I got the local scanners working," she gasped. "There's another ship approaching. A Remor ship."

Had all their fighting been for nothing? "They're going to blow us out of space."

The Alsionite was pale with fear. "Worse, I think. It looked as though they were launching small craft."

"They could be battle craft, but I doubt it," Seaborg croaked. He'd come to and obviously heard the Alsionite's grim news. "Boarding pods. They seem to really want this ship. Or what's on board."

Auditor belled like a gong struck by a hammer.

"What was that?" the Alsionite shrilled. "Are we hit?"

Seaborg shook his head, wincing as he did. "No, I don't think so."

Sue couldn't believe what she was seeing. Was that actually a smile on his face?

PACIFICA THEATER, PACIFICA ORBIT
IDLS *VON RICHTOFEN*

"Direct hit, Commander."

Stone allowed himself a grin of satisfaction. It was about the only physical sign he could give, trussed up as he was in the life-support systems that had been the first of Dr. Luwana's conditions for releasing him from sick bay so he could do what needed to be done.

"Keep on him," he ordered.

"Will do, sir," responded Captain Carmichial. "We'll get better yield on the next flight. Another volley will put this last one into hell."

Von Richtofen had been chasing this flight of Remor ships since minutes after she had taken aboard the assault shuttle carrying Stone from the near-wreck of *Auditor*. When the pursuit had been launched, Carmichial had been unaware he'd just taken on board the fleet commander. Stone had regained consciousness just as the doctor was reporting his presence, and immediately countermanded Captain Carmichial's order to abandon the pursuit. It had been impulse on Stone's part, but it had proved to be the right move.

Five enemy ships had risen from Pacifica in the enemy flight. The first two had gone down with aid from *Jack Aubrey* and CMEFS *Achilles,* but those ships had been on trajectory for a bigger battle over the planet's south pole. Only *Von Richtofen* had been able to shift vectors and chase the remaining three.

While Stone intimidated his doctor into swaddling him in the medical paraphernalia necessary to get him on the bridge, *Von Richtofen* disposed of two more of the enemy vessels. By then it was plain that the flight had been headed for *Auditor.* Flight Commander Charron reported significant numbers of survivors still aboard the nearly defenseless *Auditor*. To have let the Remor attack *Auditor* unmolested, simply to minimize the risk to Stone, would have been unconscionable.

"We have a firing solution," Carmichial reported.

"By all means, Captain, apply it."

Carmichial gave the order. As he did, the ScanTech reported, "They've launched small craft. Computer makes them as boarding pods. Inbound on *Auditor.*"

"Gunnery," Carmichial snapped. "New targets."

Von Richtofen's missiles flew true and as Carmichial predicted, they destroyed the Remor ship. The ScanTech soon reported the enemy ship dissolving. Chasing down and eliminating the boarding pods was a simple exercise in gunnery. As the last one dissolved away, the crew cheered their success.

"Sometimes I feel like we're fighting ghosts," Stone mused.

"Or maybe fairies," Carmichial said. "Don't they melt away in the sunlight?"

The cheerful mood on the bridge was dampened by Dr. Luwana's growl. "Now will you return to sick bay, Commander?"

"Dr. Luwana, I will tell you when I'm ready for your mothering."

Truth to tell, Stone had been direly in need of the doctor's attentions when he had been brought aboard *Von Richtofen,* and lucky that the patroller had been assigned as competent a physician as Luwana. Though he was not about to let on, he remained in need of the doctor's services, but he could not let his own frailty get in the way of his duty. The men and women of the fleet needed him, and he simply could not lie abed, doing nothing, while that was the situation.

"Captain Carmichial, have we achieved commo with Fleet yet?"

"Still working, sir."

The main fleet would have begun the engagement with the gathering Remor fleet by now. Despite his confidence in Chip Hollister, Stone fretted. He wanted to be *there.* Directing the action *there,* where the fate of the system was being decided.

But God put you here, didn't He?

So *here* was where he was meant to be.

While they still couldn't reach the main fleet, they were in communication with the orbital defense force, and Stone put himself to work. Mainwaring's ship commanders didn't respond as quickly as League commanders, and they questioned half his orders, but eventually they listened.

And, in the end, they won their part of the war.

Somewhere in the middle of it, communication was reestablished with *Auditor.* They too had won their part of the battle, though at steep cost.

At last, *Von Richtofen* managed a channel to the fleet.

"We have met the enemy," Chip reported. "And they are ours. Mop-up operations are ongoing."

Stone insisted on full details. It seemed that the plan had, for once, mostly survived contact with the enemy. Where it hadn't, the fleet had done well, better than he'd hoped, actually. It had cost, as it always did. And always would.

He was proud of his people.

Pacifica was not wholly free of the enemy, but it *was* back in human control.

"Tell them I'm proud of them, Chip."

"Will do, Commander."

He was suddenly very tired.

"Dr. Luwana?"

"Yes, Commander?"

"I am all yours."

PACIFICA SYSTEM
IDLS *JACK AUBREY*

The search for survivors was a necessary part of the aftermath of any battle, but it was never a part that appealed to Captain Diana Maturin. The chances of a happy ending after a space battle were too slim.

For the better part of a solar day, they had been running down the signal from an emergency suit. The transponder reported the suit to have come from CMEFS *Auditor*.

"It's a wild goose chase," her exec opined. Edlyn Fitch had a Lancastrian's bluff disregard for sensitivity. "Best we'll get is a stiff. It's been too long."

It had, in truth, been too long since the wreck of the *Auditor* for the life-support package of an emergency suit to still be functional.

"Nevertheless, we persevere," Diana responded. "If only to ascertain which of our honored dead will no longer be 'fate indeterminate.' "

"We're at ten K, Commander," ScanTech Wilson reported. "You wanted visual when we reached the mark."

She had indeed. Watching the grisly truth slowly grow in clarity was not pleasant. Better, by her, to wait until one could immediately confirm it without squinting.

"Put it on my screen."

"Will do, sir."

Ghoulishly, Fitch leaned over so she could see the monitor. When the picture came up, they both gasped.

Diana had seen the simulation that Fleet Intel had put together from Captain Seaborg's report, so she knew what she was looking at. She just couldn't believe it.

"Put me through to Fleet," she ordered. "Top priority."

PACIFICA SYSTEM
IDLS CONSTANTINE

Sick bay was quiet as Anders guided his chair through the ward toward the isolation chambers that doubled as private recovery rooms for VIPs. He didn't need to see the guard to know which one was the commander's; the day cycle traffic had more than made it clear. But the guard was there anyway, and she snapped a sharp salute before opening the door for him.

"Come in, son," Commander Stone invited.

Anders maneuvered the chair in. Before he could salute, Stone added, "At ease, son. Neither one of us is in good enough shape to stand on ceremony at the moment. Or to stand at all."

Was that a joke? It sounded like one, but Anders had to consider the source. While he did, the silence stretched out.

"Do you remember me offering you a chance to pay for your sins, Seaborg?"

"Yes, sir."

"Feel like you've done it?"

"That's not for me to say, sir."

"You said all we'd have to do was beat the unbeatable. How about that? Think we've done it?"

"They tell me the system is ours."

Stone nodded slightly. "Our fleet has beaten their fleet. If the Remor admiral was human, I'd have to say he lost control of his assets. Maybe he did. Maybe we took out their command-and-control apparatus somehow. Maybe their ASSes screwed up their commo more than they did ours.

Who knows why things went the way they did? I just thank Saint Michael that they did. The Remor deep space elements practically cooperated in allowing us to defeat them in detail, starting with that stunt their close-in squadron pulled that wrecked *Auditor.*

"They nearly got us there, sir."

"What they nearly did was get Colonel Cope and our ground forces. *Auditor*'s squadron just happened to be in the way. If Mainwaring or Lugard had been in control of *Auditor* at that point . . ." Stone trailed off. "Well, no need to speak ill of the dead, is there? The important thing is the enemy's ploy failed."

"Are you sure they weren't after *Auditor*? They did board her."

"We don't know enough about how the Remor think to be sure, but I think that enemy group alpha's apparent concentration on *Auditor* was coincidental, another example of the enemy's command breakdown. Interrogation of the species traitors you stunned suggests that the boarding contingent was expecting to take over the ship and sneak out of the system as one of our own. They wanted a way out. That, and more fodder for their unholy experiments."

Anders didn't know enough about fleet protocols to know if such a plan would have worked, but he doubted it. "That ploy failed too."

"With no little help from you."

"I did what needed doing, sir."

Stone regarded him silently for several moments. "So, now I'll ask you again, son. Did we do what we came here to do?"

"If the fighting's done, sir."

"To be sure, there are still a few stragglers out there to be mopped up, but League forces control Pacifican space. Colonel Cope has got the enemy ground forces ducking for cover, something they won't be able to find as soon as our support ships take up orbital positions. We've taken lumps.

There will likely be a few more before it's really over, but it's fair to say that the system is ours. I'm not entirely sure you and I are done."

Was that a smile lurking beneath Stone's expression? What did the commander mean about possibly not being done? "We've retaken the system. Isn't that what StratCom wanted?"

"Publicly, yes. Certainly it's what they're getting. That and more. Thanks to you, Seaborg."

This time Anders didn't know what Stone referred to. "Me, sir?"

"You, sir." Stone blinked into the heads-up display over his bed. The holotank at his bedside came to life with an image. "Recognize this?"

"Good God!" It was the Remor he'd fought on the hull of *Auditor.* He could see the emergency suit backpack he'd stuck to it. "But it's intact."

"Exactly. Intel's holy grail. You're a bona fide hero, son. Citations, medals, and promotion are foregone conclusions. I'm just giving you your early warning."

"I don't know what to say, sir."

"Were I you, son, I'd be asking directions for the deepest, darkest hole where I could jump in and pull a cover over my arse."

"I don't understand, sir."

"You will, son. You will. But that's enough for tonight." Stone's voice was weary. "Go get some rest. You've earned it."

Stone was asleep before Anders managed to get his chair turned around.

Anders rolled back to his bunk and found Sue still in the chair set beside it. She had fallen asleep with one arm stretched out to his pillow. She looked so peaceful.

Knowing he couldn't get himself back into the bed without disturbing her, he decided to stay in the chair. It was a small burden for an Eridani. A price he'd gladly pay to see that tranquil expression on her face.

Tomorrow she'd tell him how foolish he was to have done it. And maybe tomorrow he would concur. But tonight he would have his glimpse of peace.

And come tomorrow?

Why, he was up for whatever it would bring.